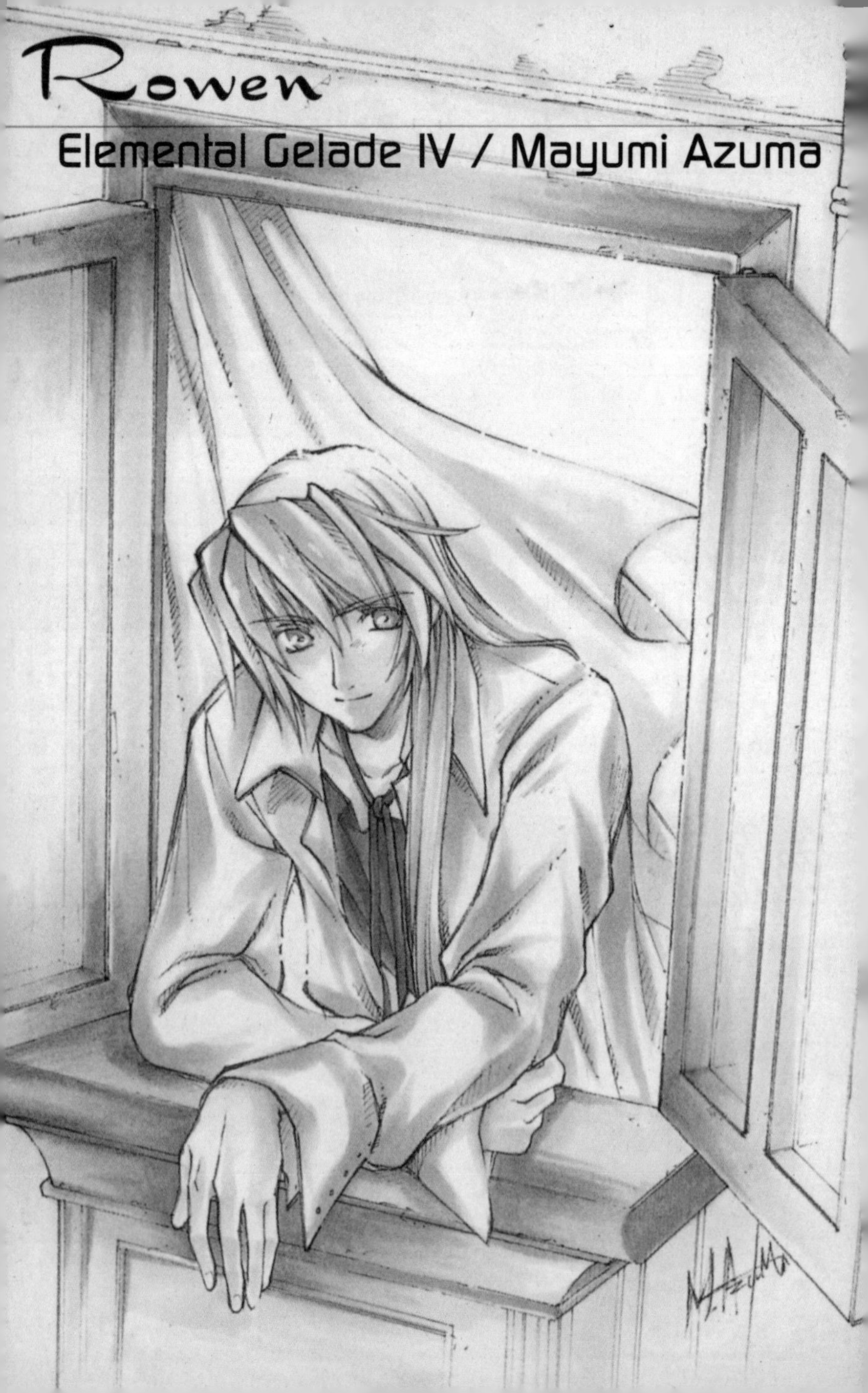
Rowen
Elemental Gelade IV / Mayumi Azuma

## *Elemental Gelade Volume 4*
## Created by Mayumi Azuma

Translation - Alethea & Athena Nibley
English Adaptation - Jordan Capell
Copy Editor - Stephanie Duchin
Retouch and Lettering - Star Print Brokers
Production Artist - Michael Paolilli
Graphic Designer - James Lee

Editor - Troy Lewter
Digital Imaging Manager - Chris Buford
Pre-Production Supervisor - Erika Terriquez
Art Director - Anne Marie Horne
Production Manager - Elisabeth Brizzi
Managing Editor - Vy Nguyen
VP of Production - Ron Klamert
Editor-in-Chief - Rob Tokar
Publisher - Mike Kiley
President and C.O.O. - John Parker
C.E.O. and Chief Creative Officer - Stuart Levy

A  Manga

TOKYOPOP Inc.
5900 Wilshire Blvd. Suite 2000
Los Angeles, CA 90036

E-mail: info@TOKYOPOP.com
Come visit us online at www.TOKYOPOP.com

ISBN: 978-1-59816-601-9

First TOKYOPOP printing: July 2007
10  9  8  7  6  5  4  3  2  1
Printed in the USA

# ELEMENTAL GELADE

## Volume 4

by
Mayumi Azuma

HAMBURG // LONDON // LOS ANGELES // TOKYO

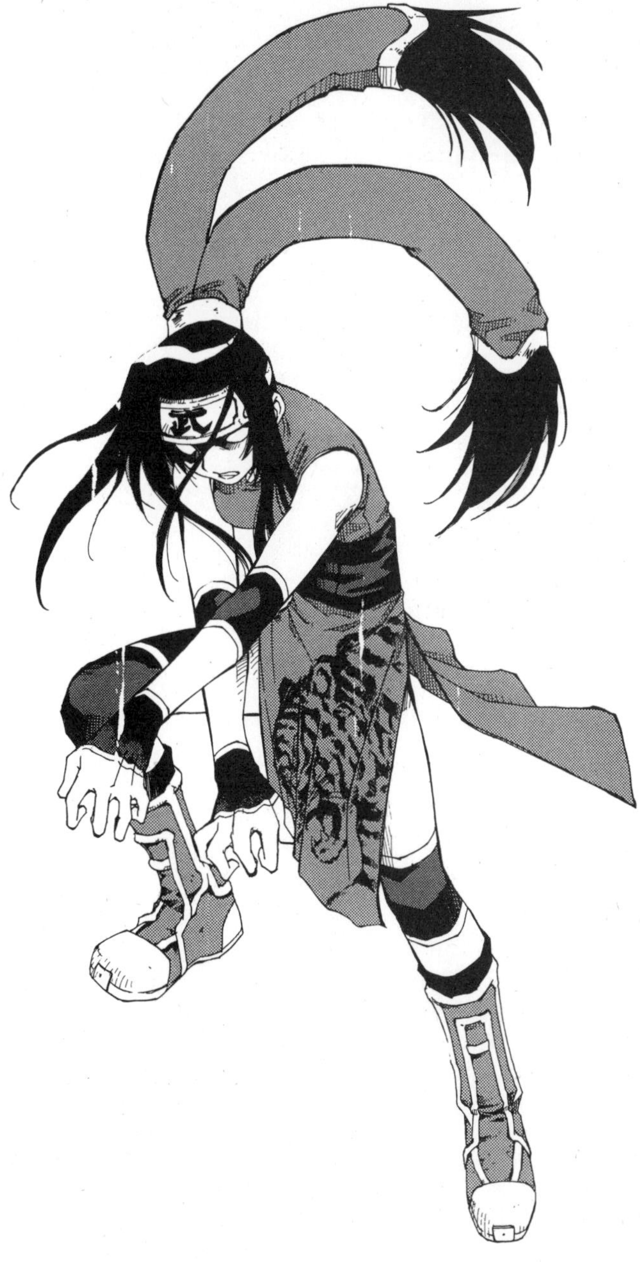

# ELEMENTAL GELADE

## Story So Far

FOLLOWING A ROUTINE RAID, SKY PIRATE COUD VAN GIRUET DISCOVERS A MOST UNUSUAL BOUNTY--A BEAUTIFUL GIRL IN A BOX NAMED REN WHO SAYS SHE NEEDS TO GO TO A PLACE CALLED EDEL GARDEN. BUT BEFORE COUD CAN MAKE SENSE OF IT ALL, A GROUP CALLED ARC AILE ARRIVES, STATING THAT THE GIRL IS IN FACT AN EDEL RAID (A LIVING WEAPON WHO REACTS WITH A HUMAN TO BECOME A FIGHTING MACHINE), AND THAT THEY WISH TO BUY HER. COU IS OUTRAGED THAT THEY WOULD TREAT HER LIKE PROPERTY, AND REFUSES TO LET THEM HAVE HER. A BATTLE BREAKS OUT, AND REN REACTS WITH COUD, BECOMING HIS WEAPON DURING THE FIGHT. REN IS SO TOUCHED BY COUD'S RESOLVE TO HELP HER THAT SHE DECIDES TO BECOME HIS PERSONAL EDEL RAID.

AFTER AN INTENSE SKY BATTLE, COUD, REN AND THE THREE MEMBERS OF ARC AILE ARE THEN LEFT TO WANDER THE FOREST BELOW WITH NO FOOD OR MONEY. CISQUA (LEADER OF THE ARC AILE TEAM) DECIDES TO FOLLOW COUD AND REN, MUCH TO COUD'S ANNOYANCE. THEY SOON REALIZE THAT EVEN THOUGH THEIR DIFFERENCES MAY BE MANY, THEIR COMMON DESIRE TO PROTECT REN MAY BE ENOUGH TO KEEP THEM FROM KILLING ONE ANOTHER. AND AFTER THEY SAVE REN FROM A BLACK MARKET EDEL RAID DEALER NAMED BEAZON, AS WELL AS FROM AN EDEL RAID HUNTER NAMED WOLX HOUND, IT BECAME PAINFULLY CLEAR PROTECTING REN IS A FULL-TIME JOB.

SPENDING TIME WITH REN MAKES CISQUA SEE HER IN A DIFFERENT LIGHT, SO SHE AGREES TO ALTER HER ORIGINAL MISSION, AND WILL INSTEAD HELP REN REACH EDEL GARDEN. HOWEVER, LACK OF MONEY FORCES THEM TO STOP AT THE BETTING GROUND MILLIARD TREY, WHERE THEY HOPE TO WIN ENOUGH MONEY BETTING ON FIGHTS TO CONTINUE THEIR JOURNEY. UNFORTUNATELY, COUD, THE ONLY ONE IN THE GROUP STRONG ENOUGH TO FIGHT, IS ALSO THE LEAST EXPERIENCED FIGHTER OF THEM ALL...

# Contents

(3:00) Going to buy snacks for Kuea.
No.238
I've been wondering about this for a long time... Cou's hair–even when he's asleep or in the bath, it stands up happily all the time! To someone with limp hair like mine, it's unbelievable that anyone would have such strong hair that it would stand up like that without using any product.
No.237
Today Cisqua-senpai left her wallet on the desk, so I picked it up to take it to her, and...it was unexpectedly light. I had thought that we had saved up quite a bit, so I was surprised.

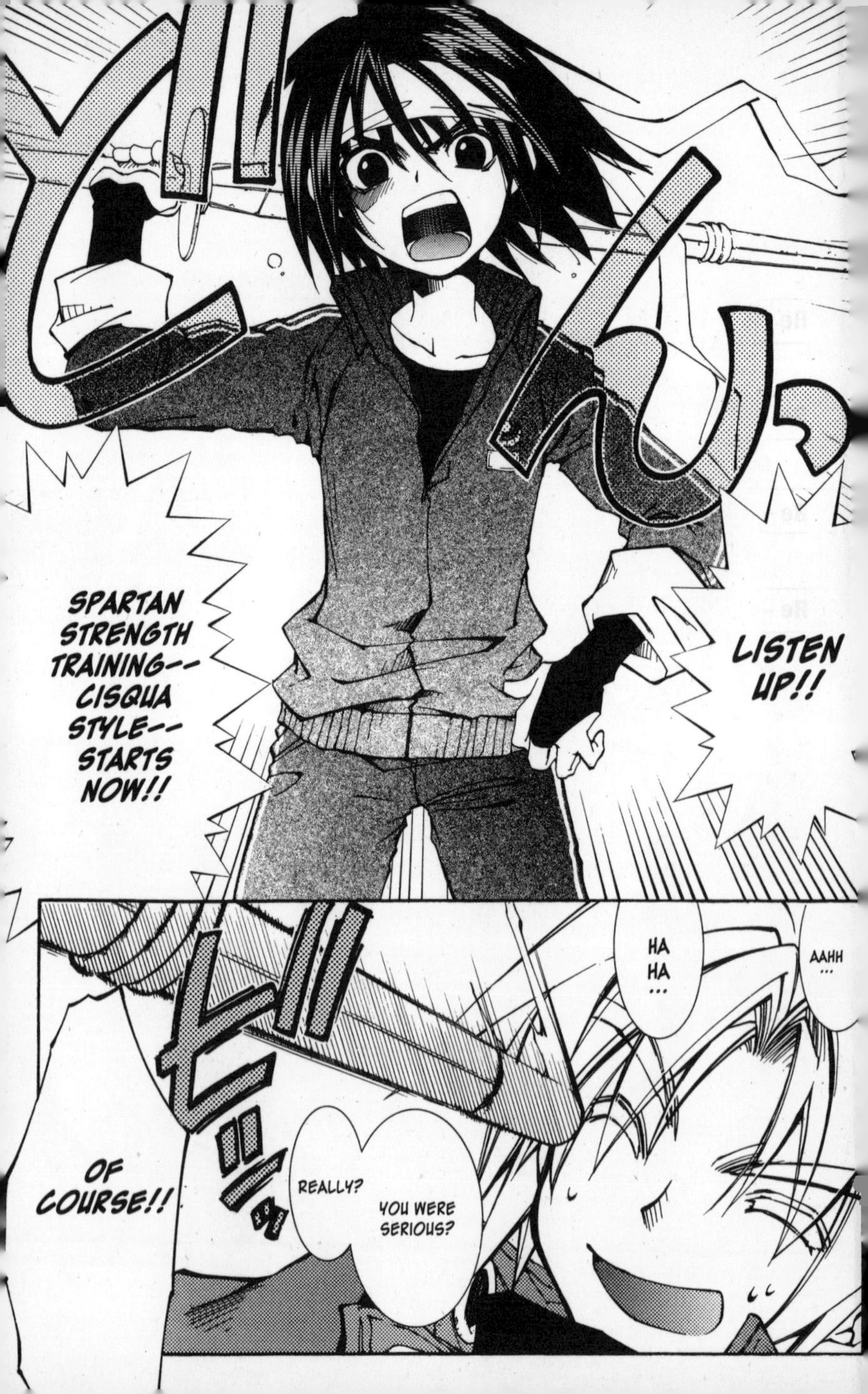
LISTEN UP!!
SPARTAN STRENGTH TRAINING-- CISQUA STYLE-- STARTS NOW!!
AAHH ...
HA HA ...
REALLY? YOU WERE SERIOUS?
OF COURSE!!

# Re-No: 13

## Milliard Trey Betting Grounds–
## The Event Dominator

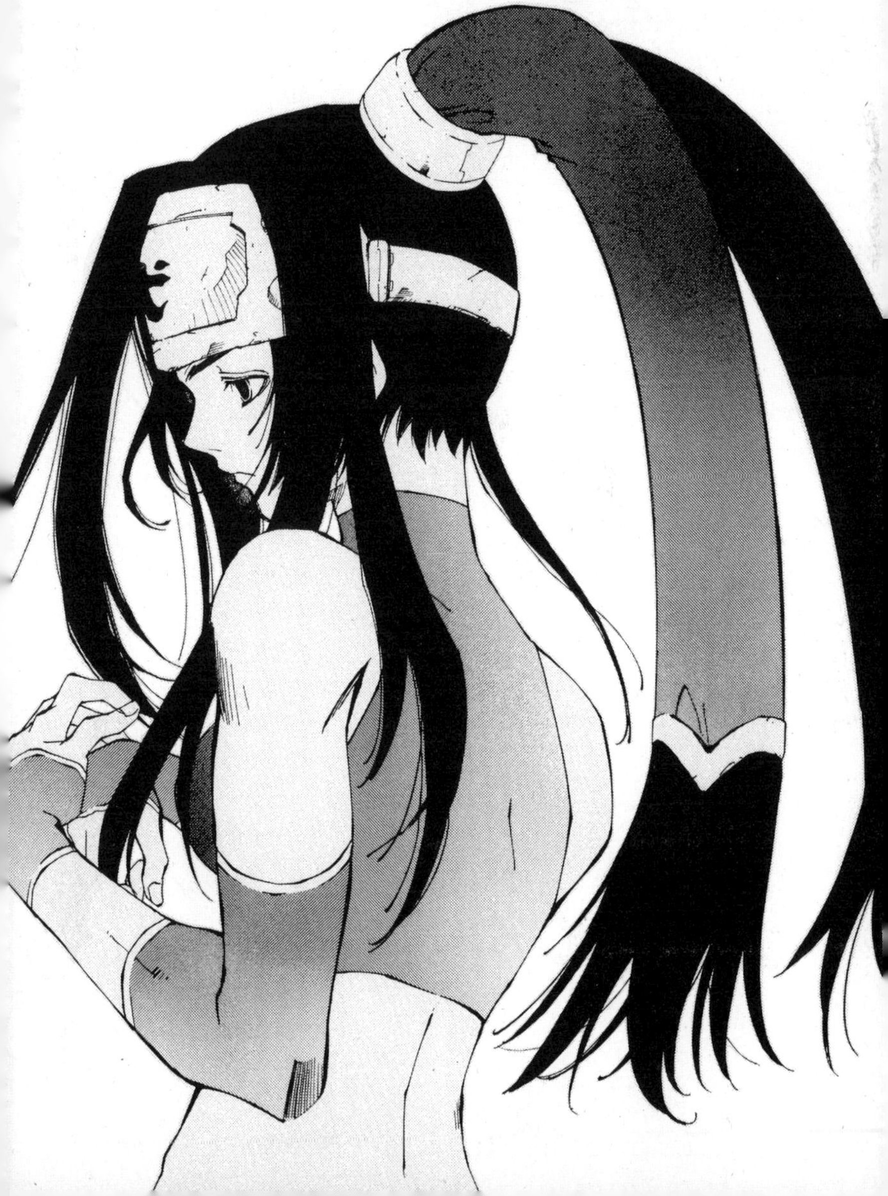

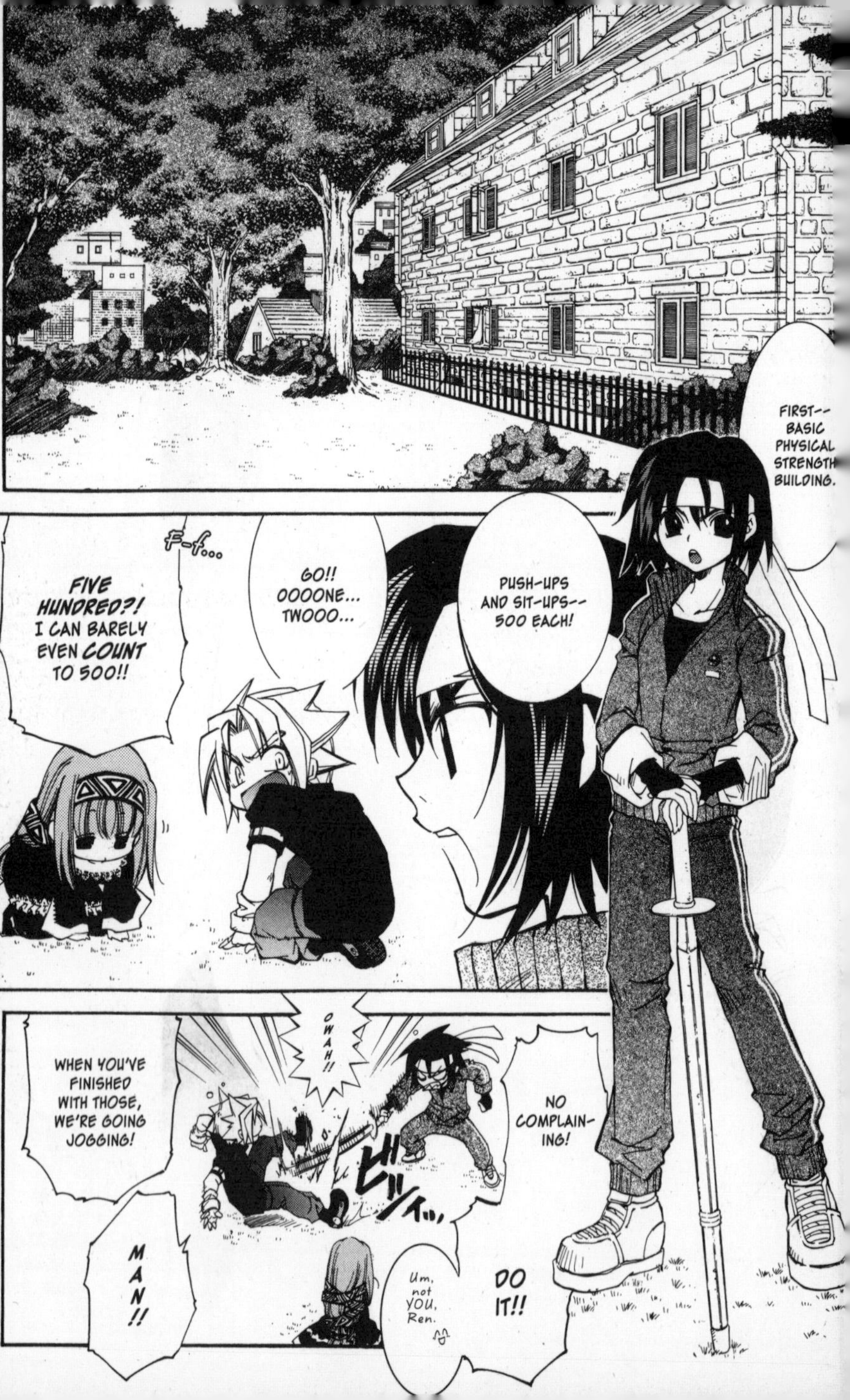
FIRST-- BASIC PHYSICAL STRENGTH BUILDING.
PUSH-UPS AND SIT-UPS-- 500 EACH!
GO!! OOOONE... TWOOO...
F-f...
FIVE HUNDRED?! I CAN BARELY EVEN COUNT TO 500!!
NO COMPLAINING!
OWAH!!
WHEN YOU'VE FINISHED WITH THOSE, WE'RE GOING JOGGING!
DO IT!!
Um, not YOU, Ren.
MAN!!

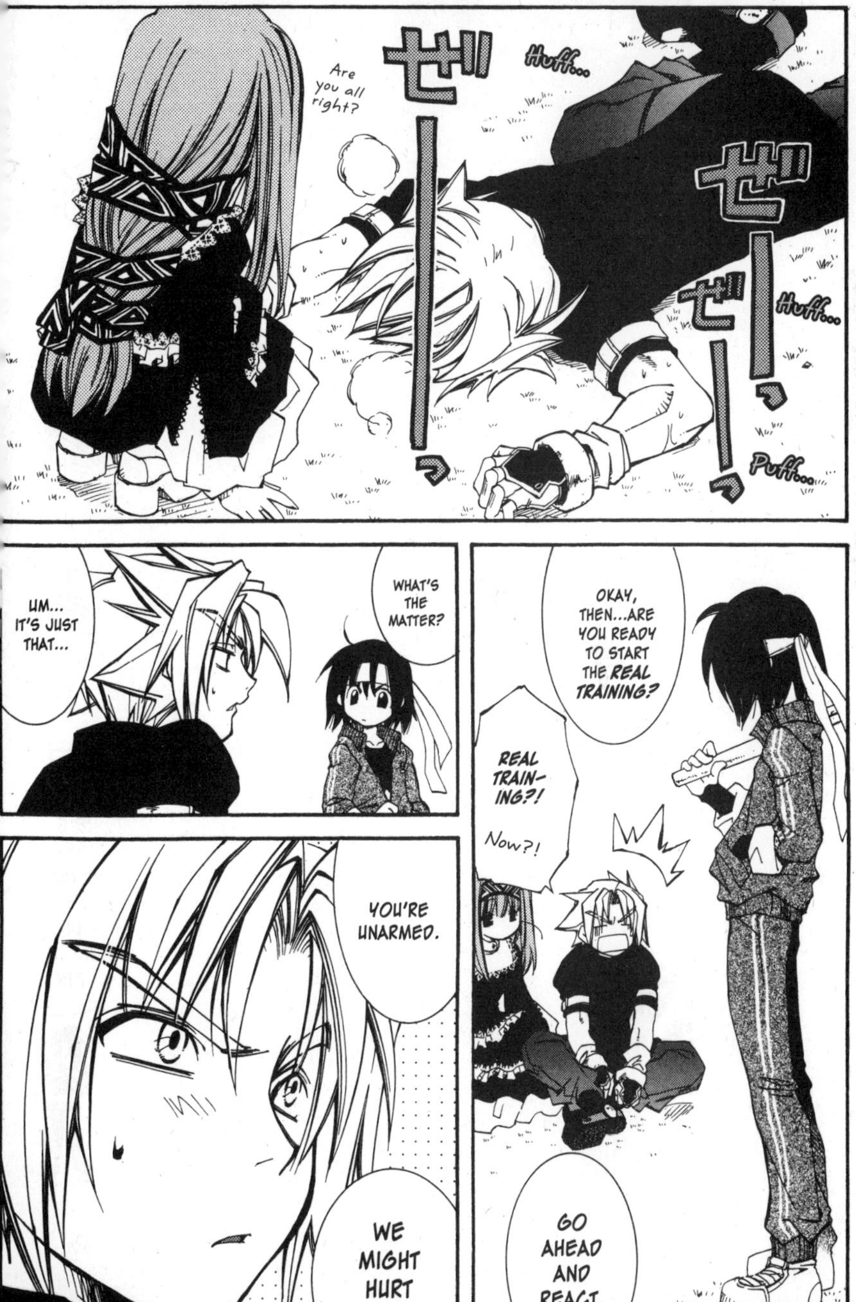
ゼー、
ゼーッ
Huff...
Puff...
ゼーッ
Huff...
Are you all right?
OKAY, THEN...ARE YOU READY TO START THE *REAL TRAINING?*
REAL TRAIN-ING?!
Now?!
GO AHEAD AND REACT.
WHAT'S THE MATTER?
UM... IT'S JUST THAT...
YOU'RE UNARMED.
WE MIGHT HURT YOU.

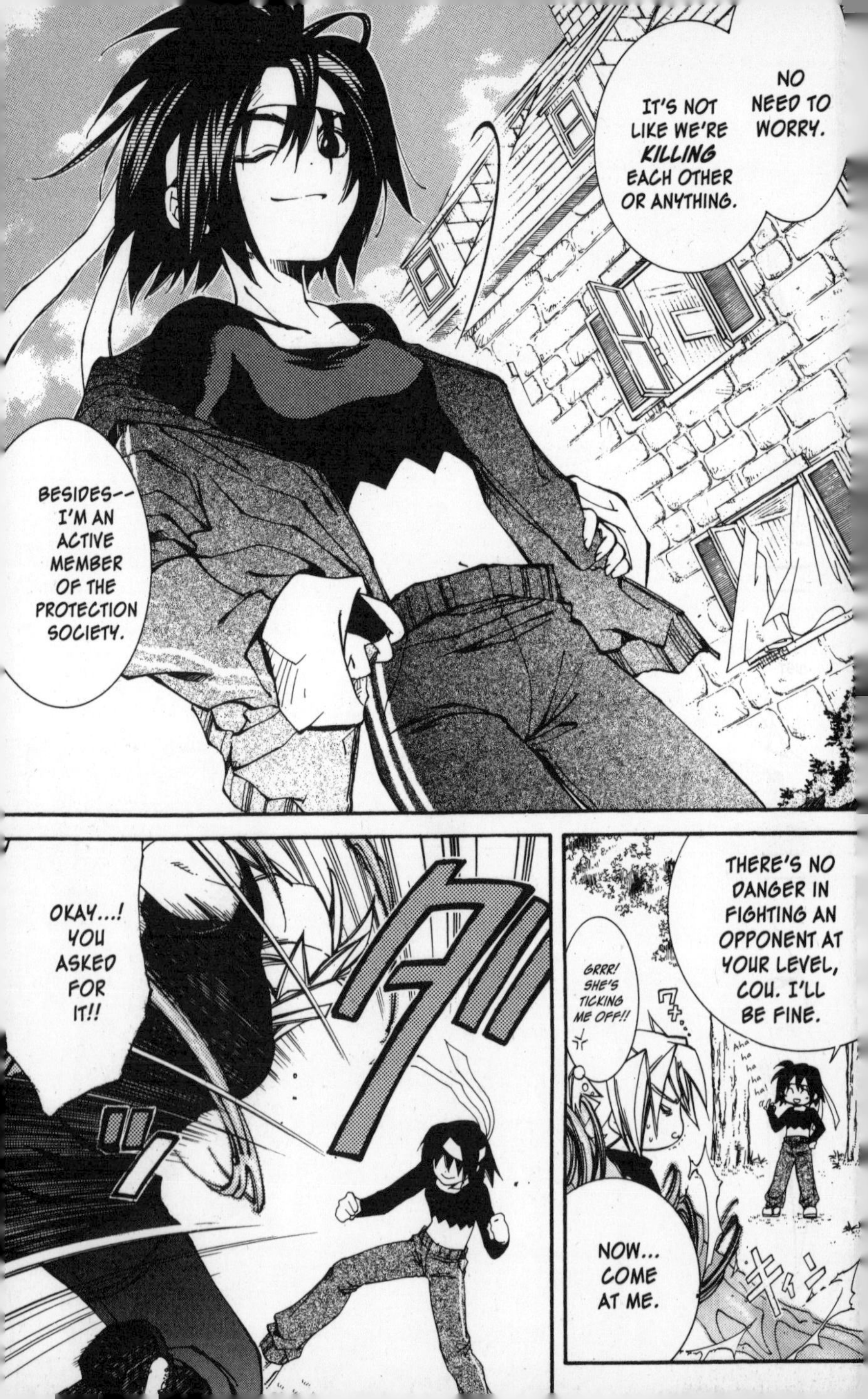
NO NEED TO WORRY.
IT'S NOT LIKE WE'RE *KILLING* EACH OTHER OR ANYTHING.
BESIDES-- I'M AN ACTIVE MEMBER OF THE PROTECTION SOCIETY.
THERE'S NO DANGER IN FIGHTING AN OPPONENT AT YOUR LEVEL, COU. I'LL BE FINE.
Aha ha ha ha ha!
GRRR! SHE'S TICKING ME OFF!!
NOW... COME AT ME.
OKAY...! YOU ASKED FOR IT!!

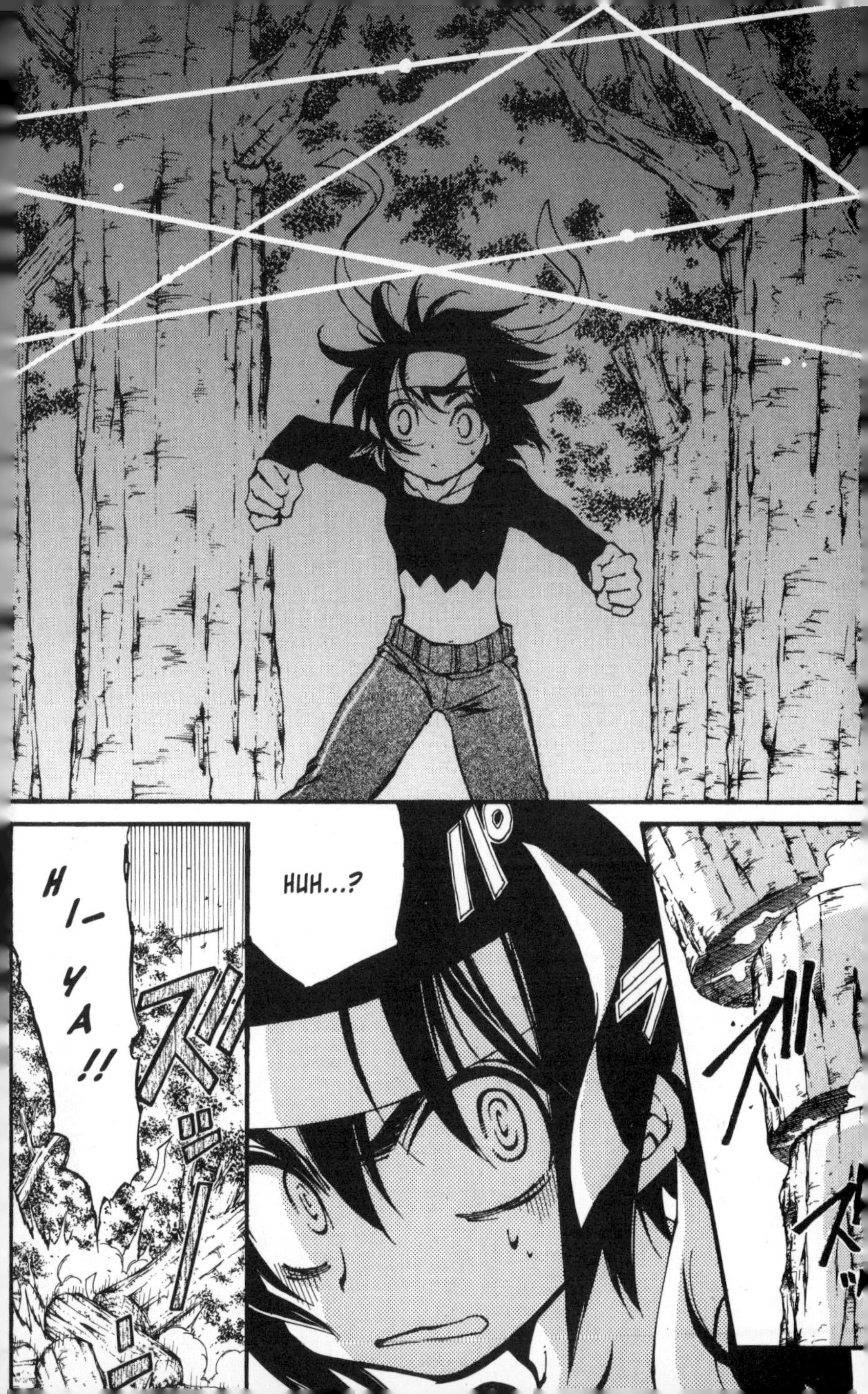
HUH...?
HI-YA!!

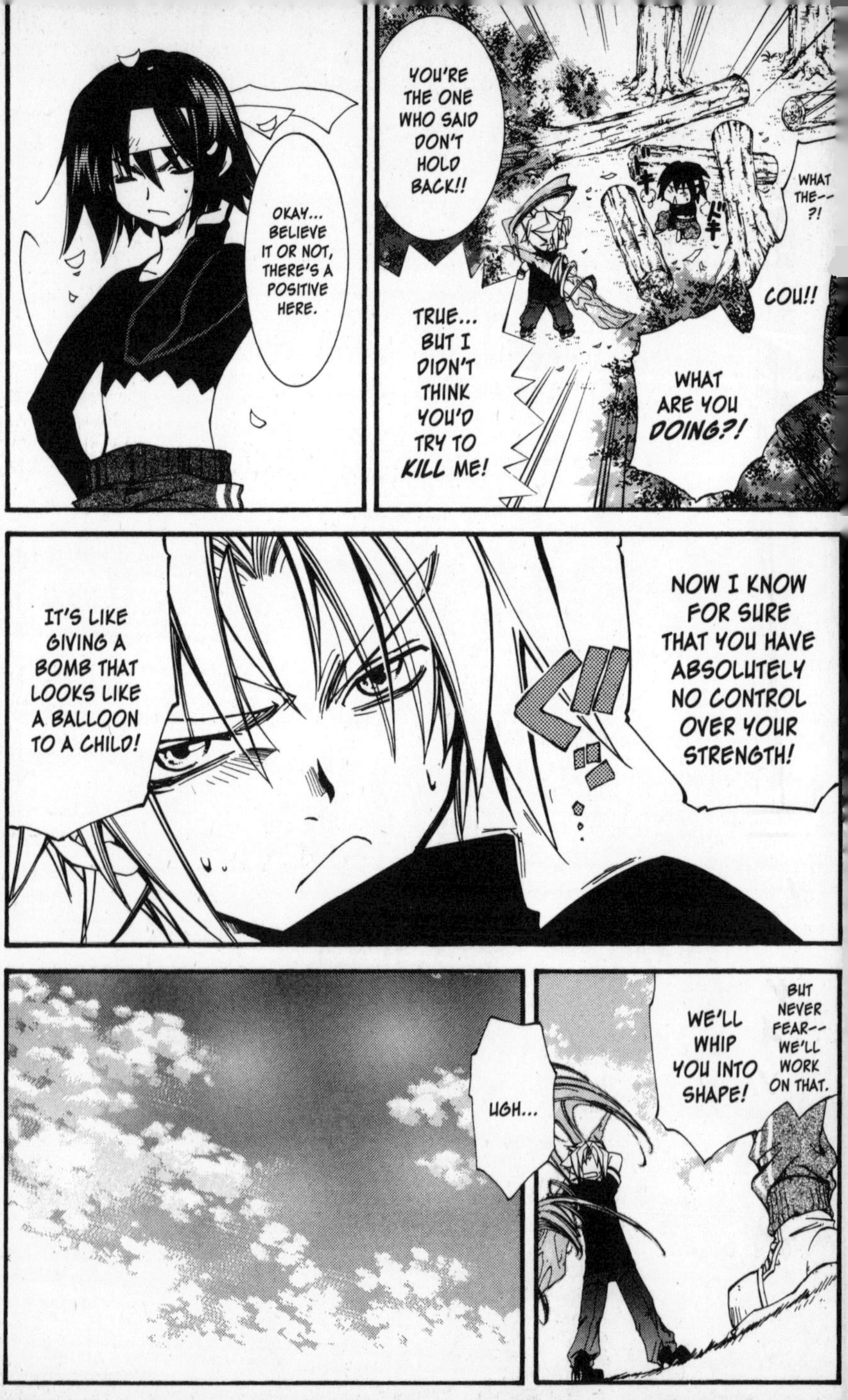
WHAT THE--?!
COU!!
WHAT ARE YOU DOING?!
YOU'RE THE ONE WHO SAID DON'T HOLD BACK!!
TRUE... BUT I DIDN'T THINK YOU'D TRY TO KILL ME!
OKAY... BELIEVE IT OR NOT, THERE'S A POSITIVE HERE.
NOW I KNOW FOR SURE THAT YOU HAVE ABSOLUTELY NO CONTROL OVER YOUR STRENGTH!
IT'S LIKE GIVING A BOMB THAT LOOKS LIKE A BALLOON TO A CHILD!
BUT NEVER FEAR-- WE'LL WORK ON THAT.
WE'LL WHIP YOU INTO SHAPE!
UGH...

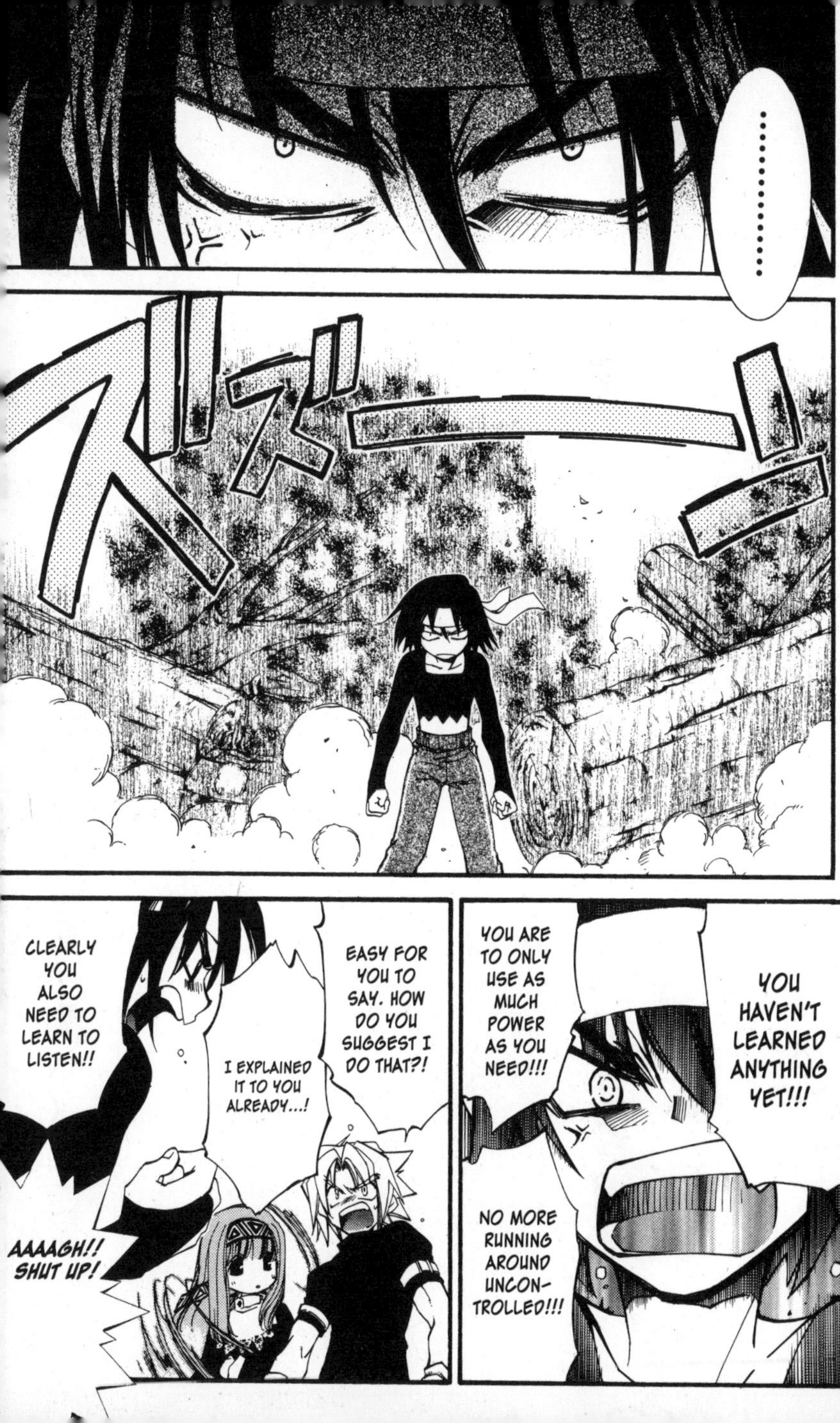
......
ズゴーン
YOU HAVEN'T LEARNED ANYTHING YET!!!
YOU ARE TO ONLY USE AS MUCH POWER AS YOU NEED!!!
NO MORE RUNNING AROUND UNCON-TROLLED!!!
EASY FOR YOU TO SAY. HOW DO YOU SUGGEST I DO THAT?!
I EXPLAINED IT TO YOU ALREADY...!
CLEARLY YOU ALSO NEED TO LEARN TO LISTEN!!
AAAAGH!! SHUT UP!

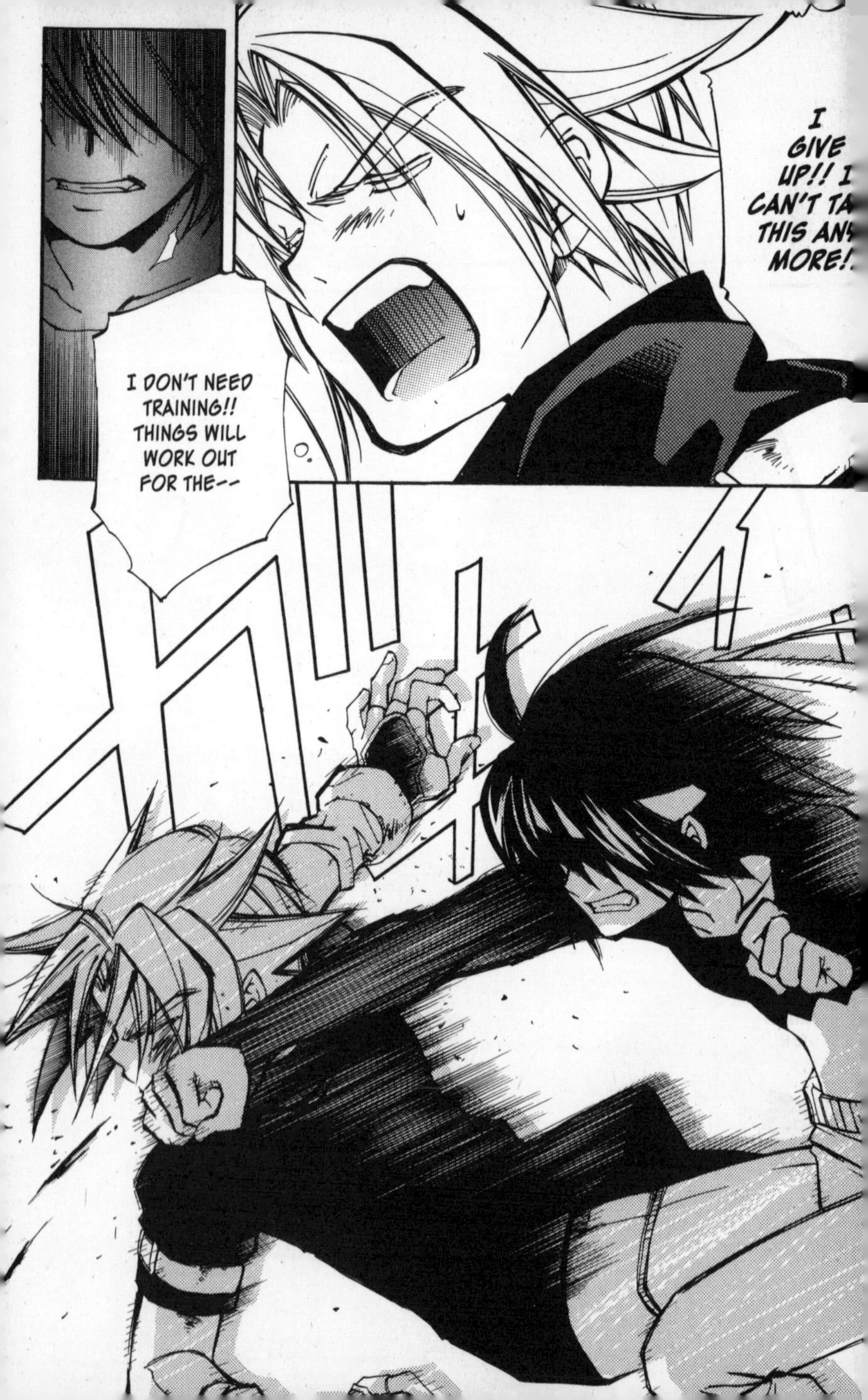
I GIVE UP!! I CAN'T TA THIS AN MORE!
I DON'T NEED TRAINING!! THINGS WILL WORK OUT FOR THE--

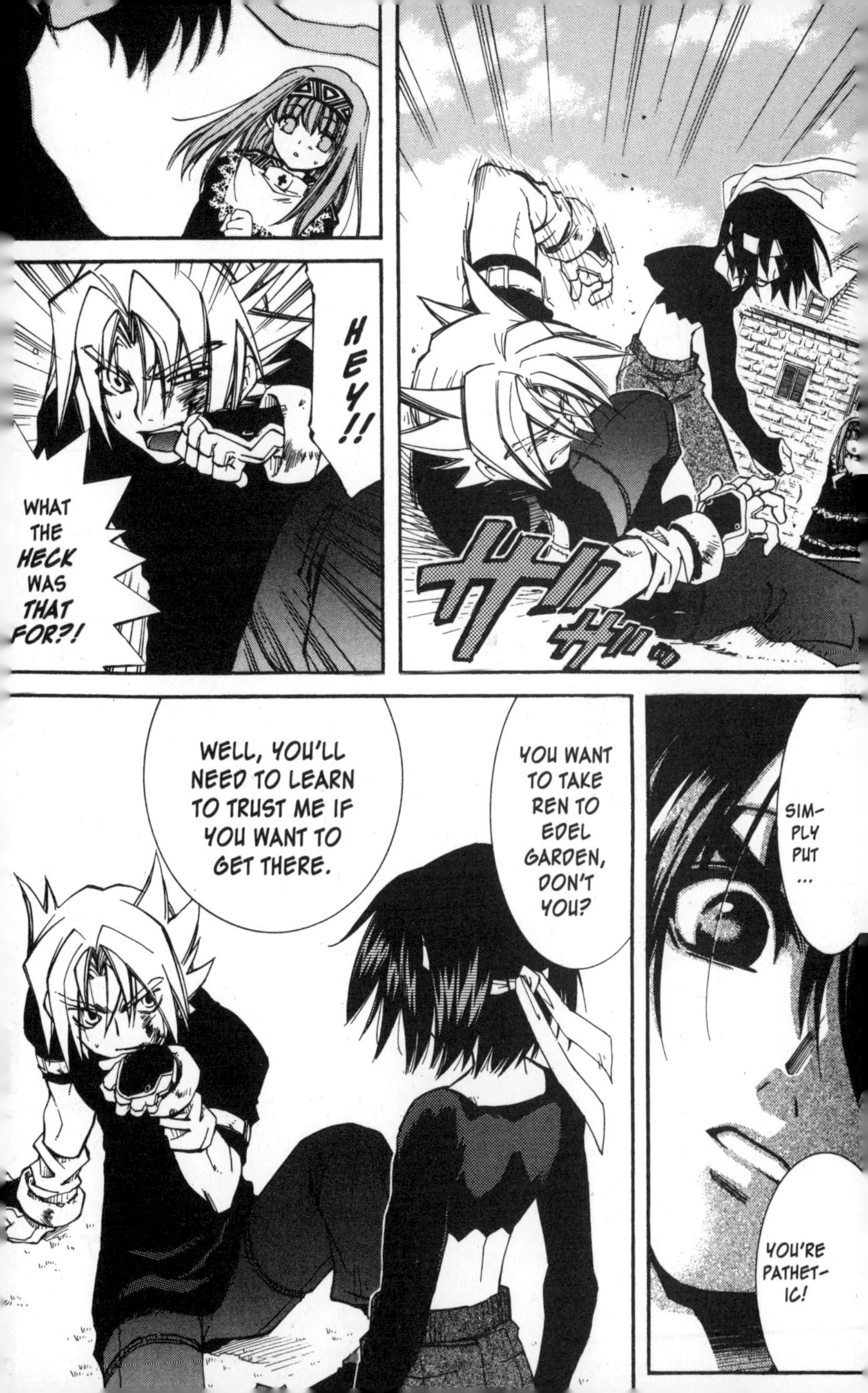
HEY!!
WHAT THE HECK WAS THAT FOR?!
SIMPLY PUT ...
YOU'RE PATHETIC!
YOU WANT TO TAKE REN TO EDEL GARDEN, DON'T YOU?
WELL, YOU'LL NEED TO LEARN TO TRUST ME IF YOU WANT TO GET THERE.

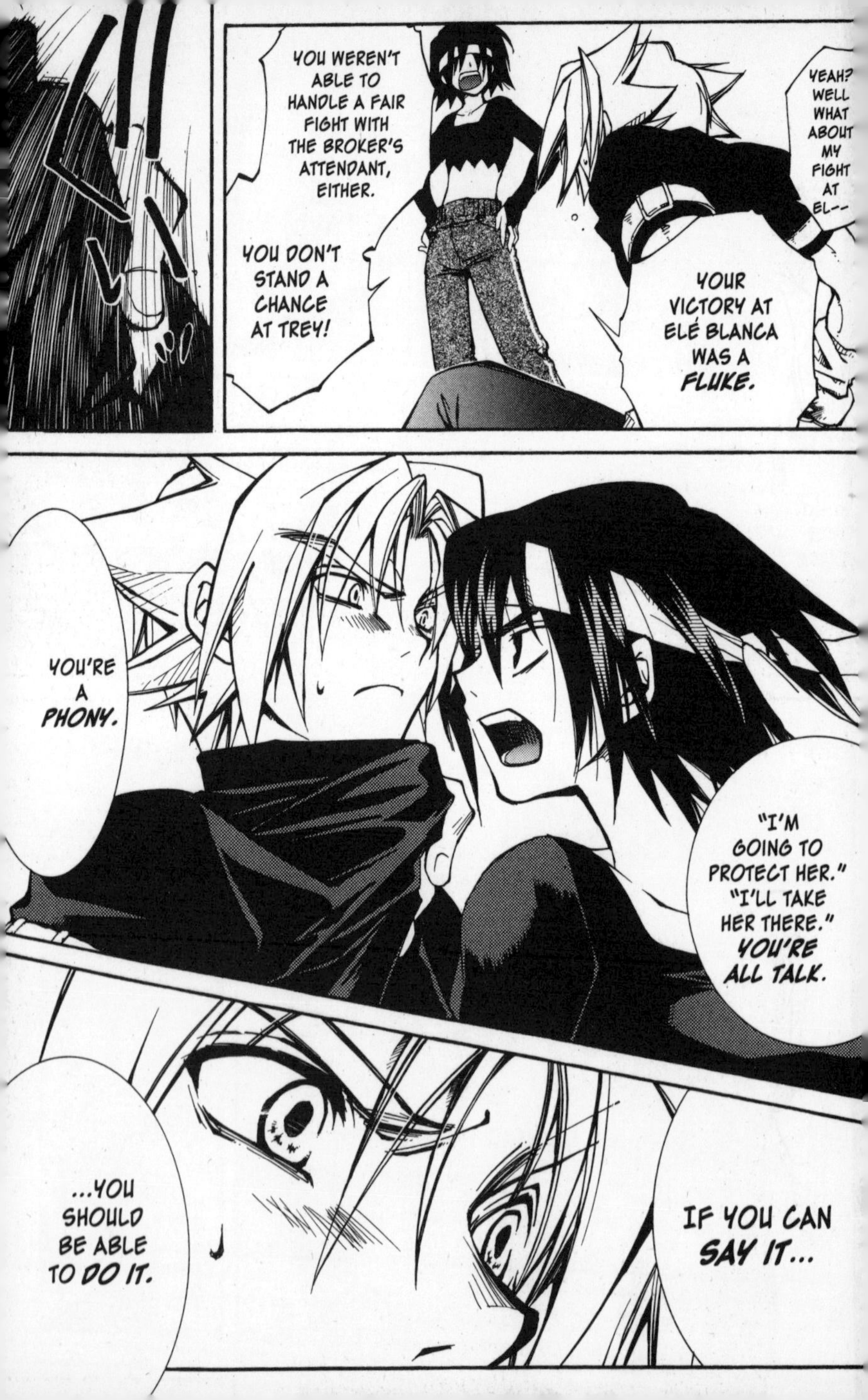
YEAH? WELL WHAT ABOUT MY FIGHT AT EL--
YOU WEREN'T ABLE TO HANDLE A FAIR FIGHT WITH THE BROKER'S ATTENDANT, EITHER.
YOUR VICTORY AT ELÉ BLANCA WAS A FLUKE.
YOU DON'T STAND A CHANCE AT TREY!
"I'M GOING TO PROTECT HER." "I'LL TAKE HER THERE." YOU'RE ALL TALK.
YOU'RE A PHONY.
IF YOU CAN SAY IT...
...YOU SHOULD BE ABLE TO DO IT.

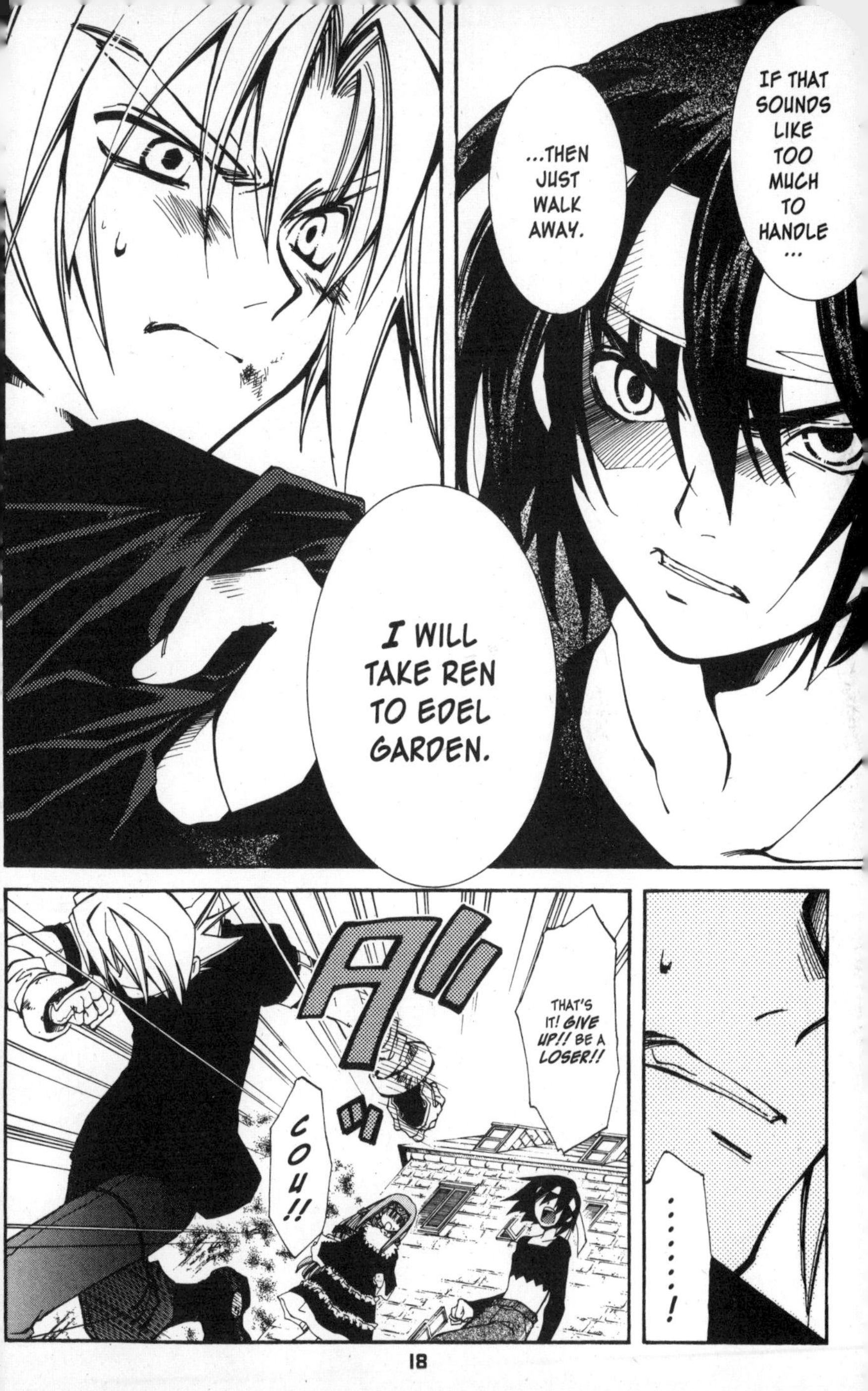
IF THAT SOUNDS LIKE TOO MUCH TO HANDLE ...
...THEN JUST WALK AWAY.
I WILL TAKE REN TO EDEL GARDEN.
........!
THAT'S IT! GIVE UP!! BE A LOSER!!
A!!
COU!!

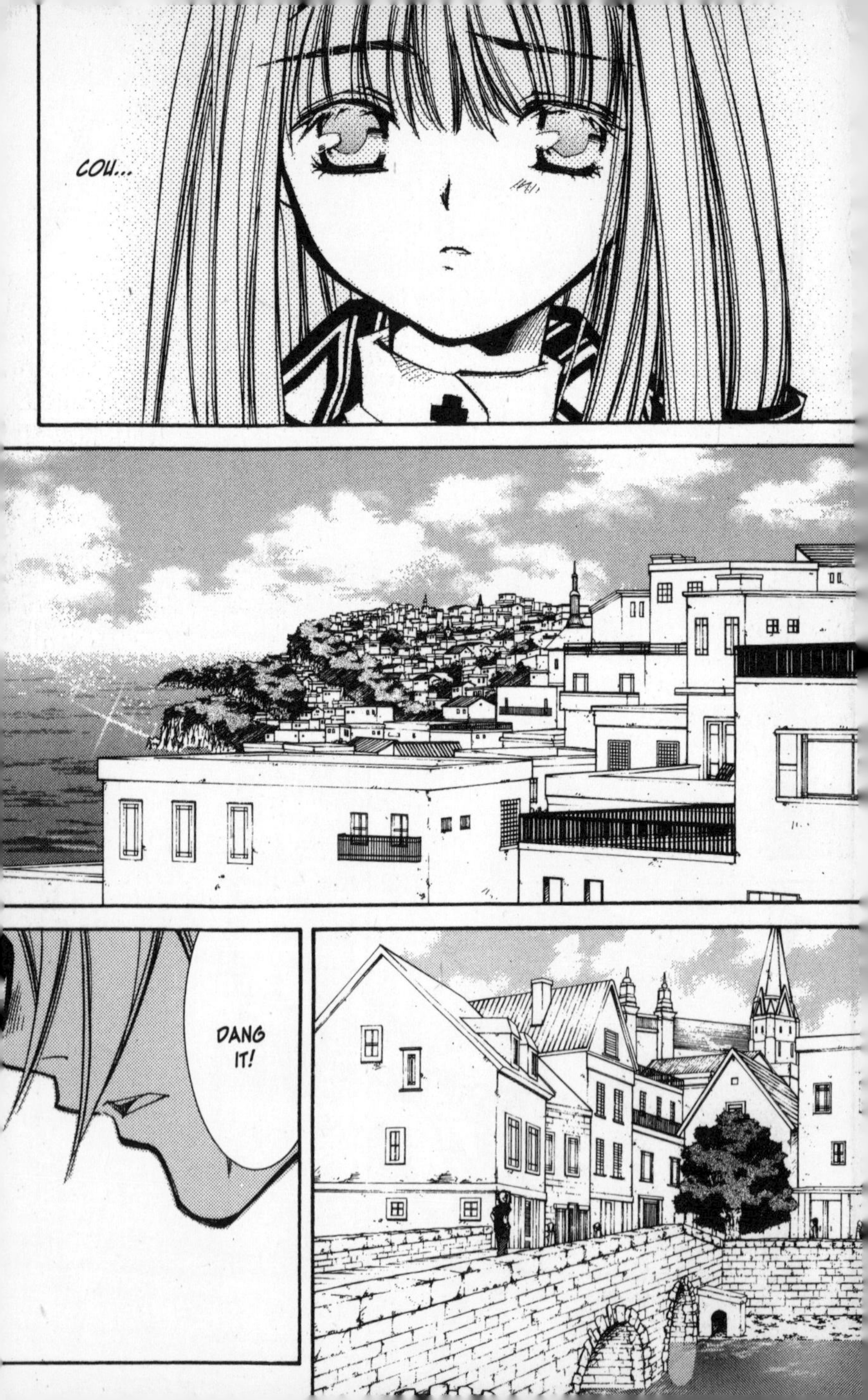
COU...
DANG IT!

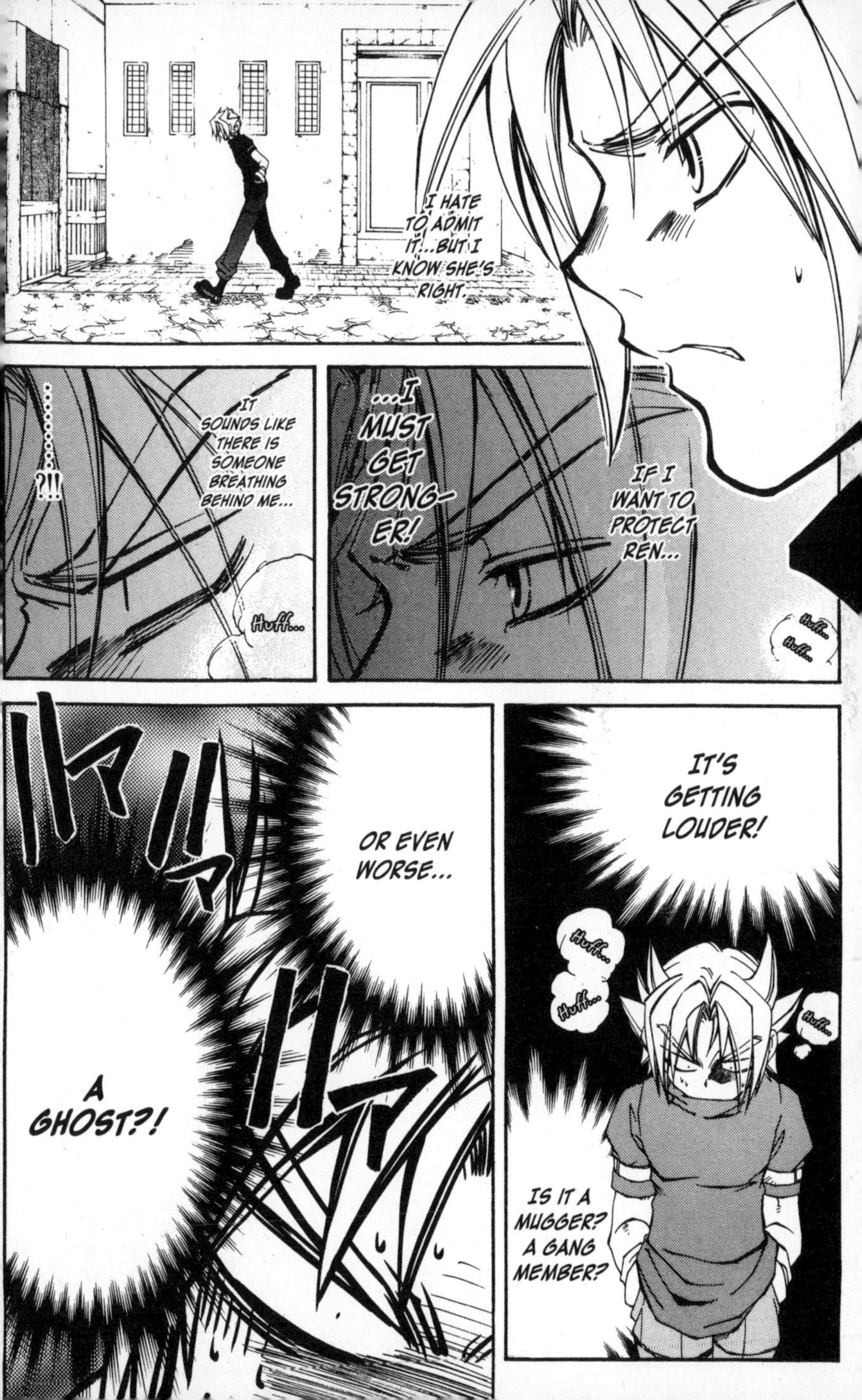

I HATE TO ADMIT IT...BUT I KNOW SHE'S RIGHT.
IF I WANT TO PROTECT REN...
...I MUST GET STRONGER!
Huff... Huff...
IT SOUNDS LIKE THERE IS SOMEONE BREATHING BEHIND ME...
Huff...
......?!!
IT'S GETTING LOUDER!
Huff... Huff...
Huff...
IS IT A MUGGER? A GANG MEMBER?
OR EVEN WORSE...
ハァ
ハァ
A GHOST?!

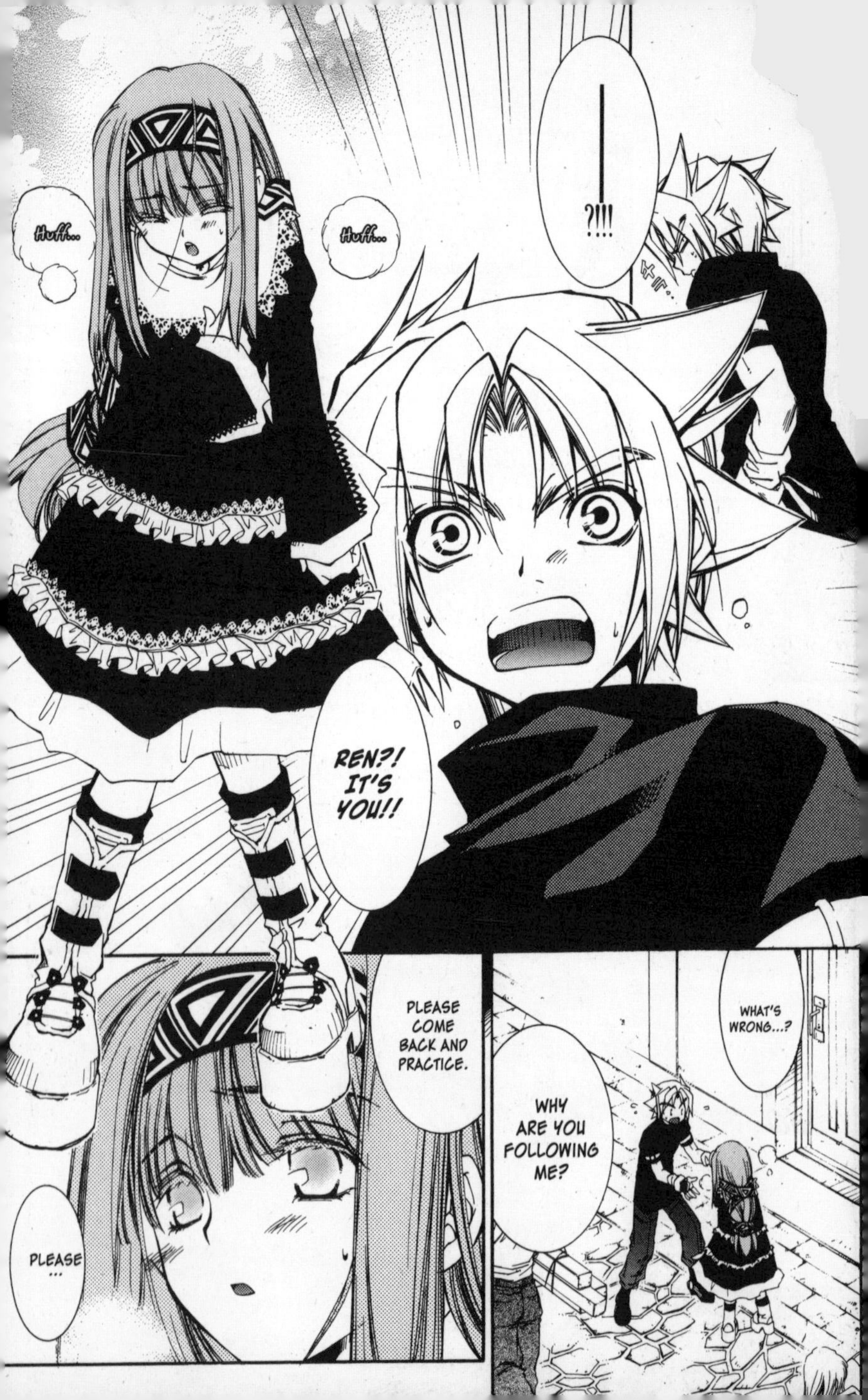
?!!!
Huff...
Huff...
REN?! IT'S YOU!!
WHAT'S WRONG...?
WHY ARE YOU FOLLOWING ME?
PLEASE COME BACK AND PRACTICE.
PLEASE ...

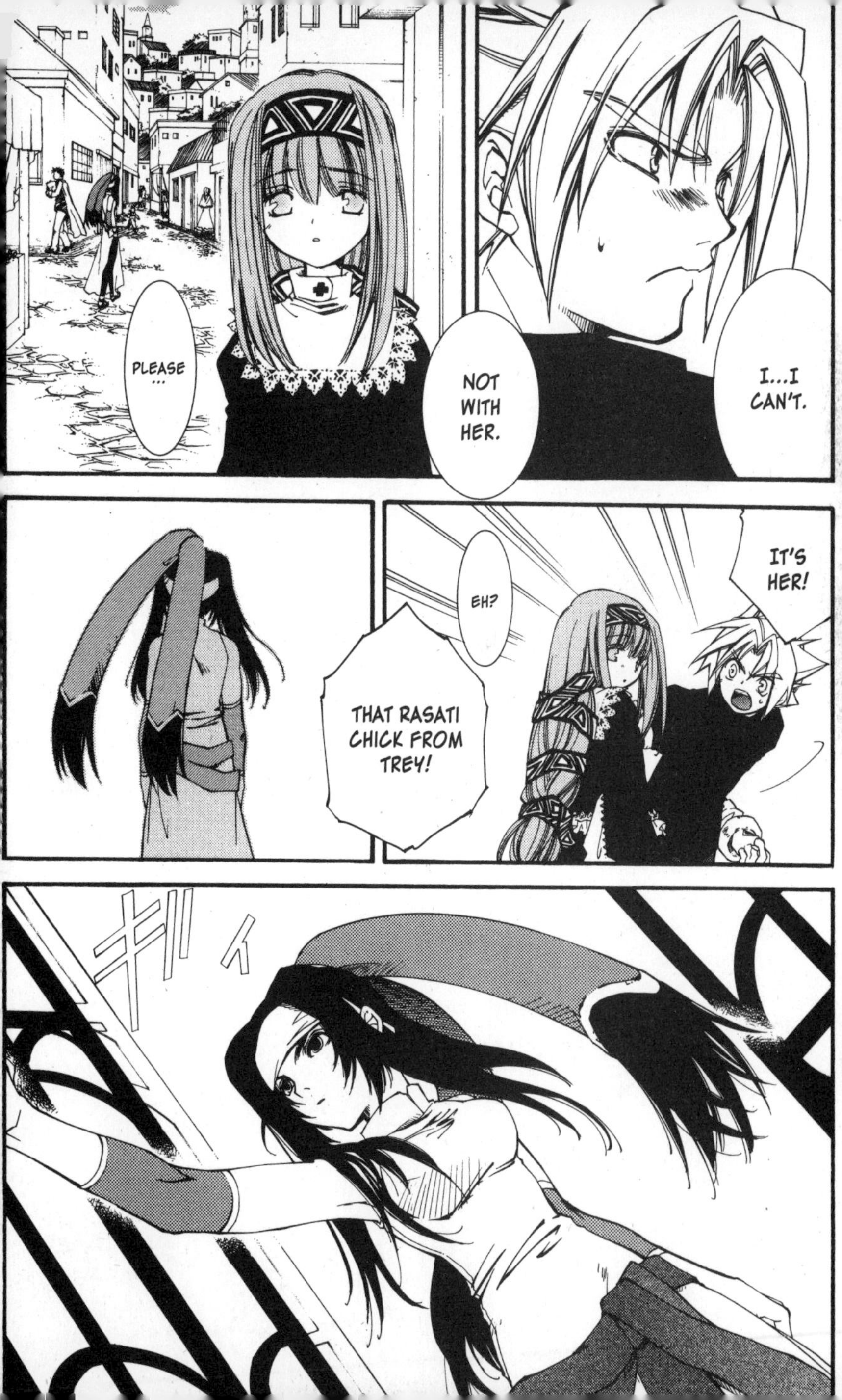
I...I CAN'T.
NOT WITH HER.
PLEASE ...
IT'S HER!
EH?
THAT RASATI CHICK FROM TREY!
キリィ

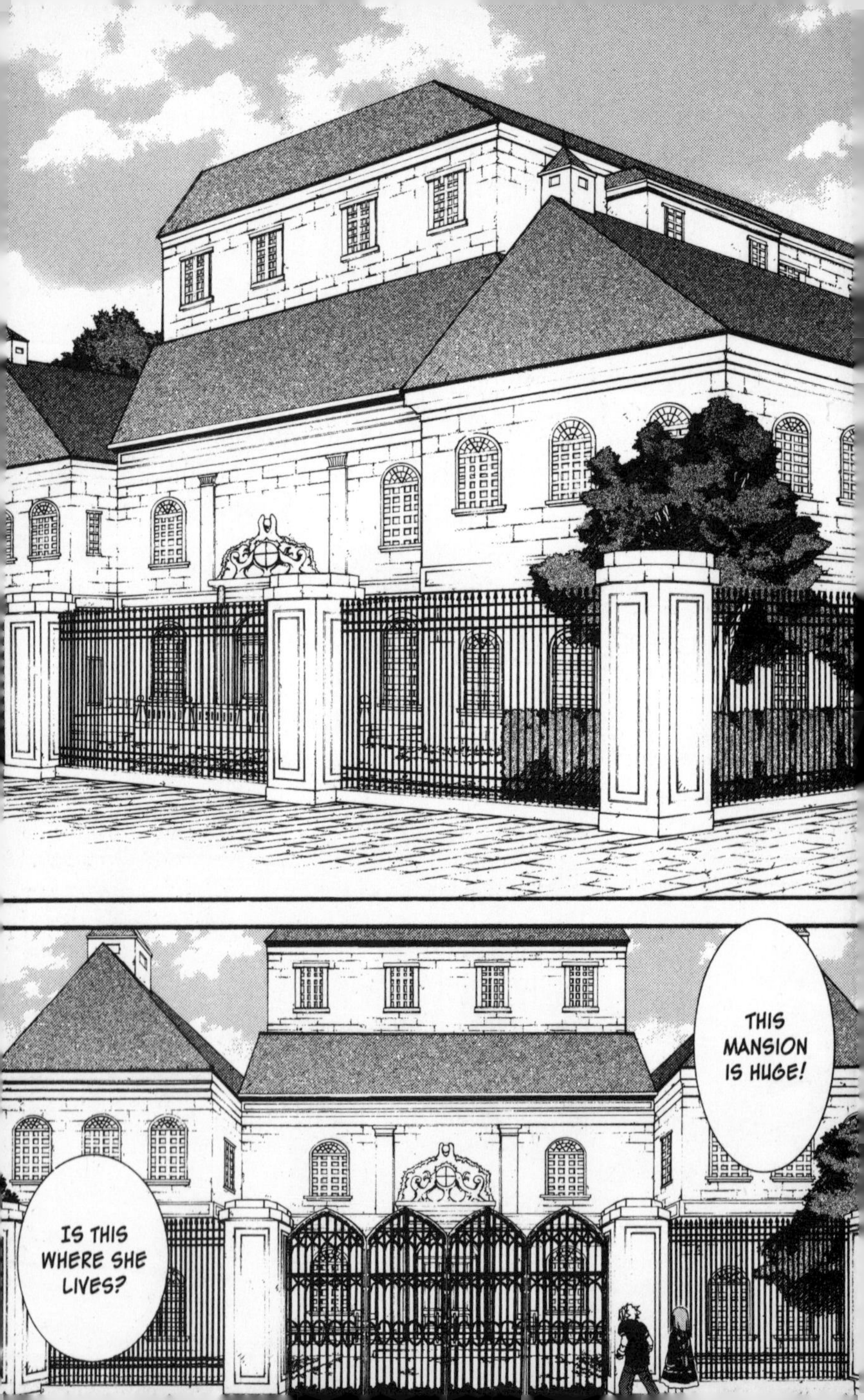
THIS MANSION IS HUGE!
IS THIS WHERE SHE LIVES?

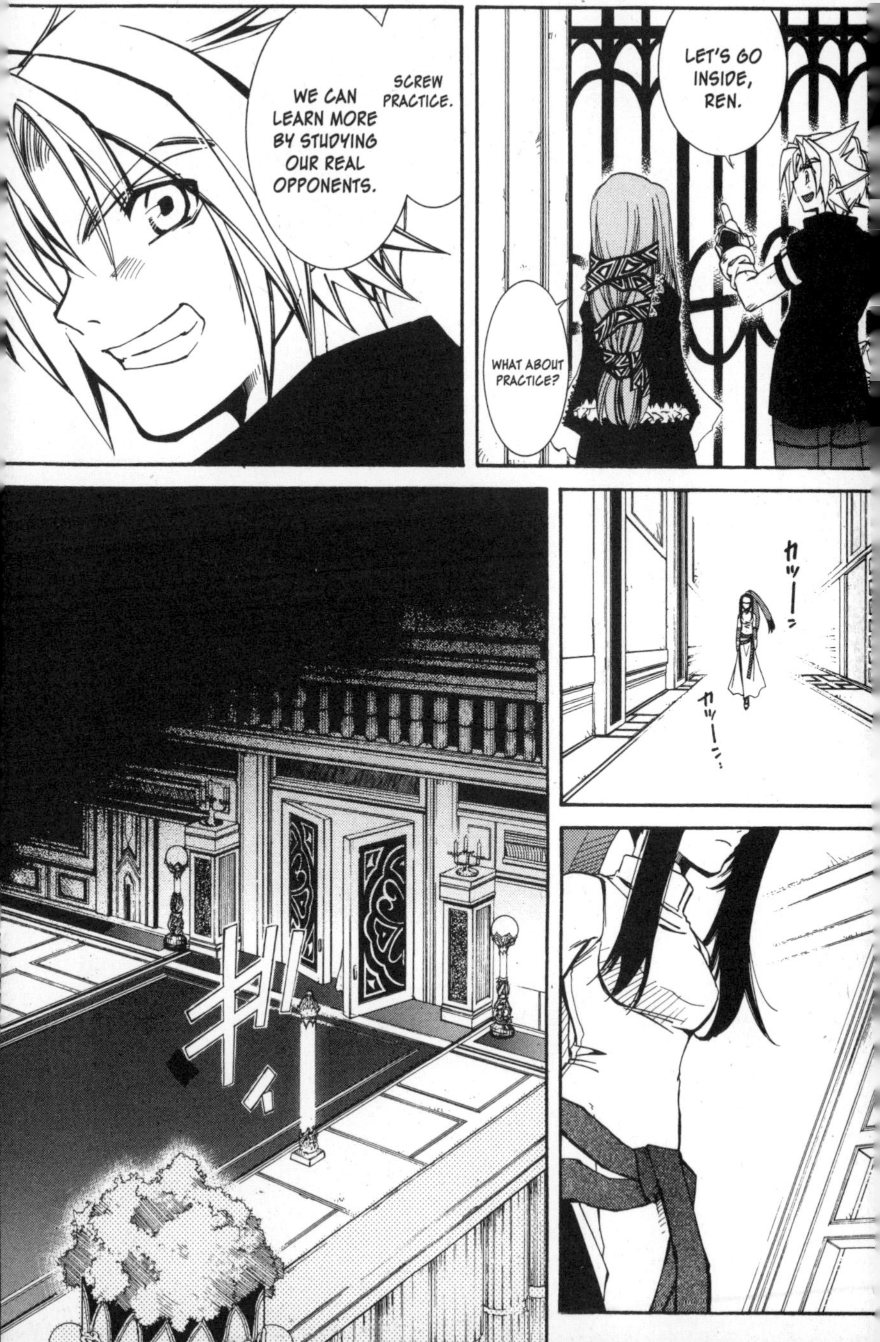
LET'S GO INSIDE, REN.
WHAT ABOUT PRACTICE?
SCREW PRACTICE.
WE CAN LEARN MORE BY STUDYING OUR REAL OPPONENTS.

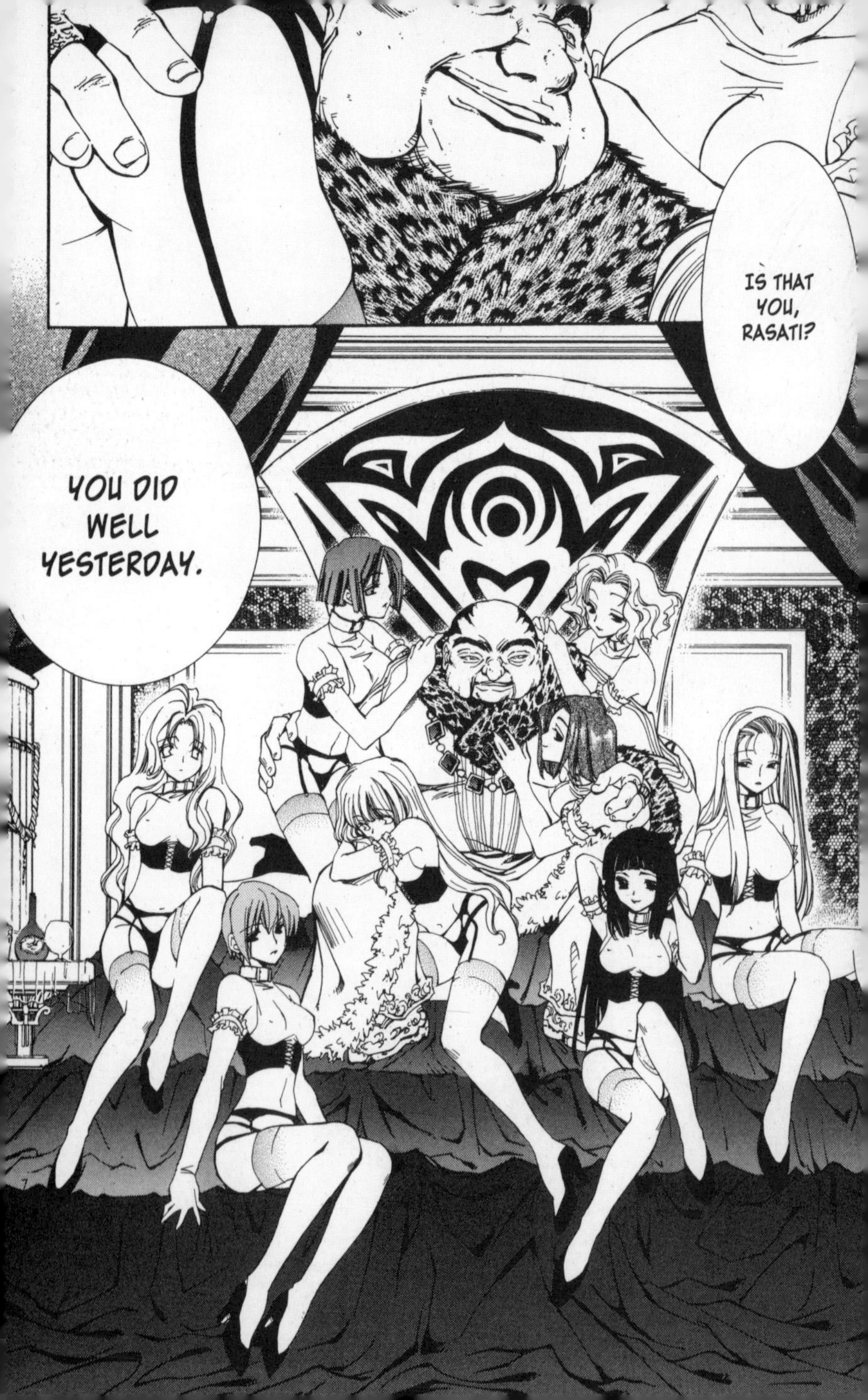
IS THAT YOU, RASATI?
YOU DID WELL YESTERDAY.

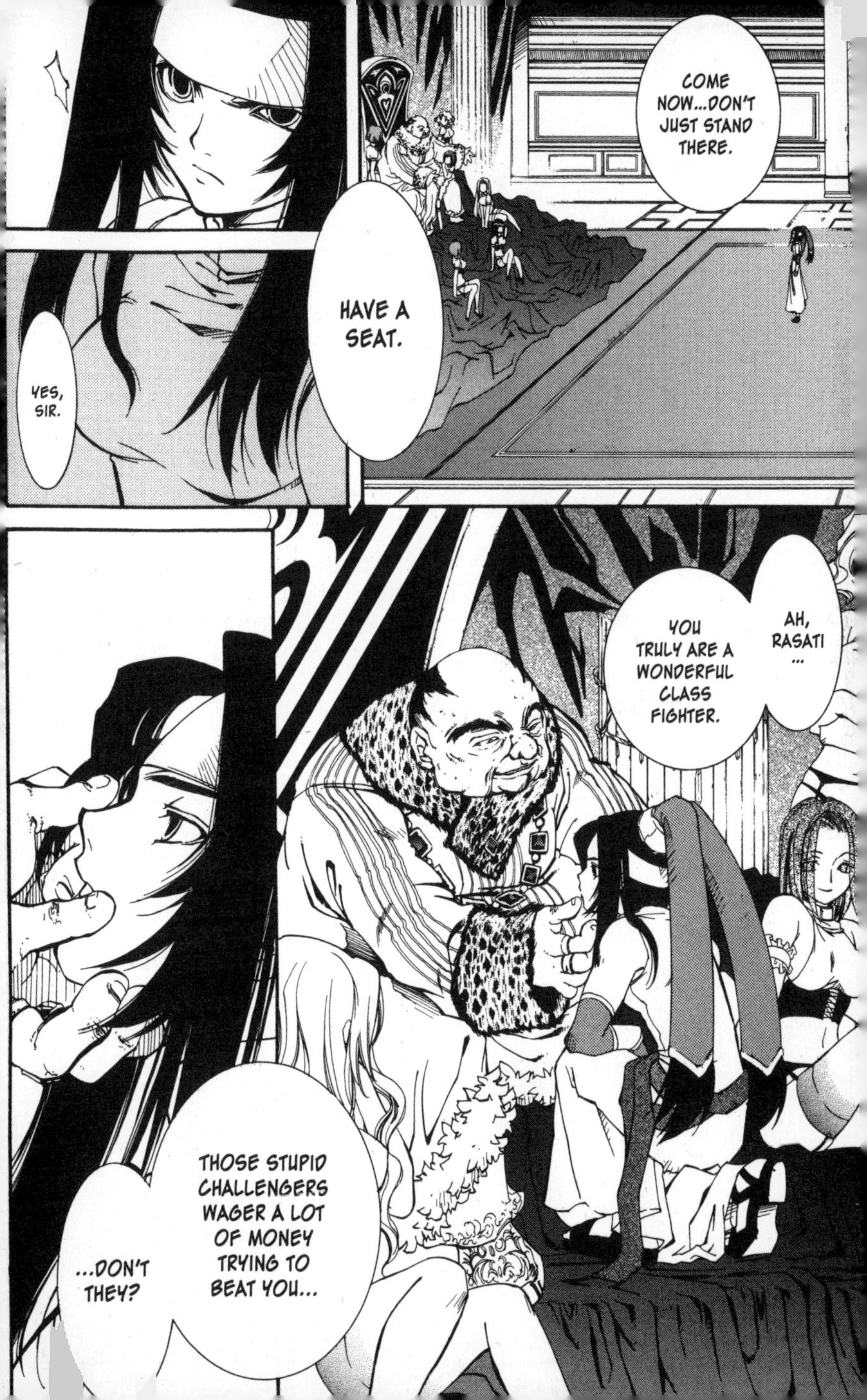
COME NOW...DON'T JUST STAND THERE.
HAVE A SEAT.
YES, SIR.
AH, RASATI ...
YOU TRULY ARE A WONDERFUL CLASS FIGHTER.
THOSE STUPID CHALLENGERS WAGER A LOT OF MONEY TRYING TO BEAT YOU...
...DON'T THEY?

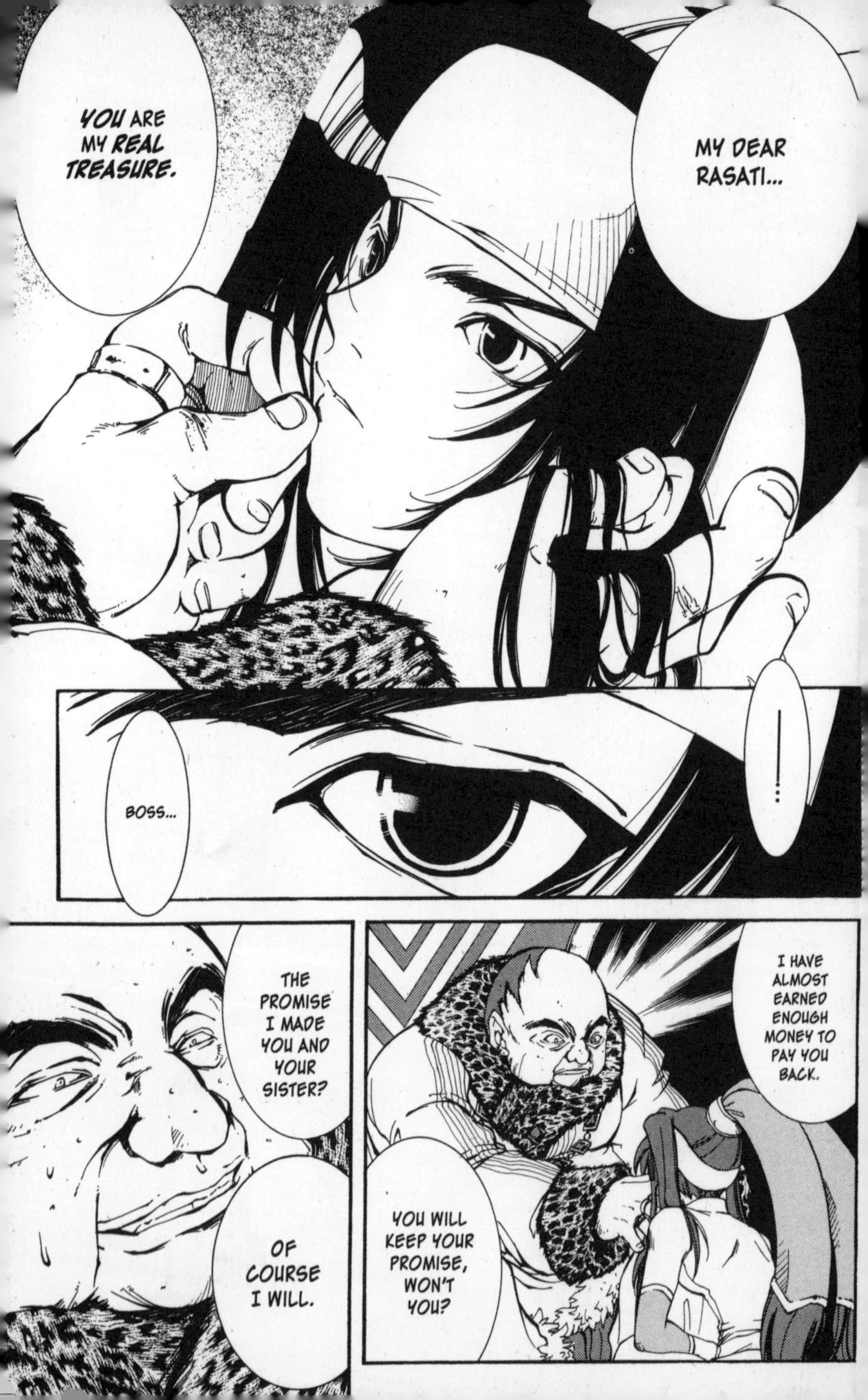
MY DEAR RASATI...
YOU ARE MY REAL TREASURE.
!......
BOSS...
I HAVE ALMOST EARNED ENOUGH MONEY TO PAY YOU BACK.
YOU WILL KEEP YOUR PROMISE, WON'T YOU?
THE PROMISE I MADE YOU AND YOUR SISTER?
OF COURSE I WILL.

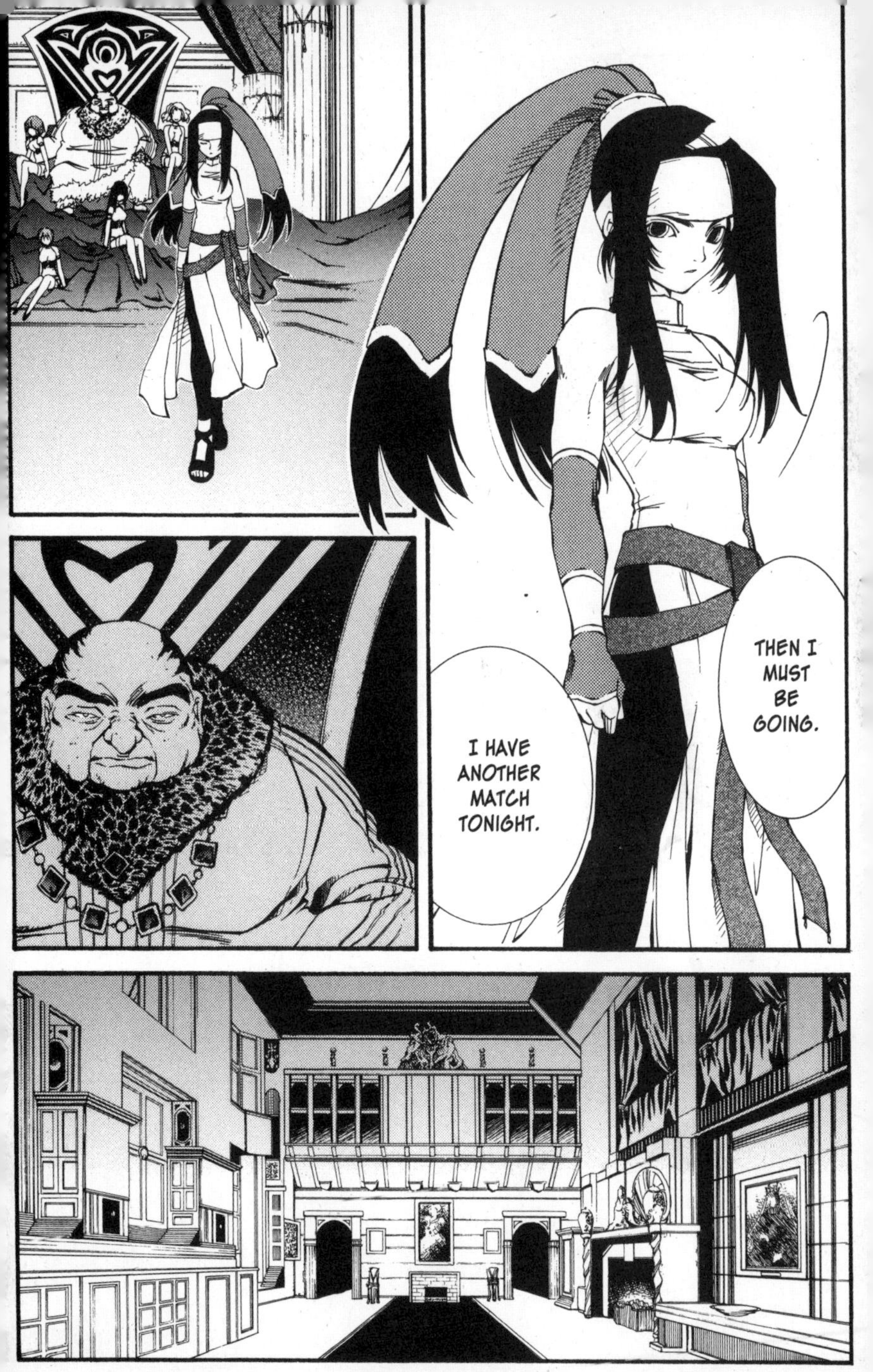
THEN I MUST BE GOING.
I HAVE ANOTHER MATCH TONIGHT.

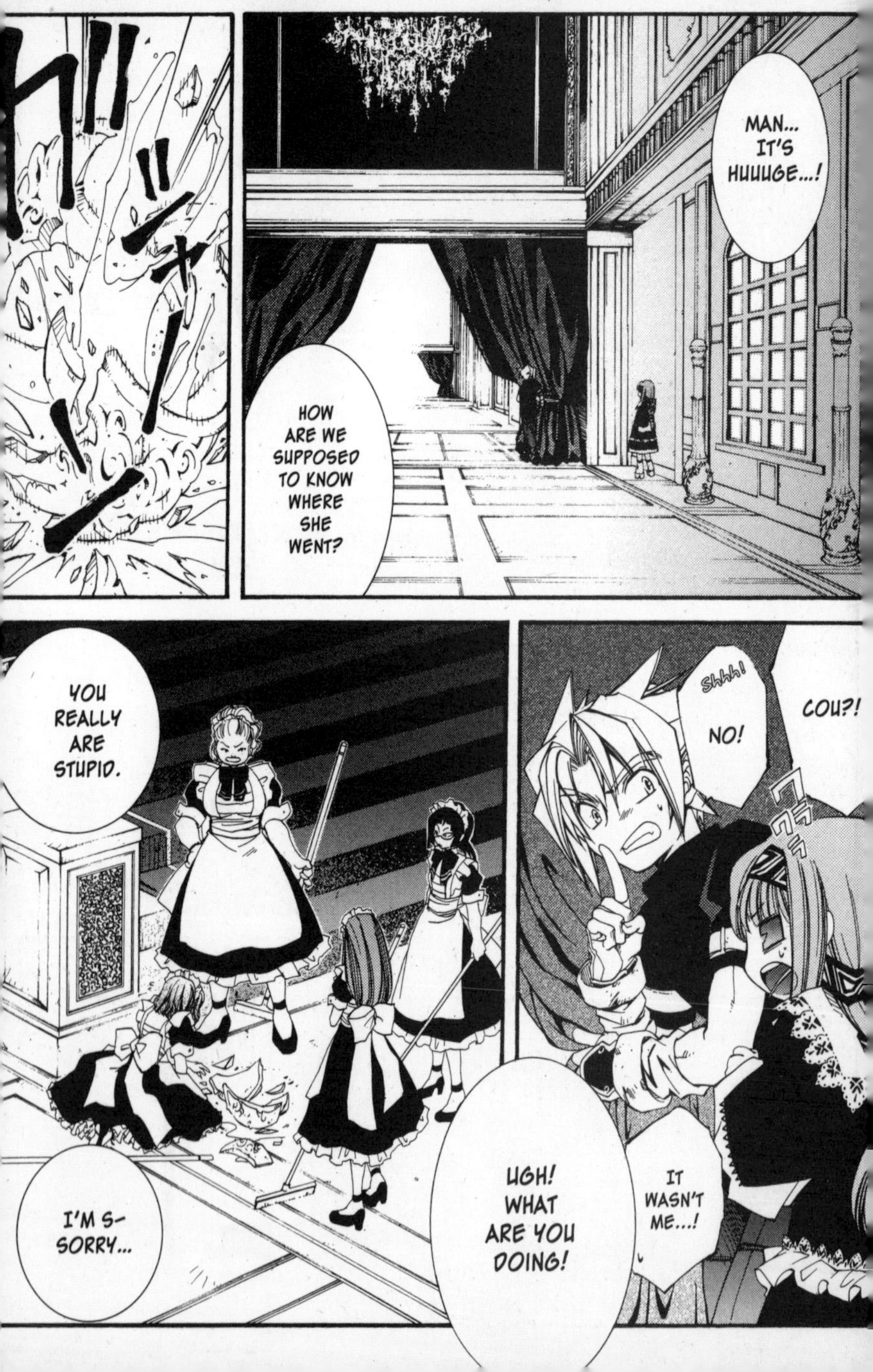
MAN... IT'S HUUUGE...!
HOW ARE WE SUPPOSED TO KNOW WHERE SHE WENT?
COU?!
Shhh!
NO!
IT WASN'T ME...!
UGH! WHAT ARE YOU DOING!
YOU REALLY ARE STUPID.
I'M S-SORRY...

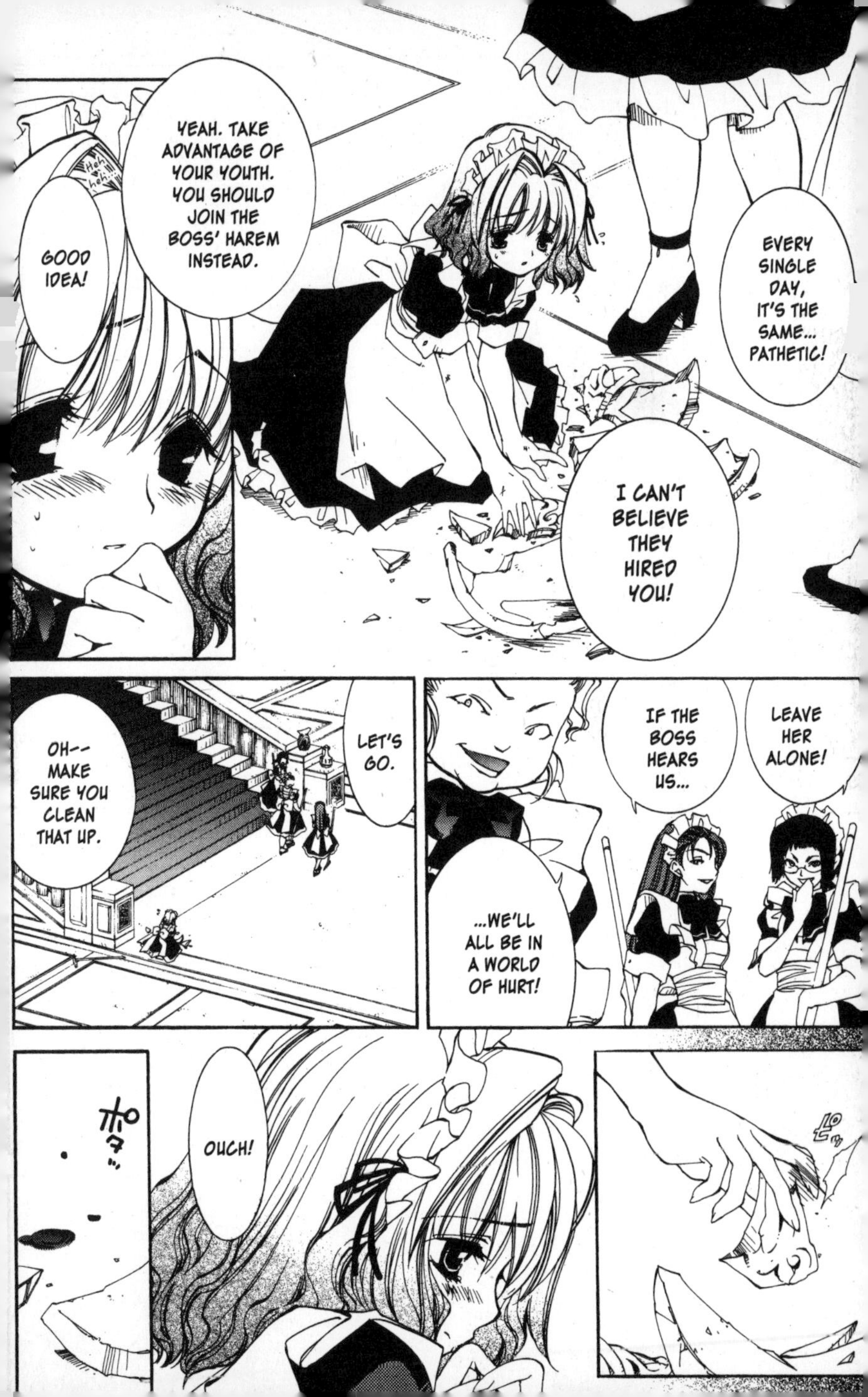
EVERY SINGLE DAY, IT'S THE SAME... PATHETIC!
I CAN'T BELIEVE THEY HIRED YOU!
YEAH. TAKE ADVANTAGE OF YOUR YOUTH. YOU SHOULD JOIN THE BOSS' HAREM INSTEAD.
Heh heh...
GOOD IDEA!
LEAVE HER ALONE!
IF THE BOSS HEARS US...
...WE'LL ALL BE IN A WORLD OF HURT!
LET'S GO.
OH-- MAKE SURE YOU CLEAN THAT UP.
OUCH!
ポタ…

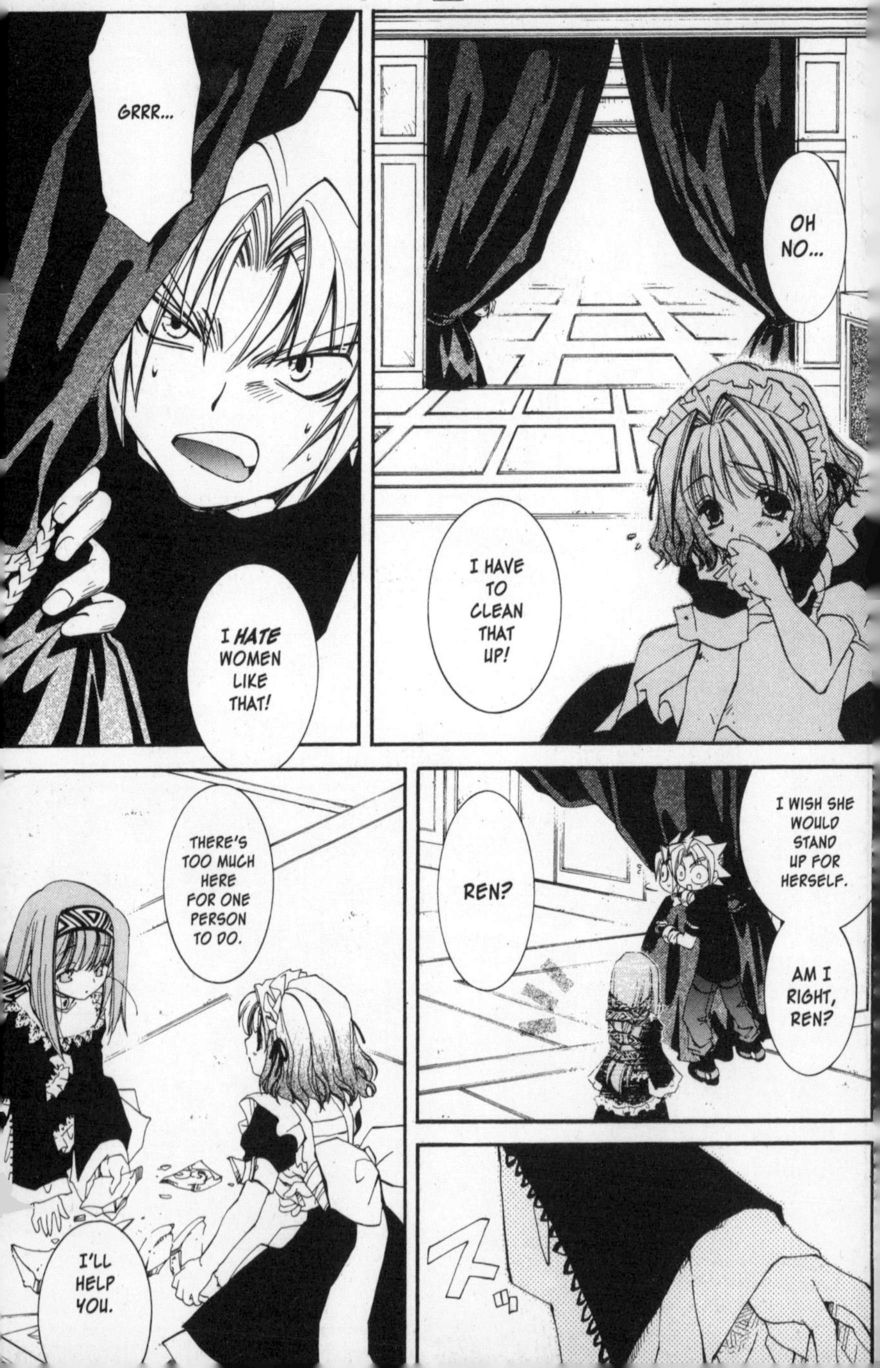
OH NO...
I HAVE TO CLEAN THAT UP!
GRRR...
I *HATE* WOMEN LIKE THAT!
I WISH SHE WOULD STAND UP FOR HERSELF.
AM I RIGHT, REN?
REN?
ス
THERE'S TOO MUCH HERE FOR ONE PERSON TO DO.
I'LL HELP YOU.

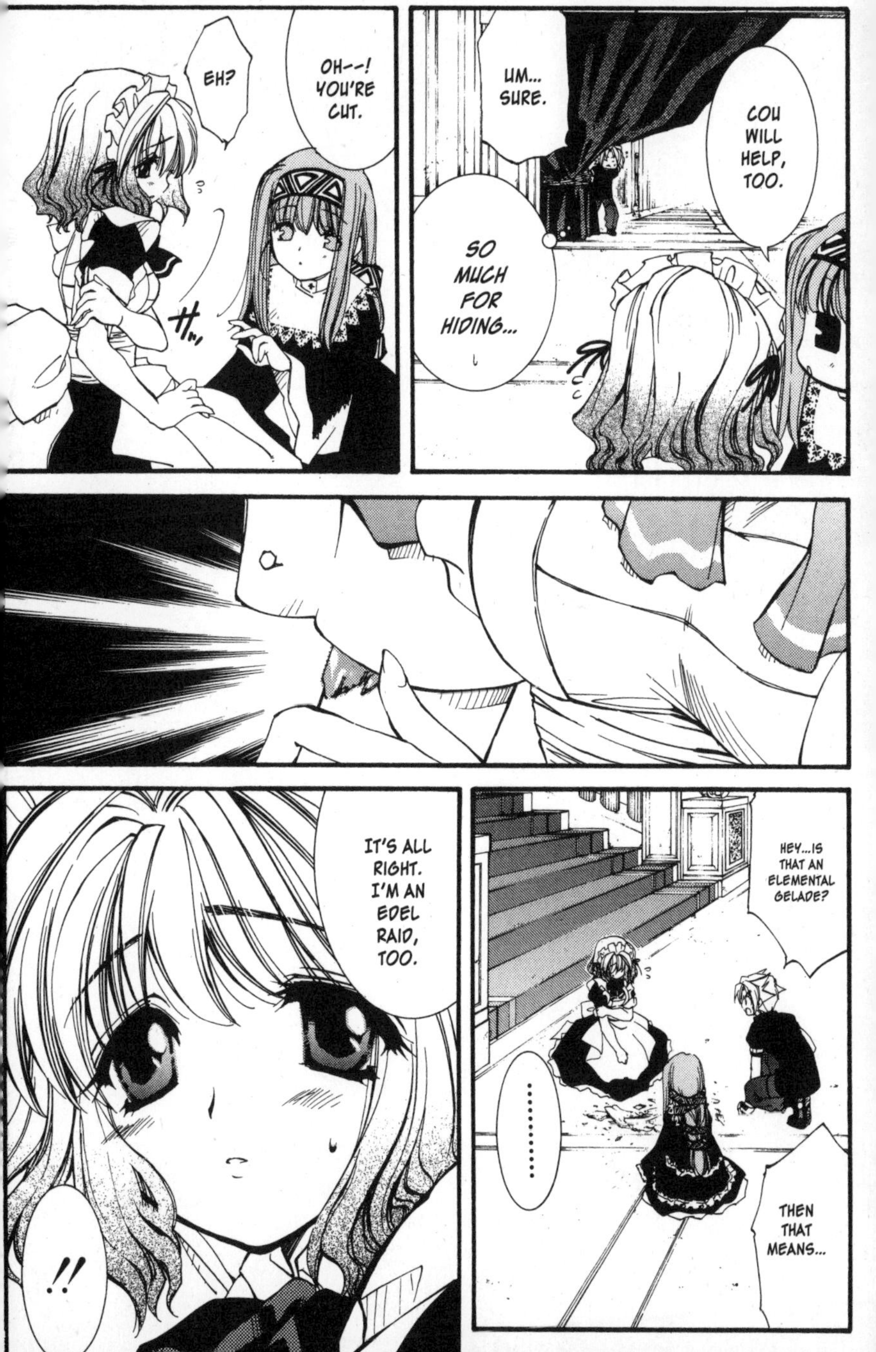
COU WILL HELP, TOO.
UM... SURE.
SO MUCH FOR HIDING...
OH--! YOU'RE CUT.
EH?
HEY...IS THAT AN ELEMENTAL GELADE?
......
THEN THAT MEANS...
IT'S ALL RIGHT. I'M AN EDEL RAID, TOO.
!!

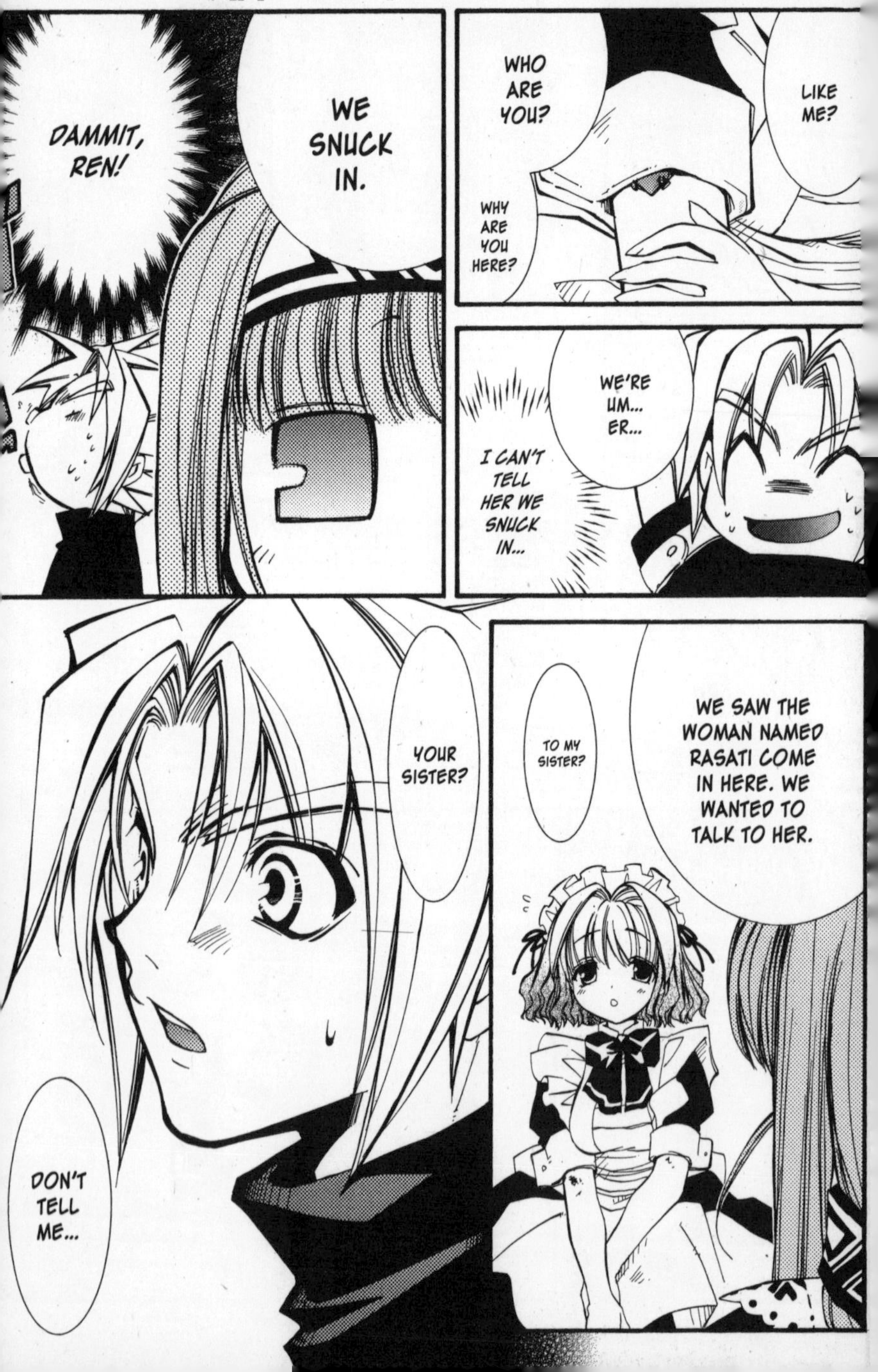
LIKE ME?
WHO ARE YOU?
WHY ARE YOU HERE?
WE'RE UM... ER...
I CAN'T TELL HER WE SNUCK IN...
WE SNUCK IN.
DAMMIT, REN!
WE SAW THE WOMAN NAMED RASATI COME IN HERE. WE WANTED TO TALK TO HER.
TO MY SISTER?
YOUR SISTER?
DON'T TELL ME...

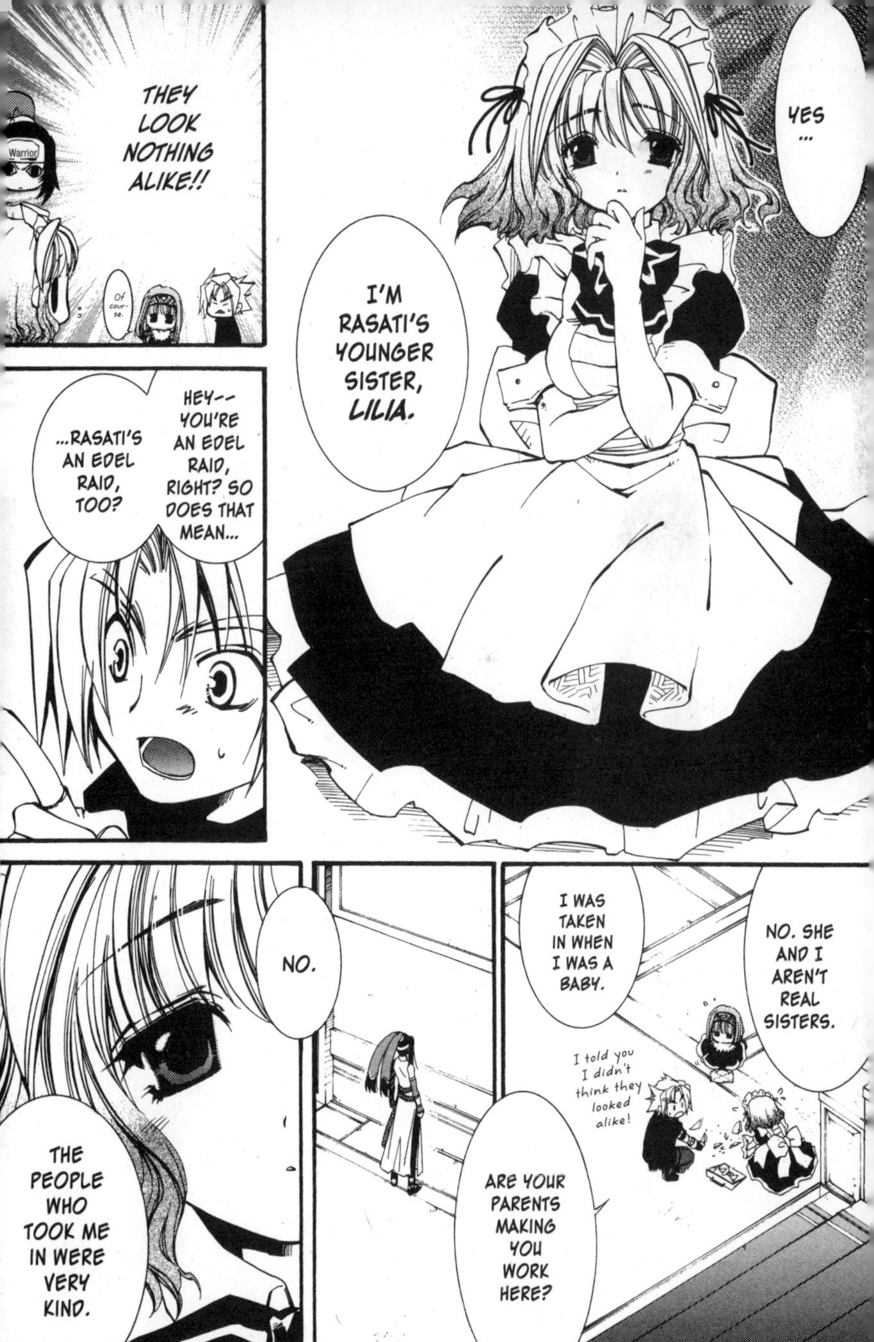
YES ...
I'M RASATI'S YOUNGER SISTER, LILIA.
THEY LOOK NOTHING ALIKE!!
Warrior
Of course.
HEY-- YOU'RE AN EDEL RAID, RIGHT? SO DOES THAT MEAN...
...RASATI'S AN EDEL RAID, TOO?
NO. SHE AND I AREN'T REAL SISTERS.
I WAS TAKEN IN WHEN I WAS A BABY.
I told you I didn't think they looked alike!
ARE YOUR PARENTS MAKING YOU WORK HERE?
NO.
THE PEOPLE WHO TOOK ME IN WERE VERY KIND.

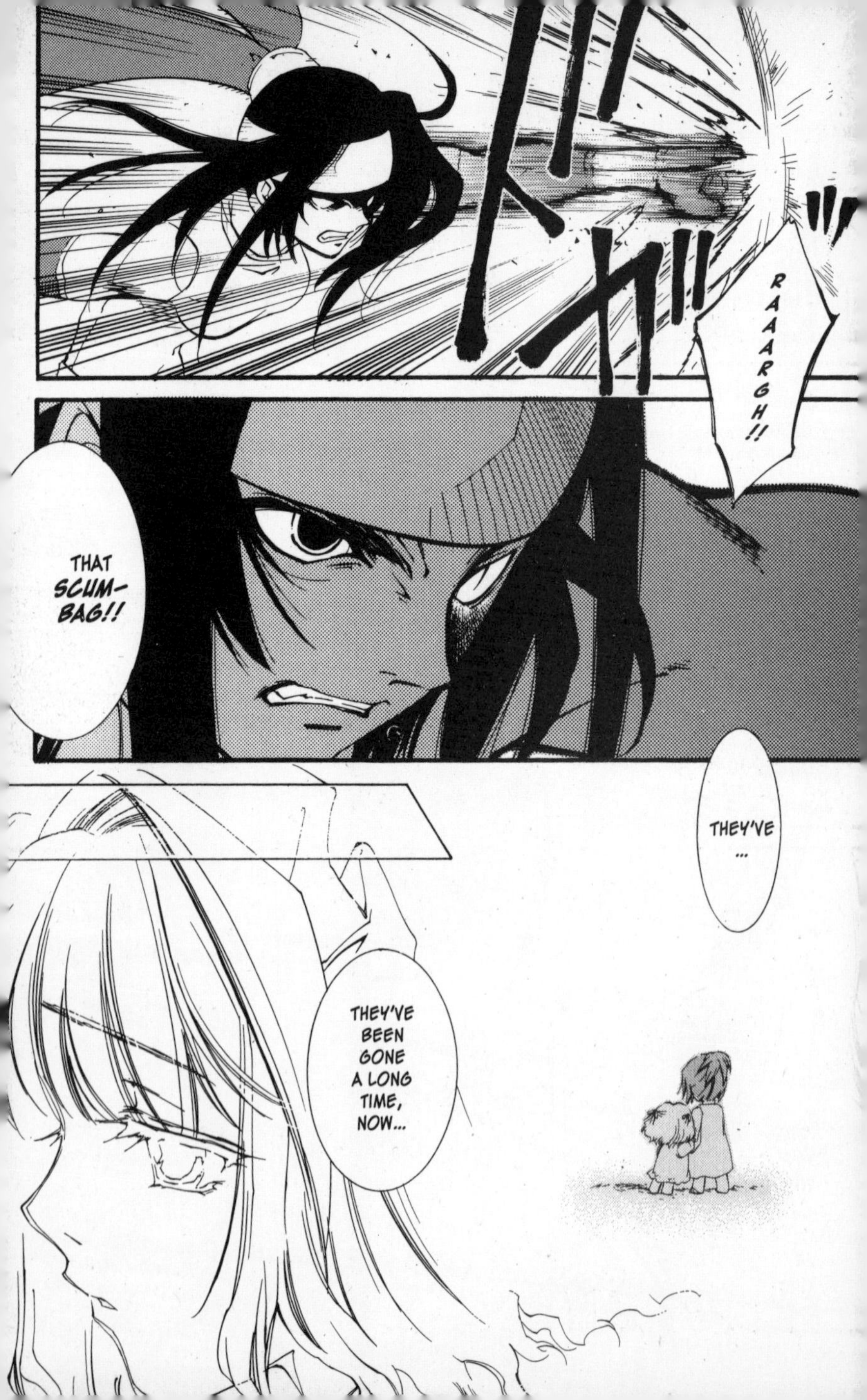
RAAARGH!!
THAT SCUM-BAG!!
THEY'VE ...
THEY'VE BEEN GONE A LONG TIME, NOW...

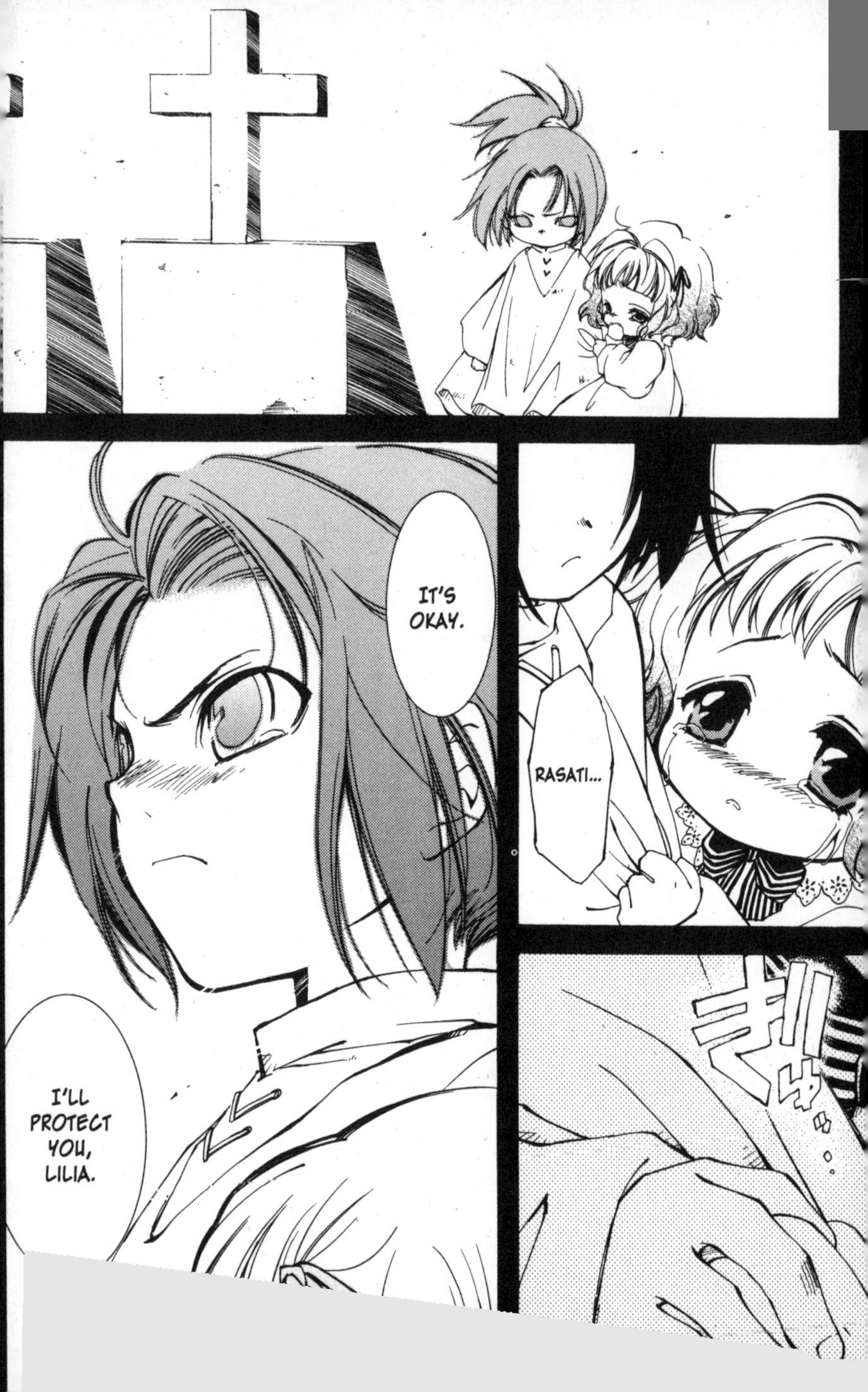
RASATI...
ぎゅ
IT'S OKAY.
I'LL PROTECT YOU, LILIA.

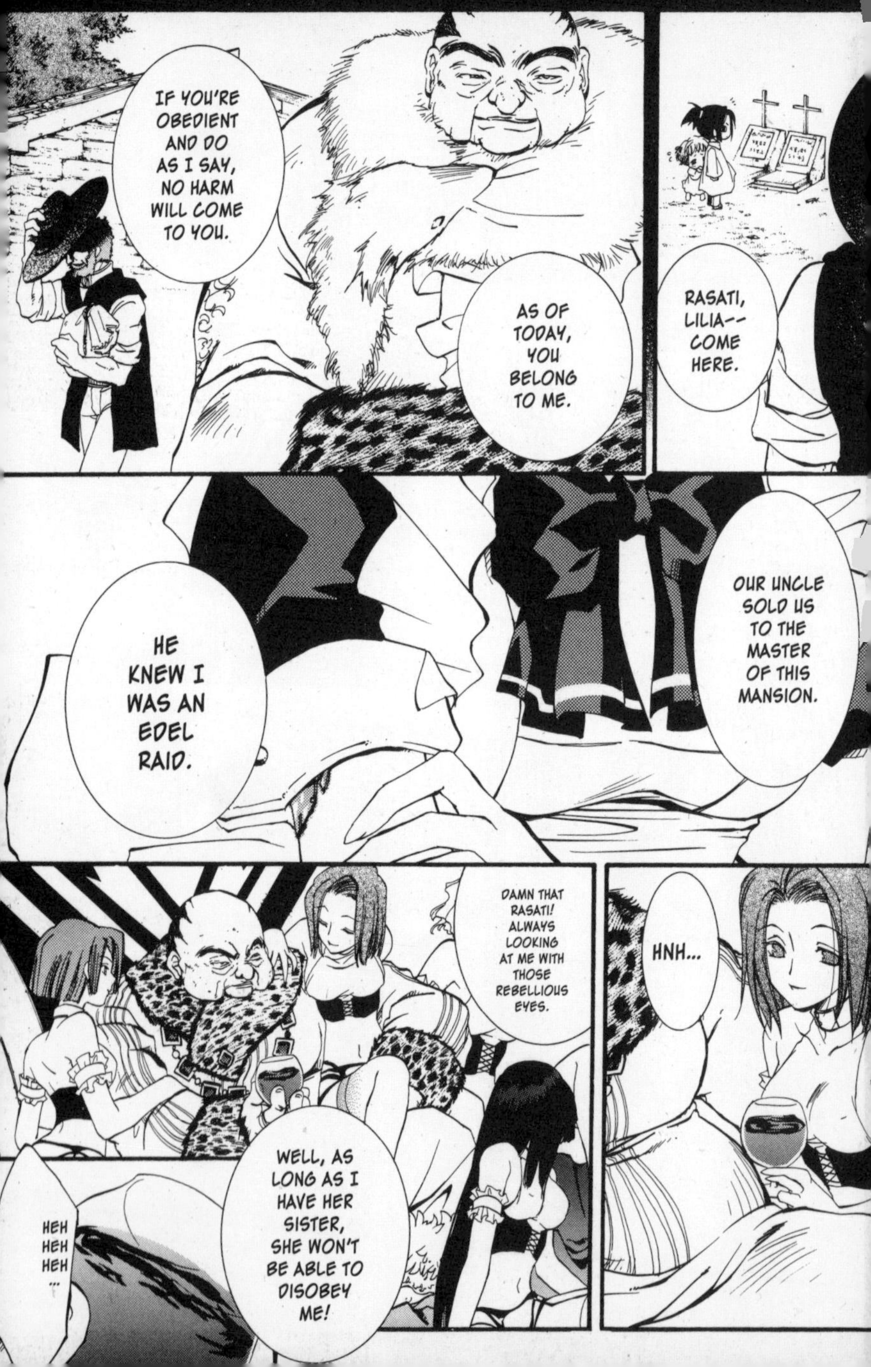
RASATI, LILIA-- COME HERE.
AS OF TODAY, YOU BELONG TO ME.
IF YOU'RE OBEDIENT AND DO AS I SAY, NO HARM WILL COME TO YOU.
OUR UNCLE SOLD US TO THE MASTER OF THIS MANSION.
HE KNEW I WAS AN EDEL RAID.
HNH...
DAMN THAT RASATI! ALWAYS LOOKING AT ME WITH THOSE REBELLIOUS EYES.
WELL, AS LONG AS I HAVE HER SISTER, SHE WON'T BE ABLE TO DISOBEY ME!
HEH HEH HEH ...

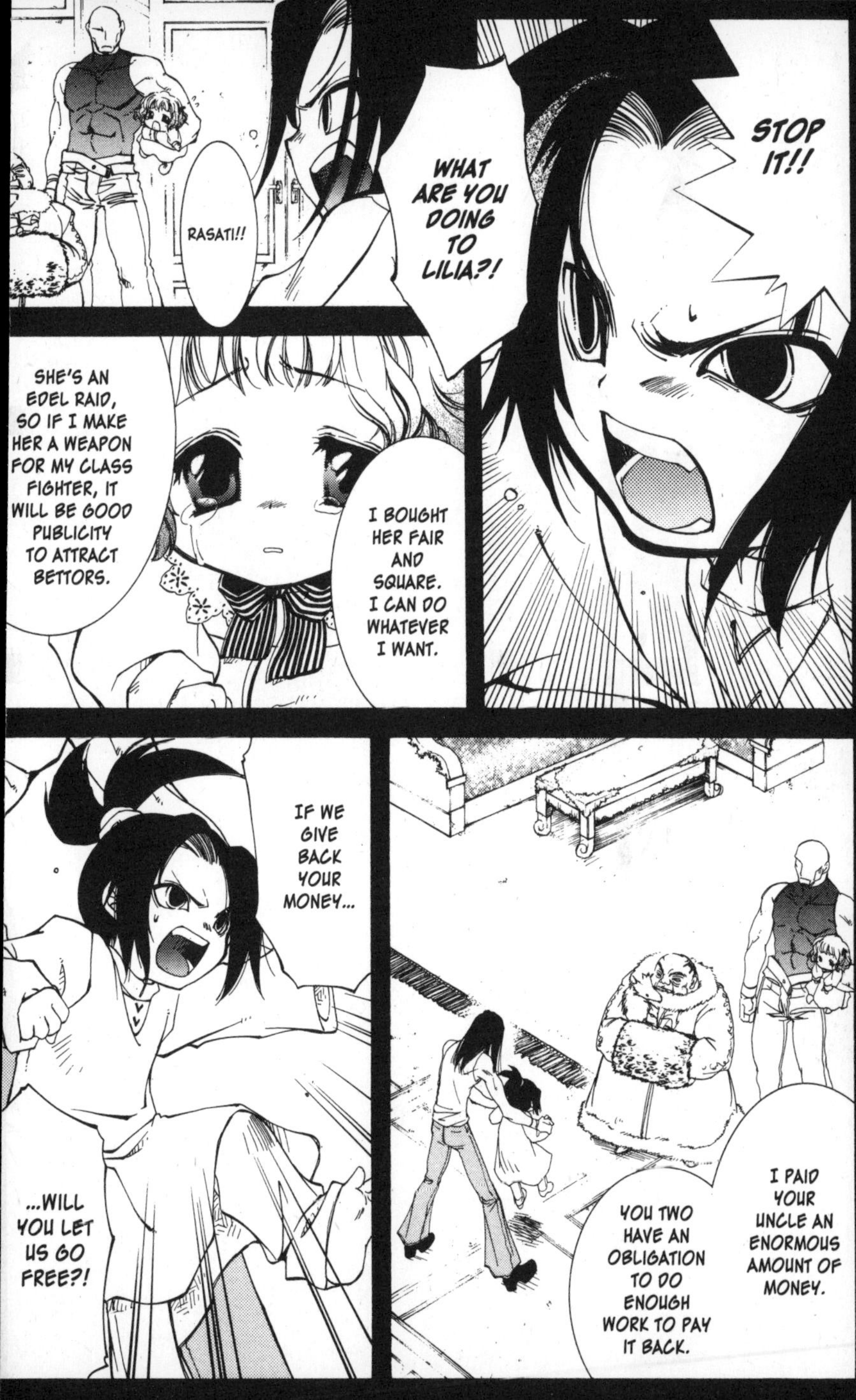

STOP IT!!
WHAT ARE YOU DOING TO LILIA?!
RASATI!!
I BOUGHT HER FAIR AND SQUARE. I CAN DO WHATEVER I WANT.
SHE'S AN EDEL RAID, SO IF I MAKE HER A WEAPON FOR MY CLASS FIGHTER, IT WILL BE GOOD PUBLICITY TO ATTRACT BETTORS.
I PAID YOUR UNCLE AN ENORMOUS AMOUNT OF MONEY.
YOU TWO HAVE AN OBLIGATION TO DO ENOUGH WORK TO PAY IT BACK.
IF WE GIVE BACK YOUR MONEY...
...WILL YOU LET US GO FREE?!

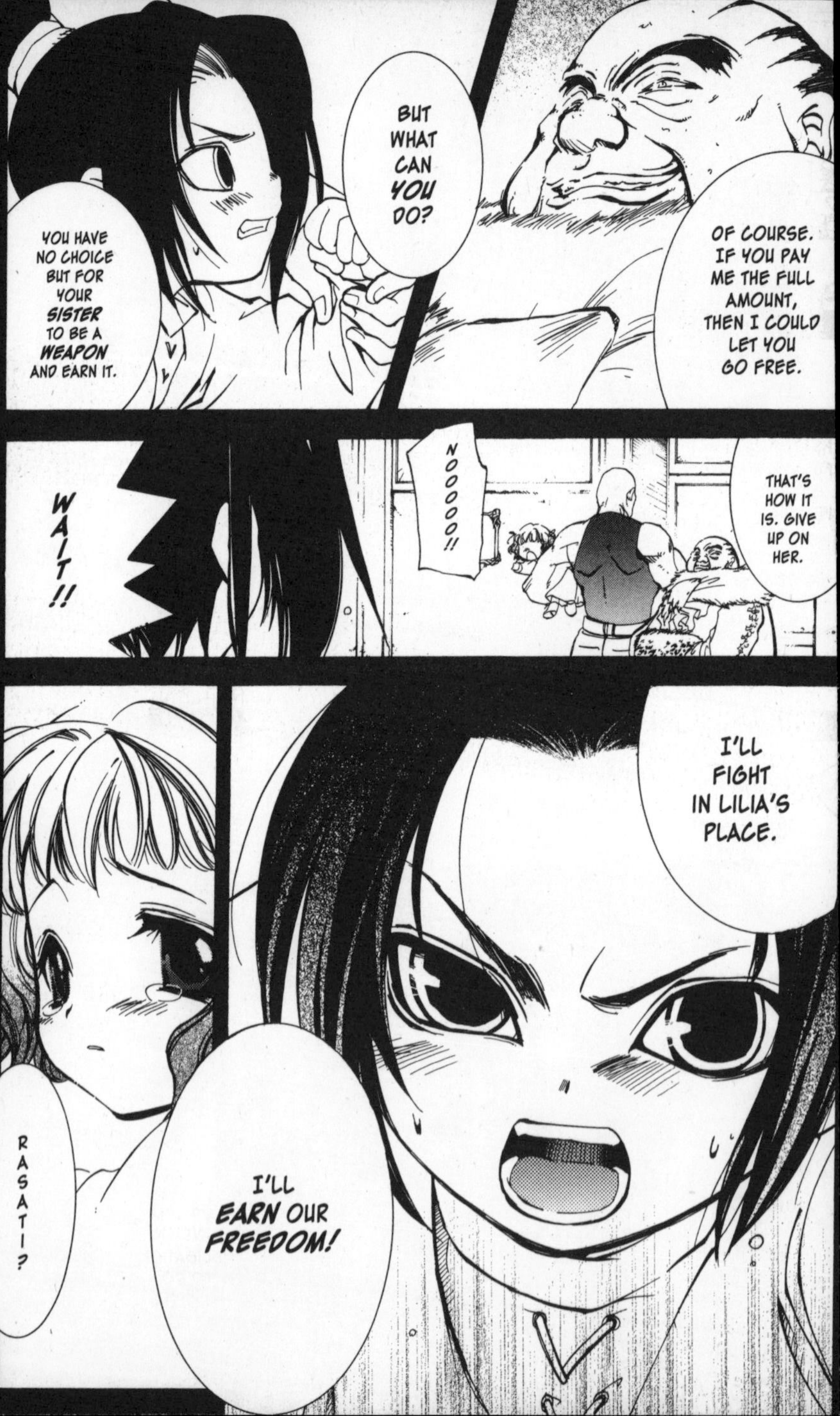
OF COURSE. IF YOU PAY ME THE FULL AMOUNT, THEN I COULD LET YOU GO FREE.
BUT WHAT CAN *YOU* DO?
YOU HAVE NO CHOICE BUT FOR YOUR *SISTER* TO BE A *WEAPON* AND EARN IT.
THAT'S HOW IT IS. GIVE UP ON HER.
NOOOOOO!!
WAIT!!
I'LL FIGHT IN LILIA'S PLACE.
I'LL *EARN* OUR *FREEDOM!*
RASATI?

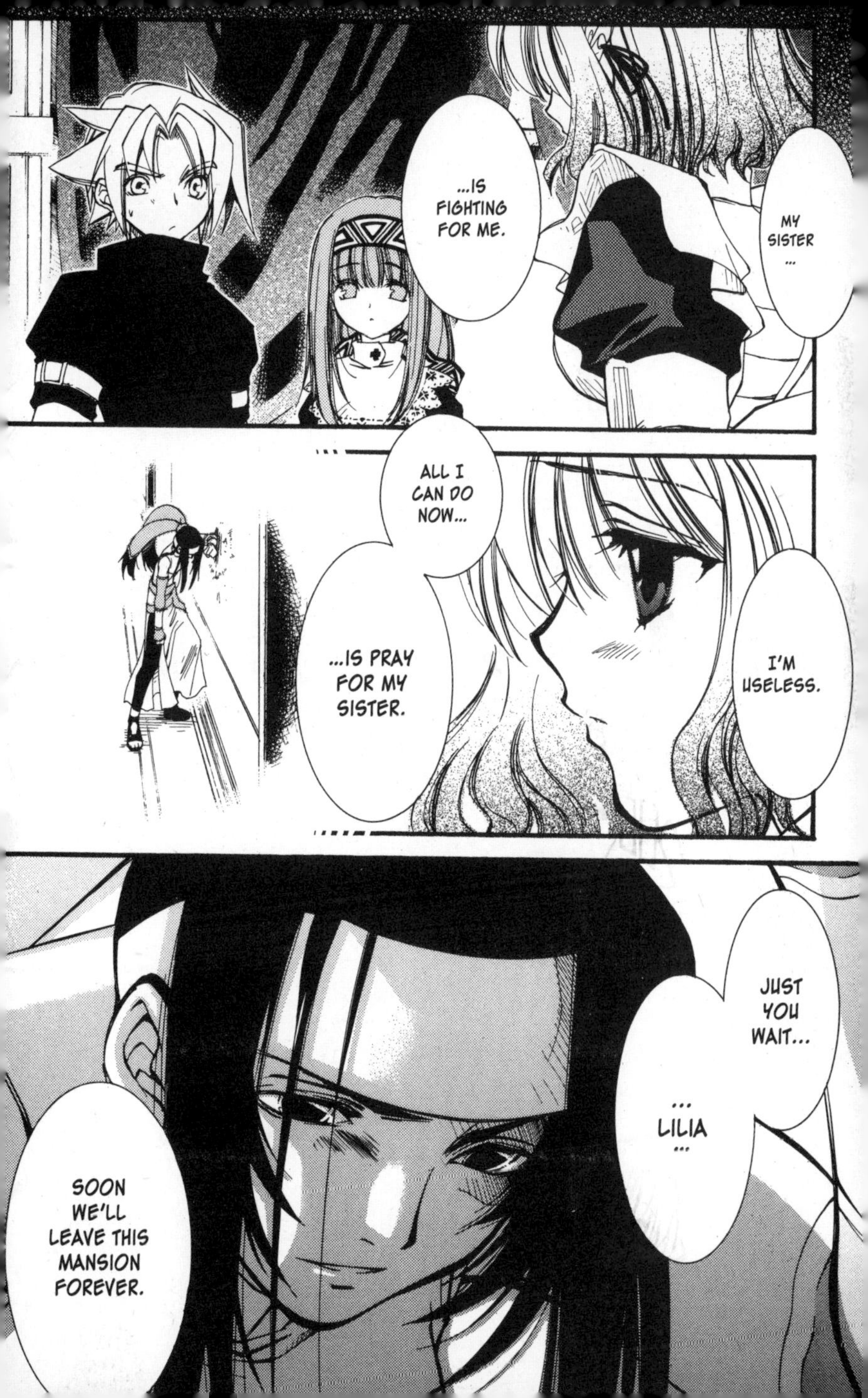
MY SISTER ...
...IS FIGHTING FOR ME.
ALL I CAN DO NOW...
...IS PRAY FOR MY SISTER.
I'M USELESS.
JUST YOU WAIT...
... LILIA ...
SOON WE'LL LEAVE THIS MANSION FOREVER.

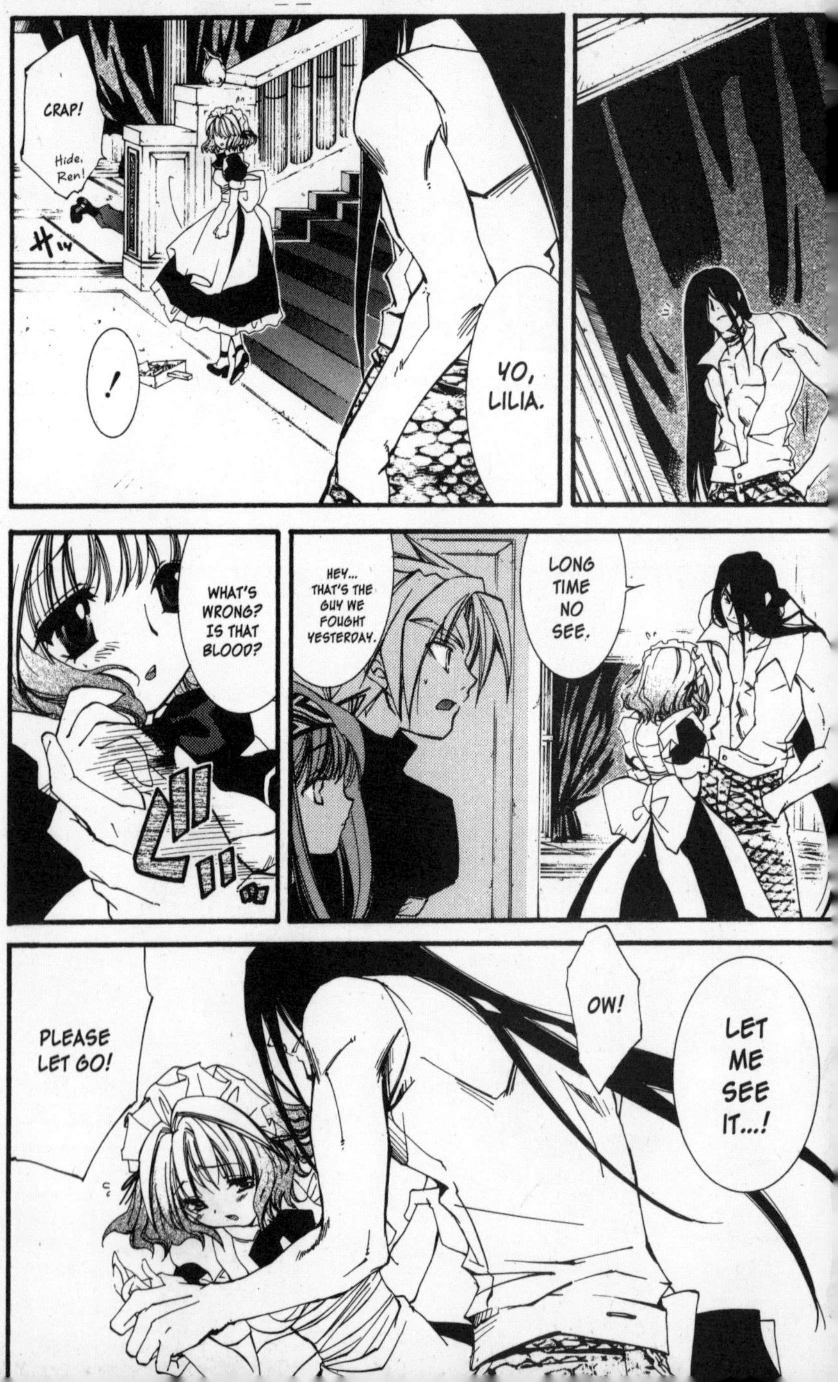
YO, LILIA.
!
CRAP!
Hide, Ren!
LONG TIME NO SEE.
HEY... THAT'S THE GUY WE FOUGHT YESTERDAY.
WHAT'S WRONG? IS THAT BLOOD?
LET ME SEE IT...!
OW!
PLEASE LET GO!

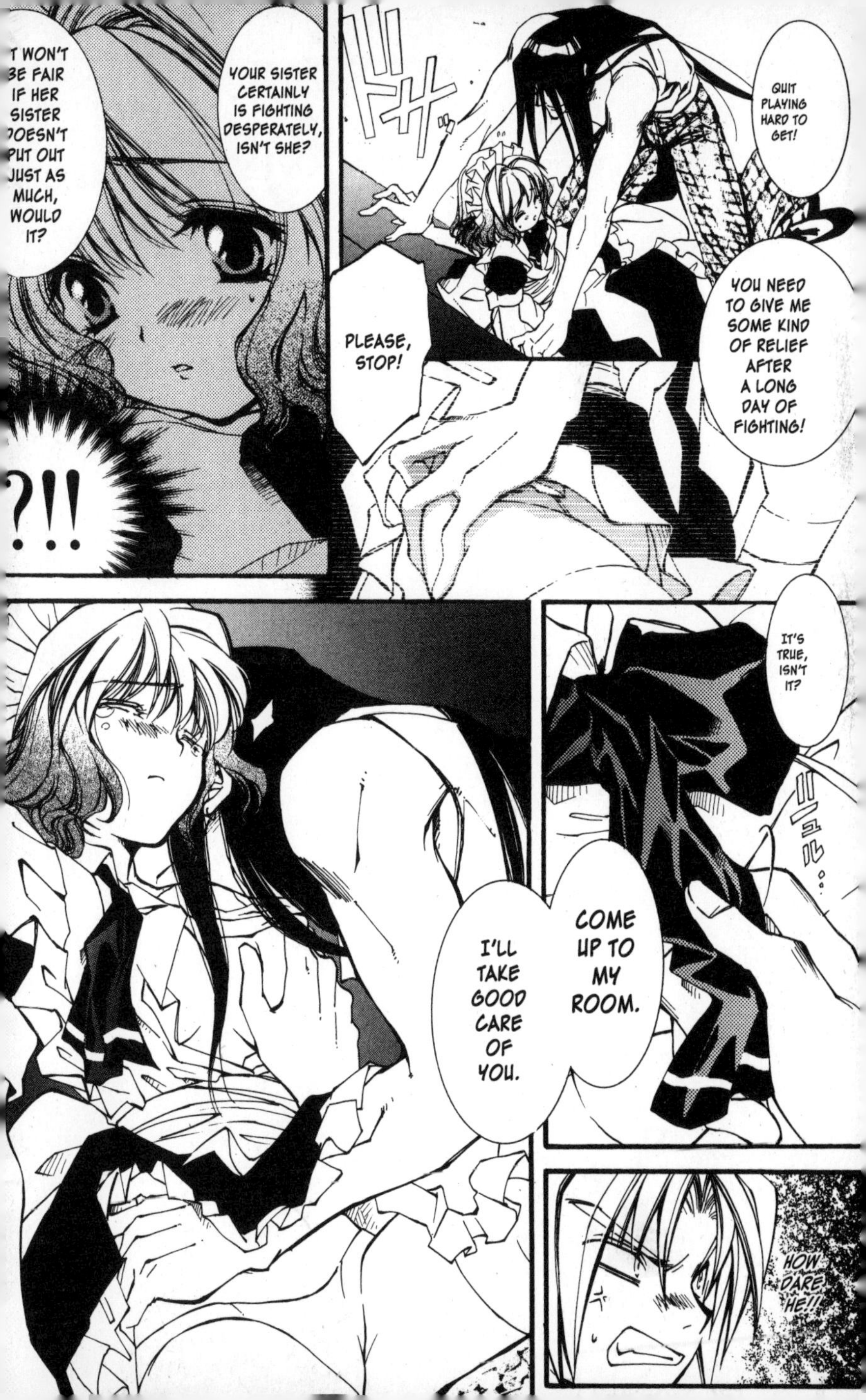
QUIT PLAYING HARD TO GET!
ドッ
YOU NEED TO GIVE ME SOME KIND OF RELIEF AFTER A LONG DAY OF FIGHTING!
PLEASE, STOP!
YOUR SISTER CERTAINLY IS FIGHTING DESPERATELY, ISN'T SHE?
T WON'T BE FAIR IF HER SISTER DOESN'T PUT OUT JUST AS MUCH, WOULD IT?
?!!
IT'S TRUE, ISN'T IT?
ニュル。。
HOW DARE HE!!
COME UP TO MY ROOM.
I'LL TAKE GOOD CARE OF YOU.

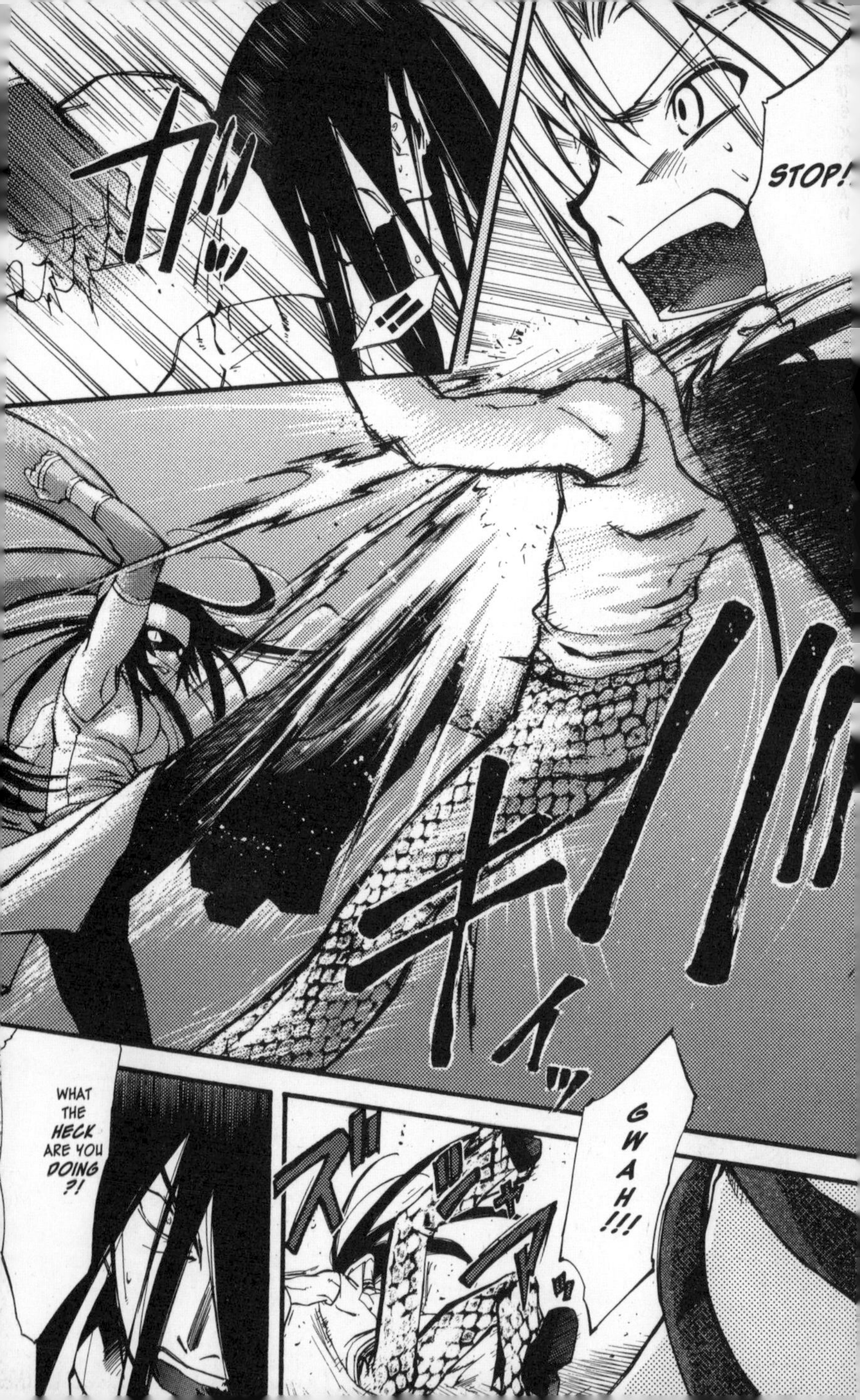
STOP!
GWAH!!!
WHAT THE HECK ARE YOU DOING?!

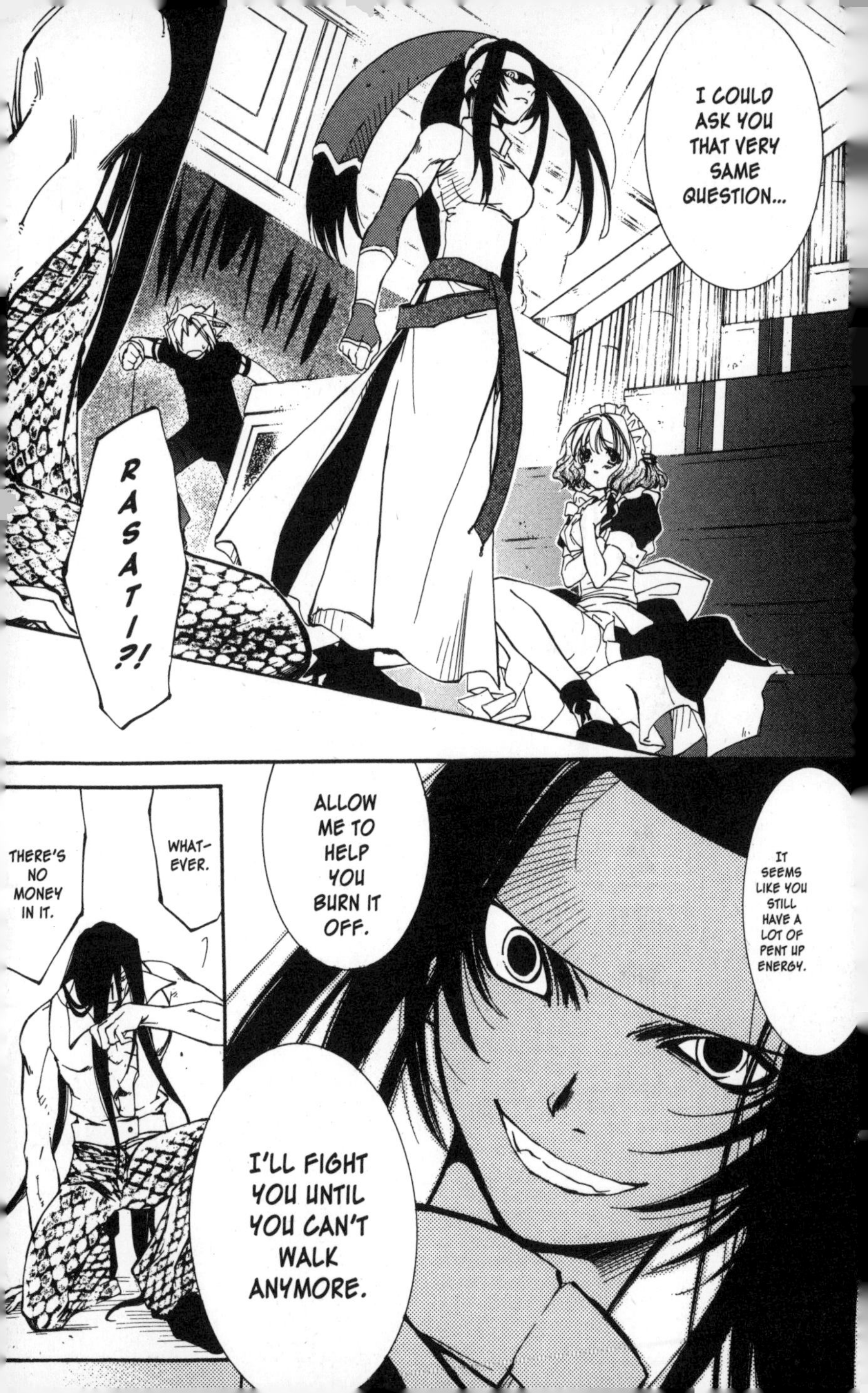
I COULD ASK YOU THAT VERY SAME QUESTION...
RASATI?!
IT SEEMS LIKE YOU STILL HAVE A LOT OF PENT UP ENERGY.
ALLOW ME TO HELP YOU BURN IT OFF.
I'LL FIGHT YOU UNTIL YOU CAN'T WALK ANYMORE.
WHAT-EVER.
THERE'S NO MONEY IN IT.

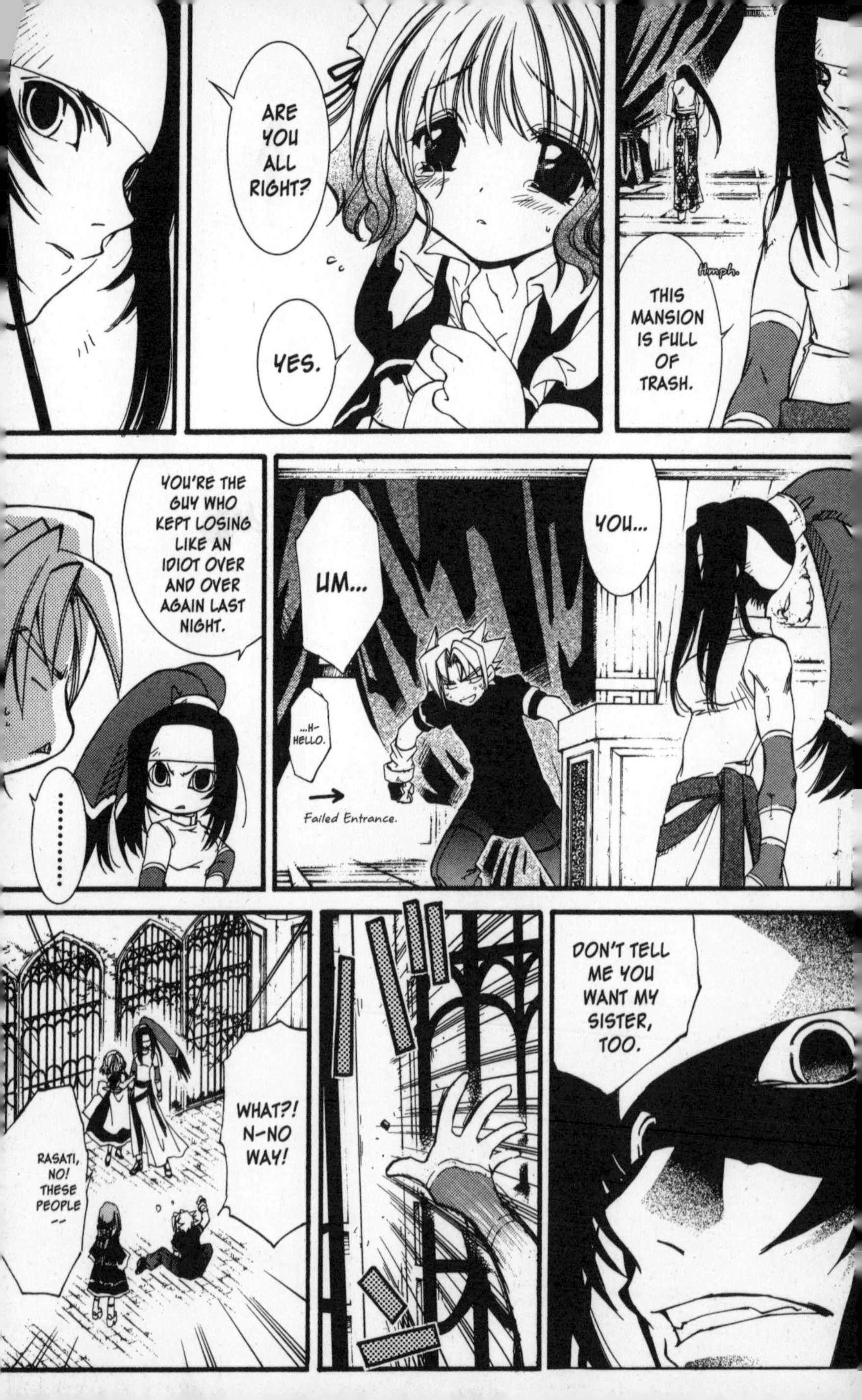
Hmph.
THIS MANSION IS FULL OF TRASH.
ARE YOU ALL RIGHT?
YES.
YOU...
UM...
...H-HELLO.
Failed Entrance.
YOU'RE THE GUY WHO KEPT LOSING LIKE AN IDIOT OVER AND OVER AGAIN LAST NIGHT.
......
DON'T TELL ME YOU WANT MY SISTER, TOO.
WHAT?! N-NO WAY!
RASATI, NO! THESE PEOPLE --

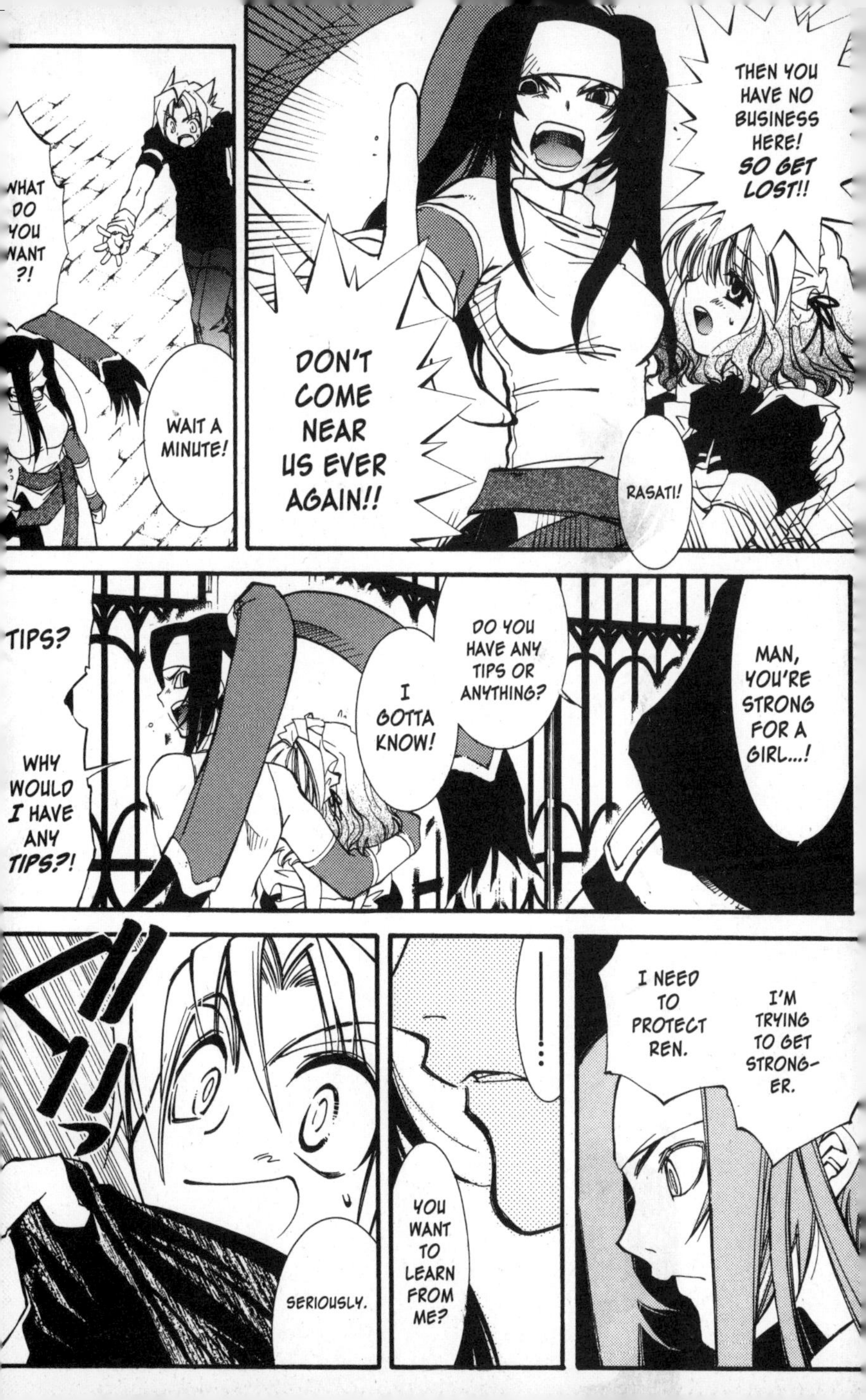
THEN YOU HAVE NO BUSINESS HERE! SO GET LOST!!
DON'T COME NEAR US EVER AGAIN!!
RASATI!
WAIT A MINUTE!
WHAT DO YOU WANT?!
MAN, YOU'RE STRONG FOR A GIRL...!
DO YOU HAVE ANY TIPS OR ANYTHING?
I GOTTA KNOW!
TIPS?
WHY WOULD I HAVE ANY TIPS?!
I'M TRYING TO GET STRONGER.
I NEED TO PROTECT REN.
......!
YOU WANT TO LEARN FROM ME?
SERIOUSLY.

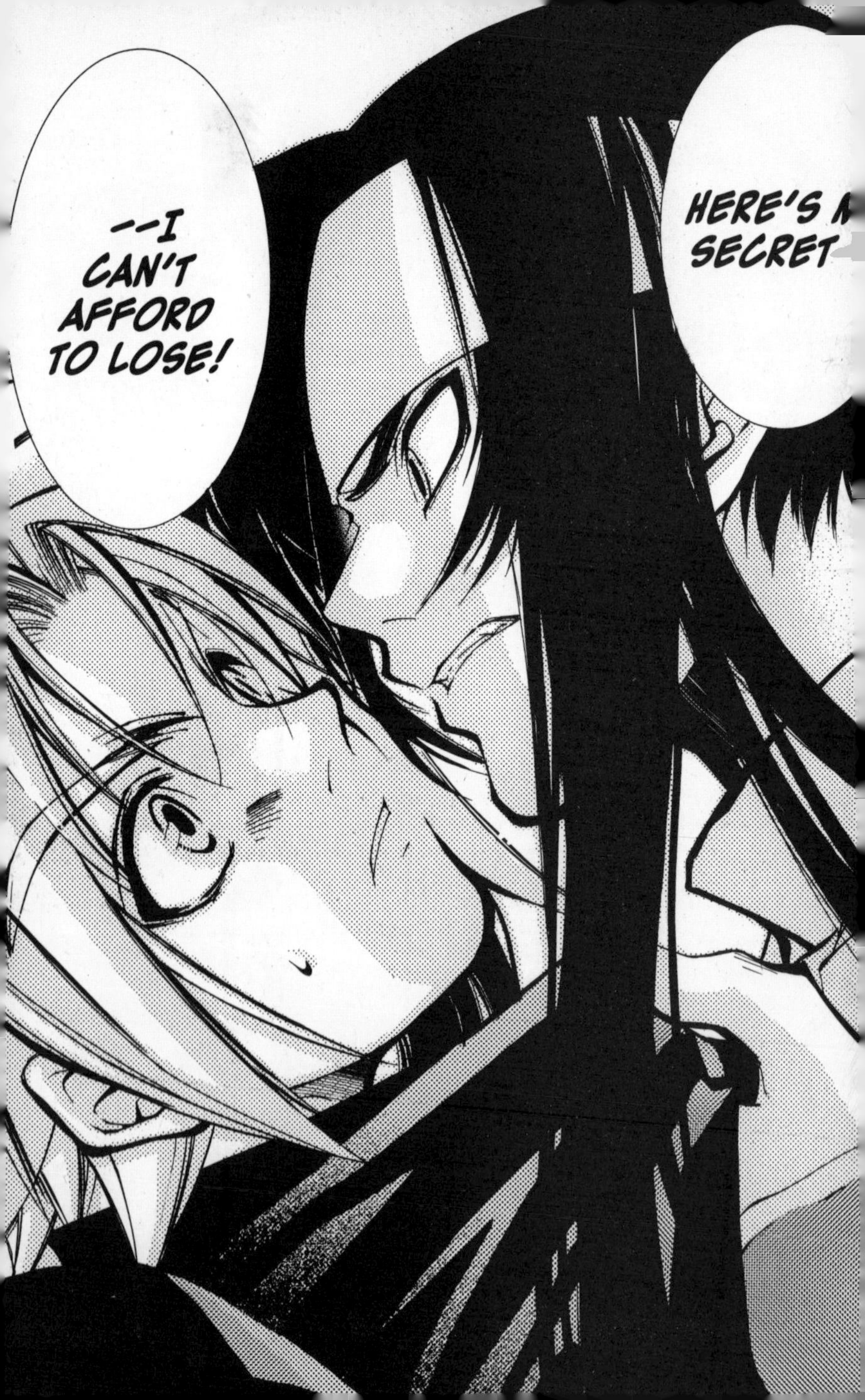
HERE'S SECRET
--I CAN'T AFFORD TO LOSE!

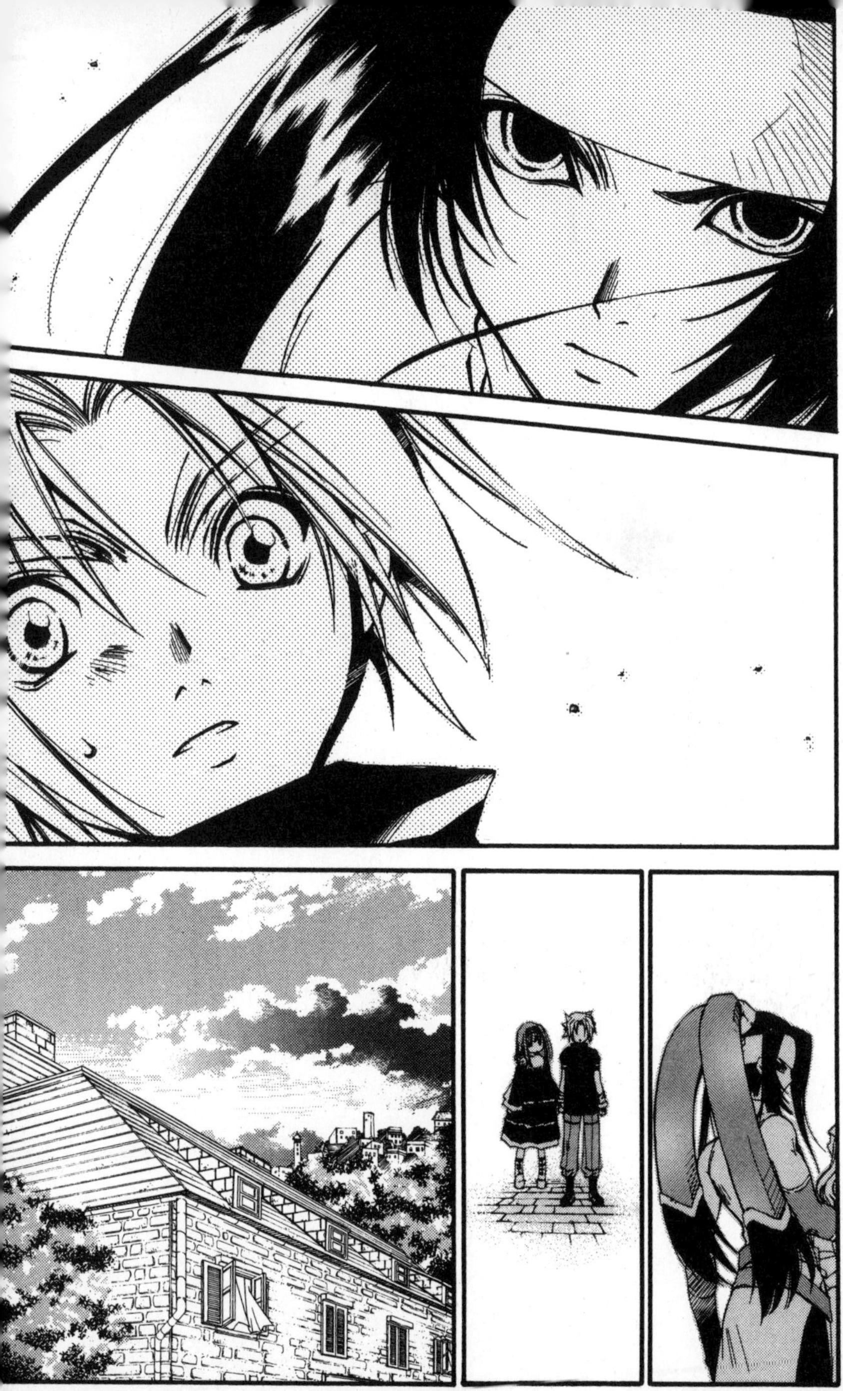

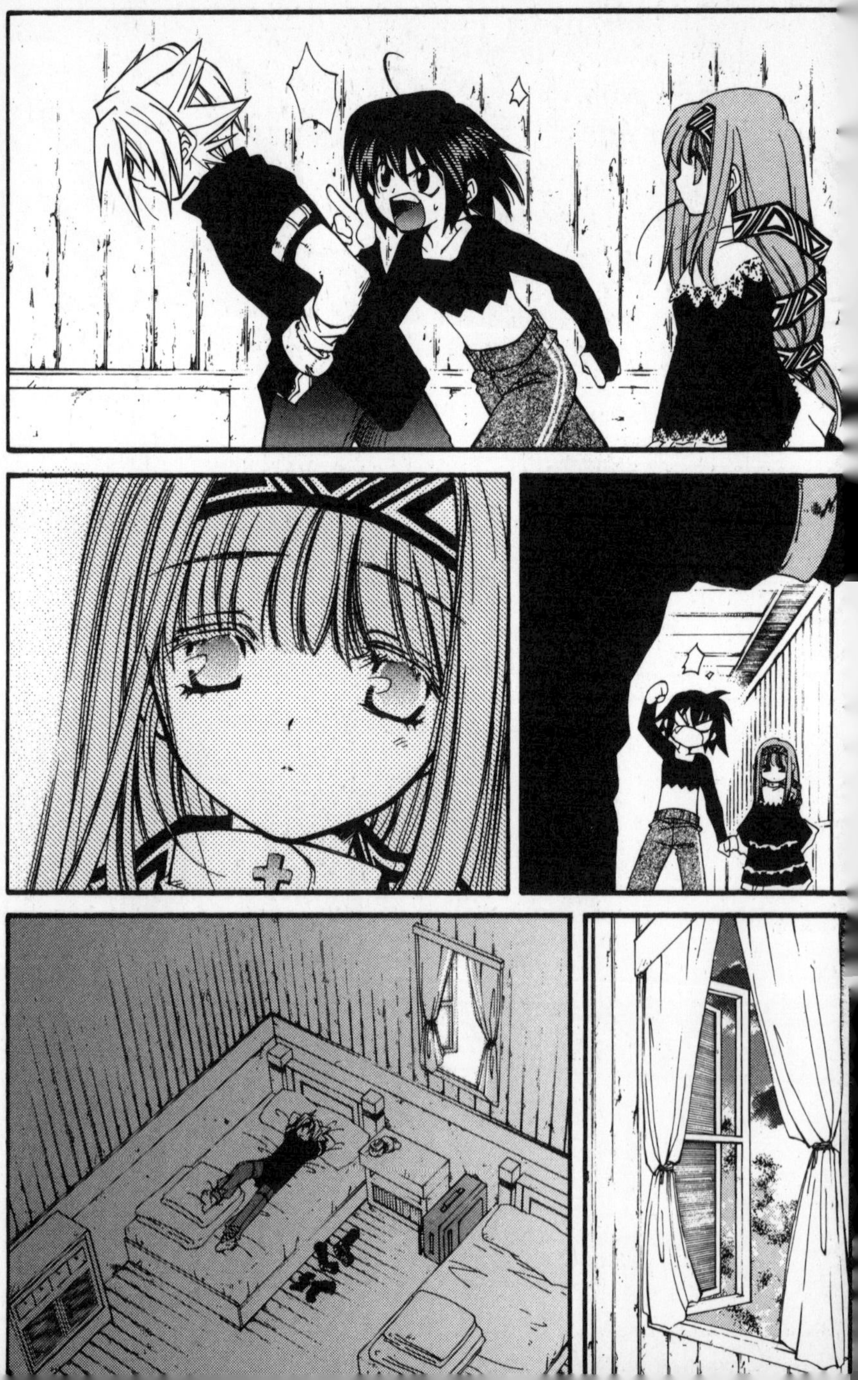

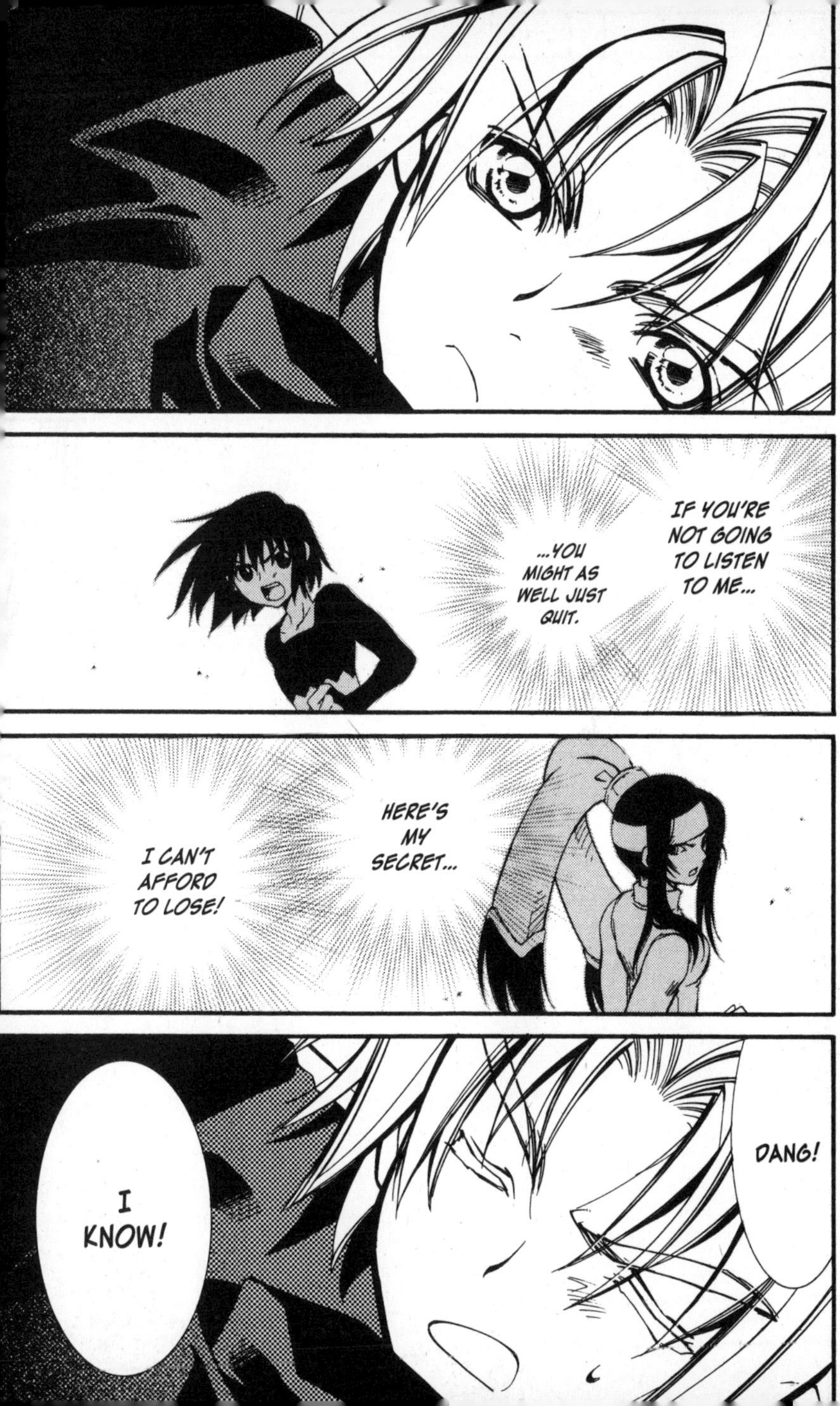
IF YOU'RE NOT GOING TO LISTEN TO ME...
...YOU MIGHT AS WELL JUST QUIT.
HERE'S MY SECRET...
I CAN'T AFFORD TO LOSE!
DANG!
I KNOW!

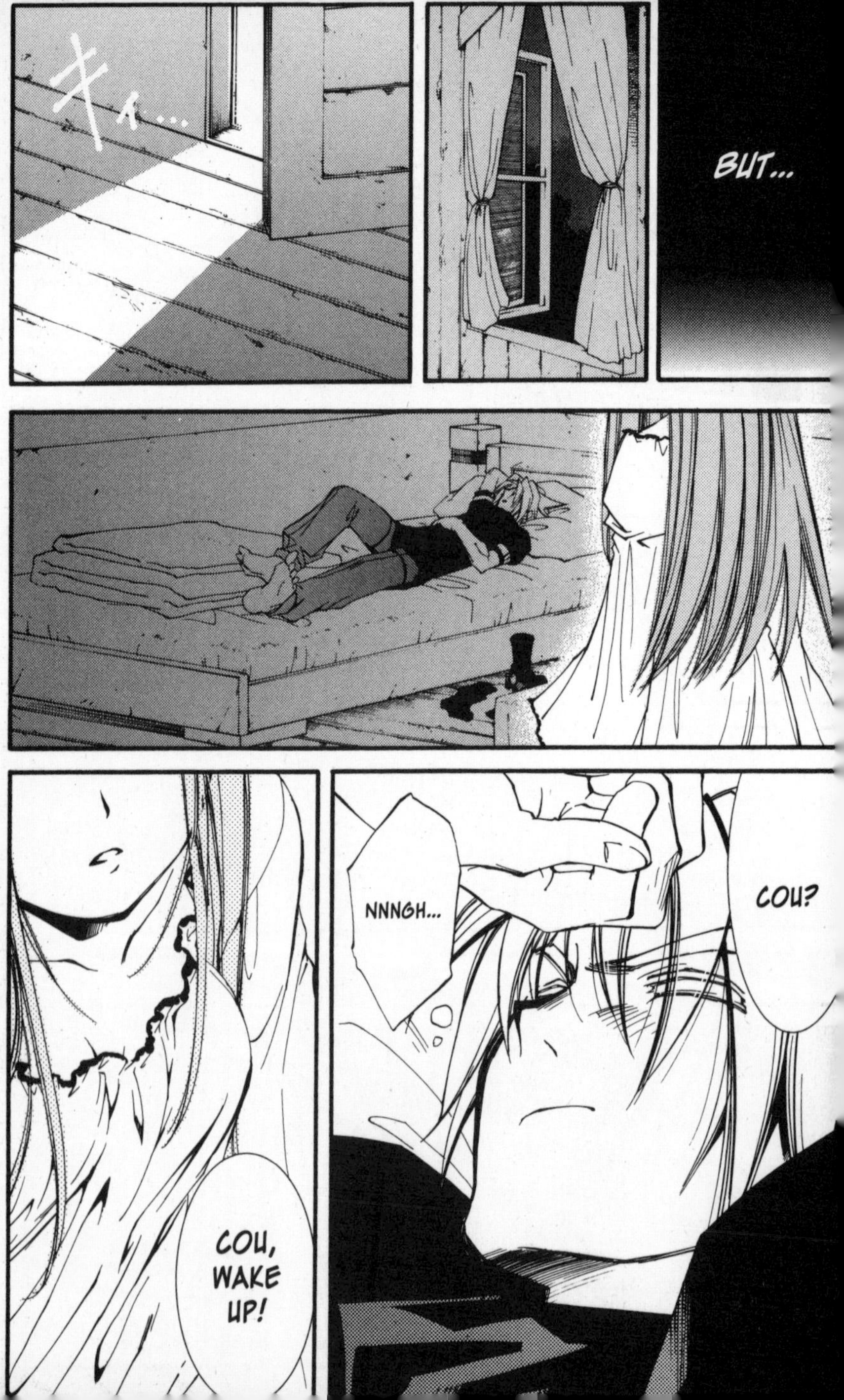
BUT...
キィ...
COU?
NNNGH...
COU, WAKE UP!

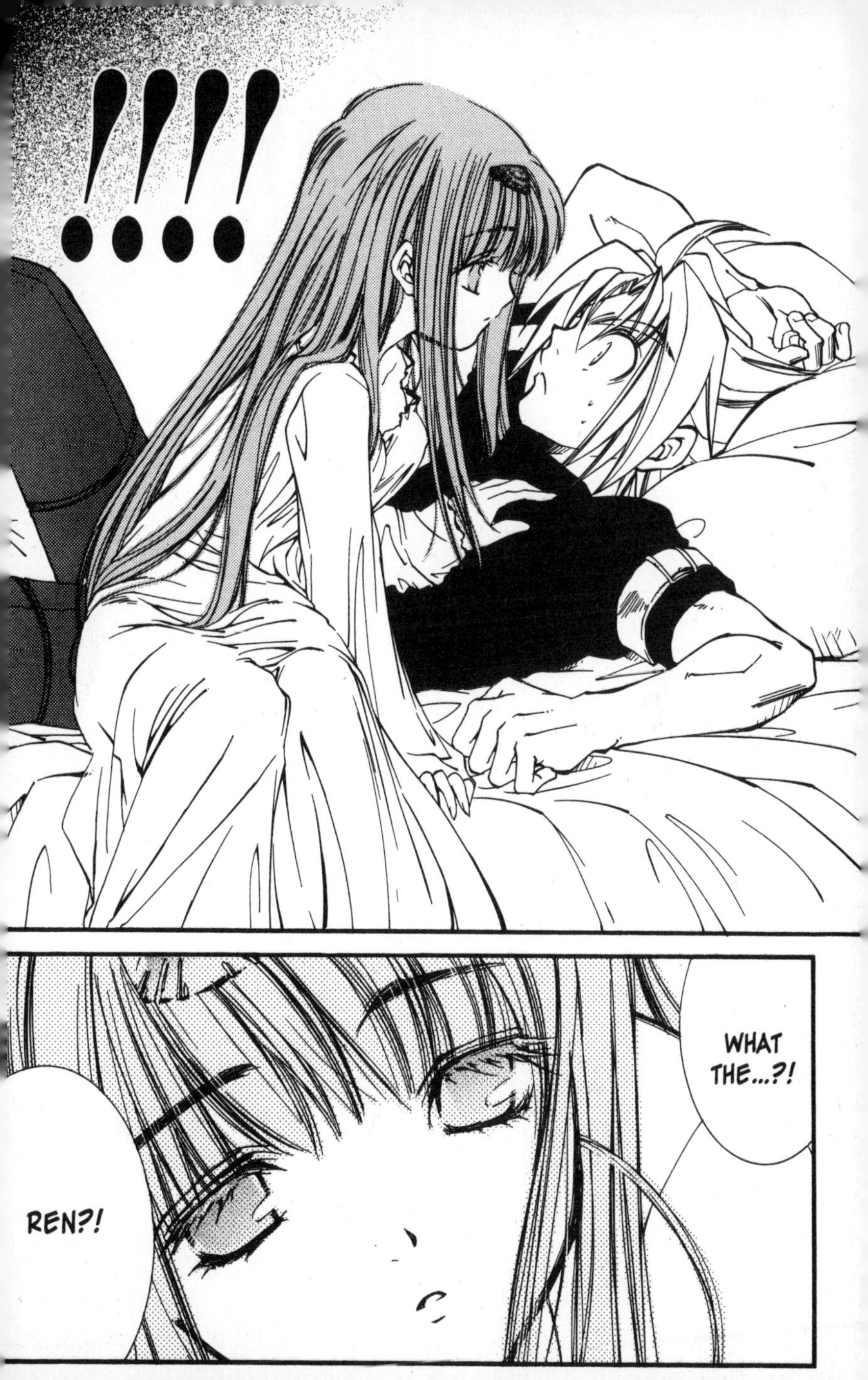
!!!!
WHAT THE...?!
REN?!

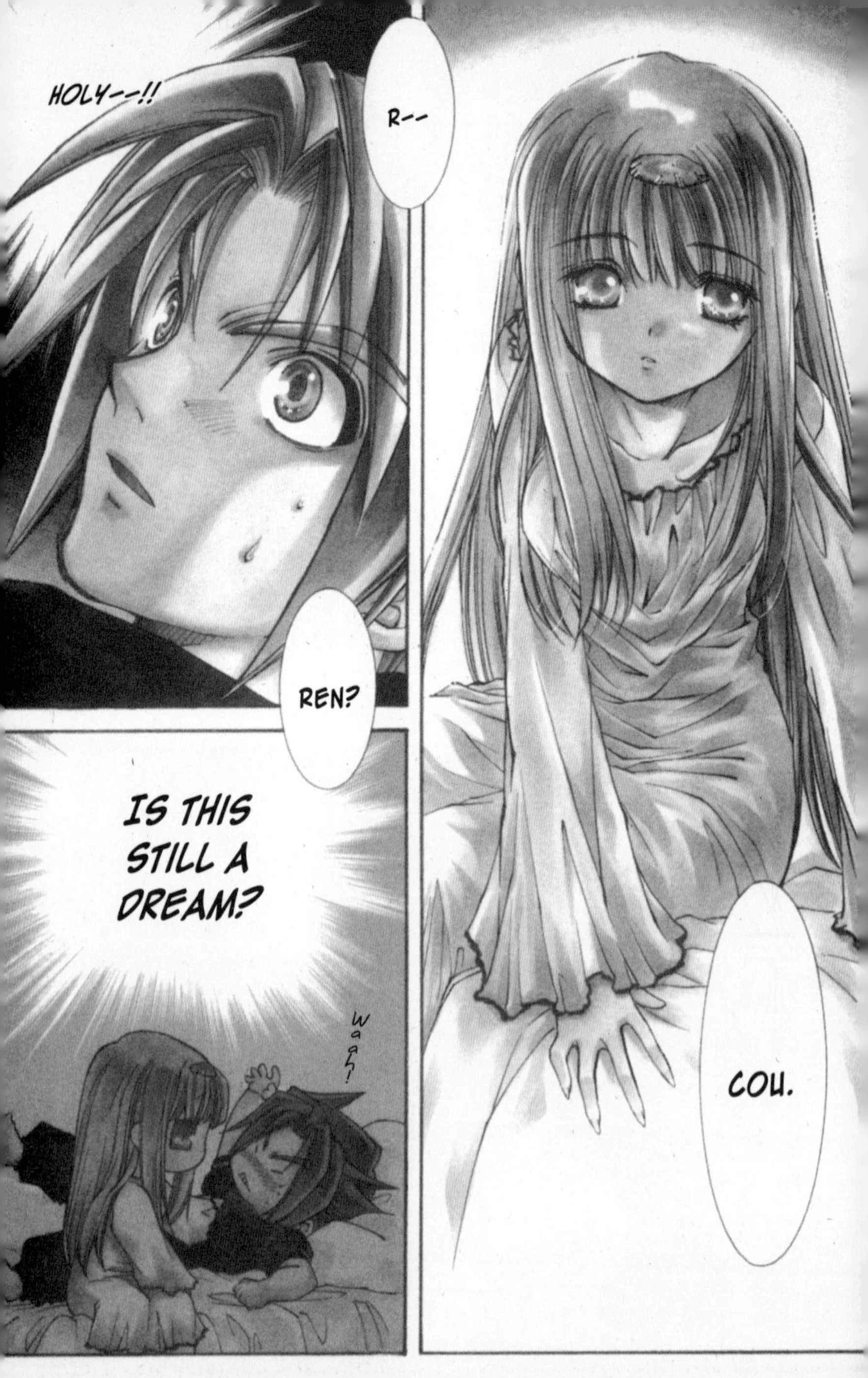
R--
REN?
COU.
HOLY--!!
IS THIS STILL A DREAM?
Waah!

# Re-No.14:
## Milliard Trey Betting Grounds–Connected Passed Sharer

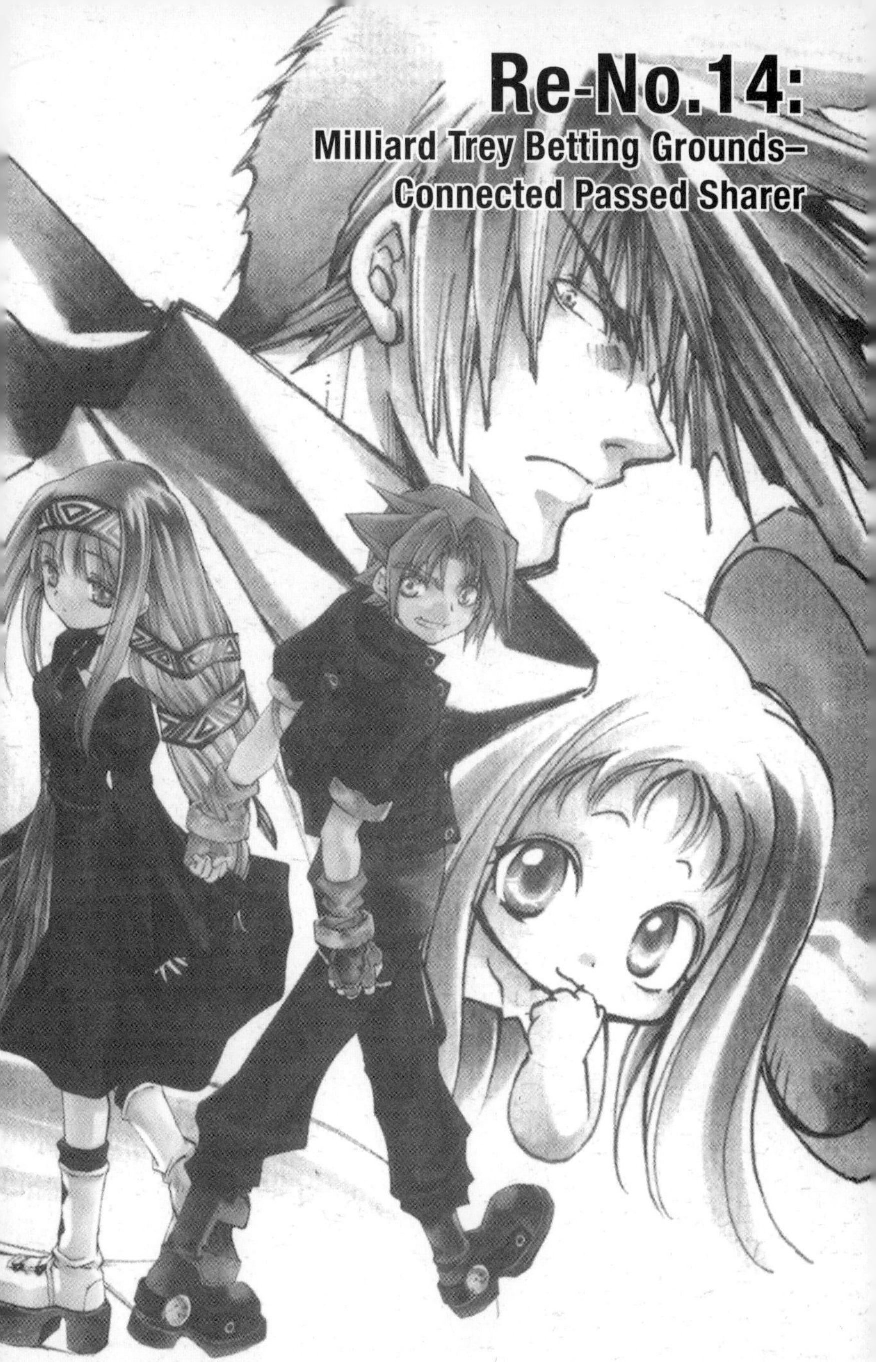

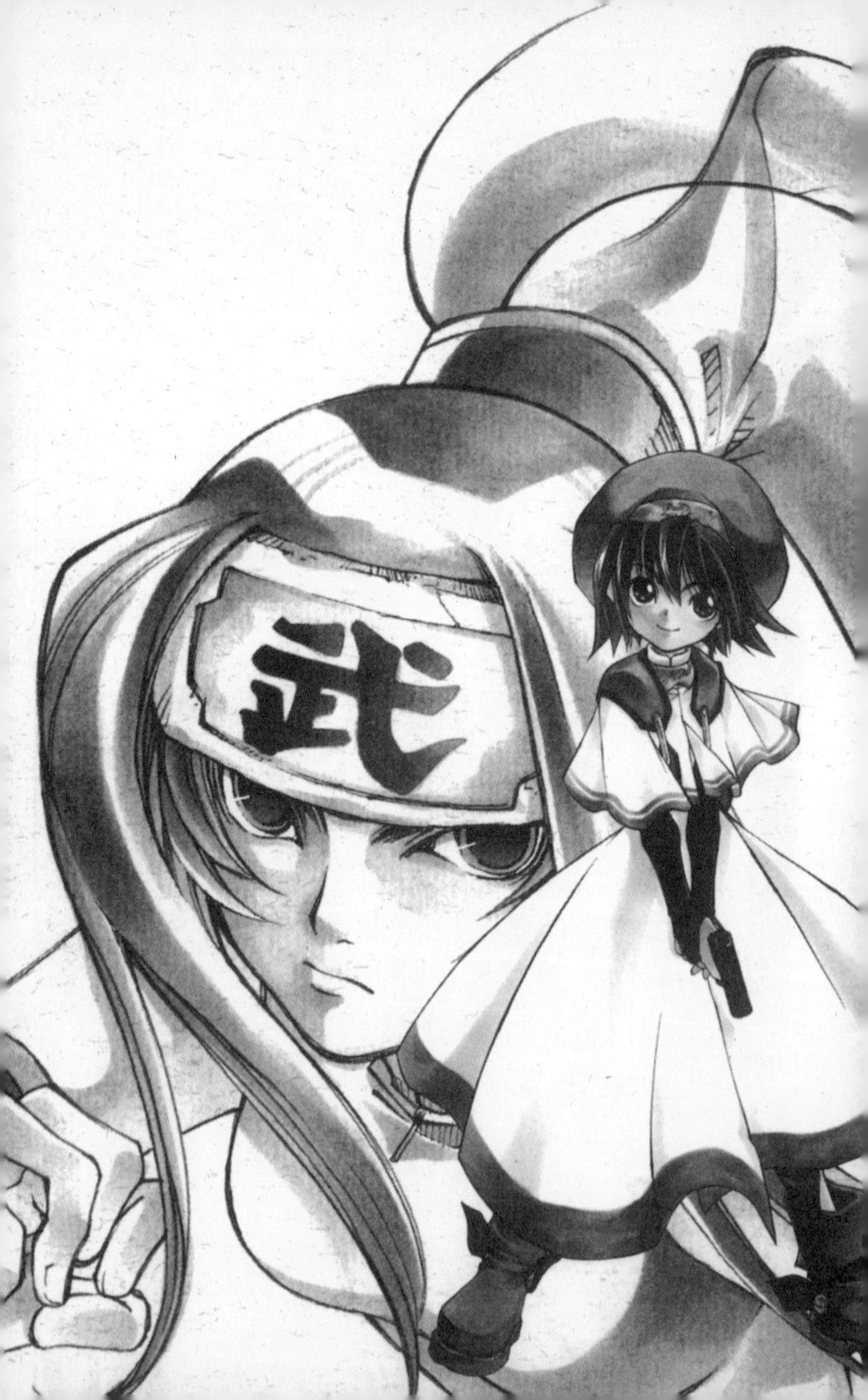
武

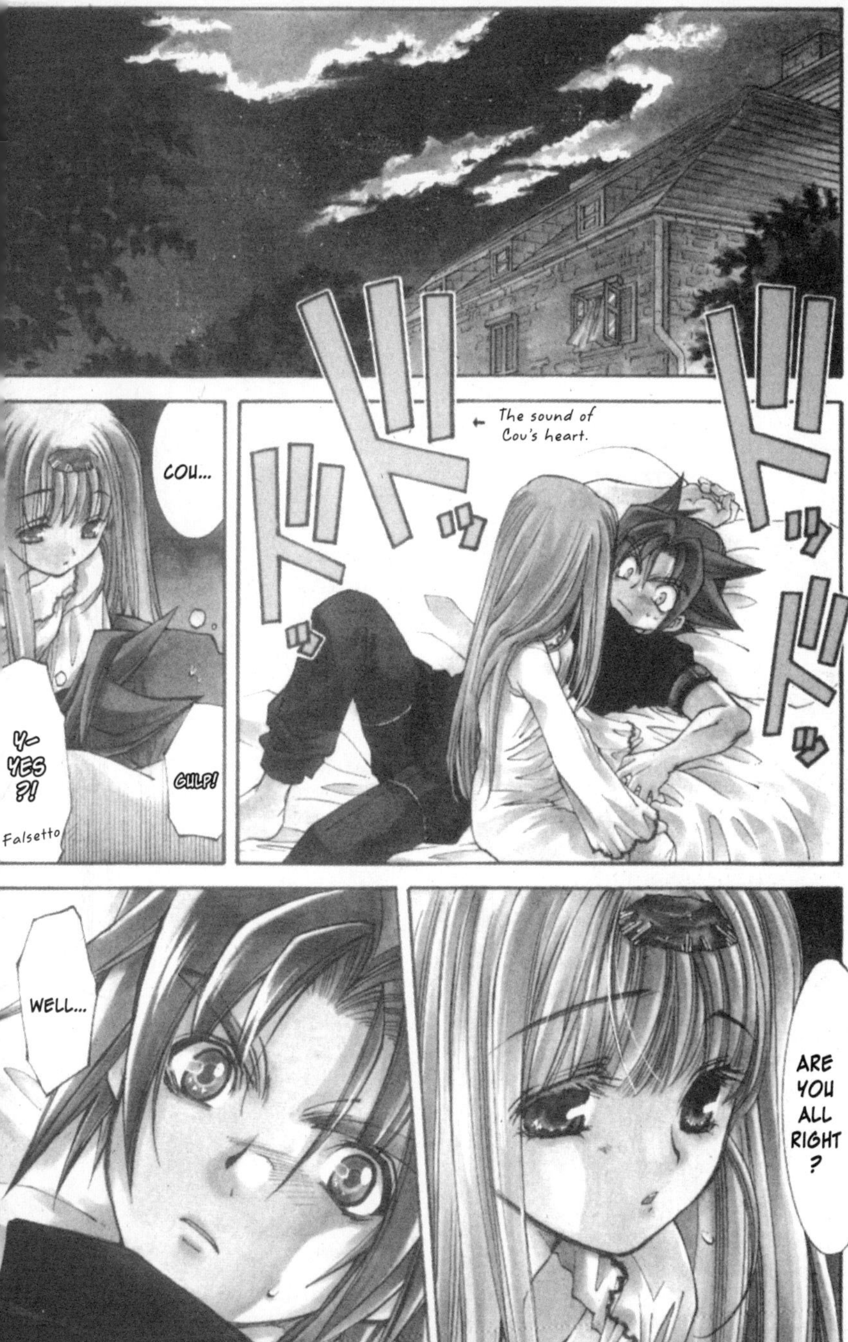

The sound of Cou's heart.
COU...
Y- YES ?!
Falsetto
GULP!
ARE YOU ALL RIGHT ?
WELL...

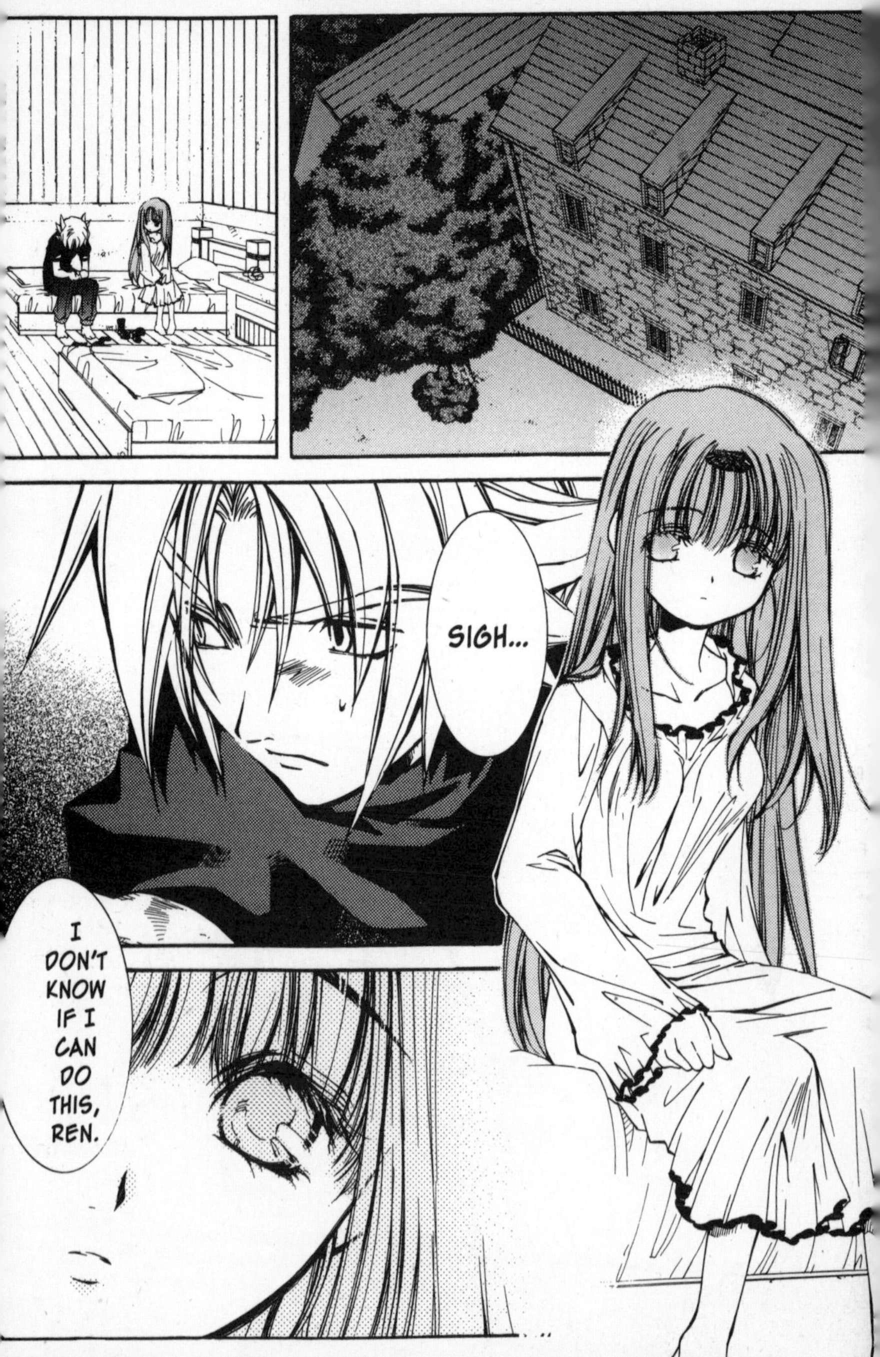
SIGH...
I DON'T KNOW IF I CAN DO THIS, REN.

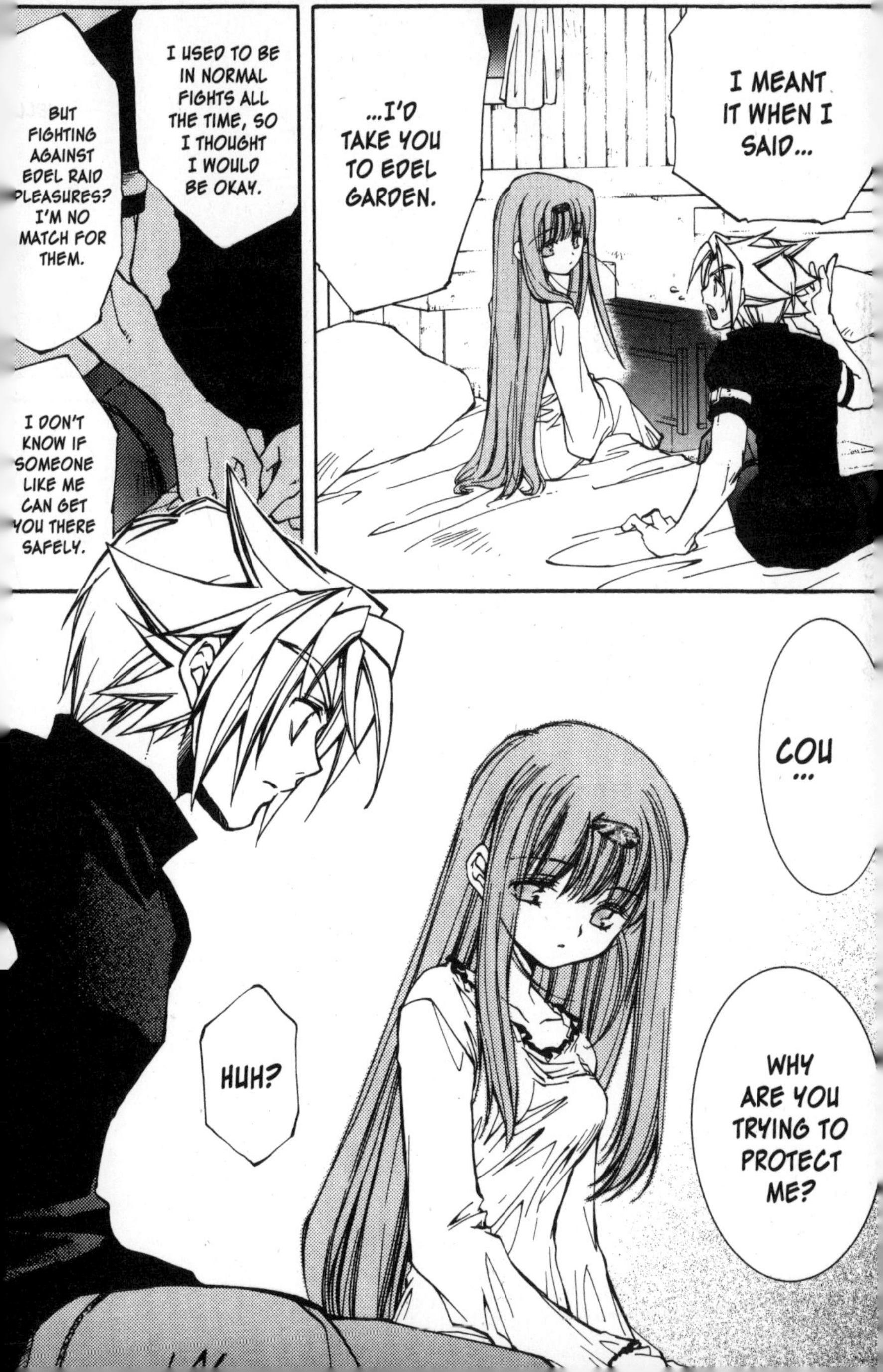
I MEANT IT WHEN I SAID...
...I'D TAKE YOU TO EDEL GARDEN.
I USED TO BE IN NORMAL FIGHTS ALL THE TIME, SO I THOUGHT I WOULD BE OKAY.
BUT FIGHTING AGAINST EDEL RAID PLEASURES? I'M NO MATCH FOR THEM.
I DON'T KNOW IF SOMEONE LIKE ME CAN GET YOU THERE SAFELY.
COU...
WHY ARE YOU TRYING TO PROTECT ME?
HUH?

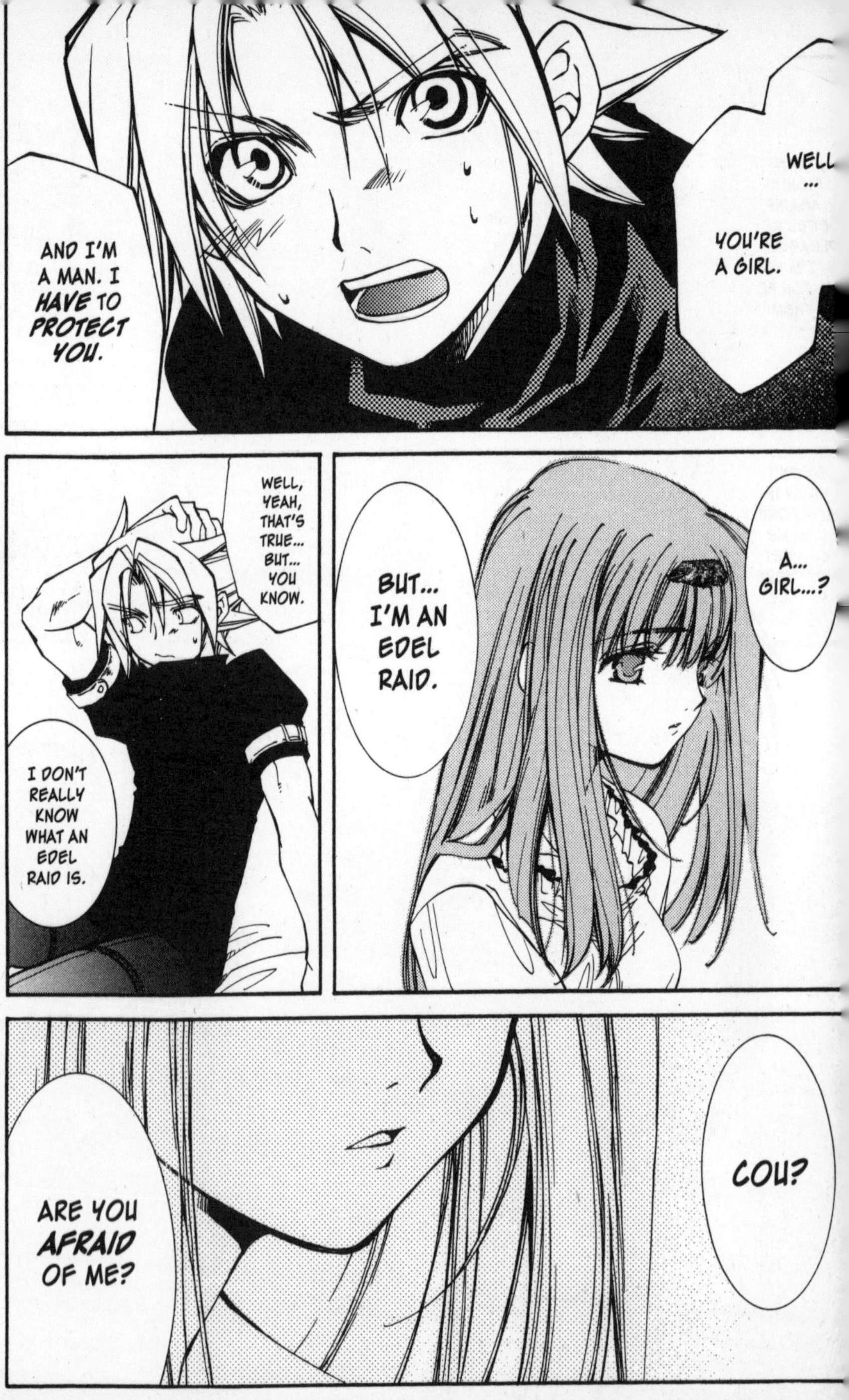
WELL ...
YOU'RE A GIRL.
AND I'M A MAN. I *HAVE* TO PROTECT YOU.
A... GIRL...?
BUT... I'M AN EDEL RAID.
WELL, YEAH, THAT'S TRUE... BUT... YOU KNOW.
I DON'T REALLY KNOW WHAT AN EDEL RAID IS.
COU?
ARE YOU *AFRAID* OF ME?

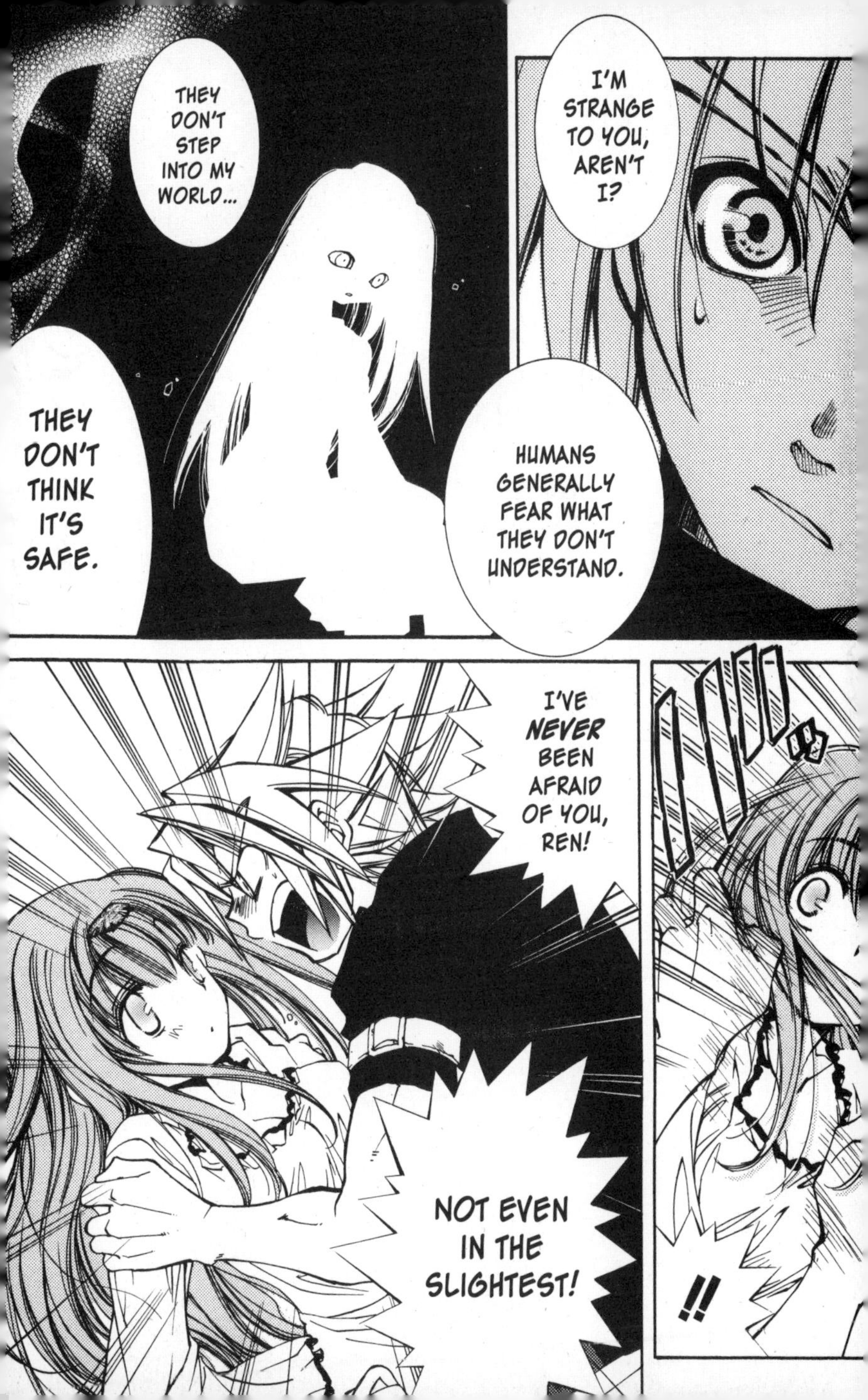
I'M STRANGE TO YOU, AREN'T I?
HUMANS GENERALLY FEAR WHAT THEY DON'T UNDERSTAND.
THEY DON'T STEP INTO MY WORLD...
THEY DON'T THINK IT'S SAFE.
!!
I'VE NEVER BEEN AFRAID OF YOU, REN!
NOT EVEN IN THE SLIGHTEST!

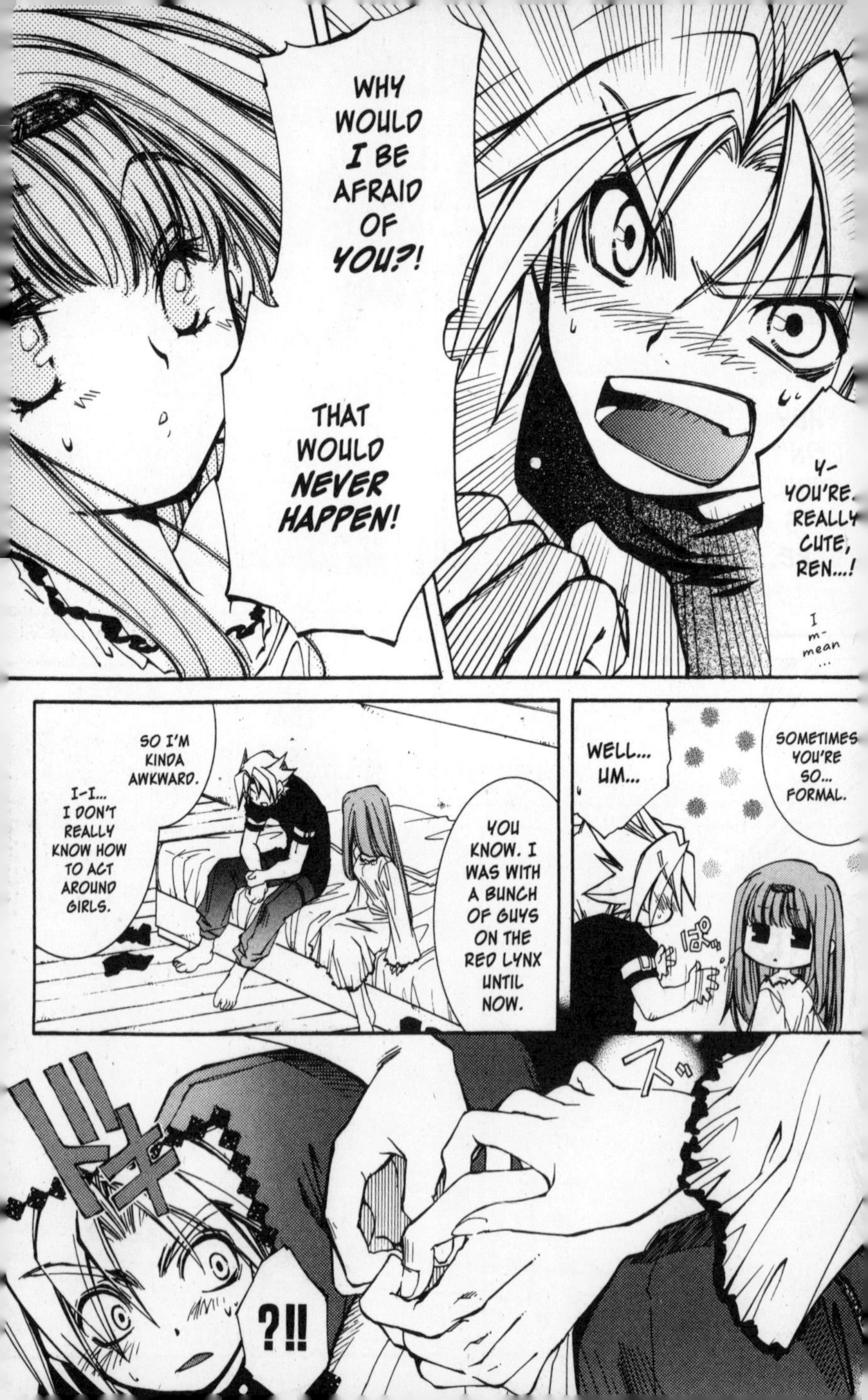
WHY WOULD I BE AFRAID OF YOU?!
THAT WOULD NEVER HAPPEN!
Y-YOU'RE... REALLY CUTE, REN...!
I m-mean ...
SOMETIMES YOU'RE SO... FORMAL.
WELL... UM...
ぱっ
YOU KNOW. I WAS WITH A BUNCH OF GUYS ON THE RED LYNX UNTIL NOW.
SO I'M KINDA AWKWARD.
I-I... I DON'T REALLY KNOW HOW TO ACT AROUND GIRLS.
スッ
ドキ
?!!

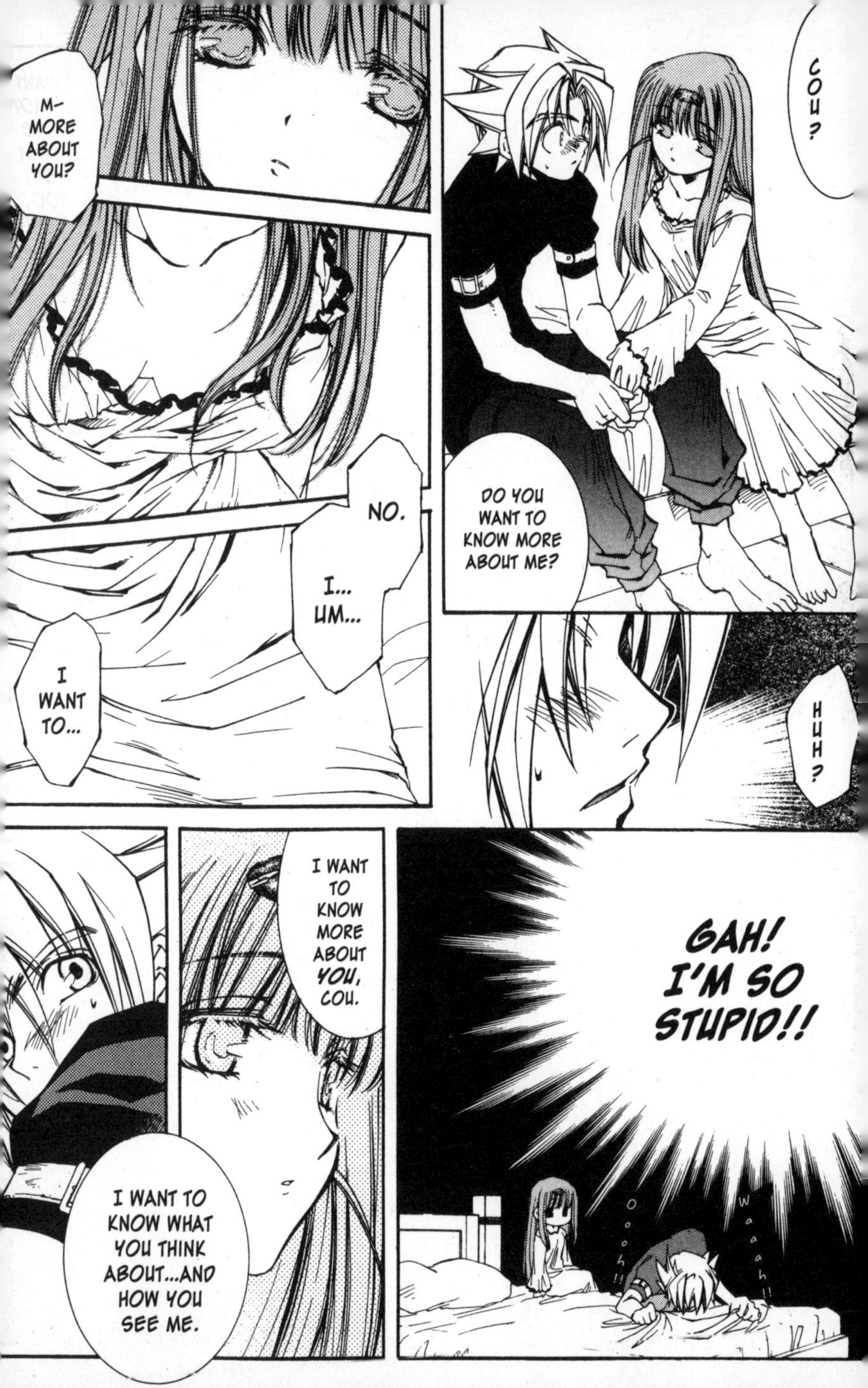
COU?
DO YOU WANT TO KNOW MORE ABOUT ME?
M-MORE ABOUT YOU?
NO.
I... UM...
HUH?
I WANT TO...
GAH! I'M SO STUPID!!
Waaah!!
Ooooh!!
I WANT TO KNOW MORE ABOUT YOU, COU.
I WANT TO KNOW WHAT YOU THINK ABOUT...AND HOW YOU SEE ME.

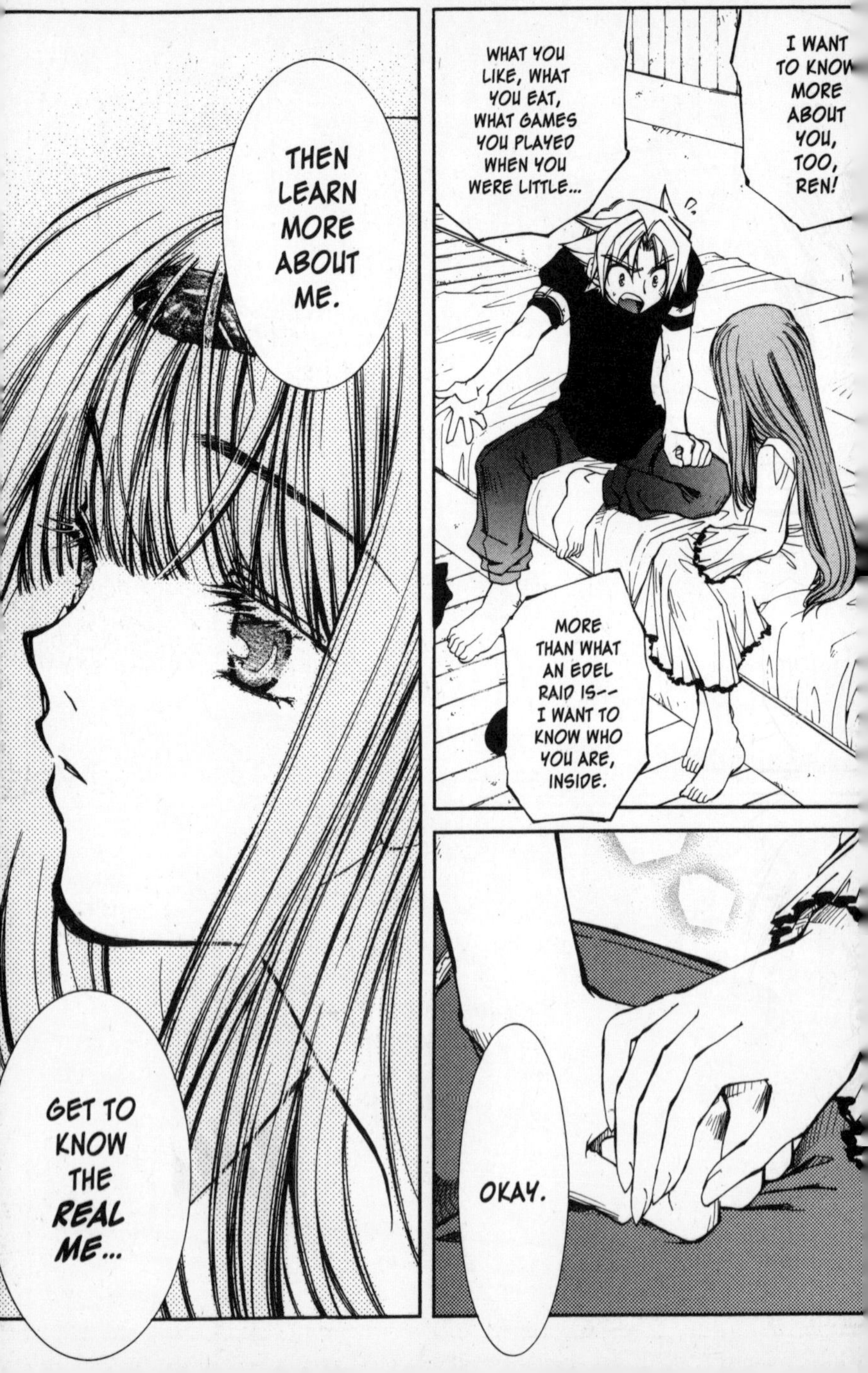
I WANT TO KNOW MORE ABOUT YOU, TOO, REN!
WHAT YOU LIKE, WHAT YOU EAT, WHAT GAMES YOU PLAYED WHEN YOU WERE LITTLE...
MORE THAN WHAT AN EDEL RAID IS-- I WANT TO KNOW WHO YOU ARE, INSIDE.
OKAY.
THEN LEARN MORE ABOUT ME.
GET TO KNOW THE *REAL ME*...

REALLY...?

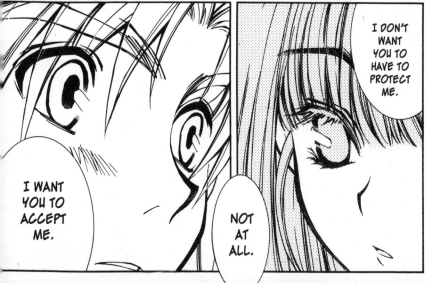

I DON'T WANT YOU TO HAVE TO PROTECT ME.

I WANT YOU TO ACCEPT ME.

NOT AT ALL.

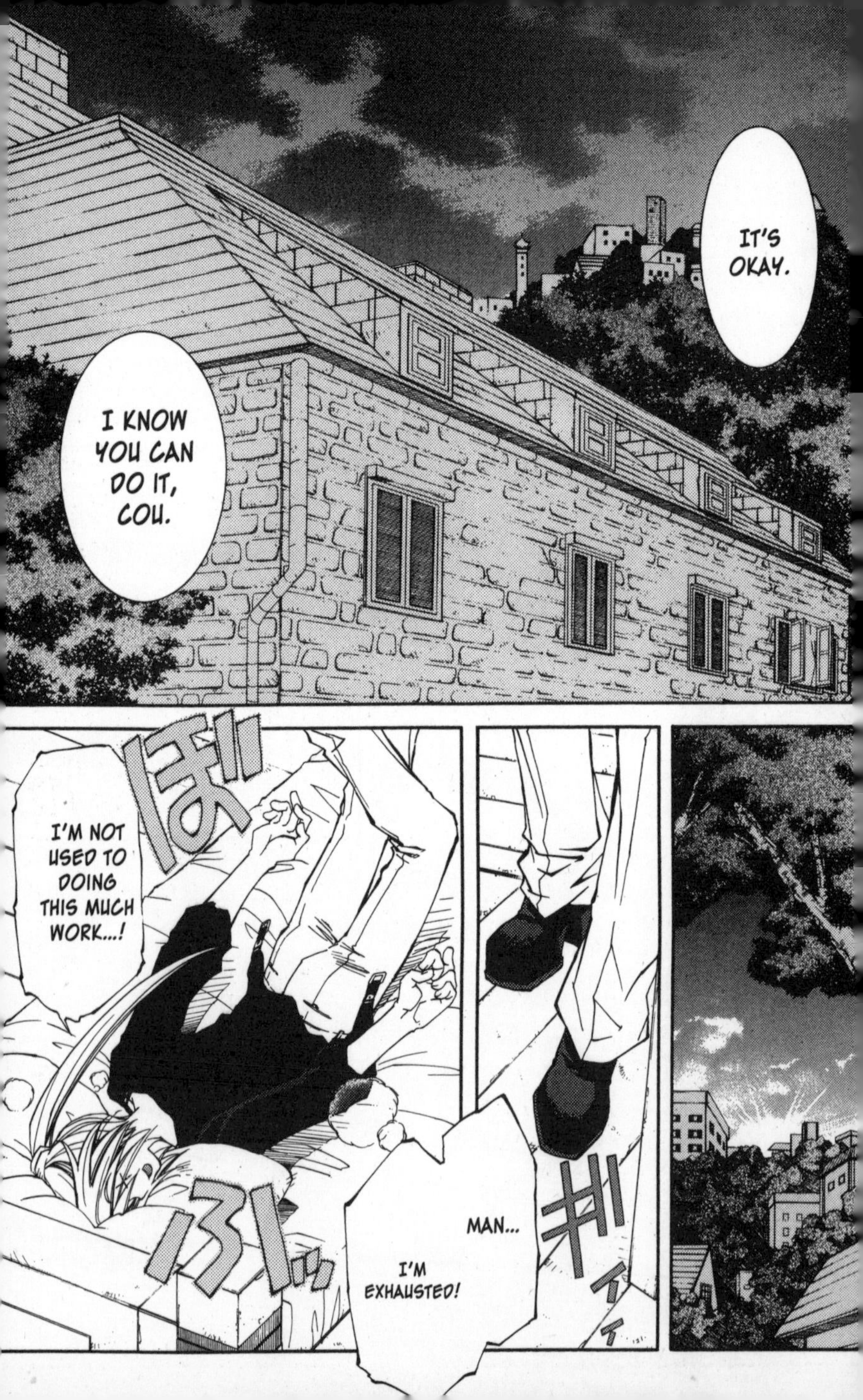
IT'S OKAY.
I KNOW YOU CAN DO IT, COU.
I'M NOT USED TO DOING THIS MUCH WORK...!
MAN... I'M EXHAUSTED!

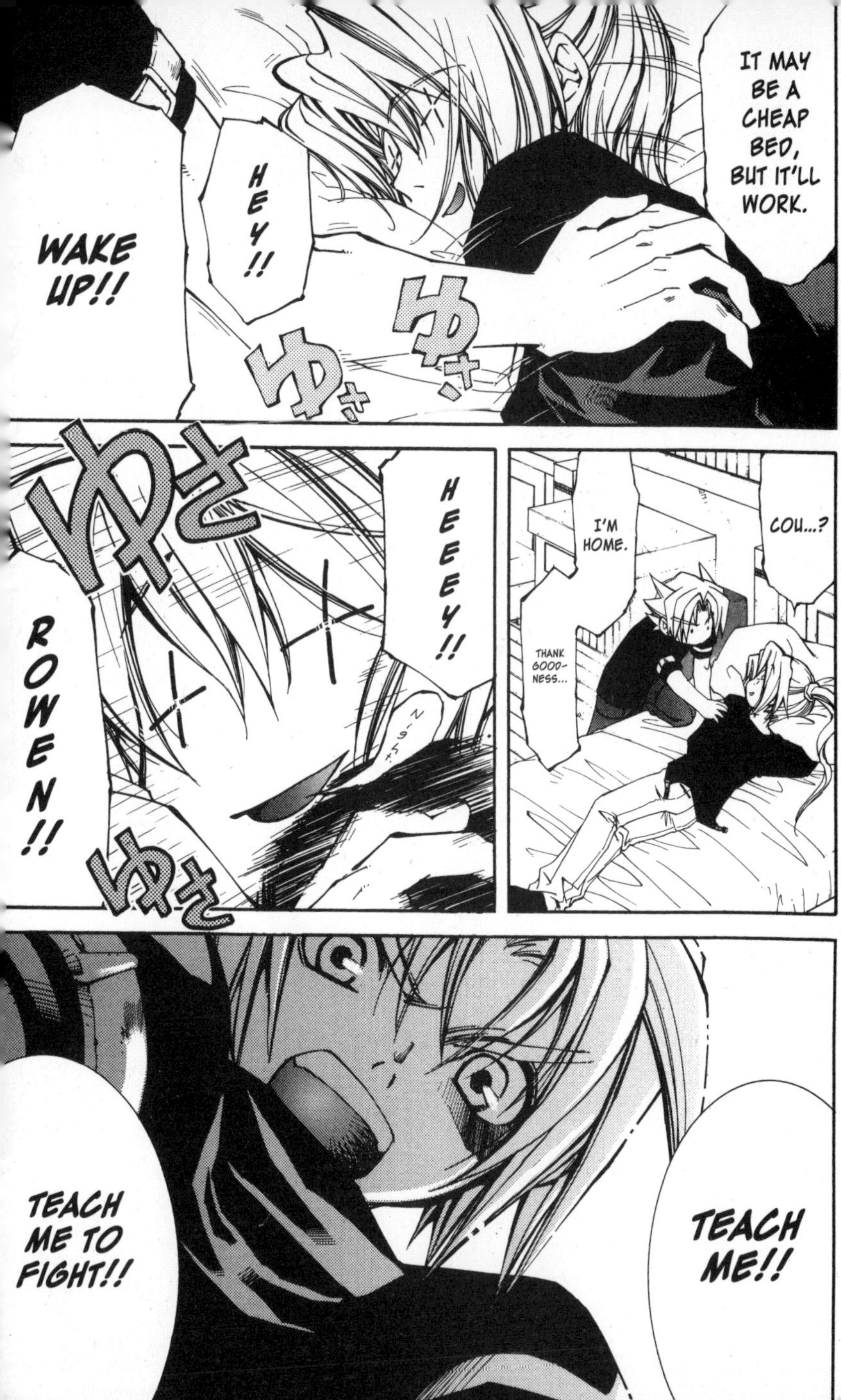
IT MAY BE A CHEAP BED, BUT IT'LL WORK.
HEY!!
WAKE UP!!
ゆさ
ゆさ
COU...?
I'M HOME.
THANK GOODNESS...
HEEEEY!!
ゆさ
ROWEN!!
ゆさ
TEACH ME!!
TEACH ME TO FIGHT!!

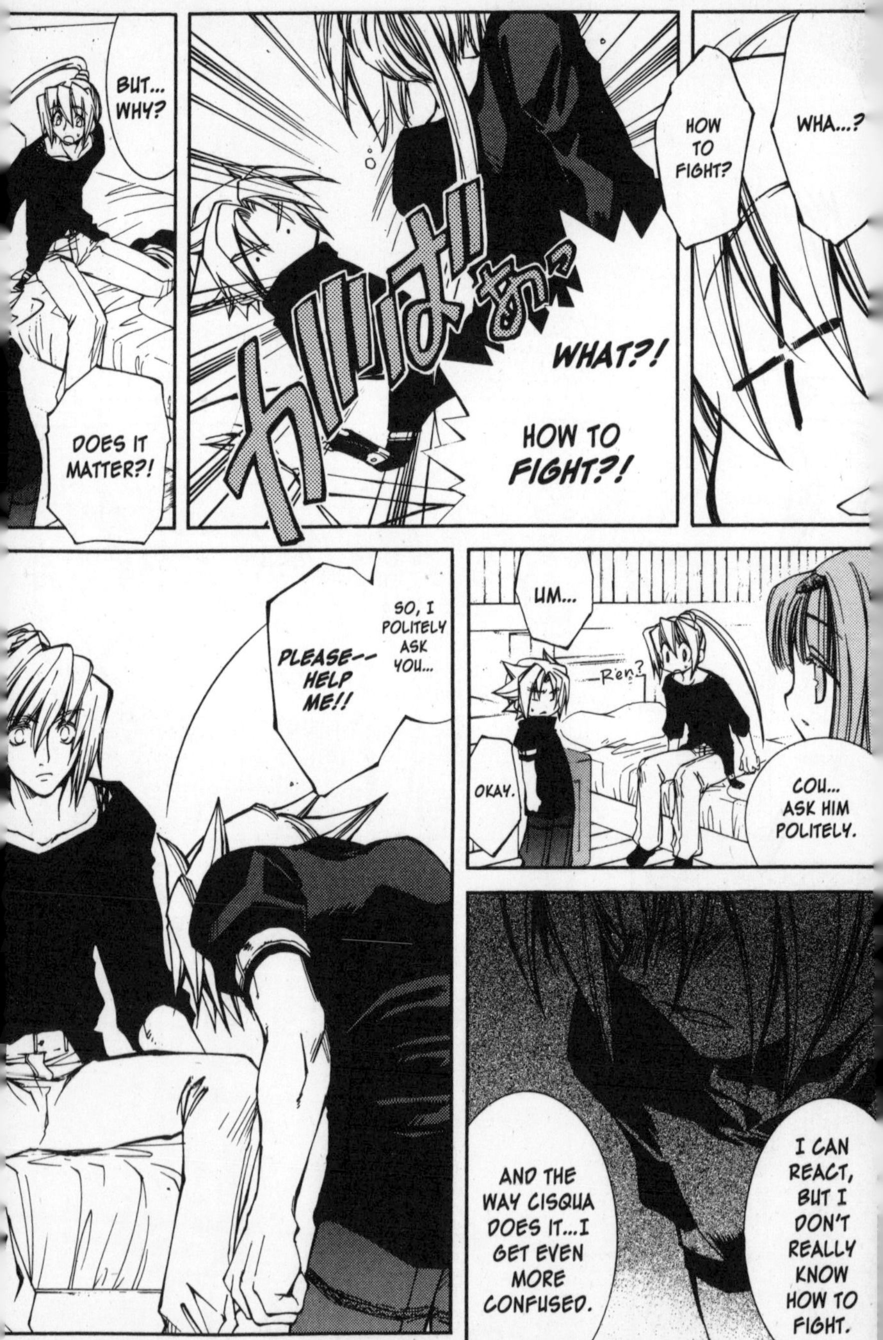
WHA...?
HOW TO FIGHT?
WHAT?!
HOW TO FIGHT?!
BUT... WHY?
DOES IT MATTER?!
UM...
Ren?
COU... ASK HIM POLITELY.
OKAY.
I CAN REACT, BUT I DON'T REALLY KNOW HOW TO FIGHT.
AND THE WAY CISQUA DOES IT...I GET EVEN MORE CONFUSED.
SO, I POLITELY ASK YOU...
PLEASE--HELP ME!!

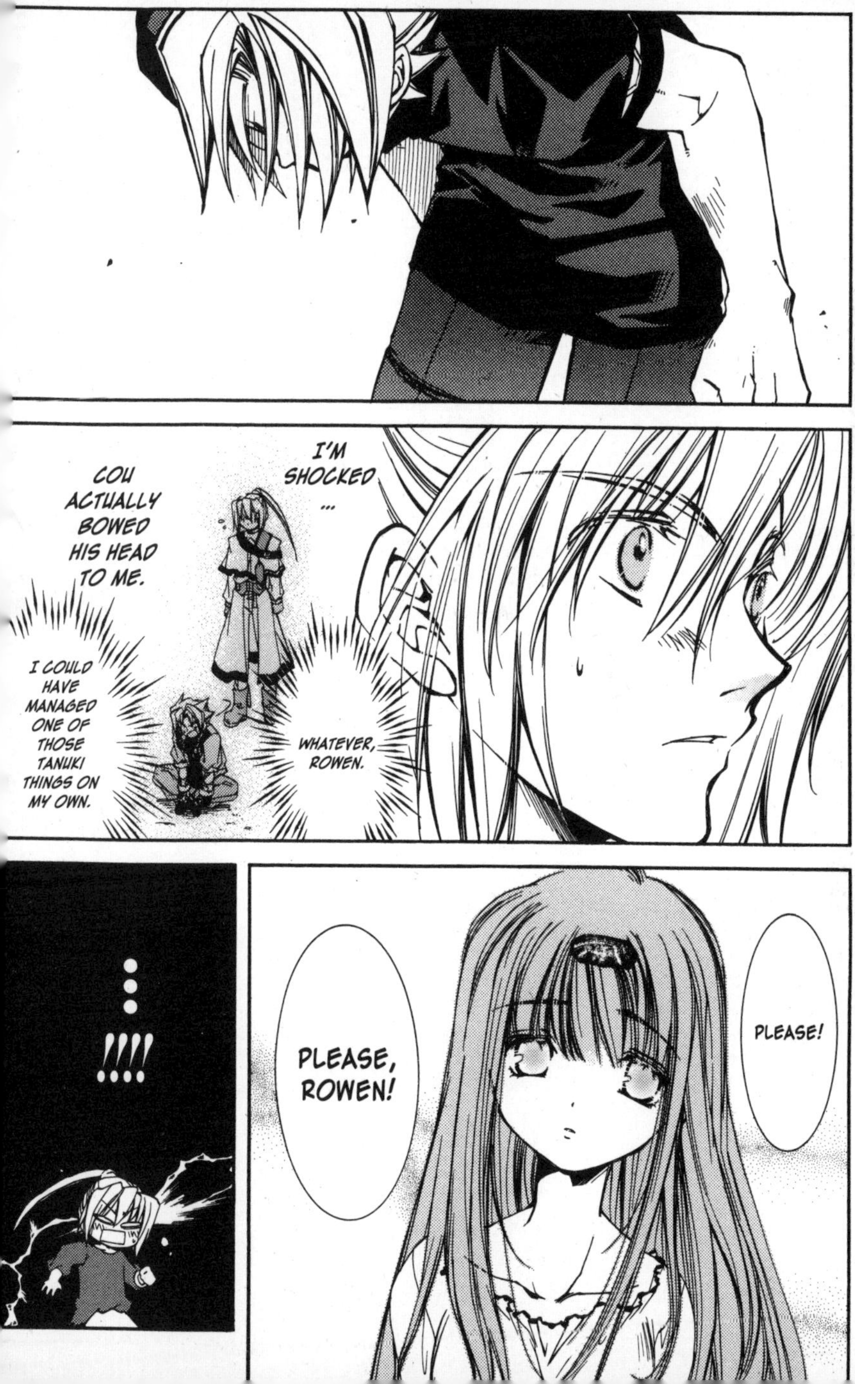
I'M SHOCKED...
COU ACTUALLY BOWED HIS HEAD TO ME.
WHATEVER, ROWEN.
I COULD HAVE MANAGED ONE OF THOSE TANUKI THINGS ON MY OWN.
PLEASE!
PLEASE, ROWEN!
...!!!!

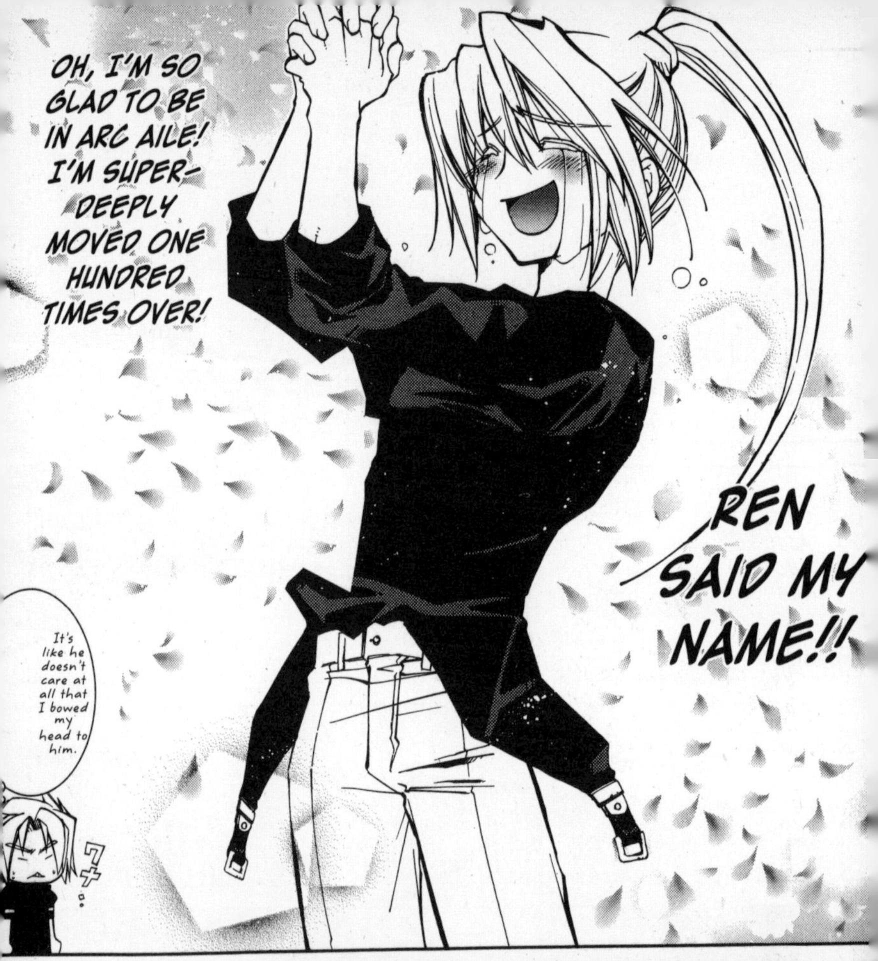
REN SAID MY NAME!!
OH, I'M SO GLAD TO BE IN ARC AILE! I'M SUPER-DEEPLY MOVED ONE HUNDRED TIMES OVER!
It's like he doesn't care at all that I bowed my head to him.
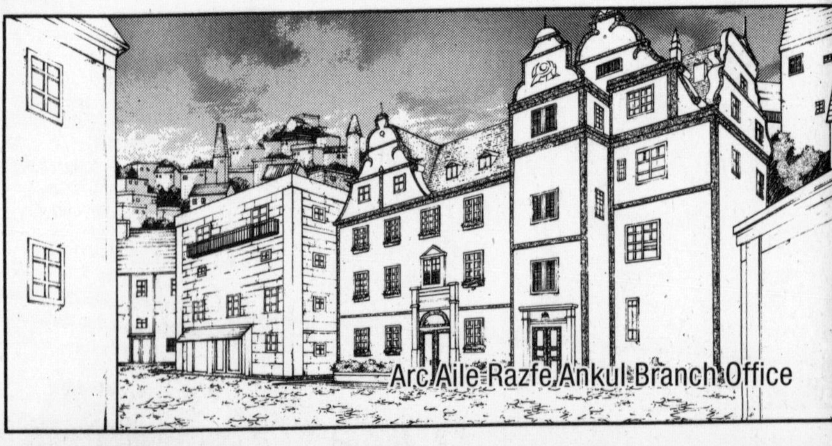
Arc Aile Razfe Ankul Branch Office

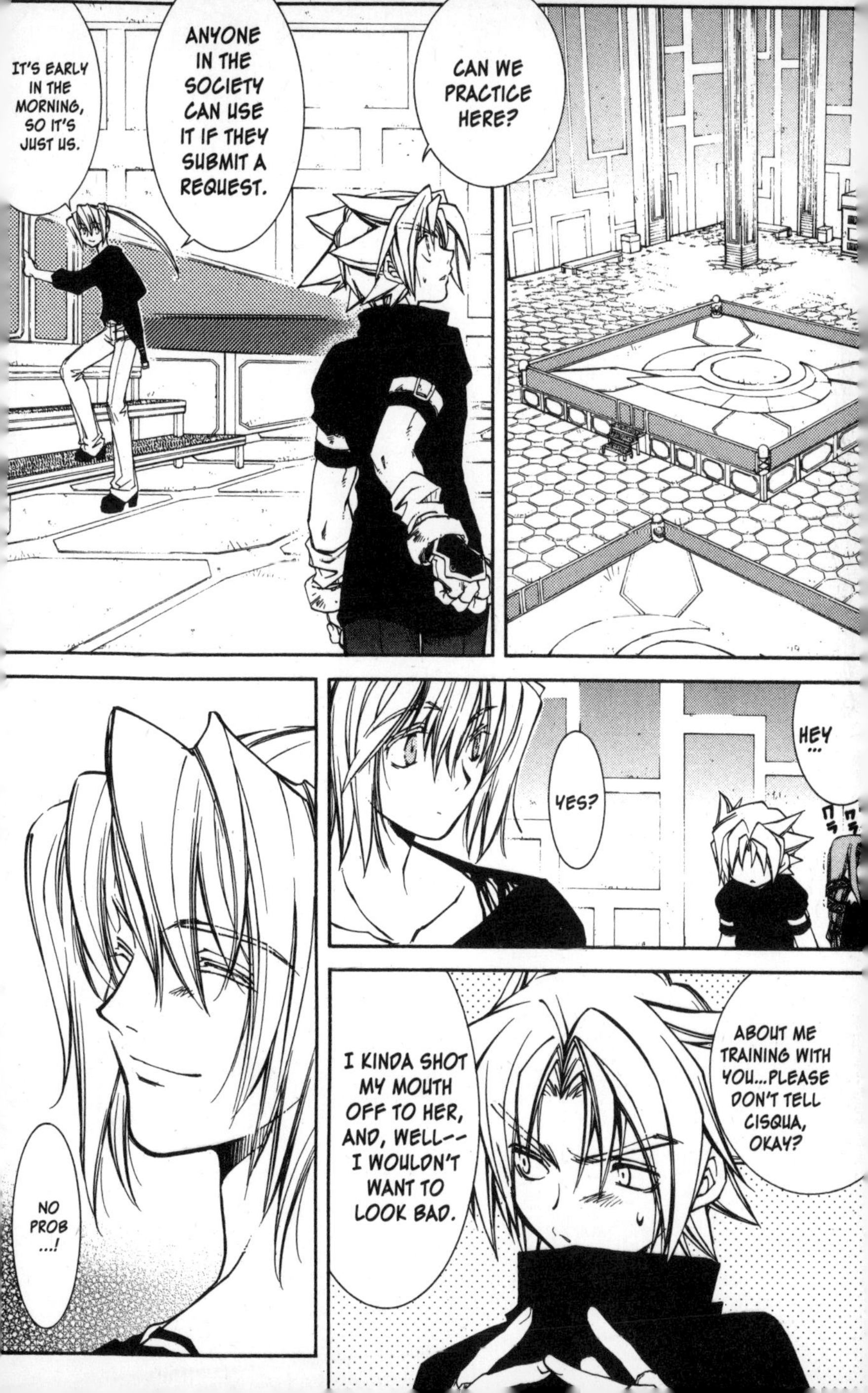
CAN WE PRACTICE HERE?
ANYONE IN THE SOCIETY CAN USE IT IF THEY SUBMIT A REQUEST.
IT'S EARLY IN THE MORNING, SO IT'S JUST US.
HEY...
YES?
ABOUT ME TRAINING WITH YOU...PLEASE DON'T TELL CISQUA, OKAY?
I KINDA SHOT MY MOUTH OFF TO HER, AND, WELL-- I WOULDN'T WANT TO LOOK BAD.
NO PROB...!

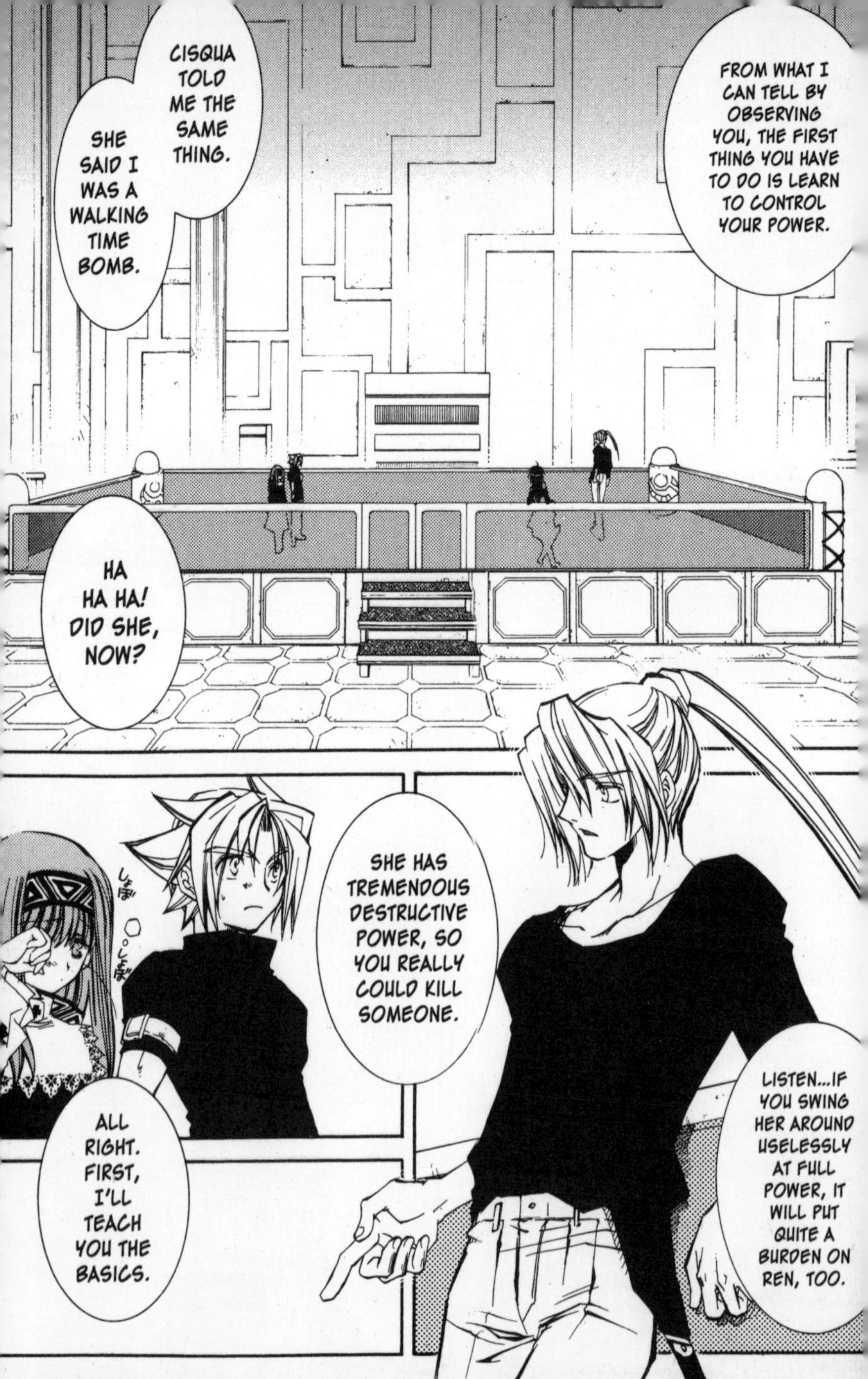
FROM WHAT I CAN TELL BY OBSERVING YOU, THE FIRST THING YOU HAVE TO DO IS LEARN TO CONTROL YOUR POWER.
CISQUA TOLD ME THE SAME THING.
SHE SAID I WAS A WALKING TIME BOMB.
HA HA HA! DID SHE, NOW?
LISTEN...IF YOU SWING HER AROUND USELESSLY AT FULL POWER, IT WILL PUT QUITE A BURDEN ON REN, TOO.
SHE HAS TREMENDOUS DESTRUCTIVE POWER, SO YOU REALLY COULD KILL SOMEONE.
しょぼ
しょぼ
ALL RIGHT. FIRST, I'LL TEACH YOU THE BASICS.

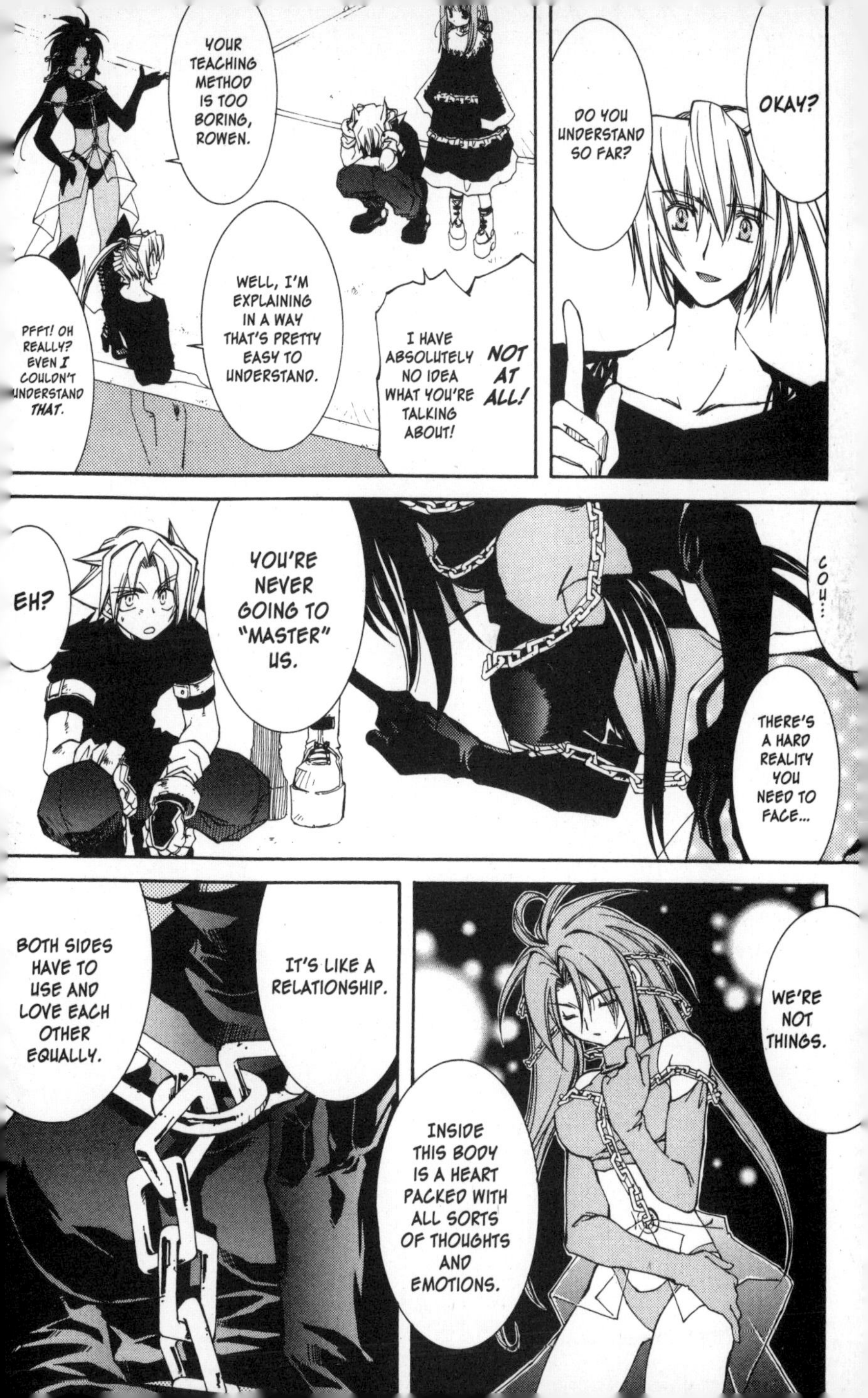
OKAY?
DO YOU UNDERSTAND SO FAR?
NOT AT ALL!
I HAVE ABSOLUTELY NO IDEA WHAT YOU'RE TALKING ABOUT!
WELL, I'M EXPLAINING IN A WAY THAT'S PRETTY EASY TO UNDERSTAND.
PFFT! OH REALLY? EVEN *I* COULDN'T UNDERSTAND *THAT*.
YOUR TEACHING METHOD IS TOO BORING, ROWEN.
COU...
THERE'S A HARD REALITY YOU NEED TO FACE...
YOU'RE NEVER GOING TO "MASTER" US.
EH?
WE'RE NOT THINGS.
INSIDE THIS BODY IS A HEART PACKED WITH ALL SORTS OF THOUGHTS AND EMOTIONS.
IT'S LIKE A RELATIONSHIP.
BOTH SIDES HAVE TO USE AND LOVE EACH OTHER EQUALLY.

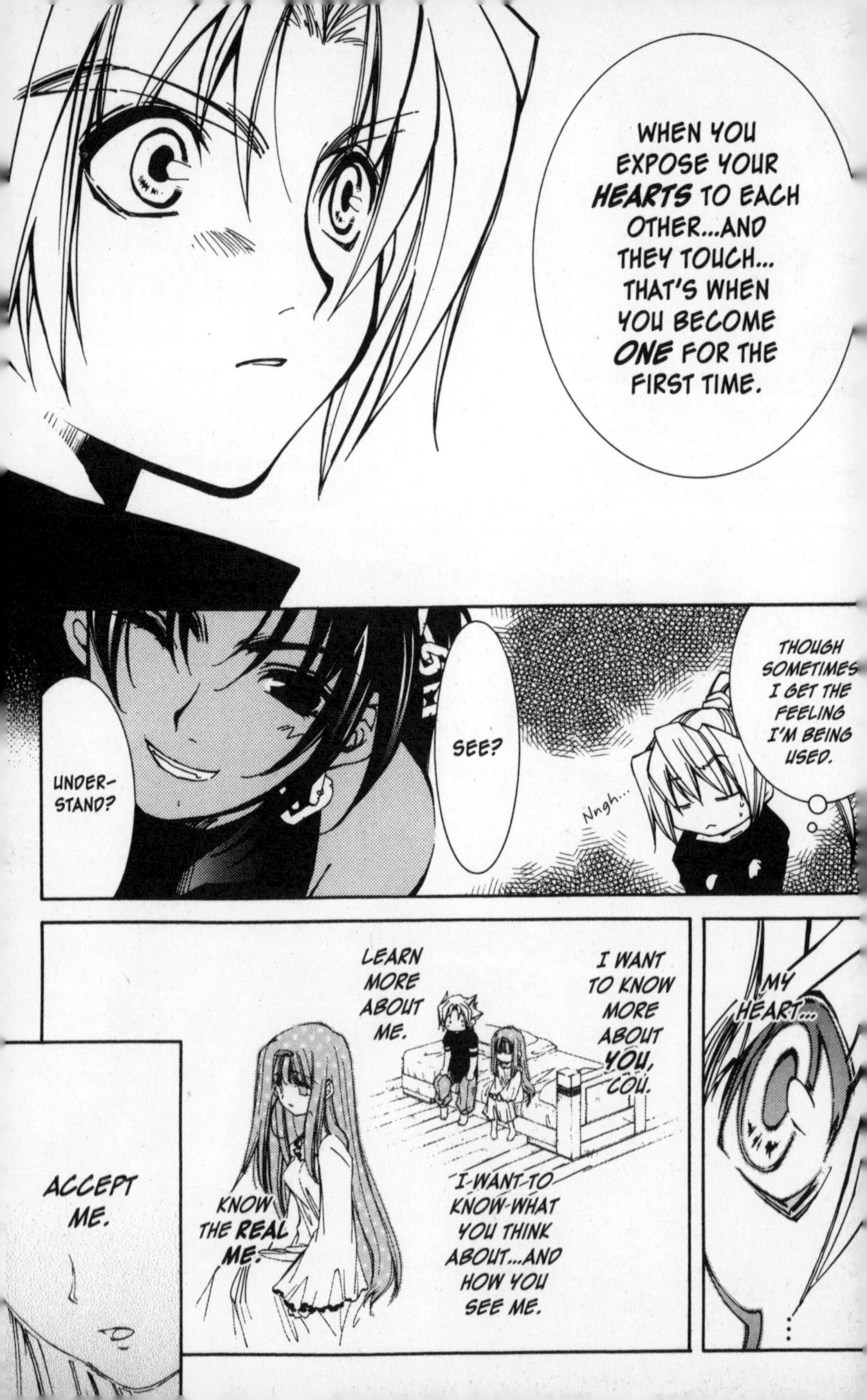
WHEN YOU EXPOSE YOUR HEARTS TO EACH OTHER...AND THEY TOUCH... THAT'S WHEN YOU BECOME ONE FOR THE FIRST TIME.
THOUGH SOMETIMES I GET THE FEELING I'M BEING USED.
SEE?
Nngh...
UNDER-STAND?
MY HEART...
I WANT TO KNOW MORE ABOUT YOU, COU.
LEARN MORE ABOUT ME.
I WANT TO KNOW WHAT YOU THINK ABOUT...AND HOW YOU SEE ME.
KNOW THE REAL ME.
ACCEPT ME.

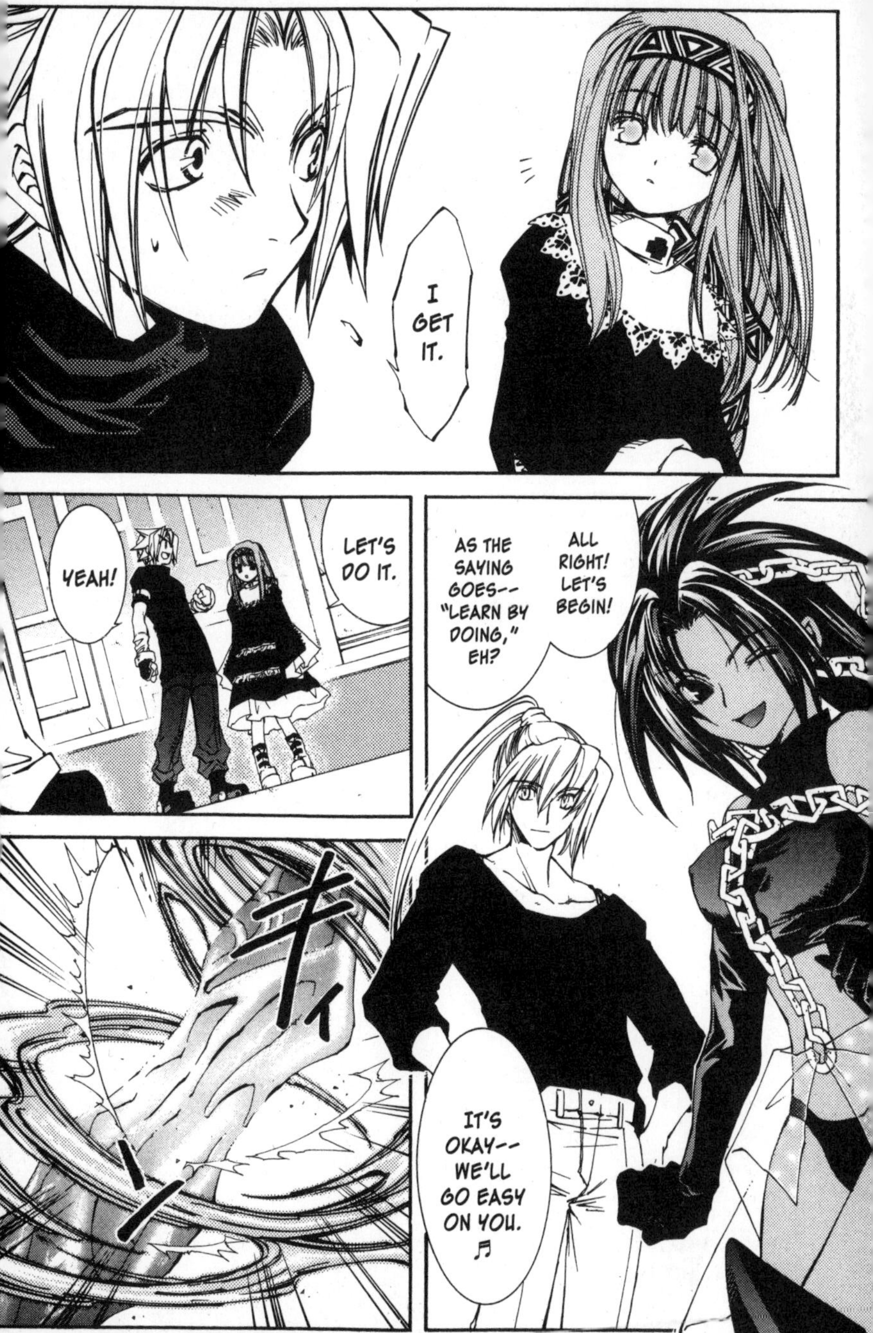
I GET IT.
ALL RIGHT! LET'S BEGIN!
AS THE SAYING GOES--"LEARN BY DOING," EH?
IT'S OKAY--WE'LL GO EASY ON YOU. ♬
LET'S DO IT.
YEAH!
キイ

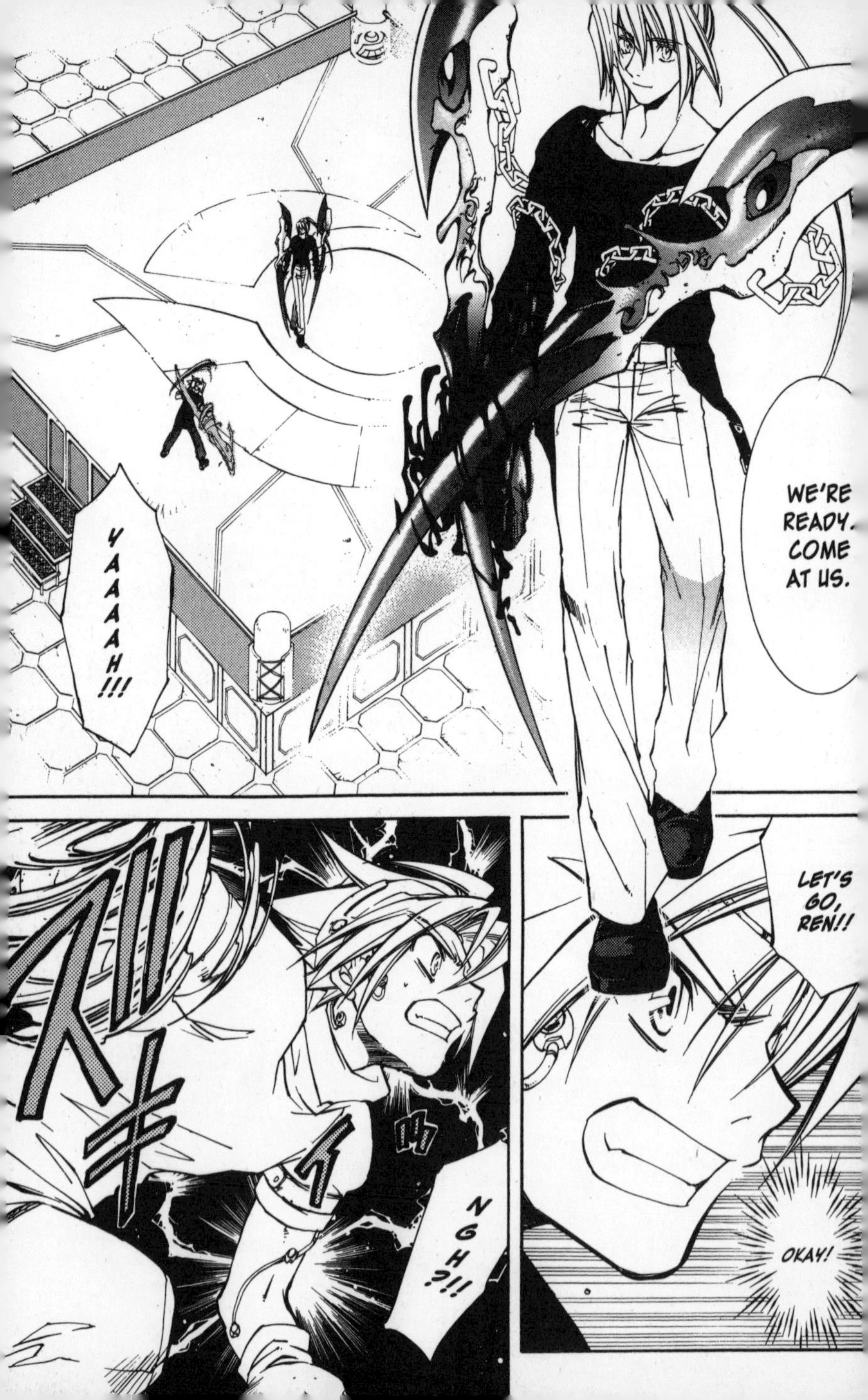
WE'RE READY. COME AT US.
YAAAAAH!!!
LET'S GO, REN!!
OKAY!
ズキィ
NGH?!!

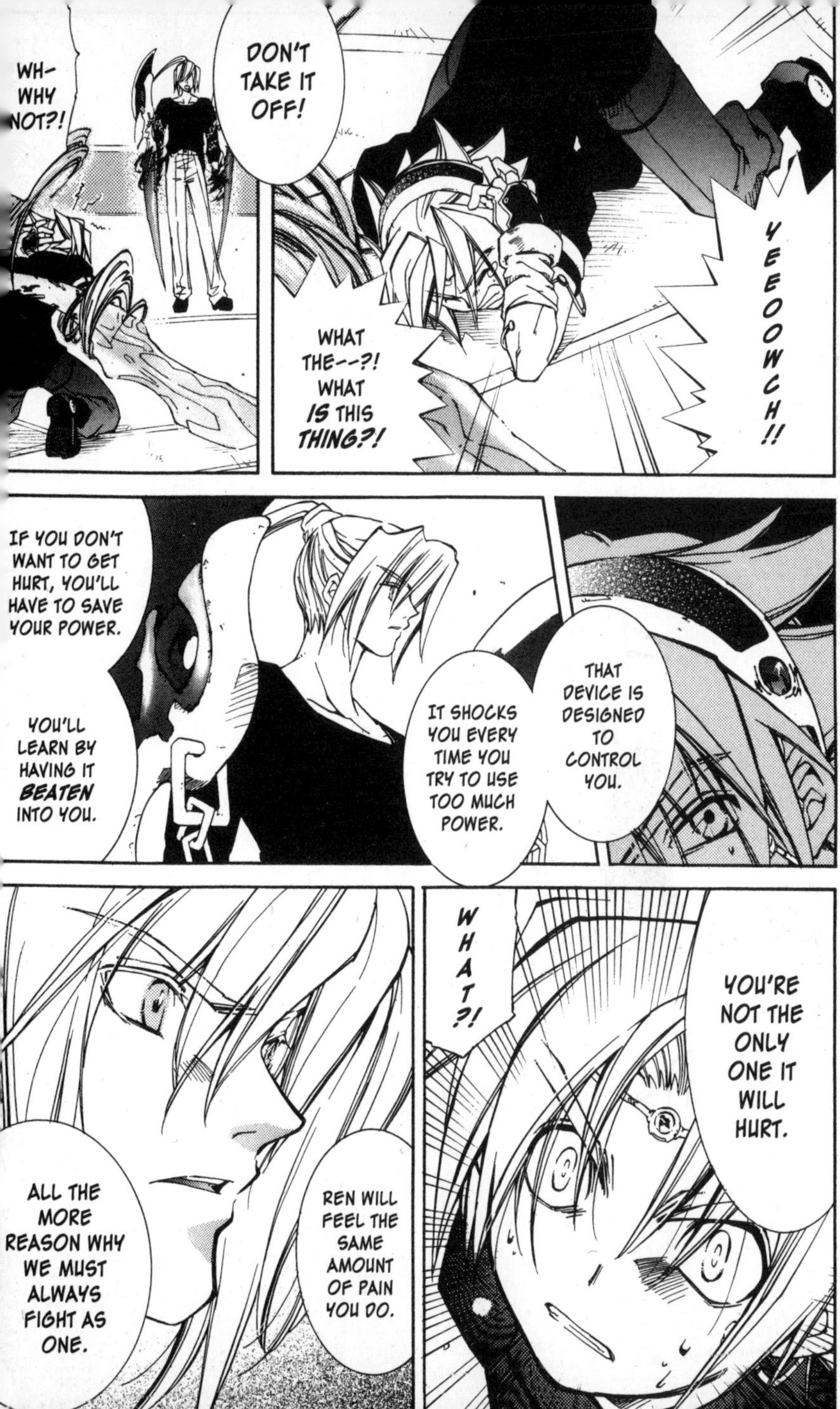
YEEOOWCH!!
WHAT THE--?! WHAT *IS* THIS *THING?!*
DON'T TAKE IT OFF!
WH- WHY NOT?!
THAT DEVICE IS DESIGNED TO CONTROL YOU.
IT SHOCKS YOU EVERY TIME YOU TRY TO USE TOO MUCH POWER.
IF YOU DON'T WANT TO GET HURT, YOU'LL HAVE TO SAVE YOUR POWER.
YOU'LL LEARN BY HAVING IT *BEATEN* INTO YOU.
YOU'RE NOT THE ONLY ONE IT WILL HURT.
WHAT?!
REN WILL FEEL THE SAME AMOUNT OF PAIN YOU DO.
ALL THE MORE REASON WHY WE MUST ALWAYS FIGHT AS ONE.

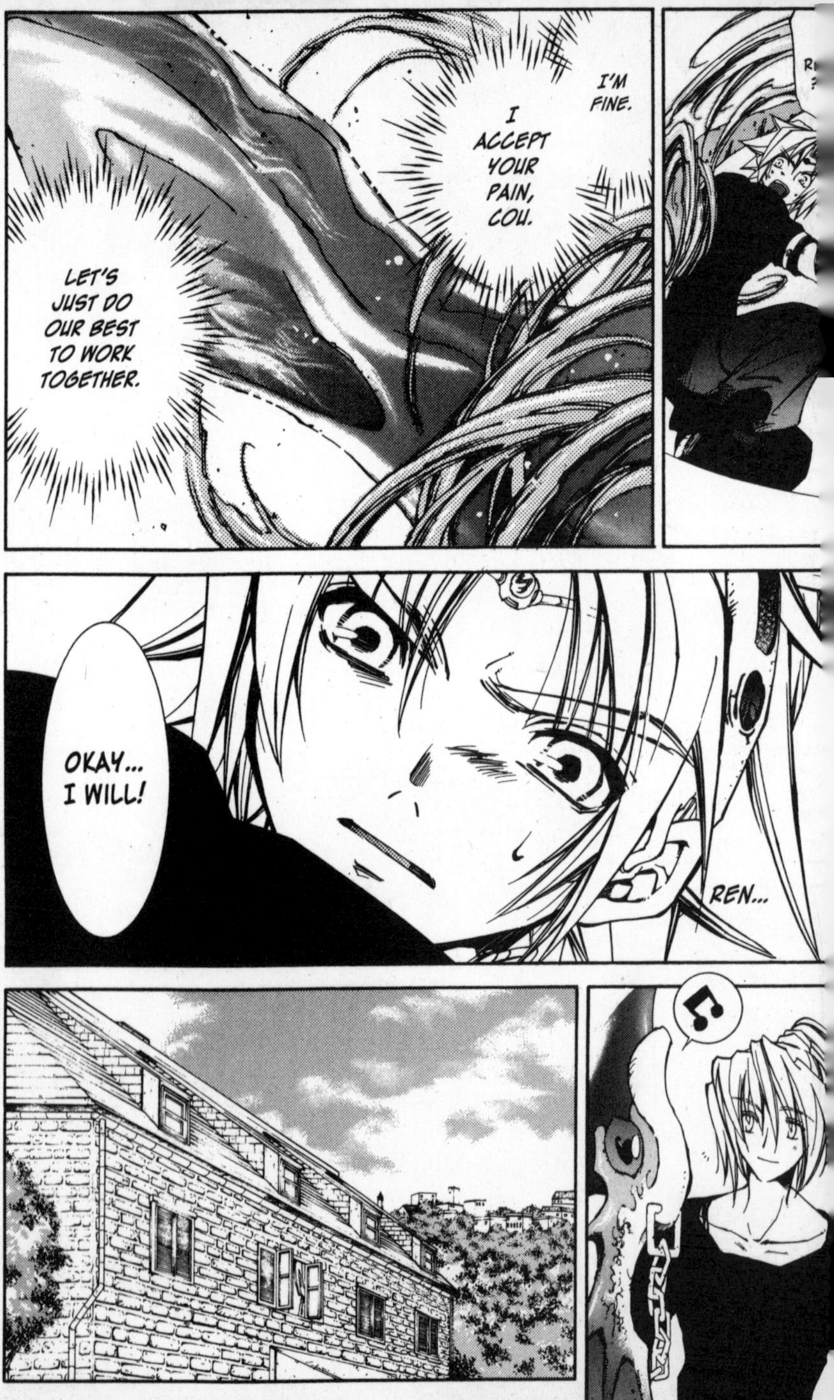
I'M FINE.
I ACCEPT YOUR PAIN, COU.
LET'S JUST DO OUR BEST TO WORK TOGETHER.
REN...
OKAY... I WILL!

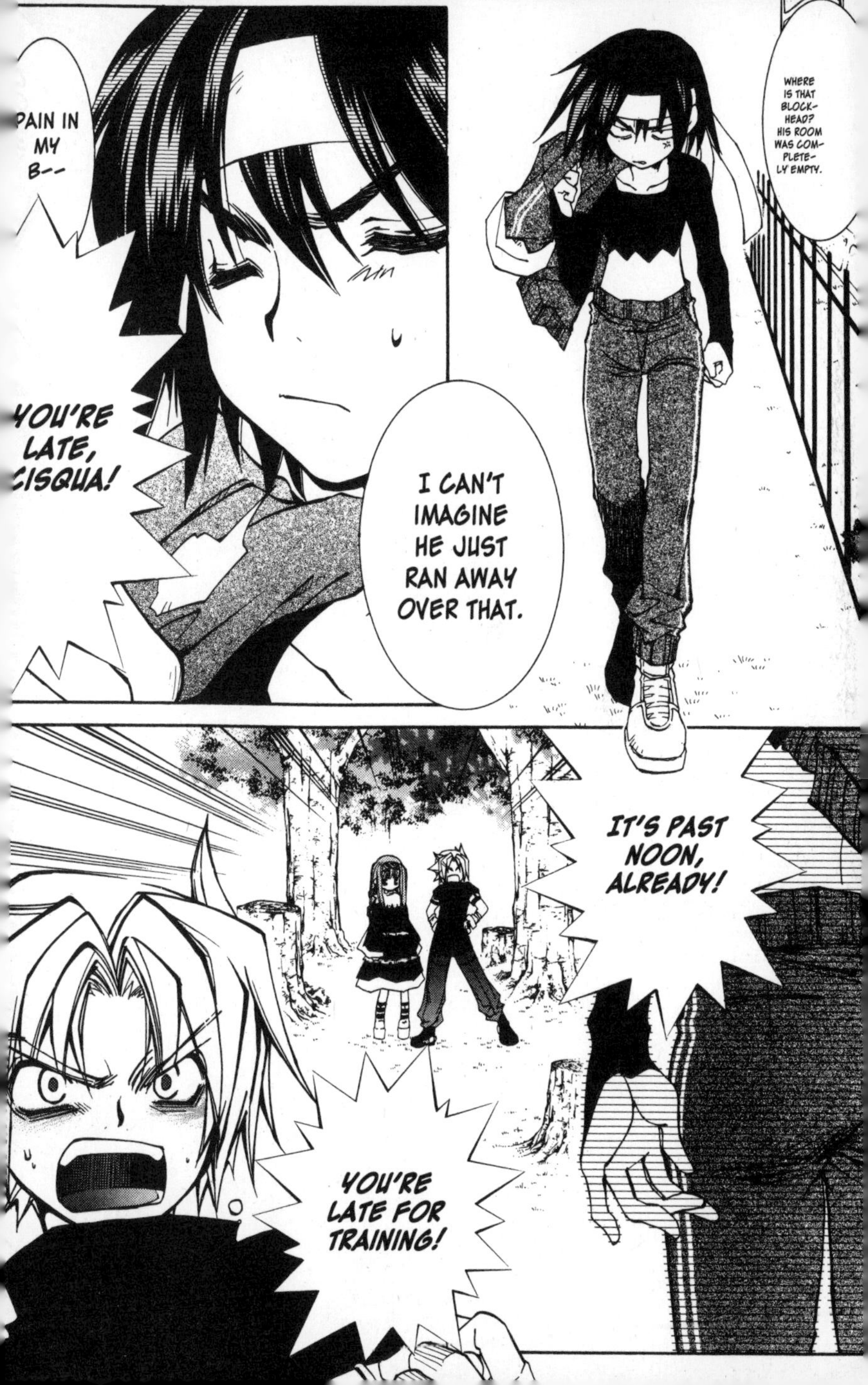

WHERE IS THAT BLOCK-HEAD? HIS ROOM WAS COMPLETELY EMPTY.
I CAN'T IMAGINE HE JUST RAN AWAY OVER THAT.
PAIN IN MY B--
YOU'RE LATE, CISQUA!
IT'S PAST NOON, ALREADY!
YOU'RE LATE FOR TRAINING!

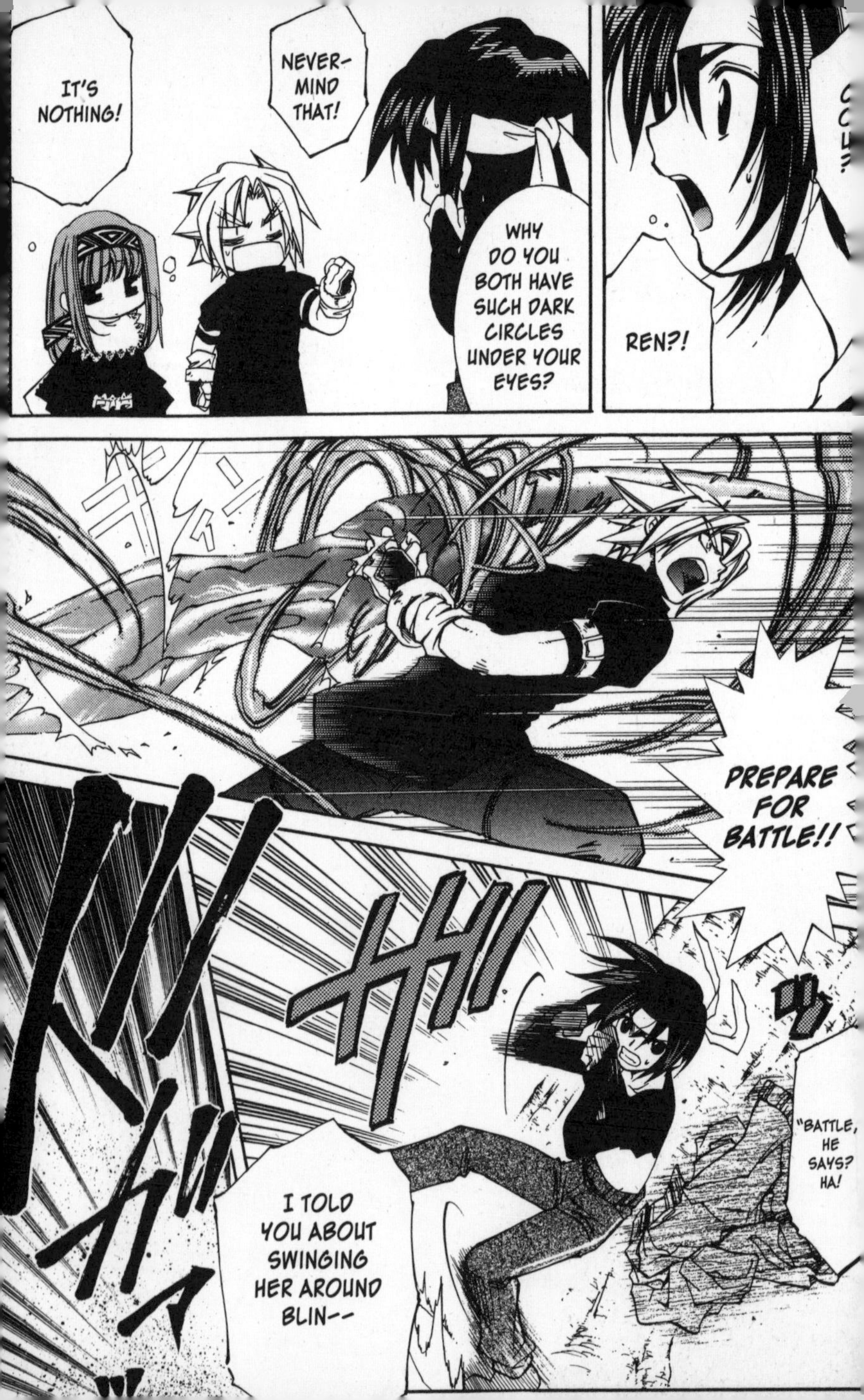
REN?!
WHY DO YOU BOTH HAVE SUCH DARK CIRCLES UNDER YOUR EYES?
NEVER-MIND THAT!
IT'S NOTHING!
PREPARE FOR BATTLE!!
"BATTLE," HE SAYS? HA!
I TOLD YOU ABOUT SWINGING HER AROUND BLIN--

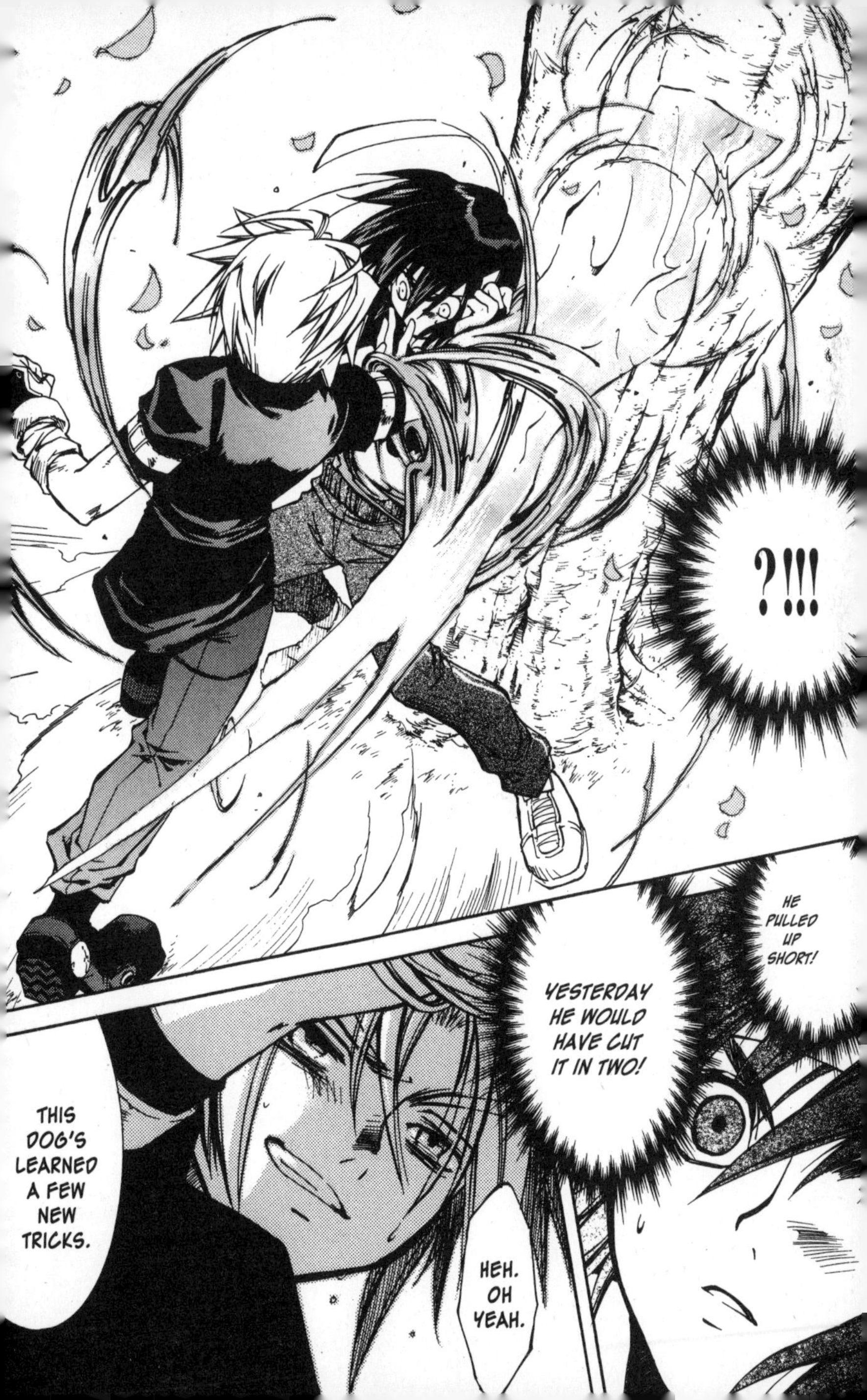
?!!!
HE PULLED UP SHORT!
YESTERDAY HE WOULD HAVE CUT IT IN TWO!
HEH. OH YEAH.
THIS DOG'S LEARNED A FEW NEW TRICKS.

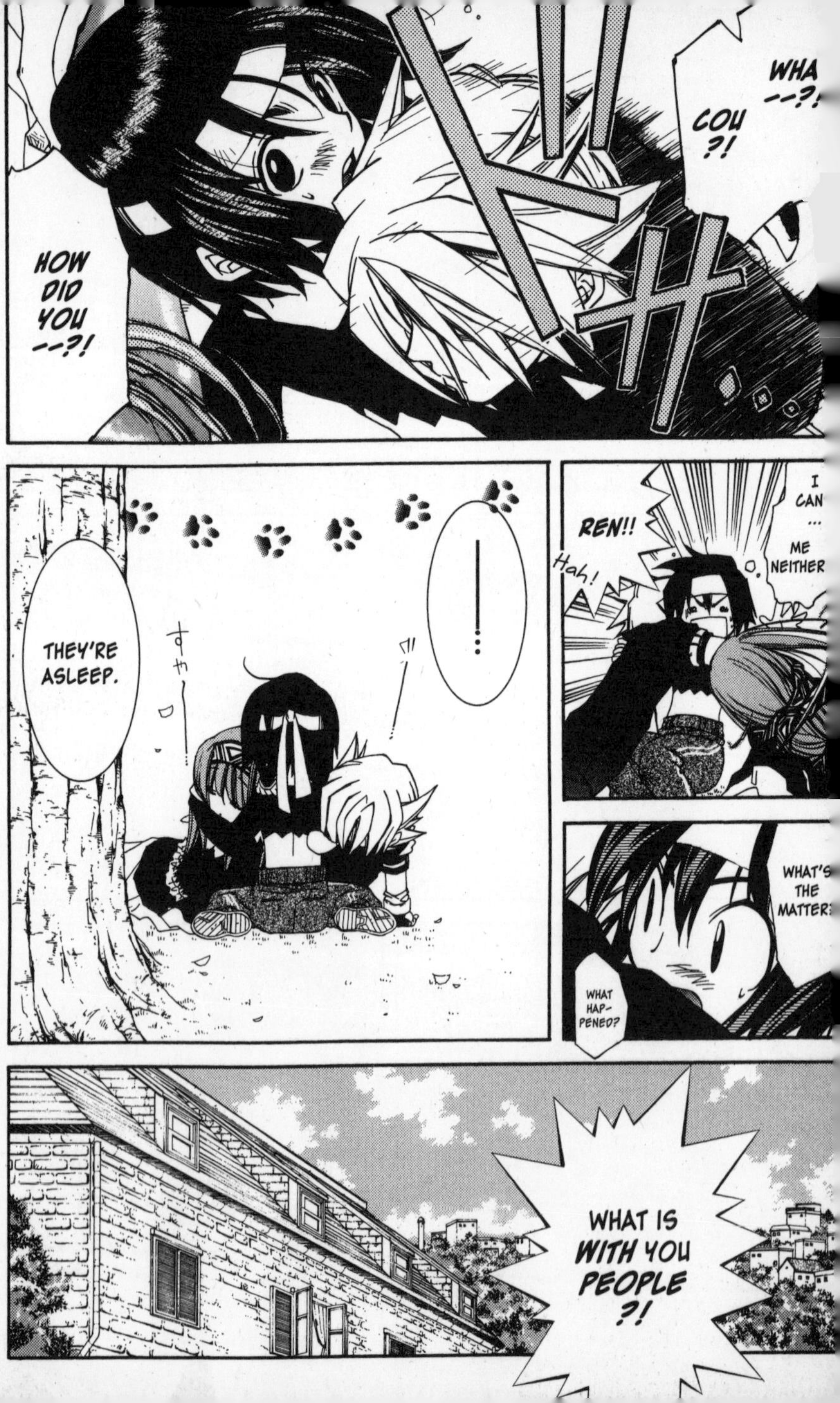
WHA--?!
COU?!
HOW DID YOU--?!
I CAN ...
ME NEITHER
REN!!
Hah!
WHAT'S THE MATTER?
WHAT HAPPENED?
—!...
THEY'RE ASLEEP.
WHAT IS WITH YOU PEOPLE?!

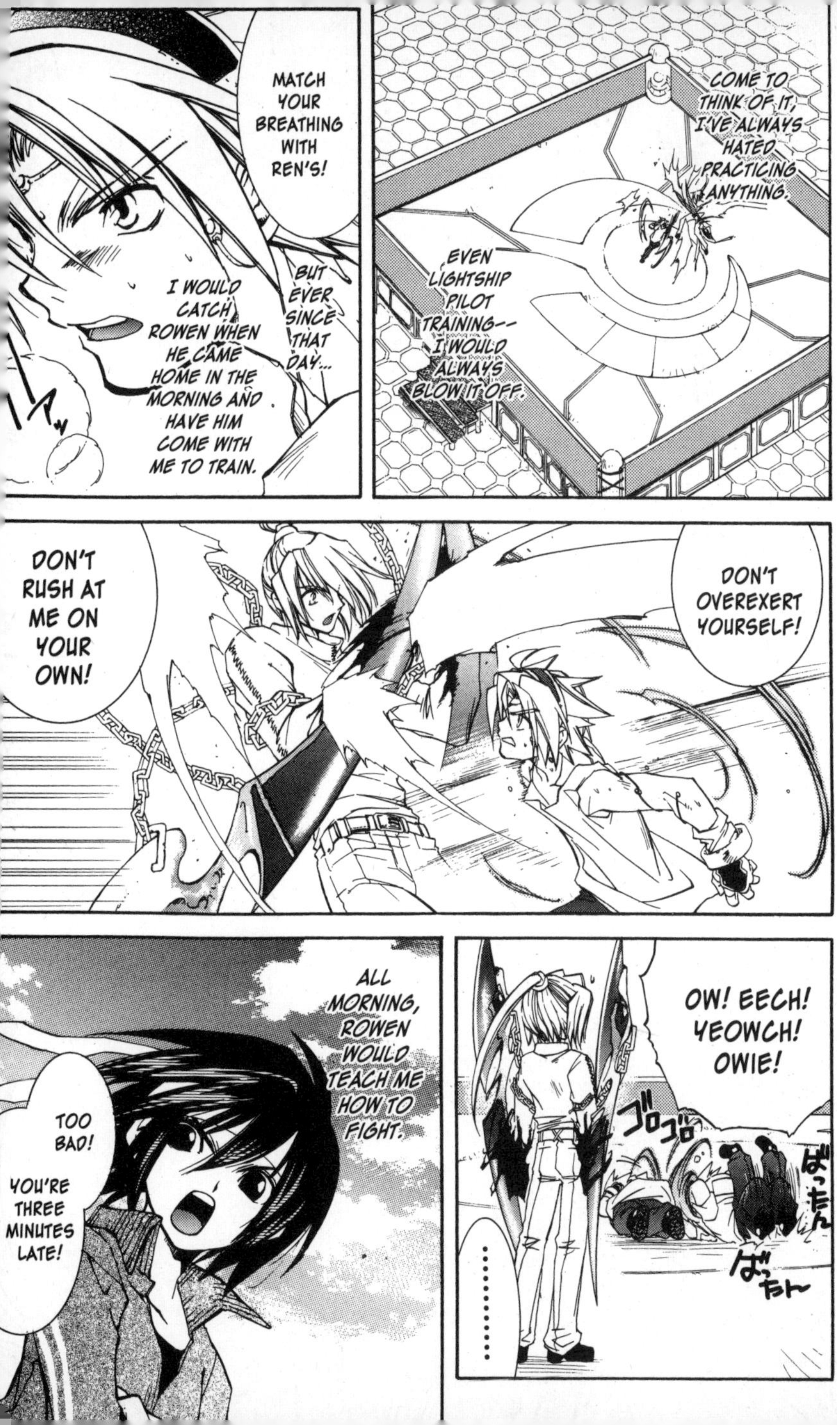
COME TO THINK OF IT, I'VE ALWAYS HATED PRACTICING ANYTHING.
EVEN LIGHTSHIP PILOT TRAINING-- I WOULD ALWAYS BLOW IT OFF.
MATCH YOUR BREATHING WITH REN'S!
BUT EVER SINCE THAT DAY...
I WOULD CATCH ROWEN WHEN HE CAME HOME IN THE MORNING AND HAVE HIM COME WITH ME TO TRAIN.
DON'T OVEREXERT YOURSELF!
DON'T RUSH AT ME ON YOUR OWN!
OW! EECH! YEOWCH! OWIE!
ゴロゴロ
ばったん
ばったん
......
ALL MORNING, ROWEN WOULD TEACH ME HOW TO FIGHT.
TOO BAD!
YOU'RE THREE MINUTES LATE!

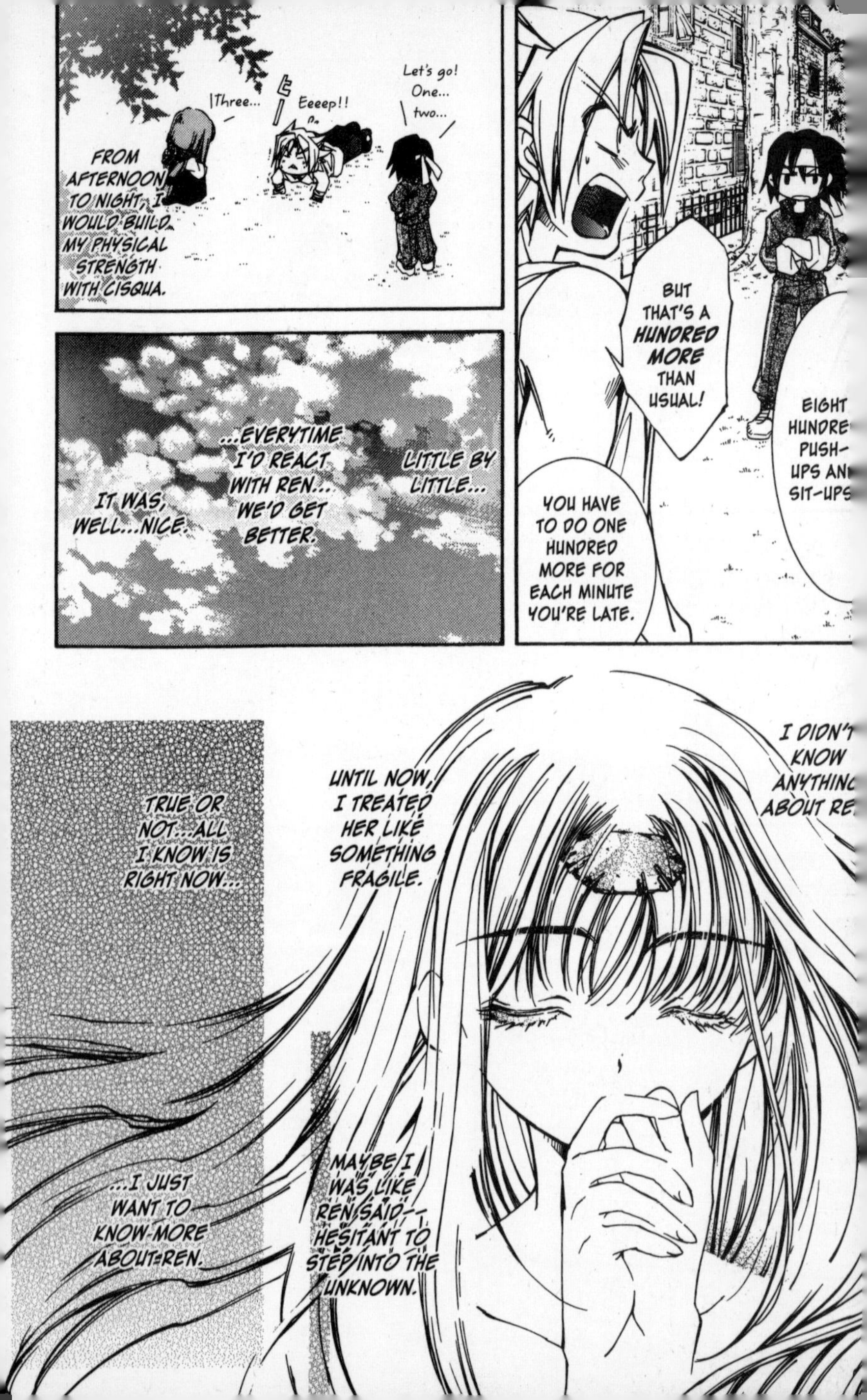
EIGHT HUNDRE PUSH-UPS AN SIT-UPS
BUT THAT'S A HUNDRED MORE THAN USUAL!
YOU HAVE TO DO ONE HUNDRED MORE FOR EACH MINUTE YOU'RE LATE.
Let's go! One... two...
Eeeep!!
Three...
FROM AFTERNOON TO NIGHT, I WOULD BUILD MY PHYSICAL STRENGTH WITH CISQUA.
LITTLE BY LITTLE...
...EVERYTIME I'D REACT WITH REN... WE'D GET BETTER.
IT WAS, WELL...NICE.
I DIDN'T KNOW ANYTHING ABOUT RE
UNTIL NOW, I TREATED HER LIKE SOMETHING FRAGILE.
TRUE OR NOT...ALL I KNOW IS RIGHT NOW...
MAYBE I WAS LIKE REN SAID—HESITANT TO STEP INTO THE UNKNOWN.
...I JUST WANT TO KNOW MORE ABOUT REN.

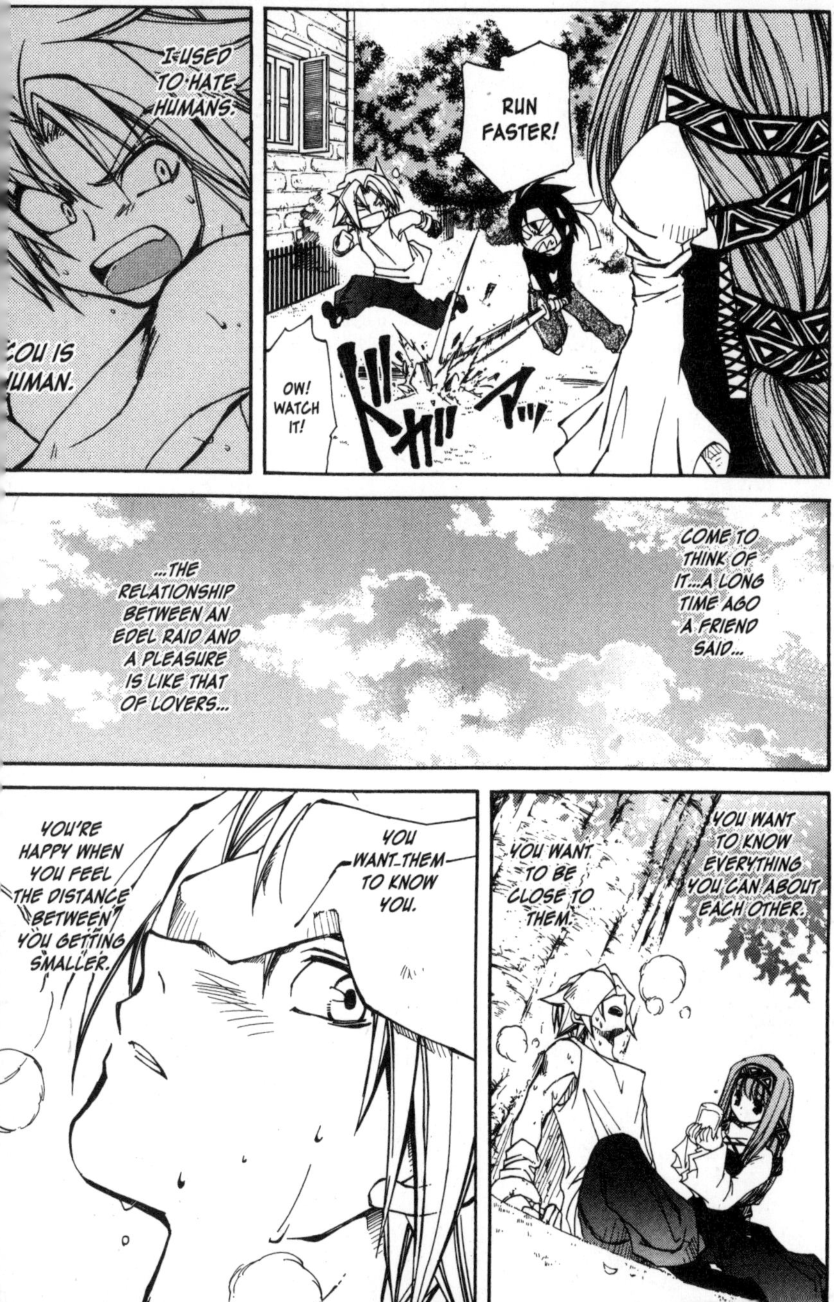
RUN FASTER!
OW! WATCH IT!
ドカッ
I USED TO HATE HUMANS.
COME TO THINK OF IT...A LONG TIME AGO A FRIEND SAID...
...THE RELATIONSHIP BETWEEN AN EDEL RAID AND A PLEASURE IS LIKE THAT OF LOVERS...
YOU WANT TO KNOW EVERYTHING YOU CAN ABOUT EACH OTHER.
YOU WANT TO BE CLOSE TO THEM.
YOU WANT THEM TO KNOW YOU.
YOU'RE HAPPY WHEN YOU FEEL THE DISTANCE BETWEEN YOU GETTING SMALLER.

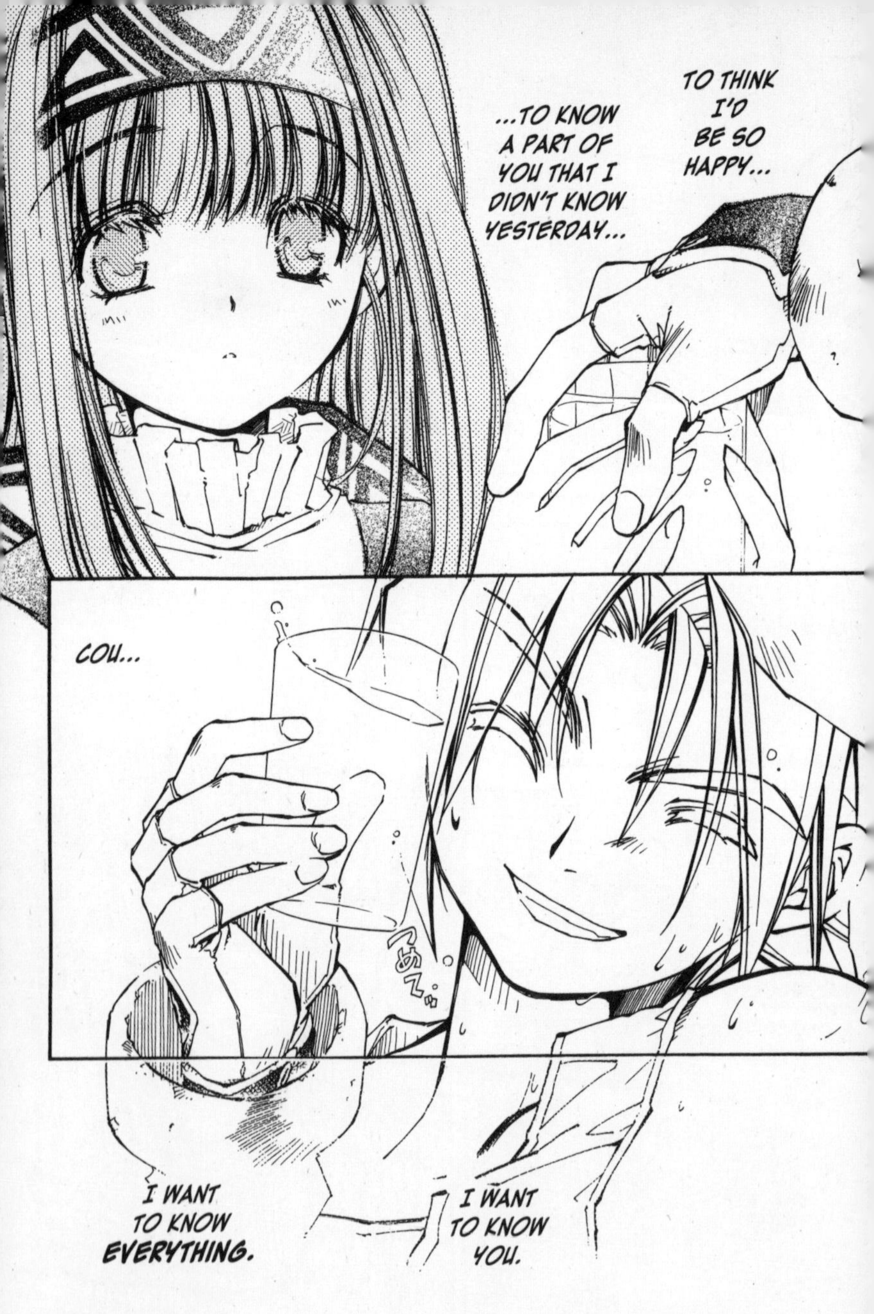
TO THINK I'D BE SO HAPPY...
...TO KNOW A PART OF YOU THAT I DIDN'T KNOW YESTERDAY...
COU...
I WANT TO KNOW YOU.
I WANT TO KNOW **EVERYTHING.**

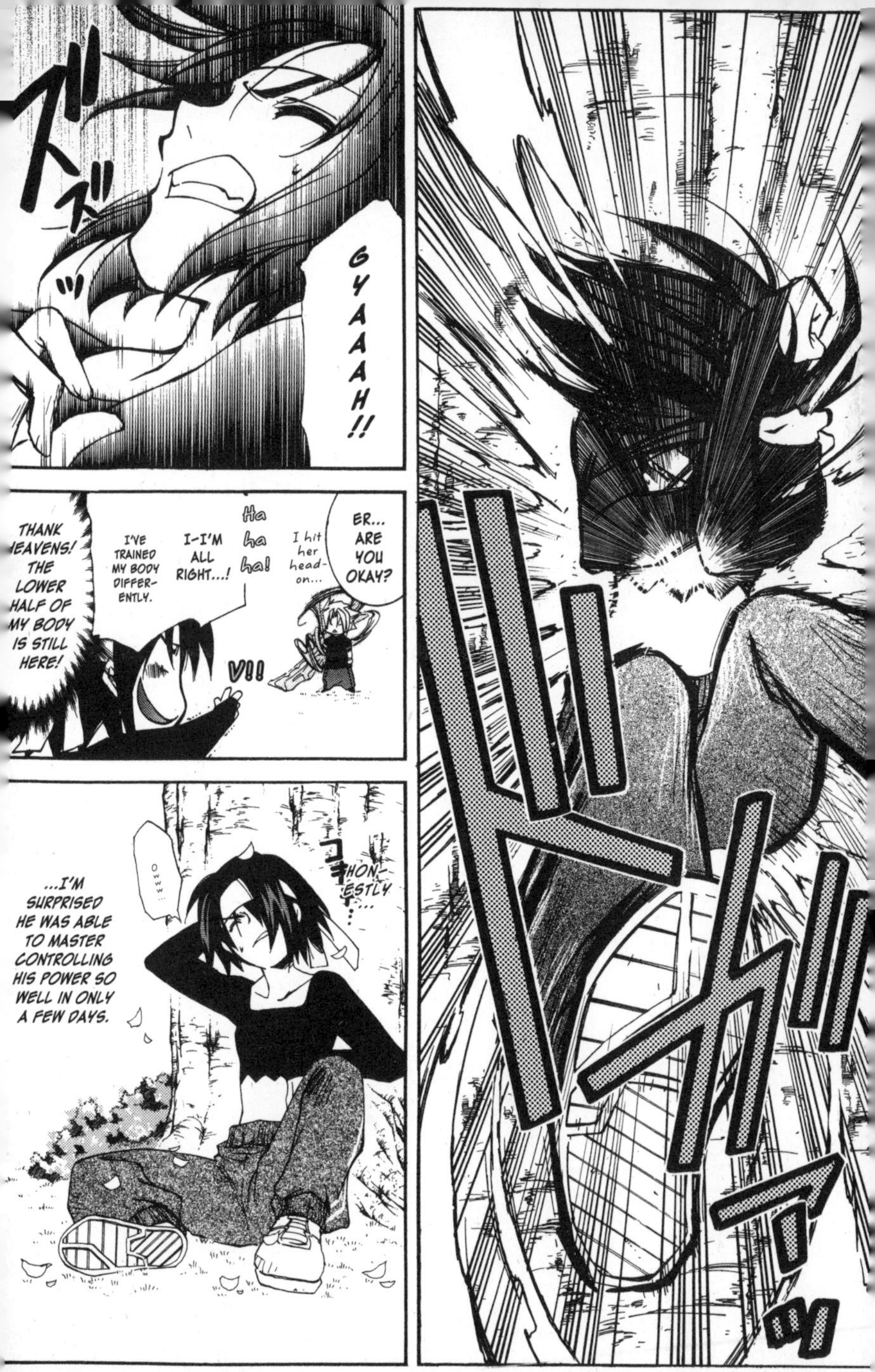
GYAAAAH!!
ER... ARE YOU OKAY?
I hit her head-on...
Ha ha ha!
I-I'M ALL RIGHT...!
I'VE TRAINED MY BODY DIFFERENTLY.
THANK HEAVENS! THE LOWER HALF OF MY BODY IS STILL HERE!
V!!
HONESTLY...
Owww...
...I'M SURPRISED HE WAS ABLE TO MASTER CONTROLLING HIS POWER SO WELL IN ONLY A FEW DAYS.

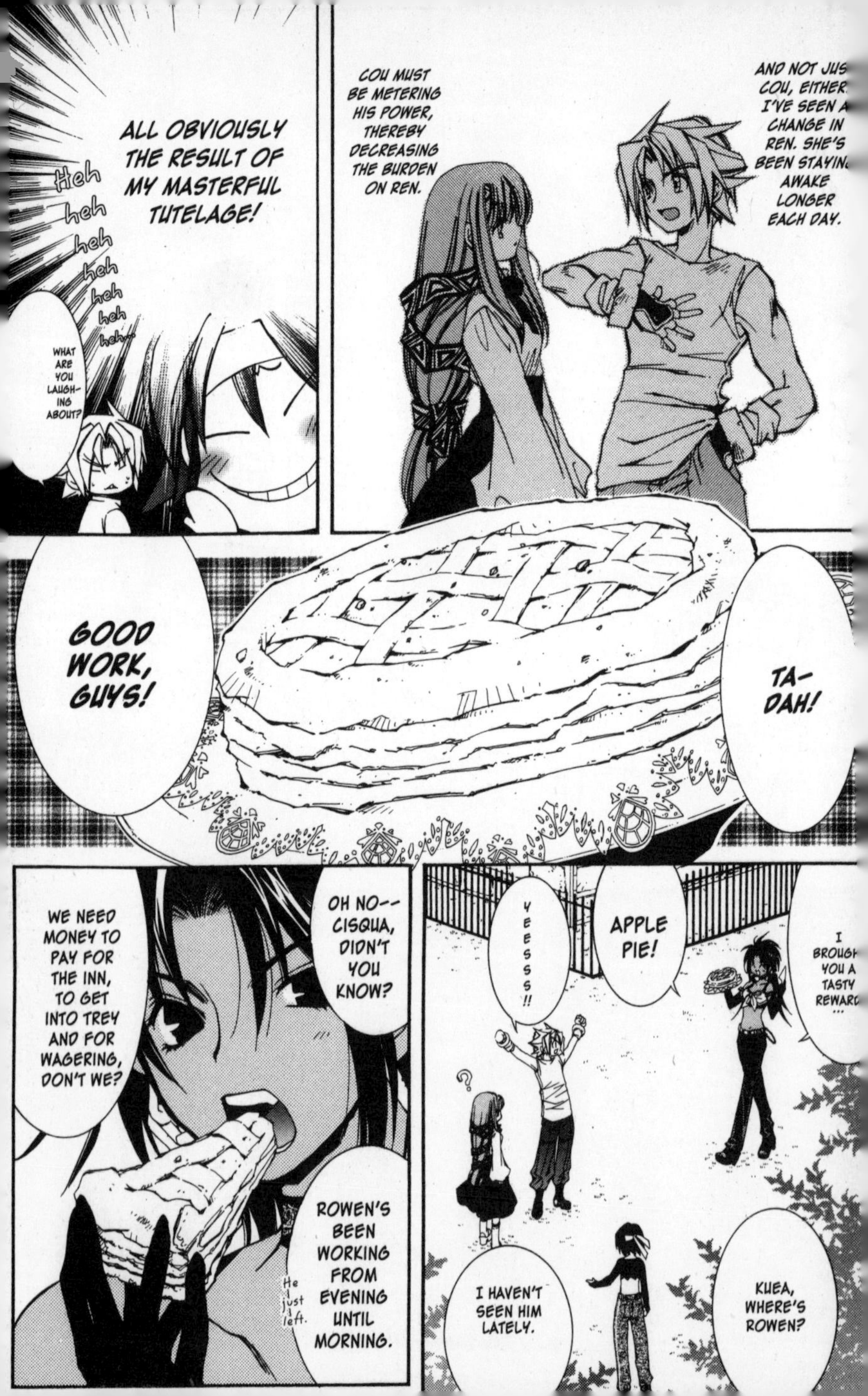
COU MUST BE METERING HIS POWER, THEREBY DECREASING THE BURDEN ON REN.
AND NOT JUS COU, EITHER I'VE SEEN A CHANGE IN REN. SHE'S BEEN STAYIN AWAKE LONGER EACH DAY.
ALL OBVIOUSLY THE RESULT OF MY MASTERFUL TUTELAGE!
Heh heh heh heh heh heh heh...
WHAT ARE YOU LAUGHING ABOUT?
TA-DAH!
GOOD WORK, GUYS!
I BROUGH YOU A TASTY REWAR...
APPLE PIE!
YEESSS!!
KUEA, WHERE'S ROWEN?
I HAVEN'T SEEN HIM LATELY.
OH NO-- CISQUA, DIDN'T YOU KNOW?
ROWEN'S BEEN WORKING FROM EVENING UNTIL MORNING.
He just left.
WE NEED MONEY TO PAY FOR THE INN, TO GET INTO TREY AND FOR WAGERING, DON'T WE?

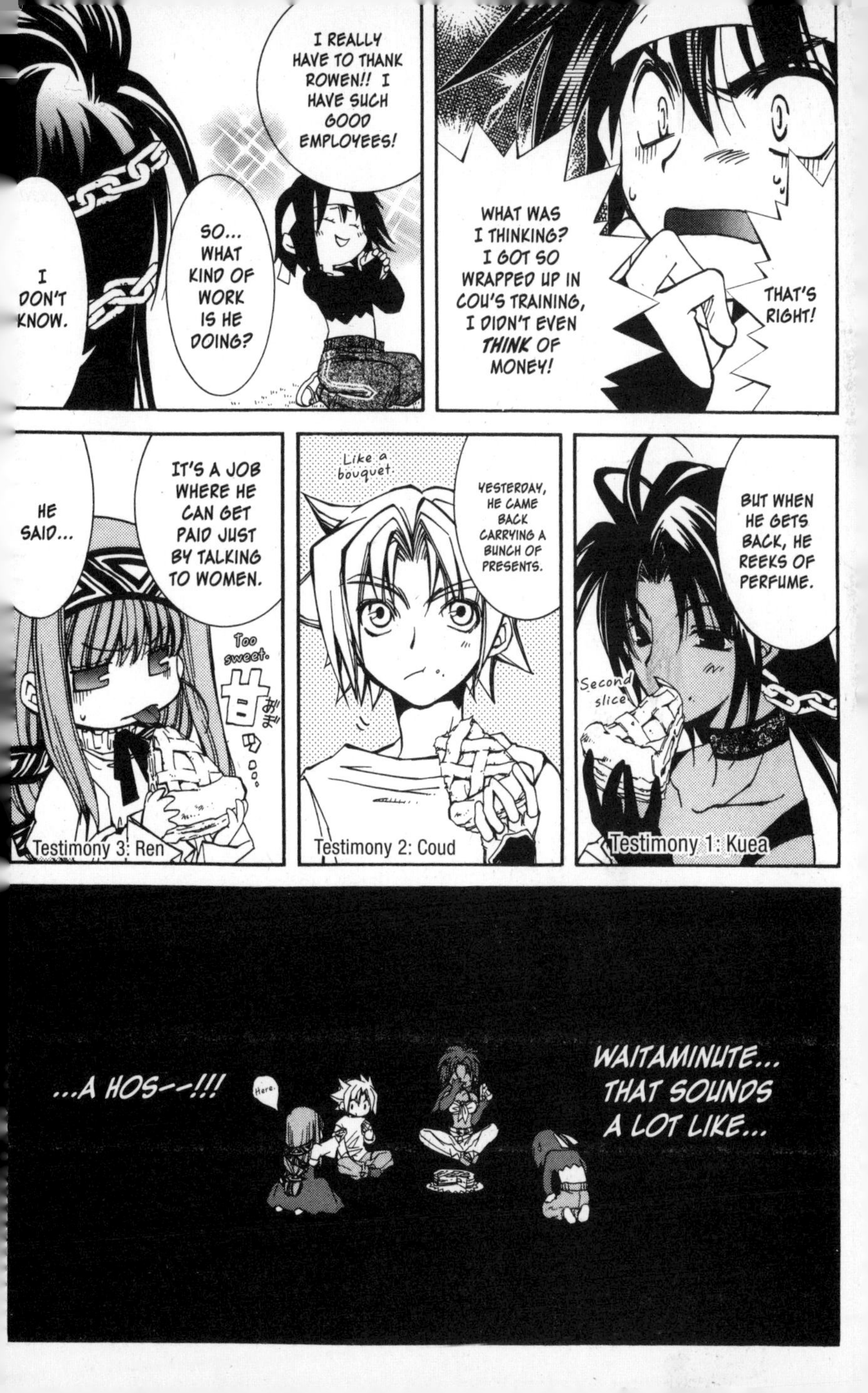
THAT'S RIGHT!
WHAT WAS I THINKING? I GOT SO WRAPPED UP IN COU'S TRAINING, I DIDN'T EVEN *THINK* OF MONEY!
I REALLY HAVE TO THANK ROWEN!! I HAVE SUCH GOOD EMPLOYEES!
SO... WHAT KIND OF WORK IS HE DOING?
I DON'T KNOW.
BUT WHEN HE GETS BACK, HE REEKS OF PERFUME.
Second slice
Testimony 1: Kuea
YESTERDAY, HE CAME BACK CARRYING A BUNCH OF PRESENTS.
Like a bouquet.
Testimony 2: Coud
HE SAID...
IT'S A JOB WHERE HE CAN GET PAID JUST BY TALKING TO WOMEN.
Too sweet.
甘
Testimony 3: Ren
WAITAMINUTE... THAT SOUNDS A LOT LIKE...
Here.
...A HOS--!!!

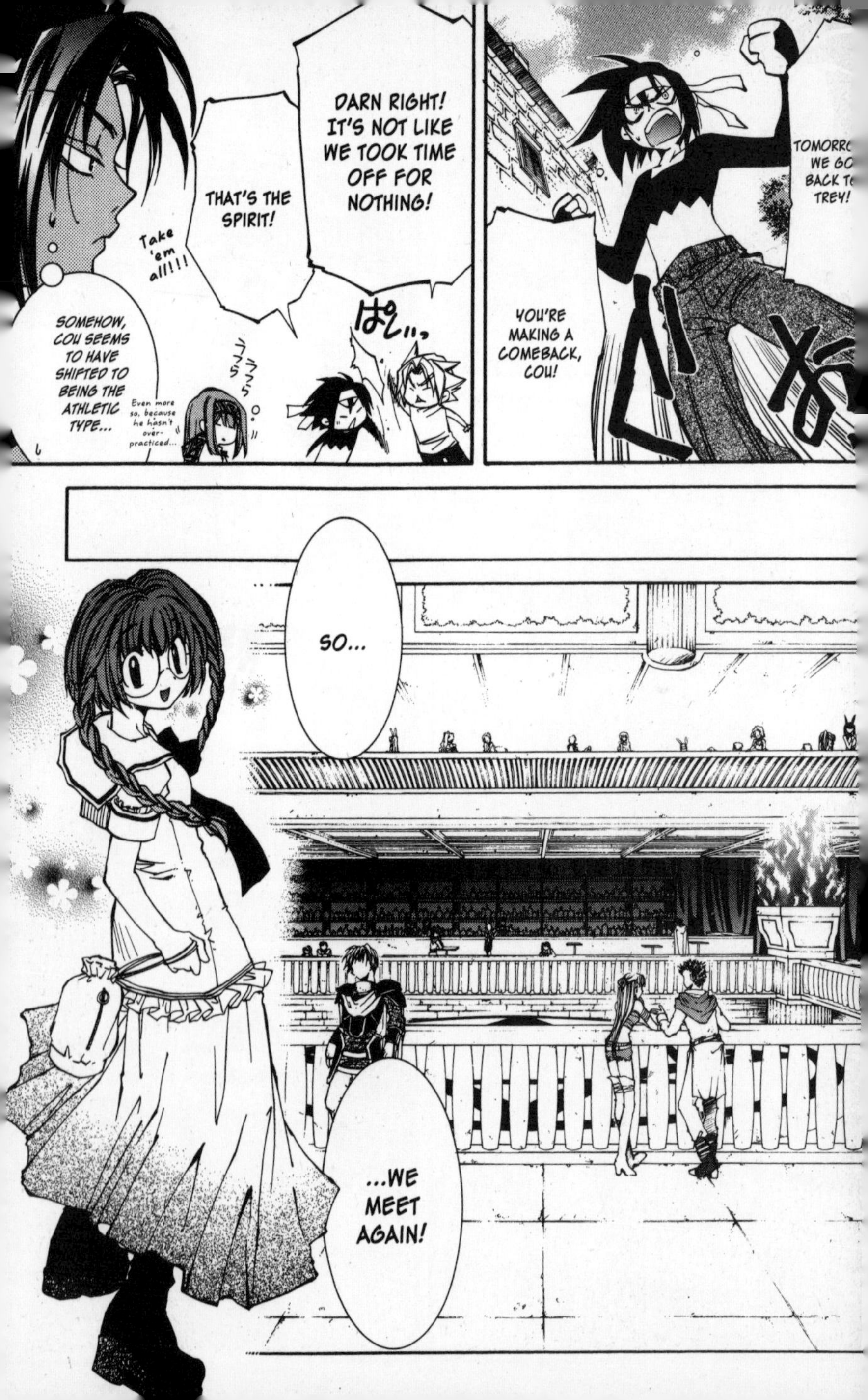
TOMORRO WE GO BACK T TREY!
YOU'RE MAKING A COMEBACK, COU!
DARN RIGHT! IT'S NOT LIKE WE TOOK TIME OFF FOR NOTHING!
THAT'S THE SPIRIT!
Take 'em all!!!
SOMEHOW, COU SEEMS TO HAVE SHIFTED TO BEING THE ATHLETIC TYPE...
Even more so, because he hasn't over-practiced...
SO...
...WE MEET AGAIN!

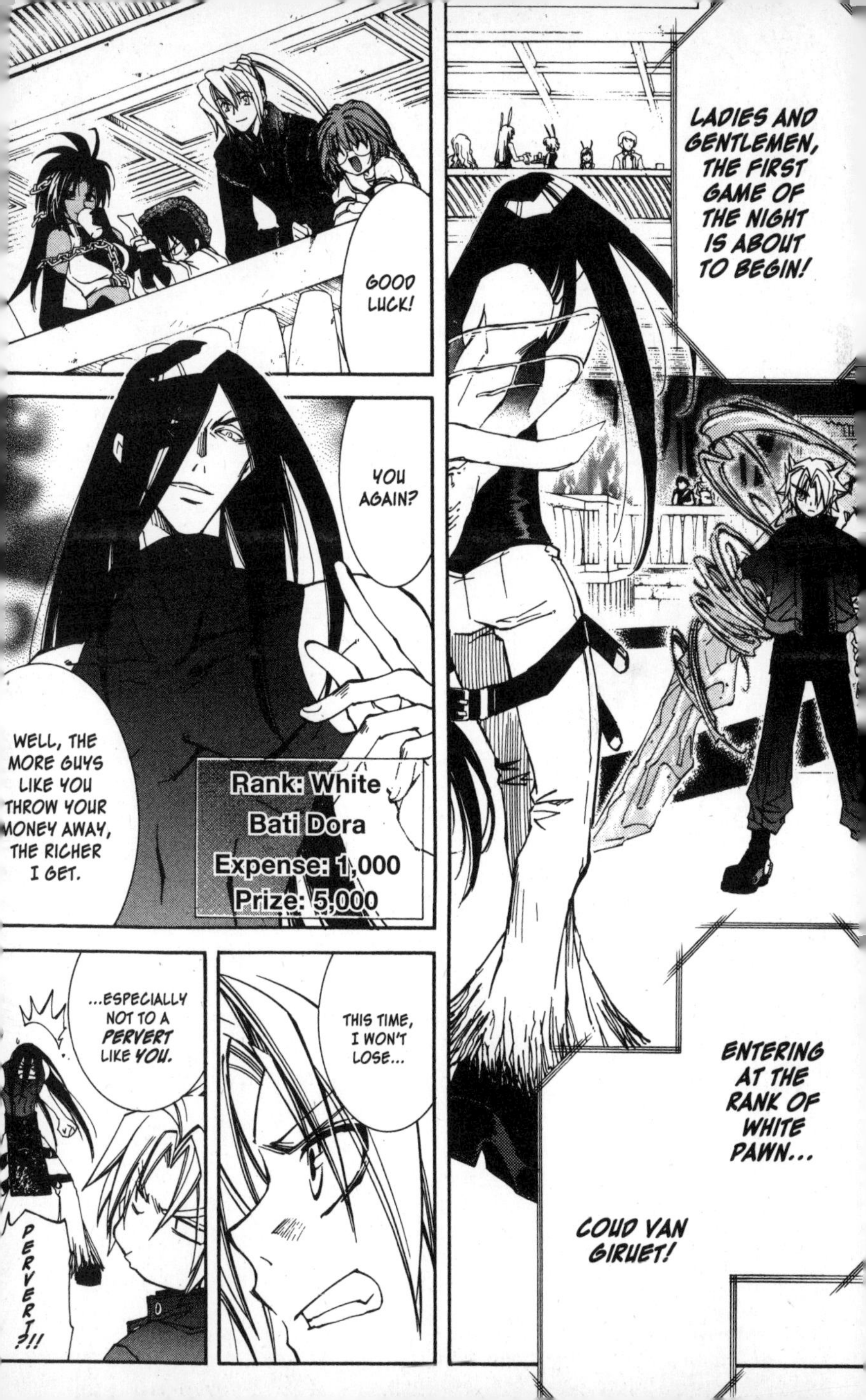
LADIES AND GENTLEMEN, THE FIRST GAME OF THE NIGHT IS ABOUT TO BEGIN!
ENTERING AT THE RANK OF WHITE PAWN...
COUD VAN GIRUET!
GOOD LUCK!
YOU AGAIN?
WELL, THE MORE GUYS LIKE YOU THROW YOUR MONEY AWAY, THE RICHER I GET.
Rank: White
Bati Dora
Expense: 1,000
Prize: 5,000
THIS TIME, I WON'T LOSE...
...ESPECIALLY NOT TO A PERVERT LIKE YOU.
PERVERT?!!

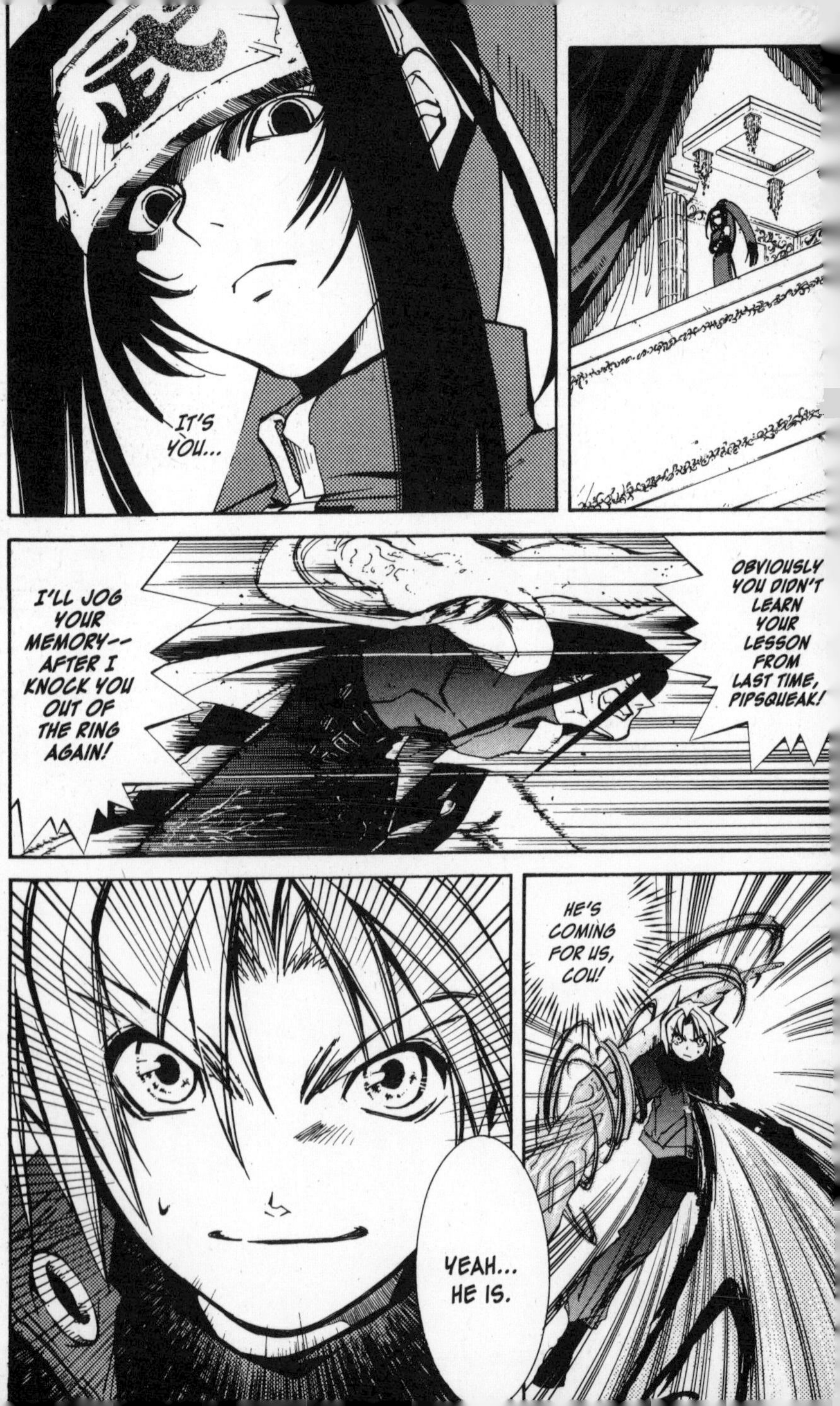
IT'S YOU...
OBVIOUSLY YOU DIDN'T LEARN YOUR LESSON FROM LAST TIME, PIPSQUEAK!
I'LL JOG YOUR MEMORY-- AFTER I KNOCK YOU OUT OF THE RING AGAIN!
HE'S COMING FOR US, COU!
YEAH... HE IS.

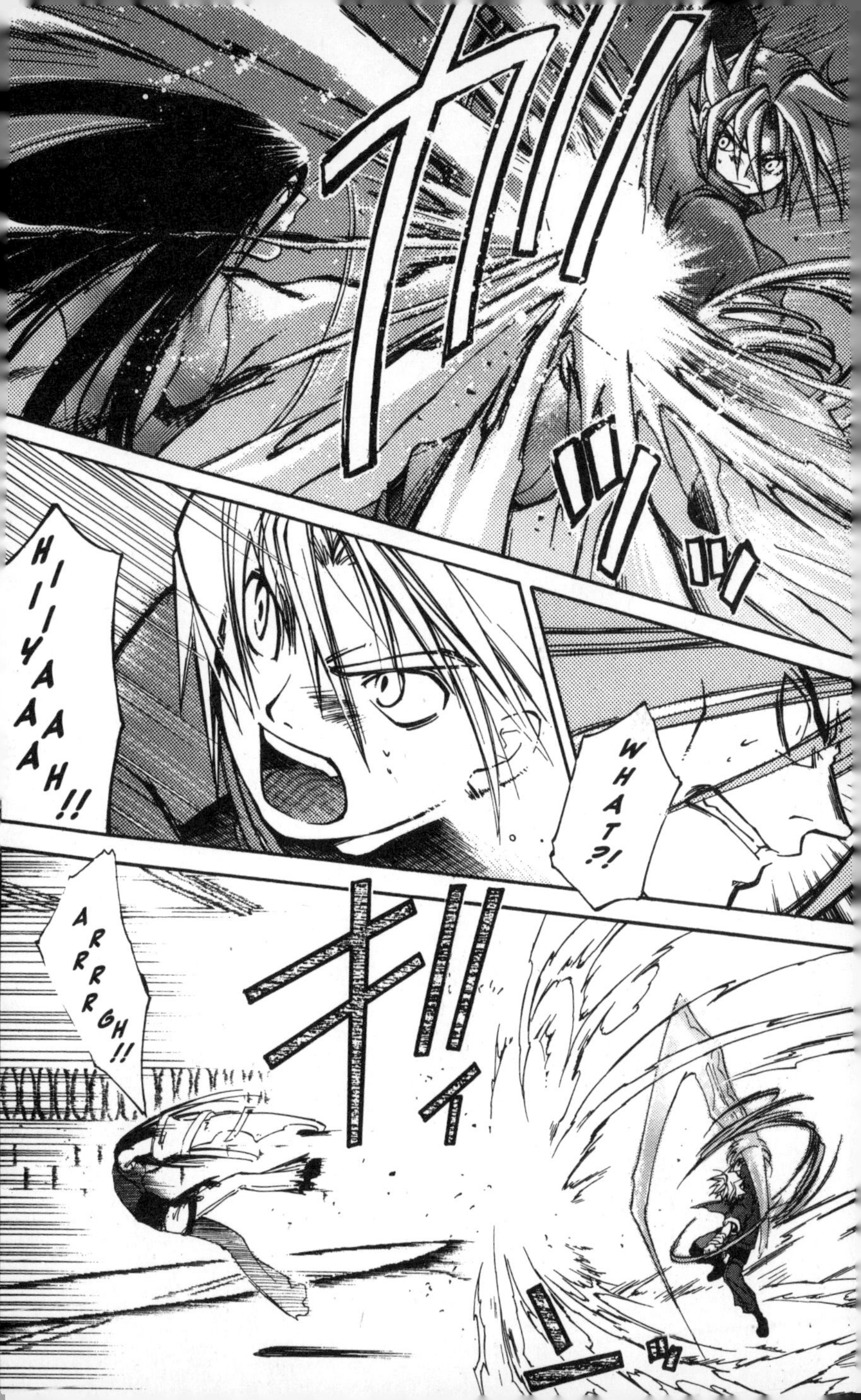
WHAT?!
HIIIYAAAAAH!!
ARRRGH!!

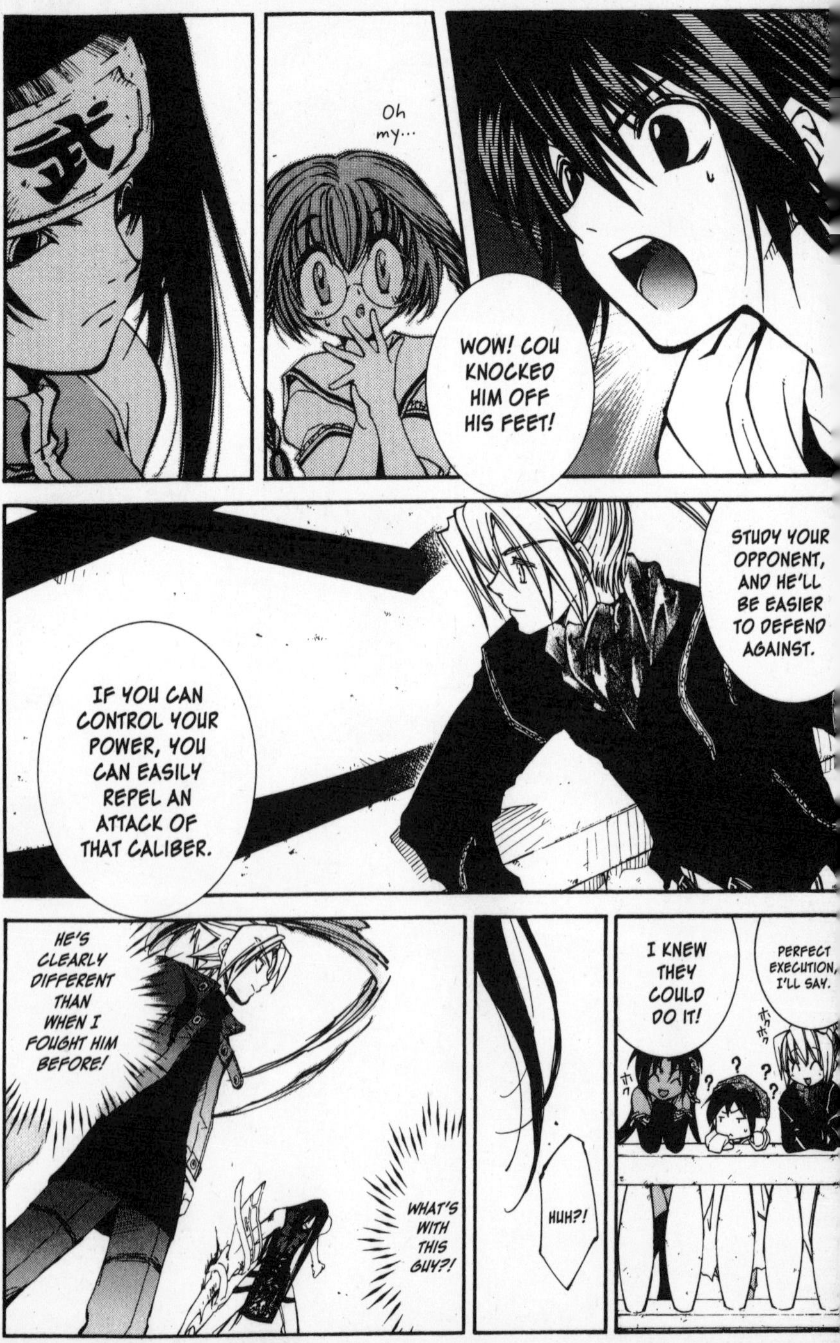
WOW! COU KNOCKED HIM OFF HIS FEET!
Oh my...
STUDY YOUR OPPONENT, AND HE'LL BE EASIER TO DEFEND AGAINST.
IF YOU CAN CONTROL YOUR POWER, YOU CAN EASILY REPEL AN ATTACK OF THAT CALIBER.
PERFECT EXECUTION, I'LL SAY.
I KNEW THEY COULD DO IT!
HUH?!
HE'S CLEARLY DIFFERENT THAN WHEN I FOUGHT HIM BEFORE!
WHAT'S WITH THIS GUY?!

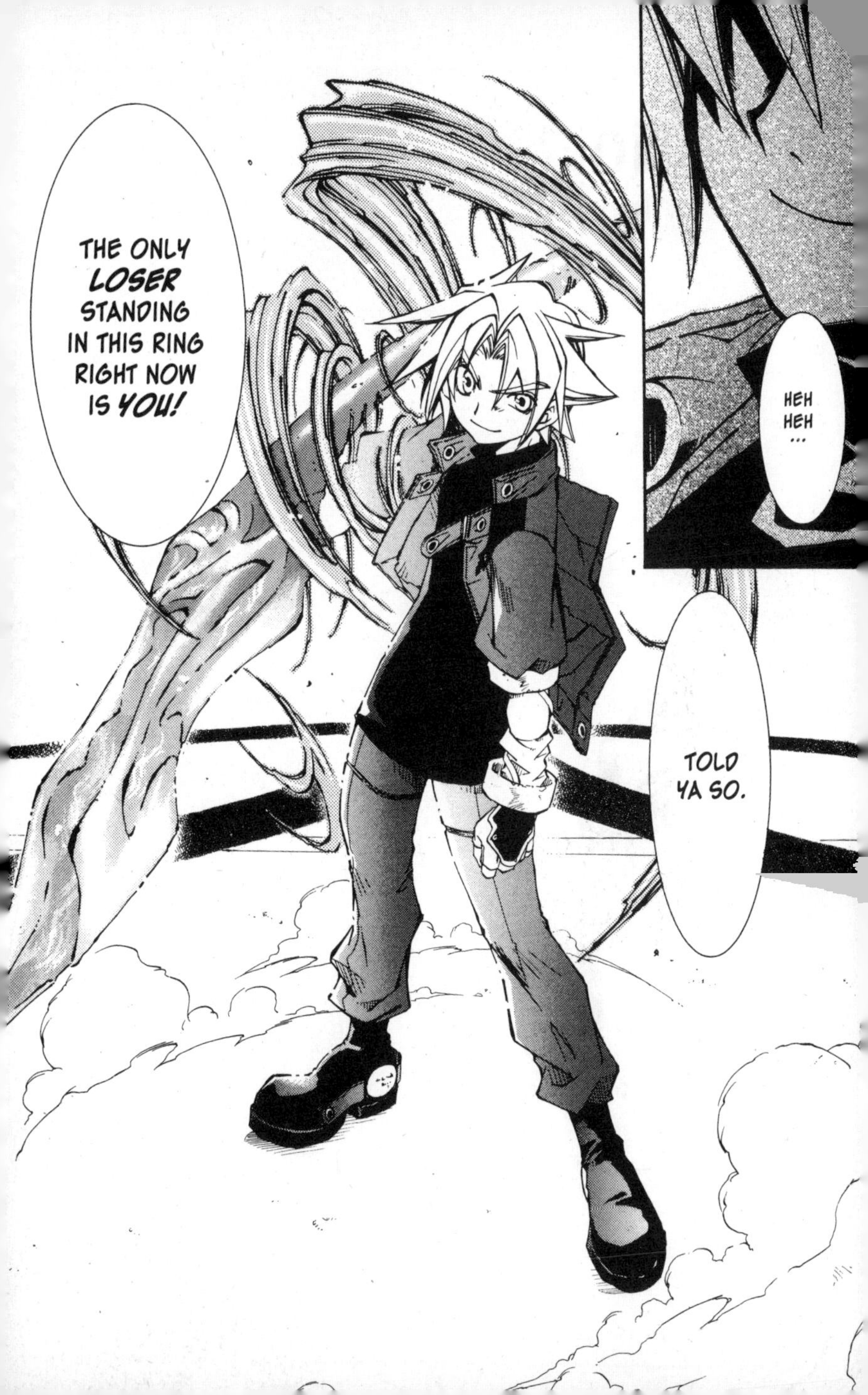
HEH HEH ...
THE ONLY LOSER STANDING IN THIS RING RIGHT NOW IS YOU!
TOLD YA SO.

# Re-No.15:
## Milliard Trey Betting Grounds—Strike Line

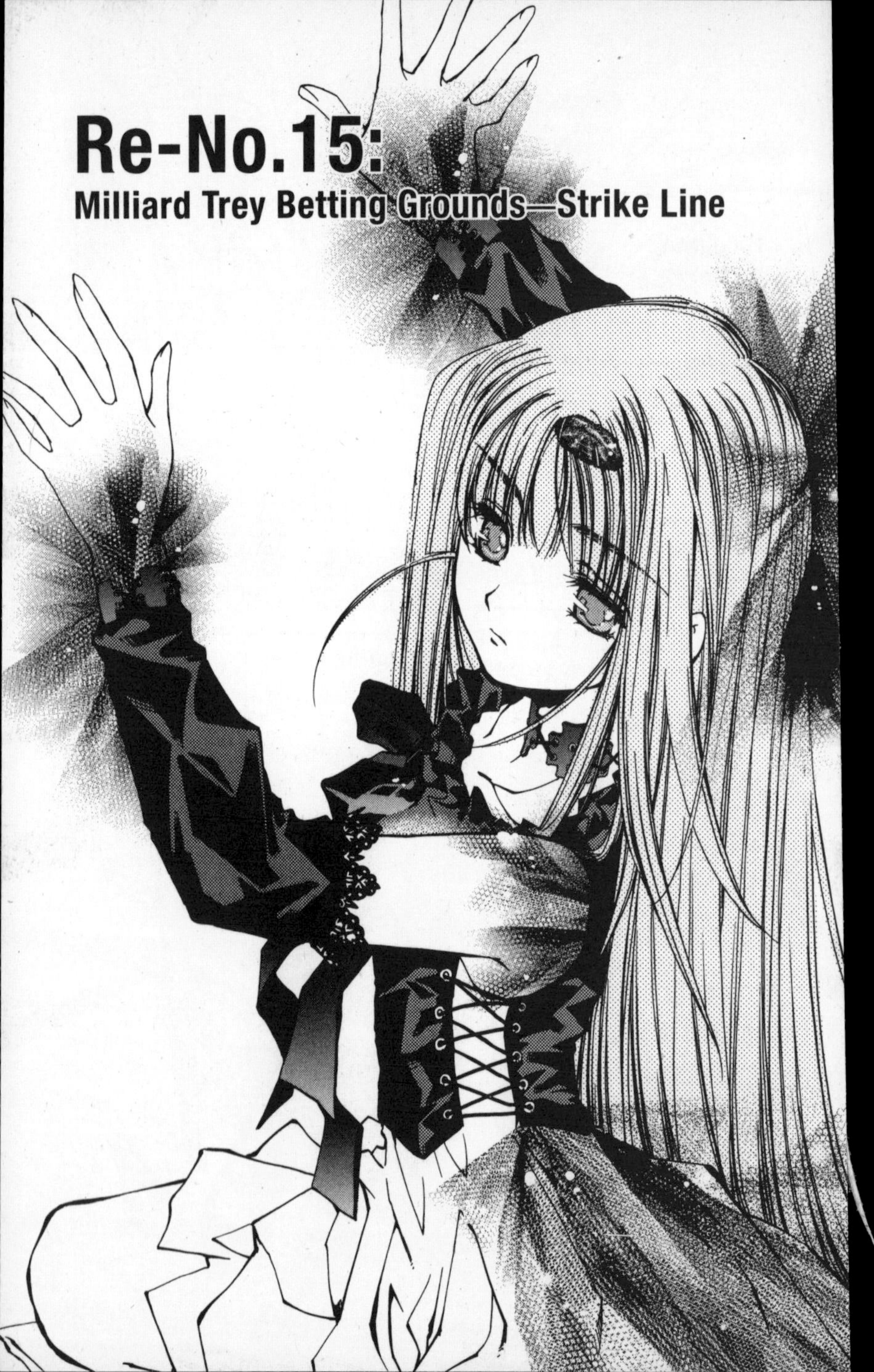

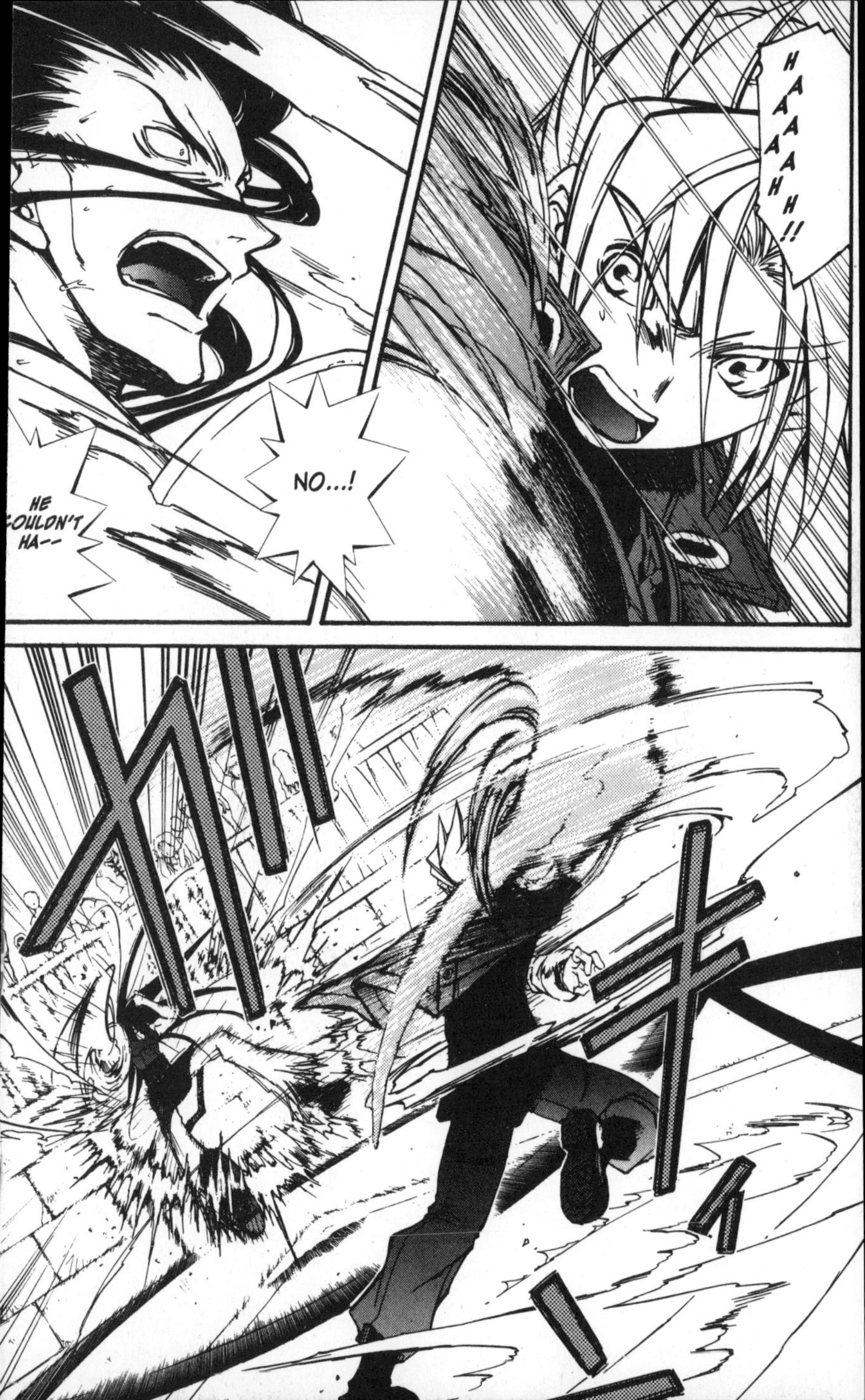
HAAAAAH!!
NO...!
HE COULDN'T HA--

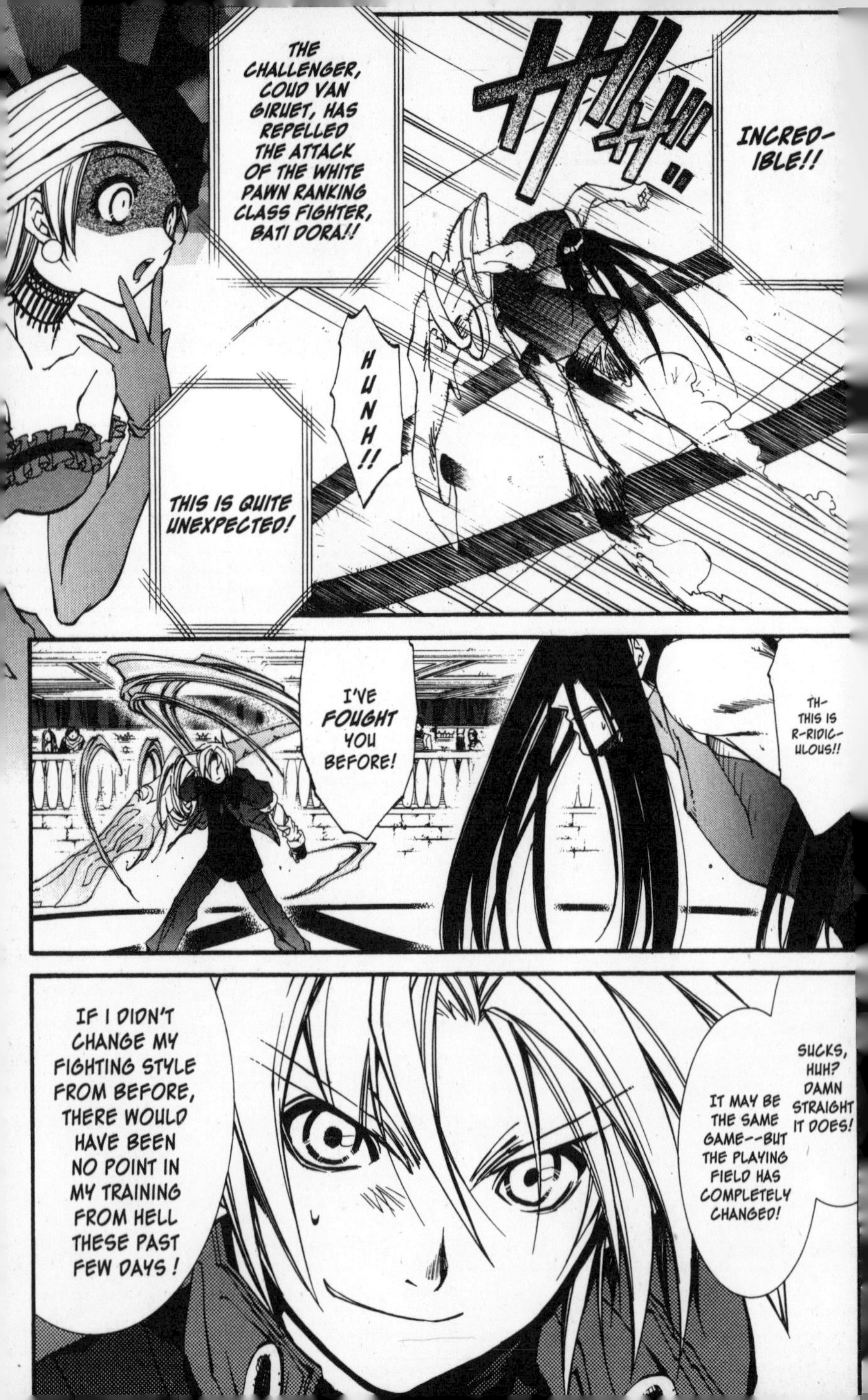
INCRED-IBLE!!
HUNH!!
THE CHALLENGER, COUD VAN GIRUET, HAS REPELLED THE ATTACK OF THE WHITE PAWN RANKING CLASS FIGHTER, BATI DORA!!
THIS IS QUITE UNEXPECTED!
TH-THIS IS R-RIDICULOUS!!
I'VE FOUGHT YOU BEFORE!
SUCKS, HUH? DAMN STRAIGHT IT DOES!
IT MAY BE THE SAME GAME--BUT THE PLAYING FIELD HAS COMPLETELY CHANGED!
IF I DIDN'T CHANGE MY FIGHTING STYLE FROM BEFORE, THERE WOULD HAVE BEEN NO POINT IN MY TRAINING FROM HELL THESE PAST FEW DAYS!

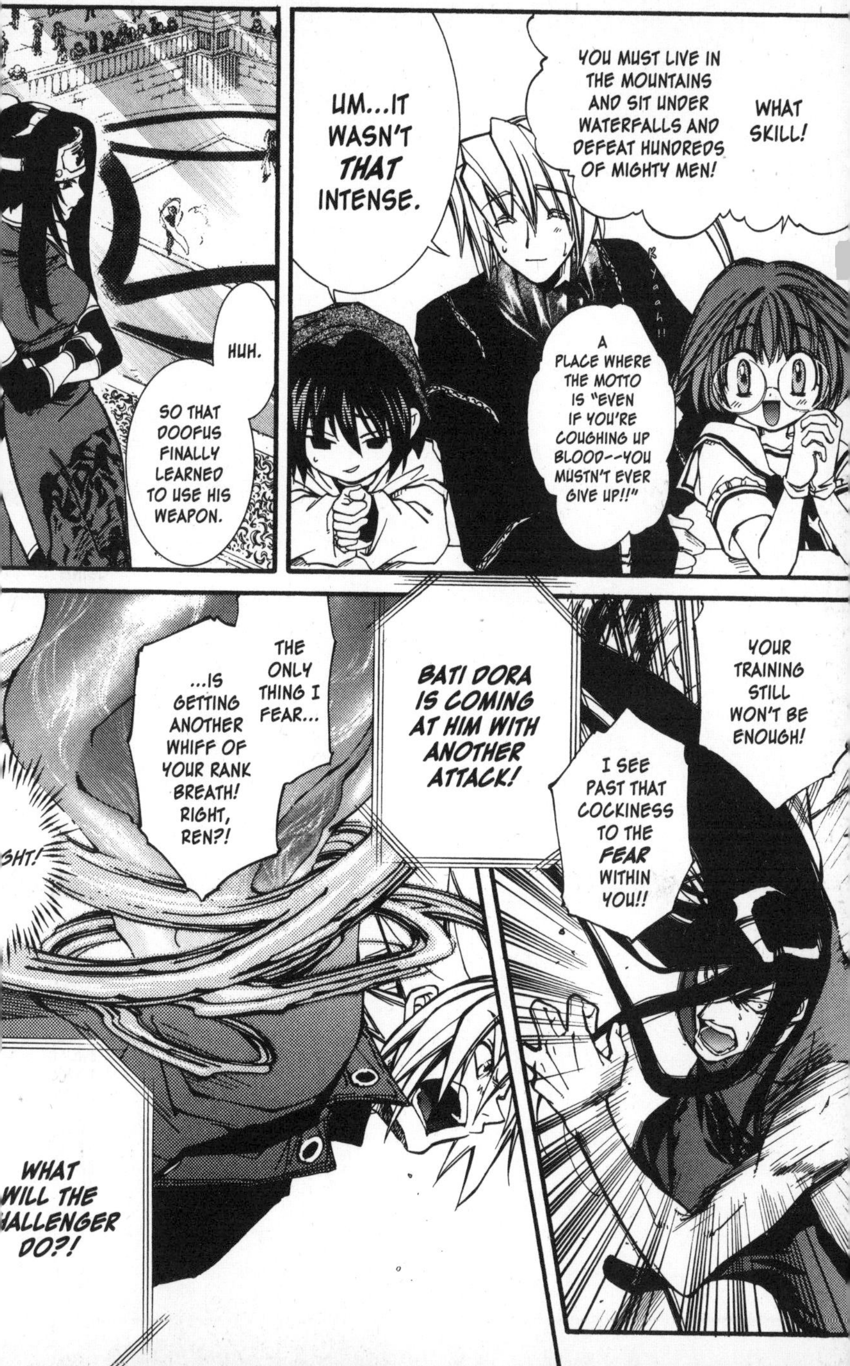
WHAT SKILL!
YOU MUST LIVE IN THE MOUNTAINS AND SIT UNDER WATERFALLS AND DEFEAT HUNDREDS OF MIGHTY MEN!
Kyaah!!
A PLACE WHERE THE MOTTO IS "EVEN IF YOU'RE COUGHING UP BLOOD--YOU MUSTN'T EVER GIVE UP!!"
UM...IT WASN'T *THAT* INTENSE.
HUH.
SO THAT DOOFUS FINALLY LEARNED TO USE HIS WEAPON.
YOUR TRAINING STILL WON'T BE ENOUGH!
I SEE PAST THAT COCKINESS TO THE *FEAR* WITHIN YOU!!
BATI DORA IS COMING AT HIM WITH ANOTHER ATTACK!
THE ONLY THING I FEAR...
...IS GETTING ANOTHER WHIFF OF YOUR RANK BREATH! RIGHT, REN?!
WHAT WILL THE HALLENGER DO?!

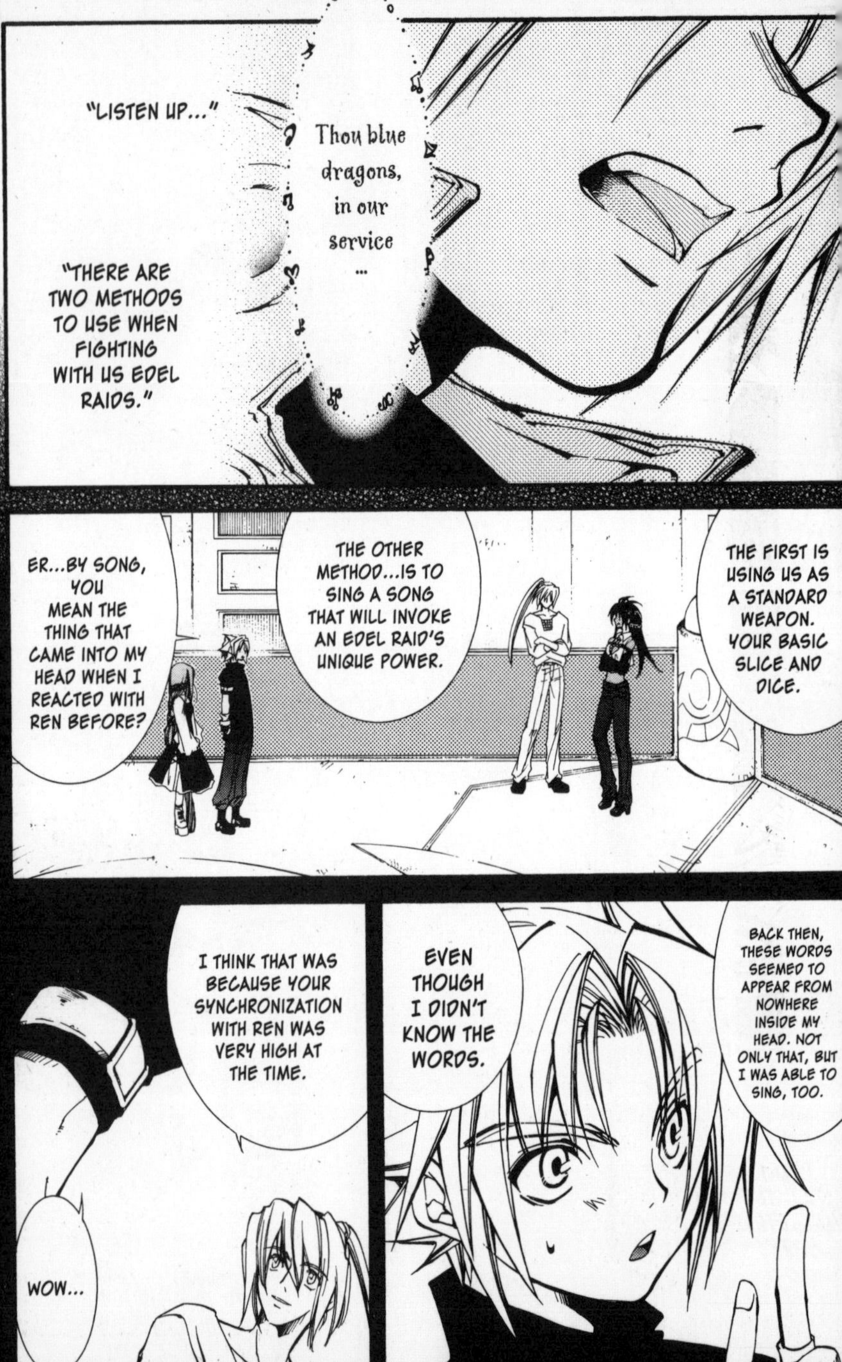
Thou blue dragons, in our service ...
"LISTEN UP..."
"THERE ARE TWO METHODS TO USE WHEN FIGHTING WITH US EDEL RAIDS."
THE FIRST IS USING US AS A STANDARD WEAPON. YOUR BASIC SLICE AND DICE.
THE OTHER METHOD...IS TO SING A SONG THAT WILL INVOKE AN EDEL RAID'S UNIQUE POWER.
ER...BY SONG, YOU MEAN THE THING THAT CAME INTO MY HEAD WHEN I REACTED WITH REN BEFORE?
BACK THEN, THESE WORDS SEEMED TO APPEAR FROM NOWHERE INSIDE MY HEAD. NOT ONLY THAT, BUT I WAS ABLE TO SING, TOO.
EVEN THOUGH I DIDN'T KNOW THE WORDS.
I THINK THAT WAS BECAUSE YOUR SYNCHRONIZATION WITH REN WAS VERY HIGH AT THE TIME.
WOW...

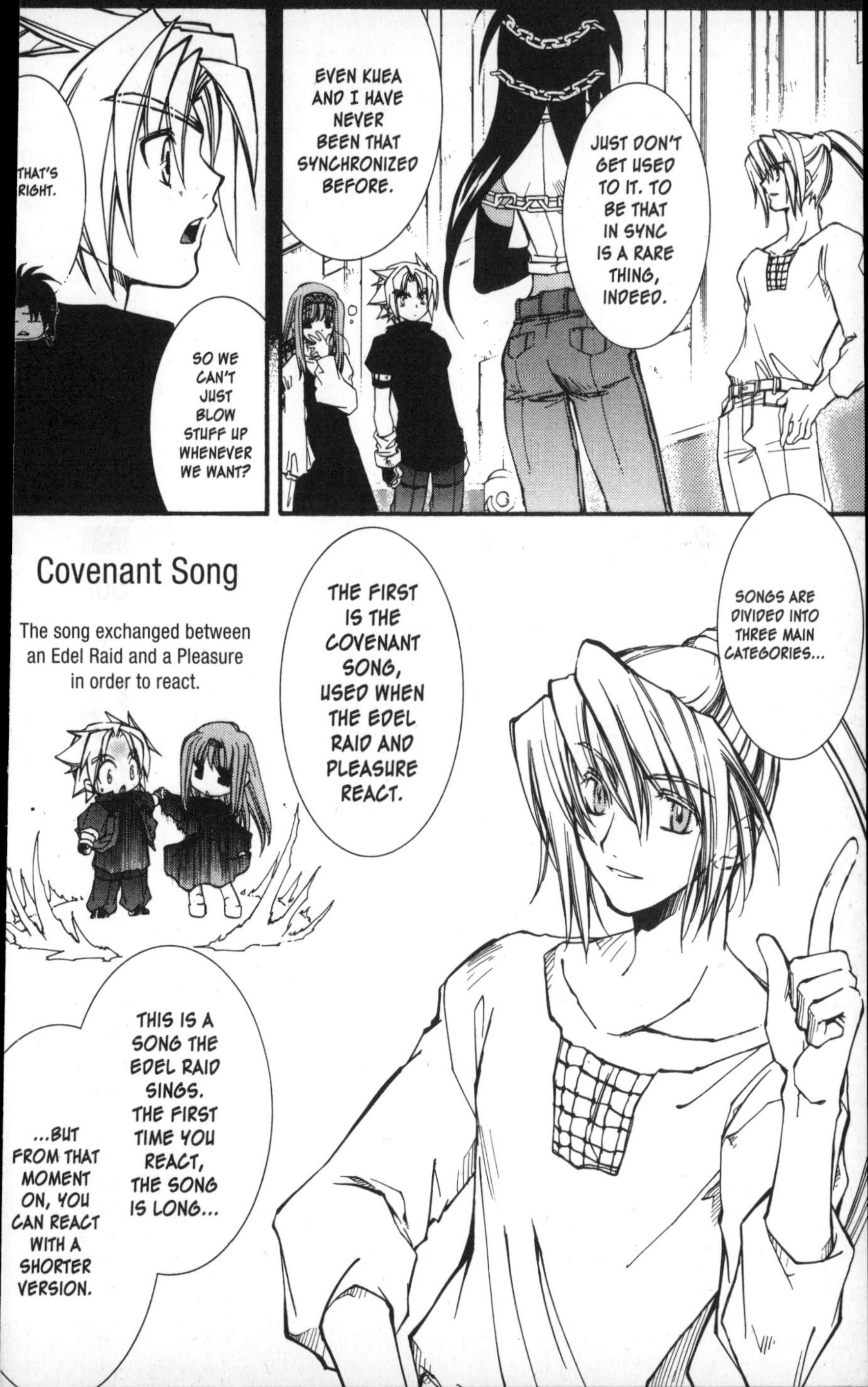
EVEN KUEA AND I HAVE NEVER BEEN THAT SYNCHRONIZED BEFORE.
JUST DON'T GET USED TO IT. TO BE THAT IN SYNC IS A RARE THING, INDEED.
SO WE CAN'T JUST BLOW STUFF UP WHENEVER WE WANT?
THAT'S RIGHT.
SONGS ARE DIVIDED INTO THREE MAIN CATEGORIES...
THE FIRST IS THE COVENANT SONG, USED WHEN THE EDEL RAID AND PLEASURE REACT.
Covenant Song
The song exchanged between an Edel Raid and a Pleasure in order to react.
THIS IS A SONG THE EDEL RAID SINGS. THE FIRST TIME YOU REACT, THE SONG IS LONG...
...BUT FROM THAT MOMENT ON, YOU CAN REACT WITH A SHORTER VERSION.

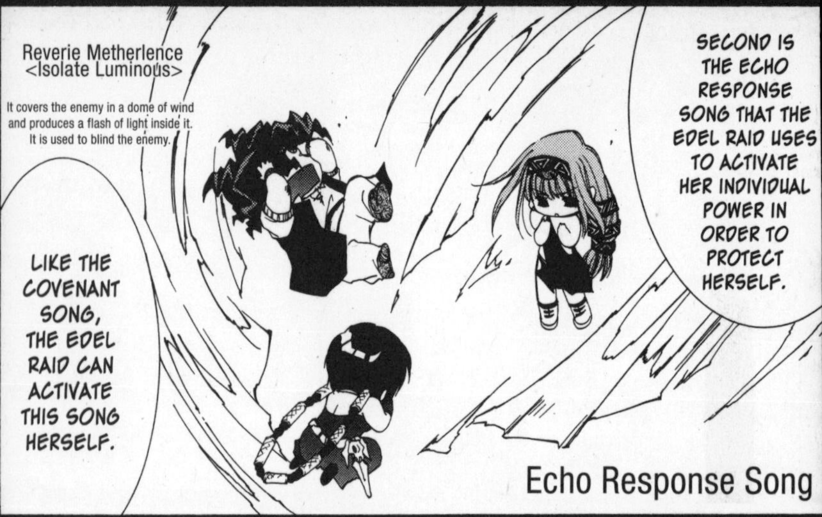
SECOND IS THE ECHO RESPONSE SONG THAT THE EDEL RAID USES TO ACTIVATE HER INDIVIDUAL POWER IN ORDER TO PROTECT HERSELF.
Reverie Metherlence
<Isolate Luminous>
It covers the enemy in a dome of wind and produces a flash of light inside it. It is used to blind the enemy.
LIKE THE COVENANT SONG, THE EDEL RAID CAN ACTIVATE THIS SONG HERSELF.
Echo Response Song

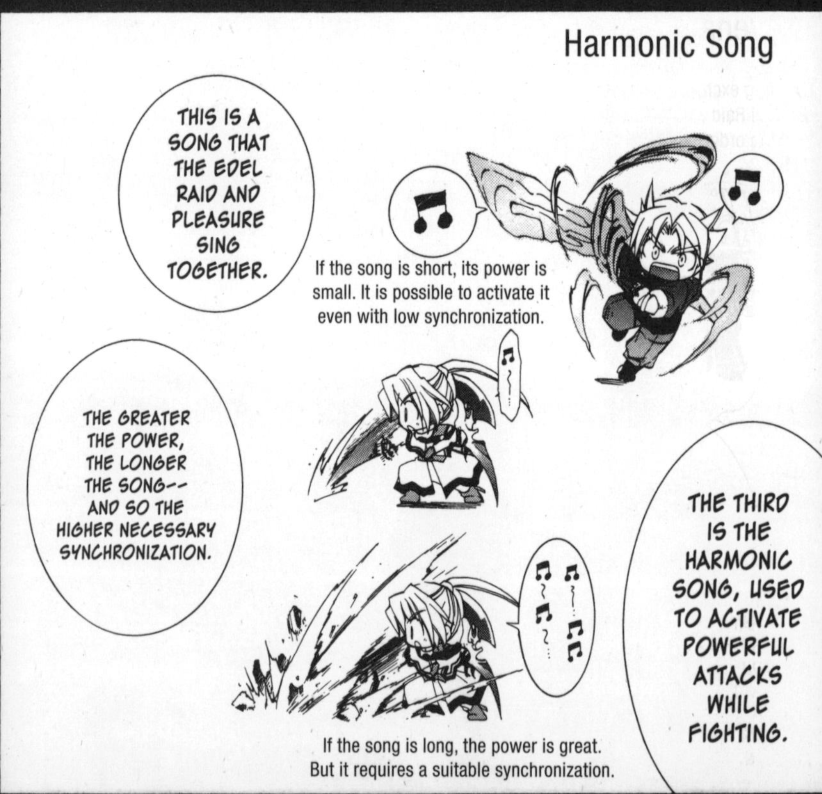
Harmonic Song
THIS IS A SONG THAT THE EDEL RAID AND PLEASURE SING TOGETHER.
If the song is short, its power is small. It is possible to activate it even with low synchronization.
THE THIRD IS THE HARMONIC SONG, USED TO ACTIVATE POWERFUL ATTACKS WHILE FIGHTING.
THE GREATER THE POWER, THE LONGER THE SONG--AND SO THE HIGHER NECESSARY SYNCHRONIZATION.
If the song is long, the power is great. But it requires a suitable synchronization.

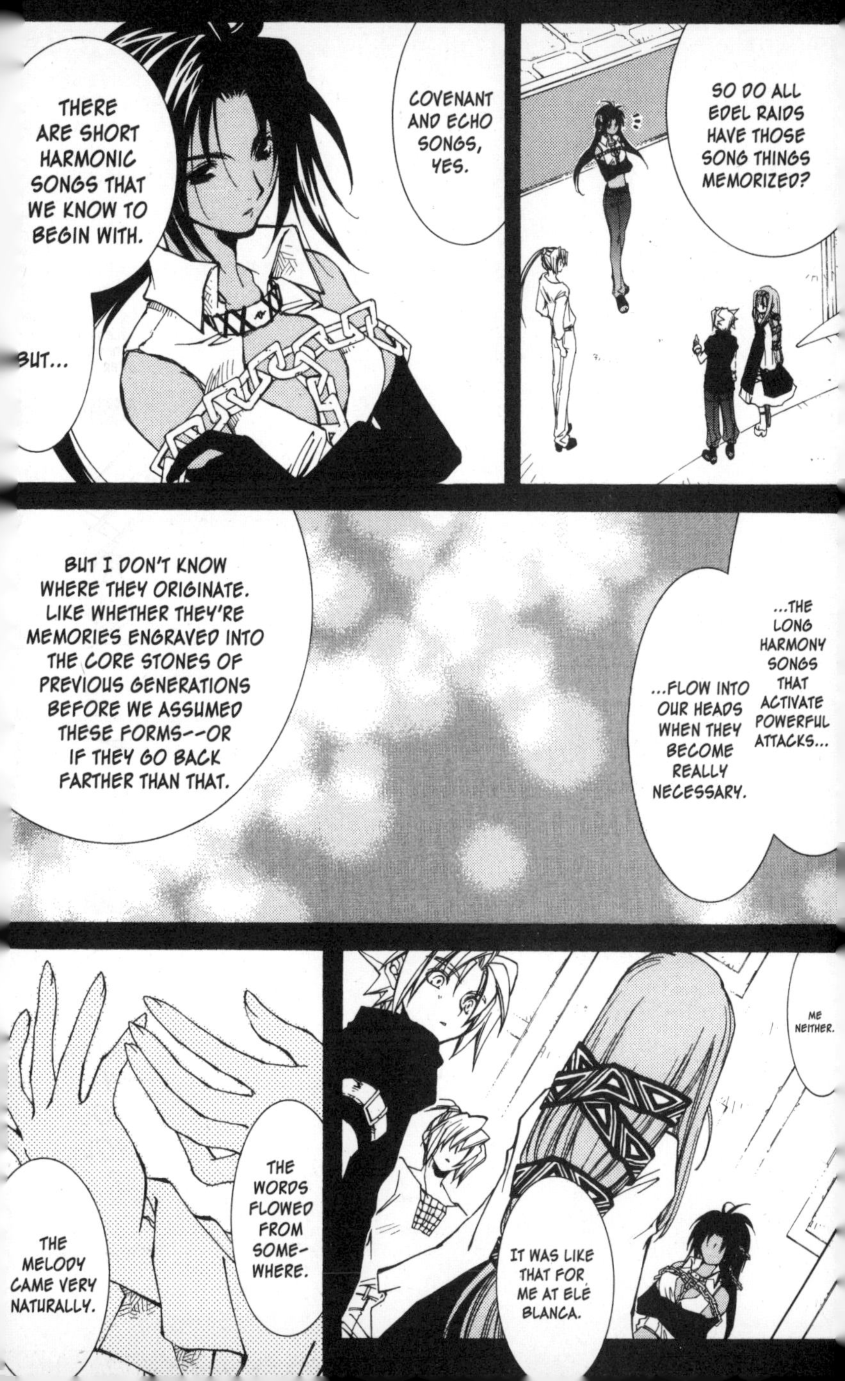
SO DO ALL EDEL RAIDS HAVE THOSE SONG THINGS MEMORIZED?
COVENANT AND ECHO SONGS, YES.
THERE ARE SHORT HARMONIC SONGS THAT WE KNOW TO BEGIN WITH.
BUT...
...THE LONG HARMONY SONGS THAT ACTIVATE POWERFUL ATTACKS...
...FLOW INTO OUR HEADS WHEN THEY BECOME REALLY NECESSARY.
BUT I DON'T KNOW WHERE THEY ORIGINATE. LIKE WHETHER THEY'RE MEMORIES ENGRAVED INTO THE CORE STONES OF PREVIOUS GENERATIONS BEFORE WE ASSUMED THESE FORMS--OR IF THEY GO BACK FARTHER THAN THAT.
ME NEITHER.
IT WAS LIKE THAT FOR ME AT ELÉ BLANCA.
THE WORDS FLOWED FROM SOME-WHERE.
THE MELODY CAME VERY NATURALLY.

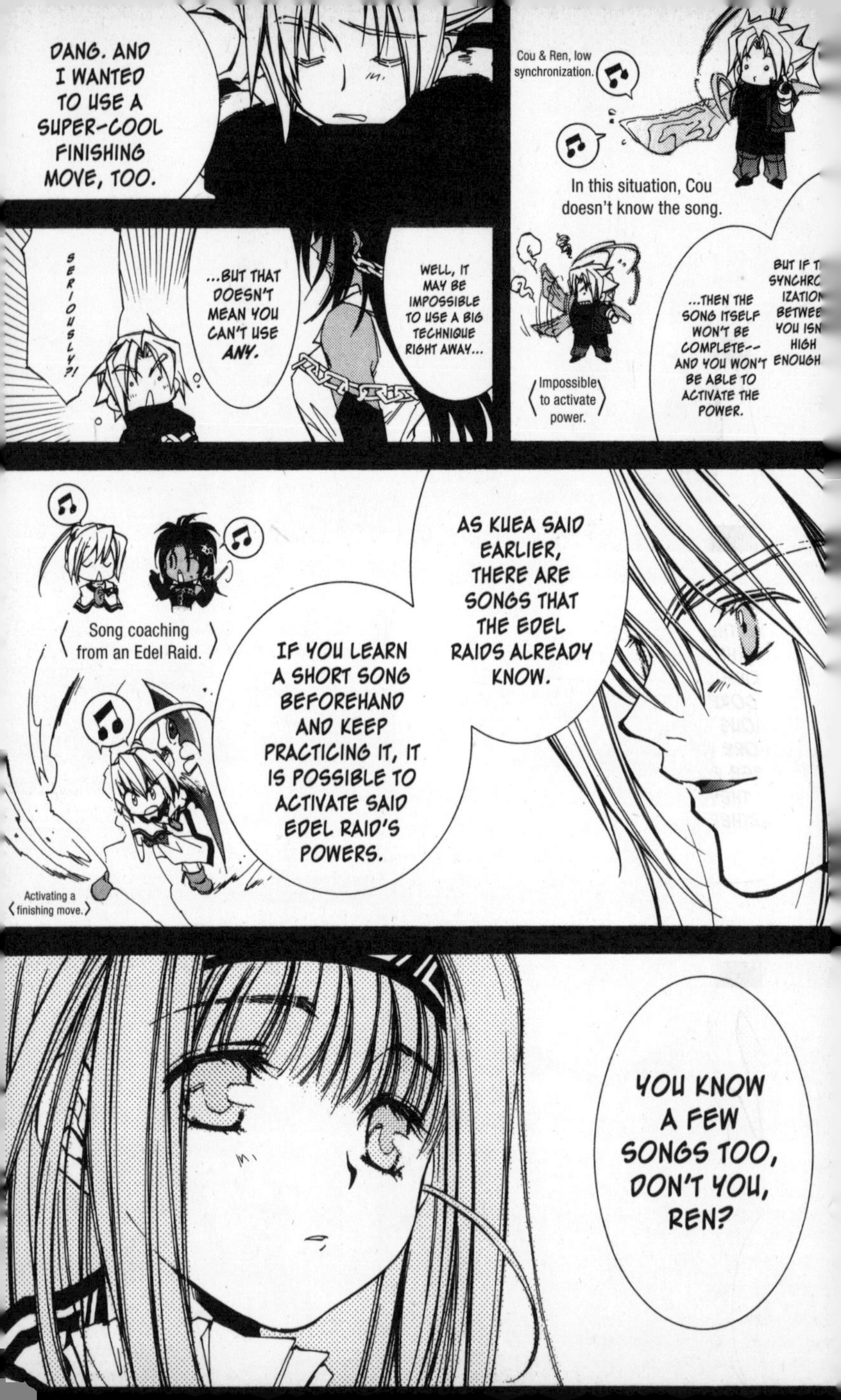
Cou & Ren, low synchronization.
In this situation, Cou doesn't know the song.
BUT IF T SYNCHRC IZATION BETWEE YOU ISN HIGH ENOUGH
...THEN THE SONG ITSELF WON'T BE COMPLETE-- AND YOU WON'T BE ABLE TO ACTIVATE THE POWER.
〈Impossible to activate power.〉
DANG. AND I WANTED TO USE A SUPER-COOL FINISHING MOVE, TOO.
WELL, IT MAY BE IMPOSSIBLE TO USE A BIG TECHNIQUE RIGHT AWAY...
...BUT THAT DOESN'T MEAN YOU CAN'T USE *ANY*.
SERIOUSLY?!
AS KUEA SAID EARLIER, THERE ARE SONGS THAT THE EDEL RAIDS ALREADY KNOW.
IF YOU LEARN A SHORT SONG BEFOREHAND AND KEEP PRACTICING IT, IT IS POSSIBLE TO ACTIVATE SAID EDEL RAID'S POWERS.
〈Song coaching from an Edel Raid.〉
〈Activating a finishing move.〉
YOU KNOW A FEW SONGS TOO, DON'T YOU, REN?

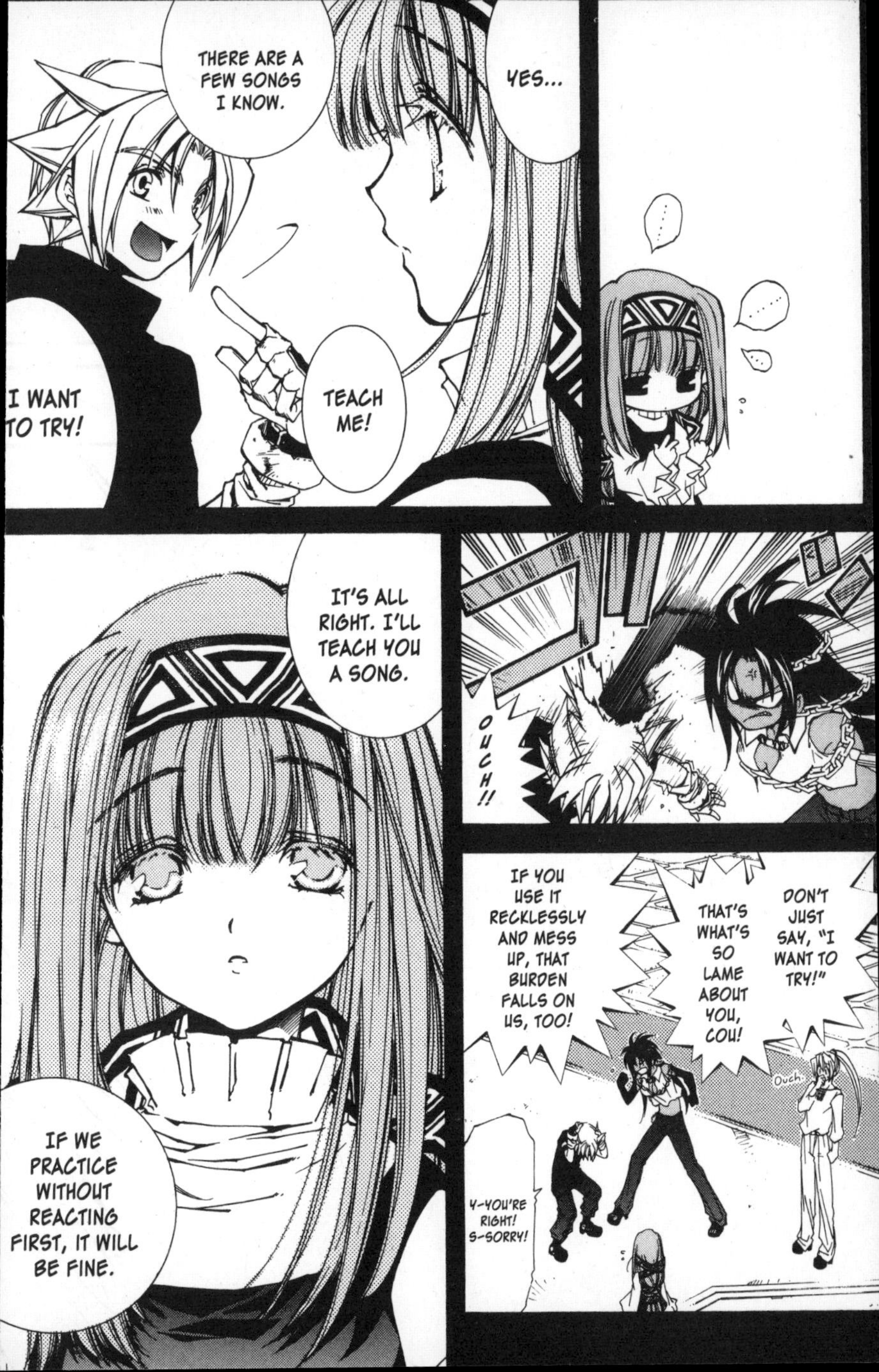

...
...
..
YES...
THERE ARE A FEW SONGS I KNOW.
TEACH ME!
I WANT TO TRY!
OUCH!!
DON'T JUST SAY, "I WANT TO TRY!"
THAT'S WHAT'S SO LAME ABOUT YOU, COU!
IF YOU USE IT RECKLESSLY AND MESS UP, THAT BURDEN FALLS ON US, TOO!
Ouch.
Y-YOU'RE RIGHT! S-SORRY!
IT'S ALL RIGHT. I'LL TEACH YOU A SONG.
IF WE PRACTICE WITHOUT REACTING FIRST, IT WILL BE FINE.

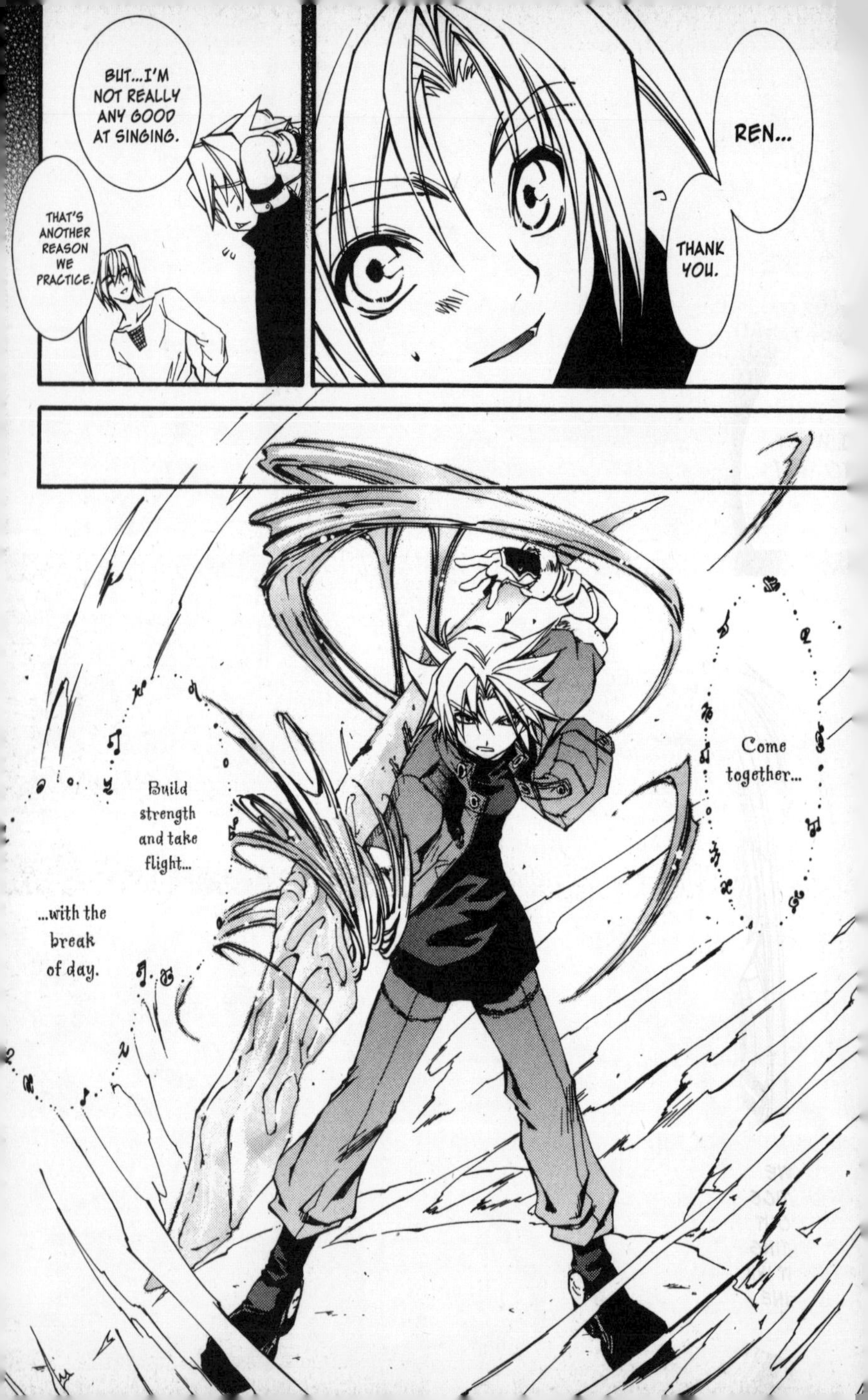
REN...
THANK YOU.
BUT...I'M NOT REALLY ANY GOOD AT SINGING.
THAT'S ANOTHER REASON WE PRACTICE.
Come together...
Build strength and take flight...
...with the break of day.

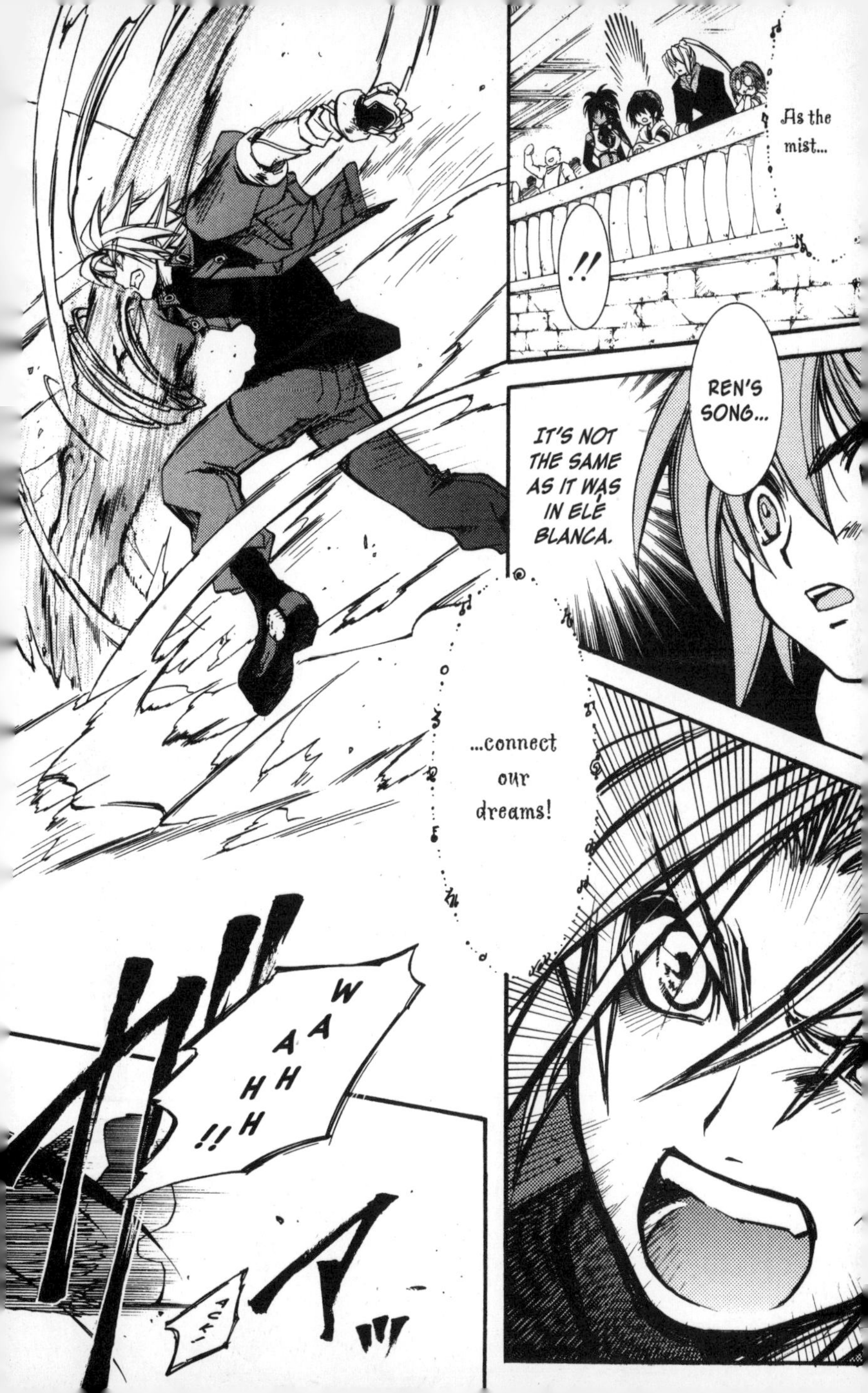
As the mist...
!!
REN'S SONG...
IT'S NOT THE SAME AS IT WAS IN ELÉ BLANCA.
...connect our dreams!
WAAAHHH!!
AUK!

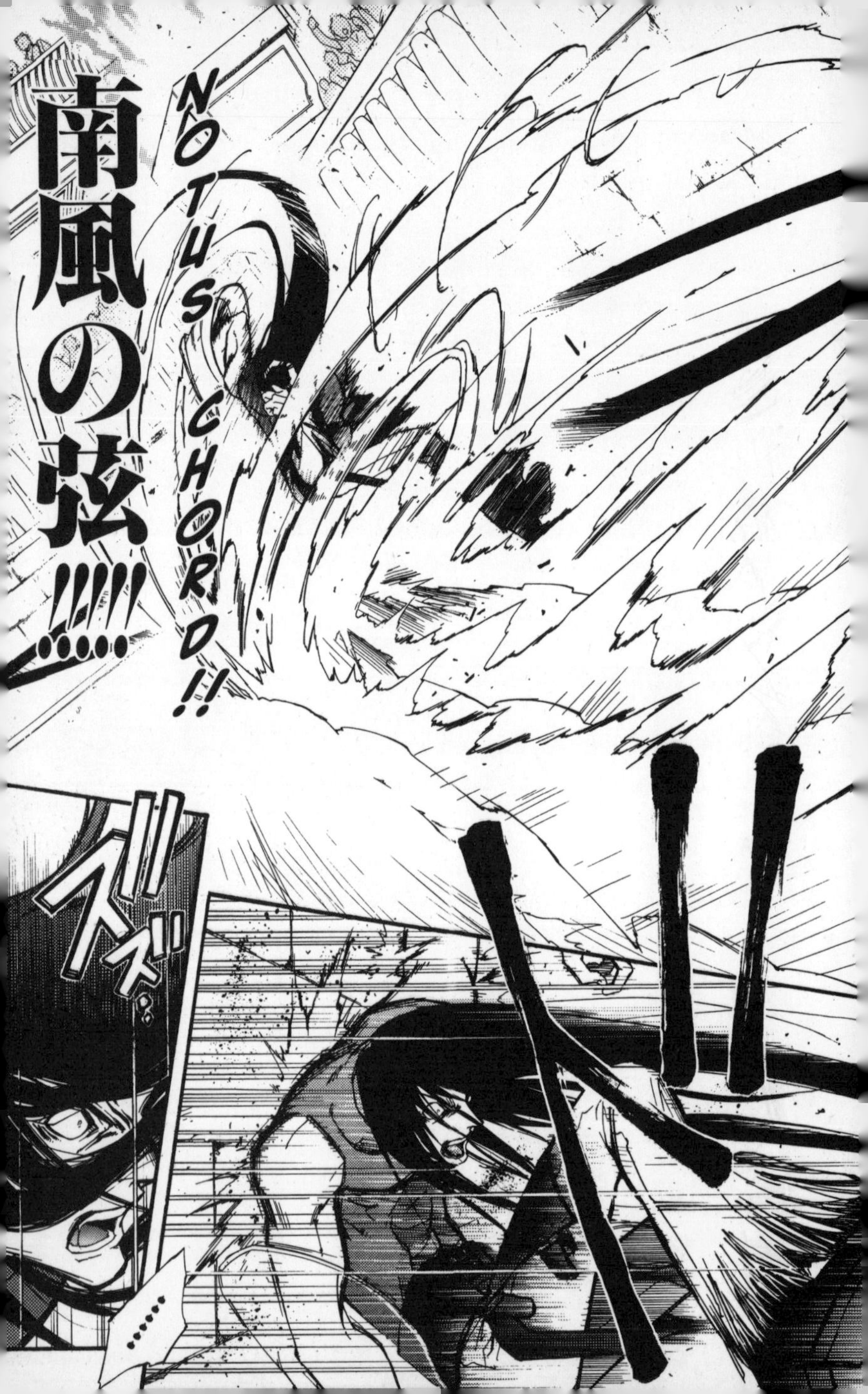
NOTUS CHORD!!
南風の弦!!!!!
ズズ..
......

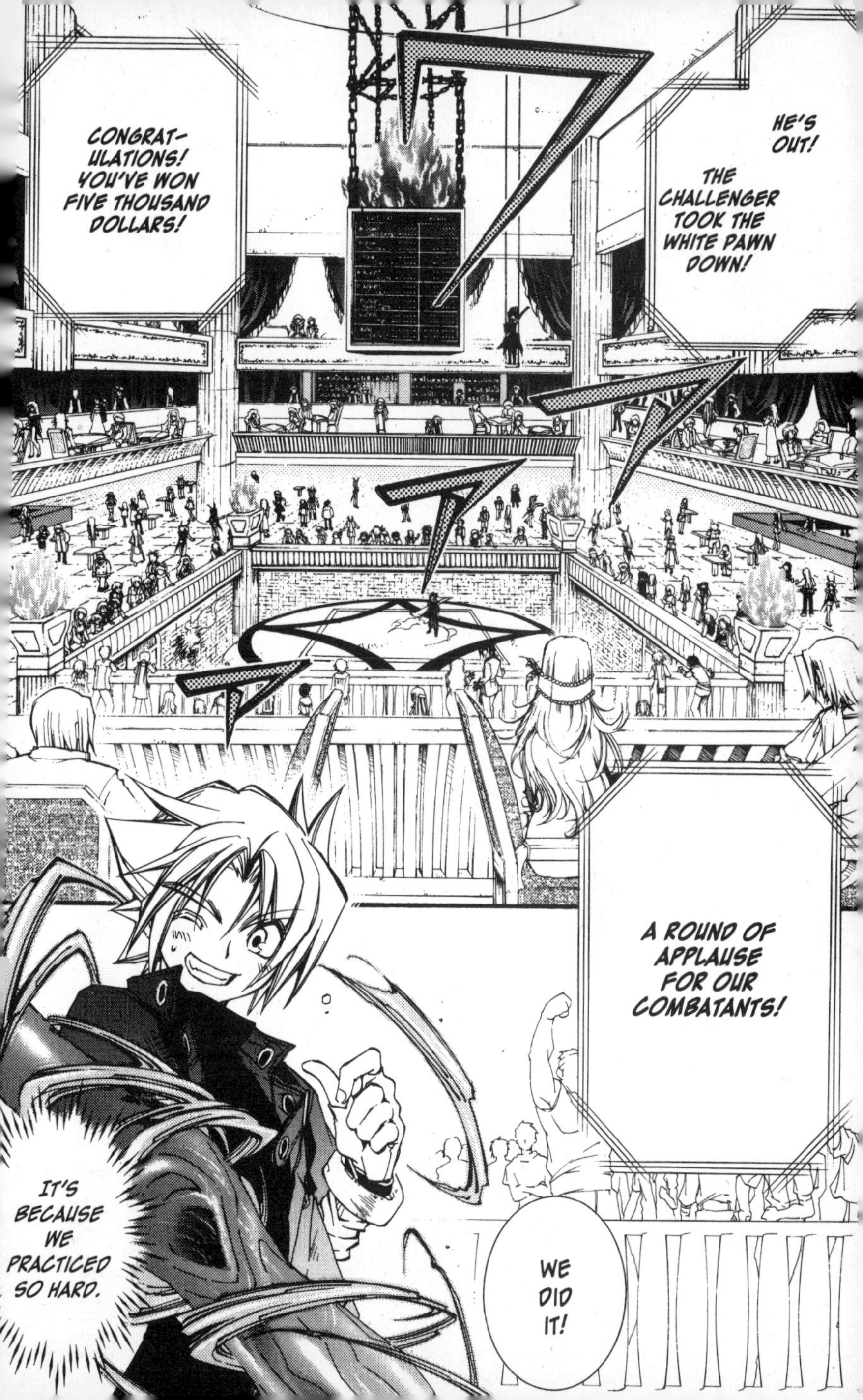

HE'S OUT!
THE CHALLENGER TOOK THE WHITE PAWN DOWN!
CONGRAT-ULATIONS! YOU'VE WON FIVE THOUSAND DOLLARS!
A ROUND OF APPLAUSE FOR OUR COMBATANTS!
WE DID IT!
IT'S BECAUSE WE PRACTICED SO HARD.

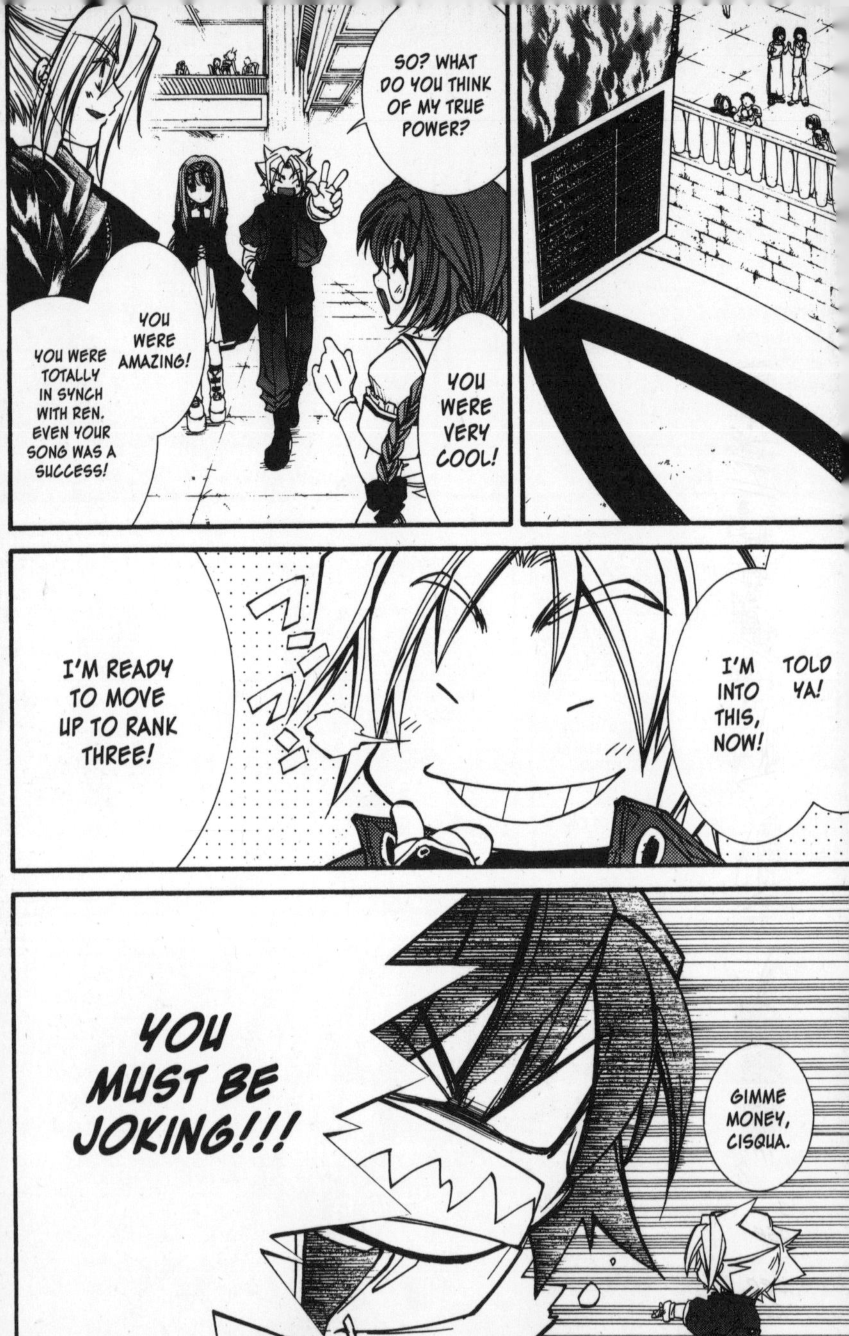
SO? WHAT DO YOU THINK OF MY TRUE POWER?
YOU WERE VERY COOL!
YOU WERE AMAZING!
YOU WERE TOTALLY IN SYNCH WITH REN. EVEN YOUR SONG WAS A SUCCESS!
TOLD YA!
I'M INTO THIS, NOW!
I'M READY TO MOVE UP TO RANK THREE!
GIMME MONEY, CISQUA.
YOU MUST BE JOKING!!!

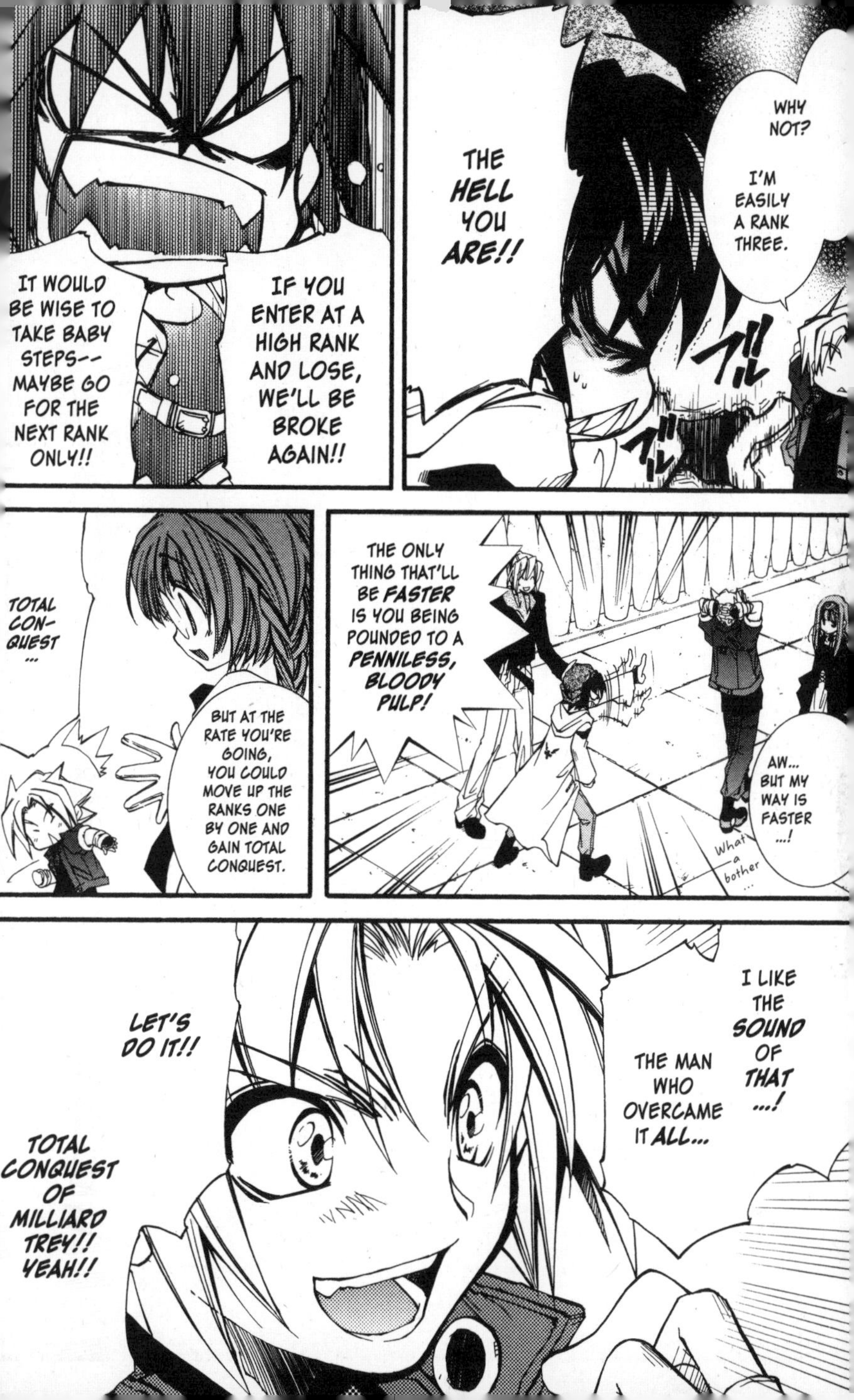
WHY NOT?
I'M EASILY A RANK THREE.
THE HELL YOU ARE!!
IF YOU ENTER AT A HIGH RANK AND LOSE, WE'LL BE BROKE AGAIN!!
IT WOULD BE WISE TO TAKE BABY STEPS-- MAYBE GO FOR THE NEXT RANK ONLY!!
AW... BUT MY WAY IS FASTER ...!
What a bother ...
THE ONLY THING THAT'LL BE FASTER IS YOU BEING POUNDED TO A PENNILESS, BLOODY PULP!
BUT AT THE RATE YOU'RE GOING, YOU COULD MOVE UP THE RANKS ONE BY ONE AND GAIN TOTAL CONQUEST.
TOTAL CON-QUEST ...
I LIKE THE SOUND OF THAT ...!
THE MAN WHO OVERCAME IT ALL...
LET'S DO IT!!
TOTAL CONQUEST OF MILLIARD TREY!! YEAH!!

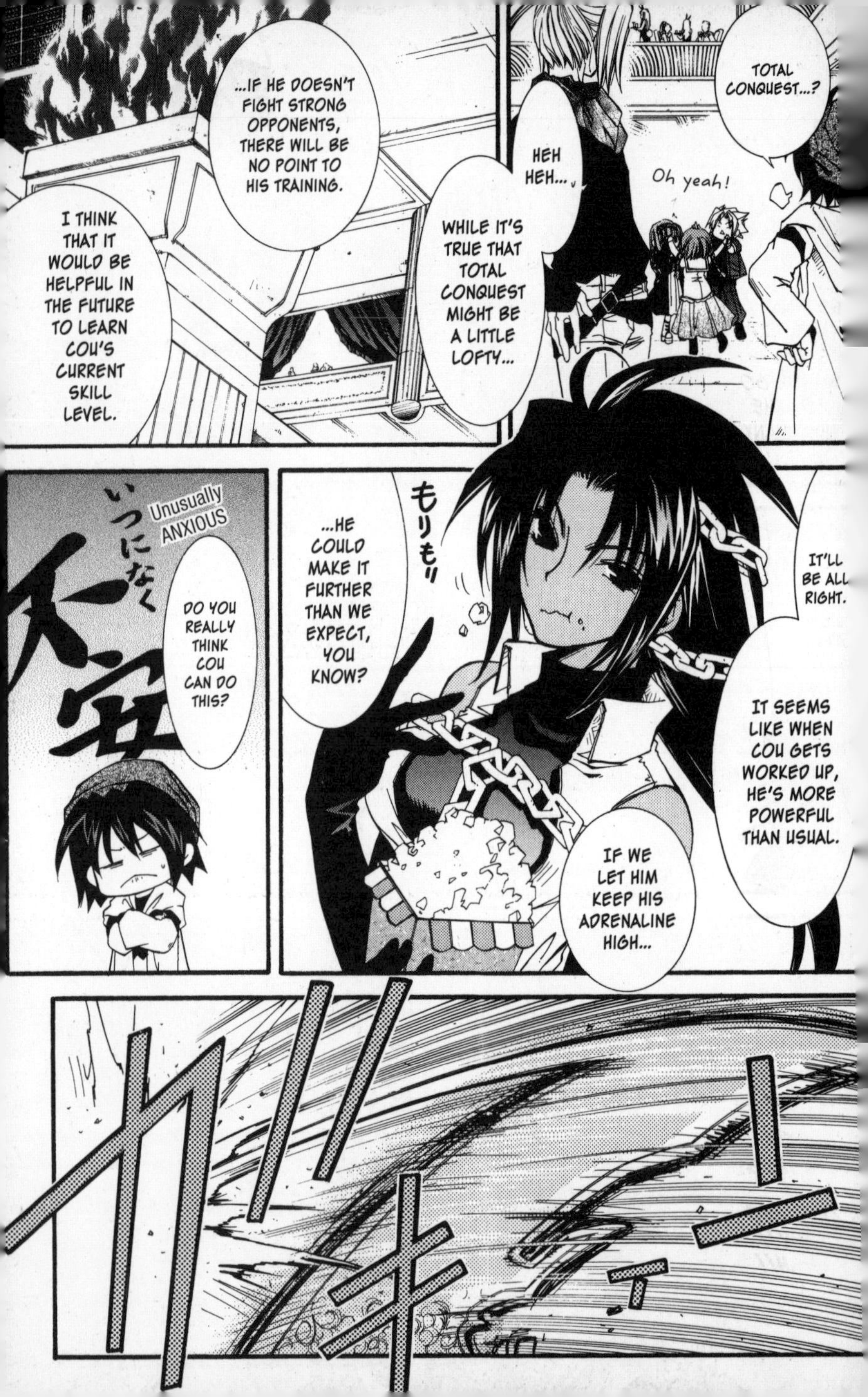
TOTAL CONQUEST...?
Oh yeah!
HEH HEH...
WHILE IT'S TRUE THAT TOTAL CONQUEST MIGHT BE A LITTLE LOFTY...
...IF HE DOESN'T FIGHT STRONG OPPONENTS, THERE WILL BE NO POINT TO HIS TRAINING.
I THINK THAT IT WOULD BE HELPFUL IN THE FUTURE TO LEARN COU'S CURRENT SKILL LEVEL.
IT'LL BE ALL RIGHT.
IT SEEMS LIKE WHEN COU GETS WORKED UP, HE'S MORE POWERFUL THAN USUAL.
IF WE LET HIM KEEP HIS ADRENALINE HIGH...
もりもり
...HE COULD MAKE IT FURTHER THAN WE EXPECT, YOU KNOW?
いつになく不安
Unusually ANXIOUS
DO YOU REALLY THINK COU CAN DO THIS?

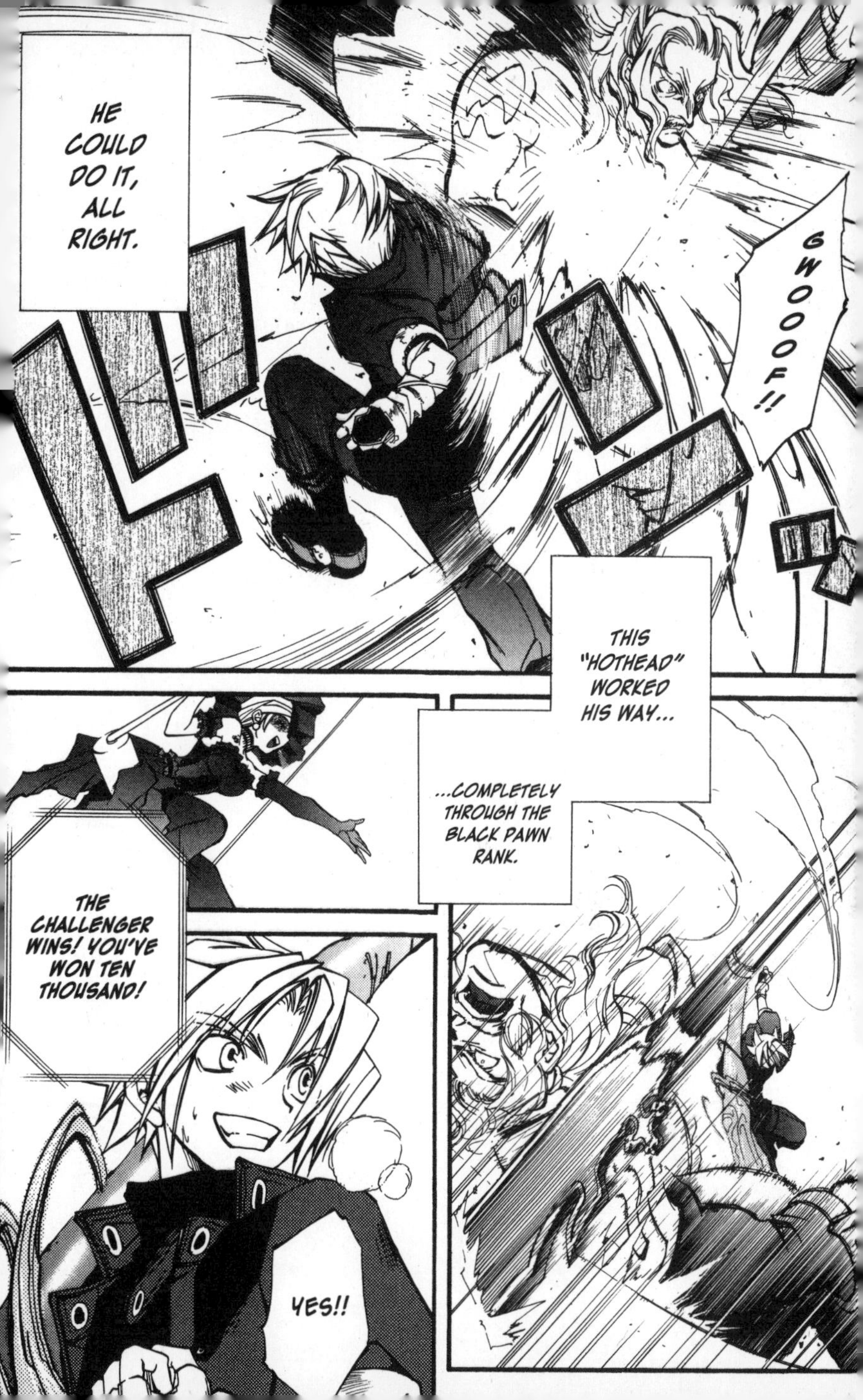
HE COULD DO IT, ALL RIGHT.
GWOOOOF!!
THIS "HOTHEAD" WORKED HIS WAY...
...COMPLETELY THROUGH THE BLACK PAWN RANK.
THE CHALLENGER WINS! YOU'VE WON TEN THOUSAND!
YES!!

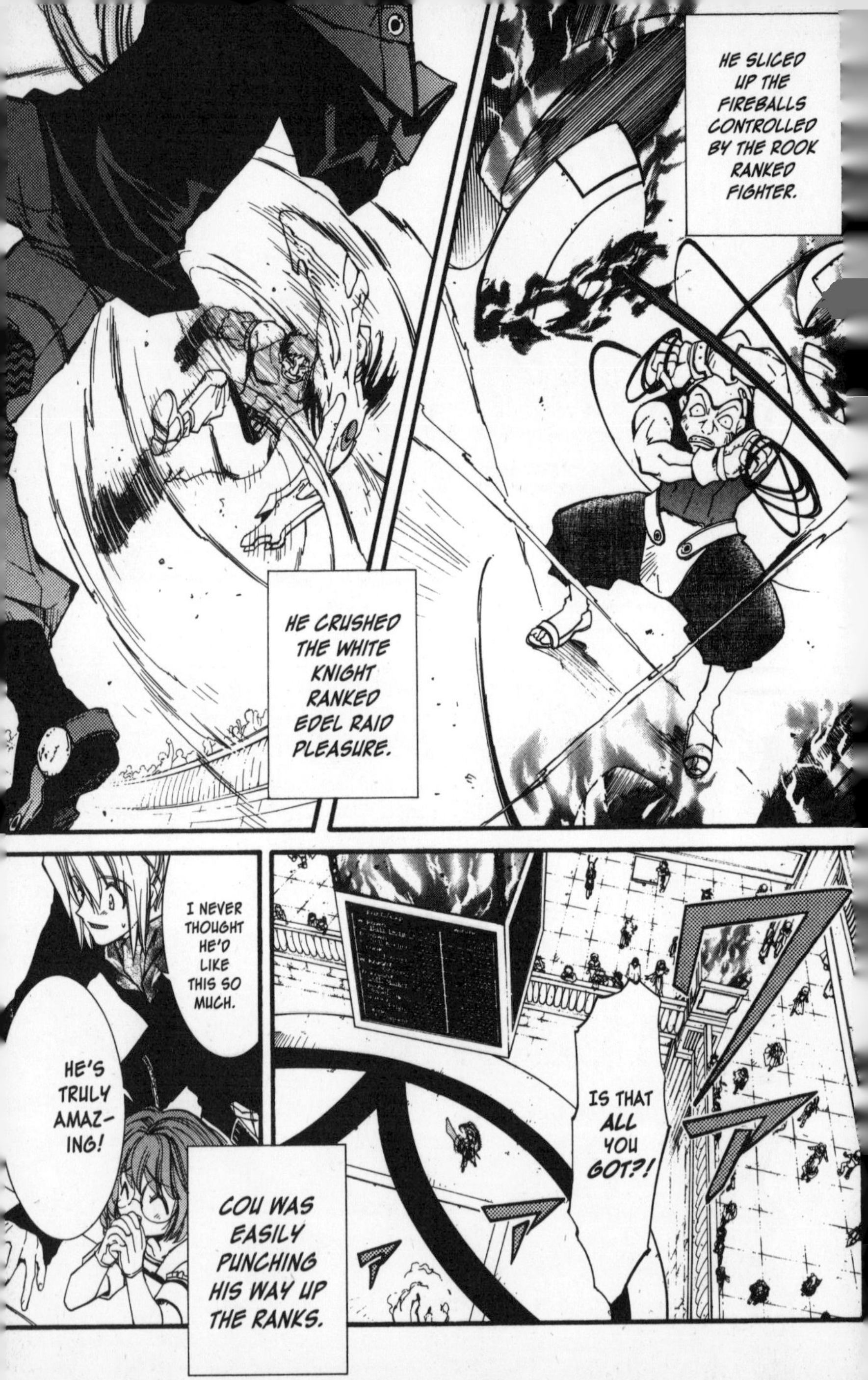
HE SLICED UP THE FIREBALLS CONTROLLED BY THE ROOK RANKED FIGHTER.
HE CRUSHED THE WHITE KNIGHT RANKED EDEL RAID PLEASURE.
IS THAT ALL YOU GOT?!
I NEVER THOUGHT HE'D LIKE THIS SO MUCH.
HE'S TRULY AMAZ-ING!
COU WAS EASILY PUNCHING HIS WAY UP THE RANKS.

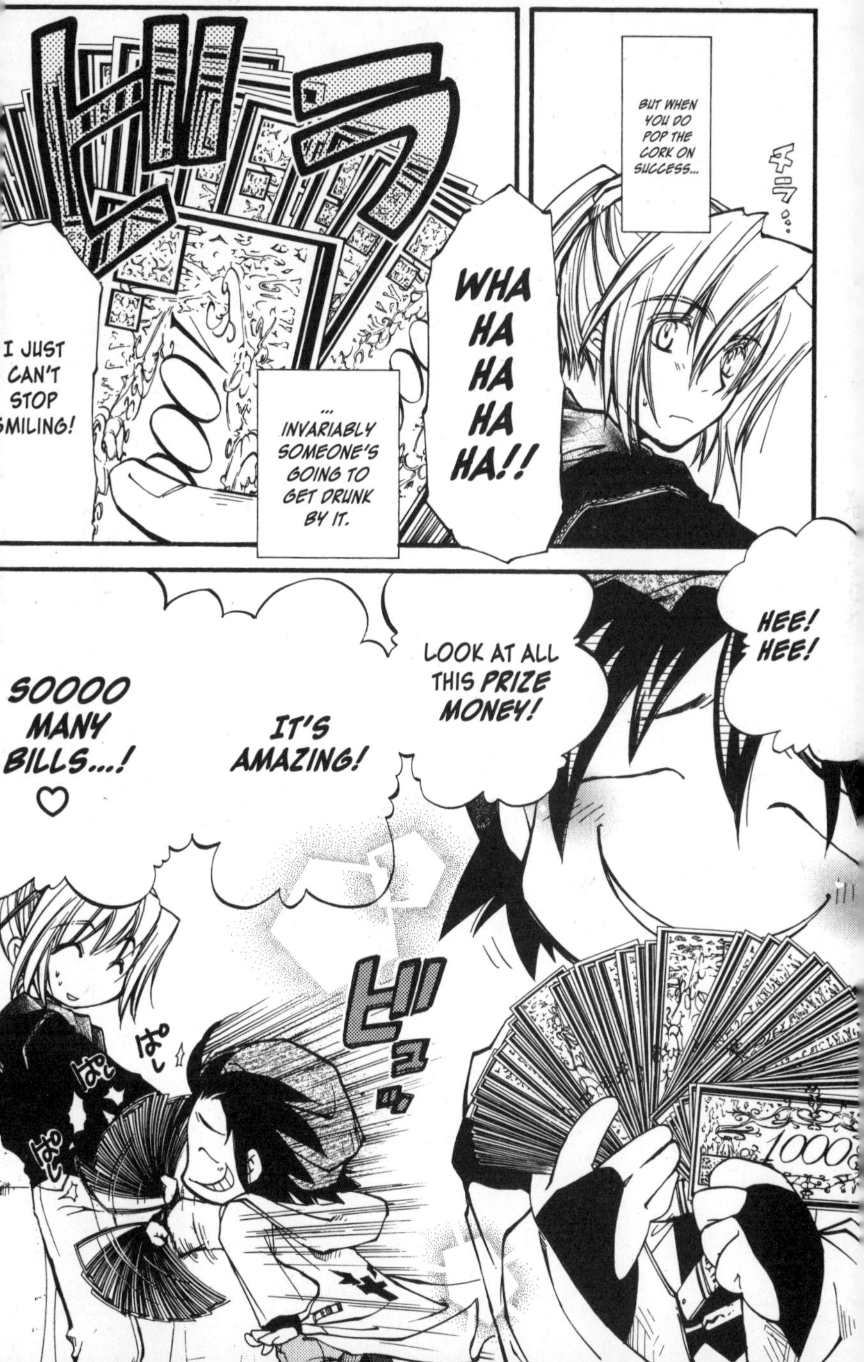
BUT WHEN YOU DO POP THE CORK ON SUCCESS...
チラ。。
WHA HA HA HA HA!!
...INVARIABLY SOMEONE'S GOING TO GET DRUNK BY IT.
I JUST CAN'T STOP SMILING!
HEE! HEE!
LOOK AT ALL THIS PRIZE MONEY!
IT'S AMAZING!
SOOOO MANY BILLS...! ♡
1000
ピュッ
ぱし
ぱし
ぱし

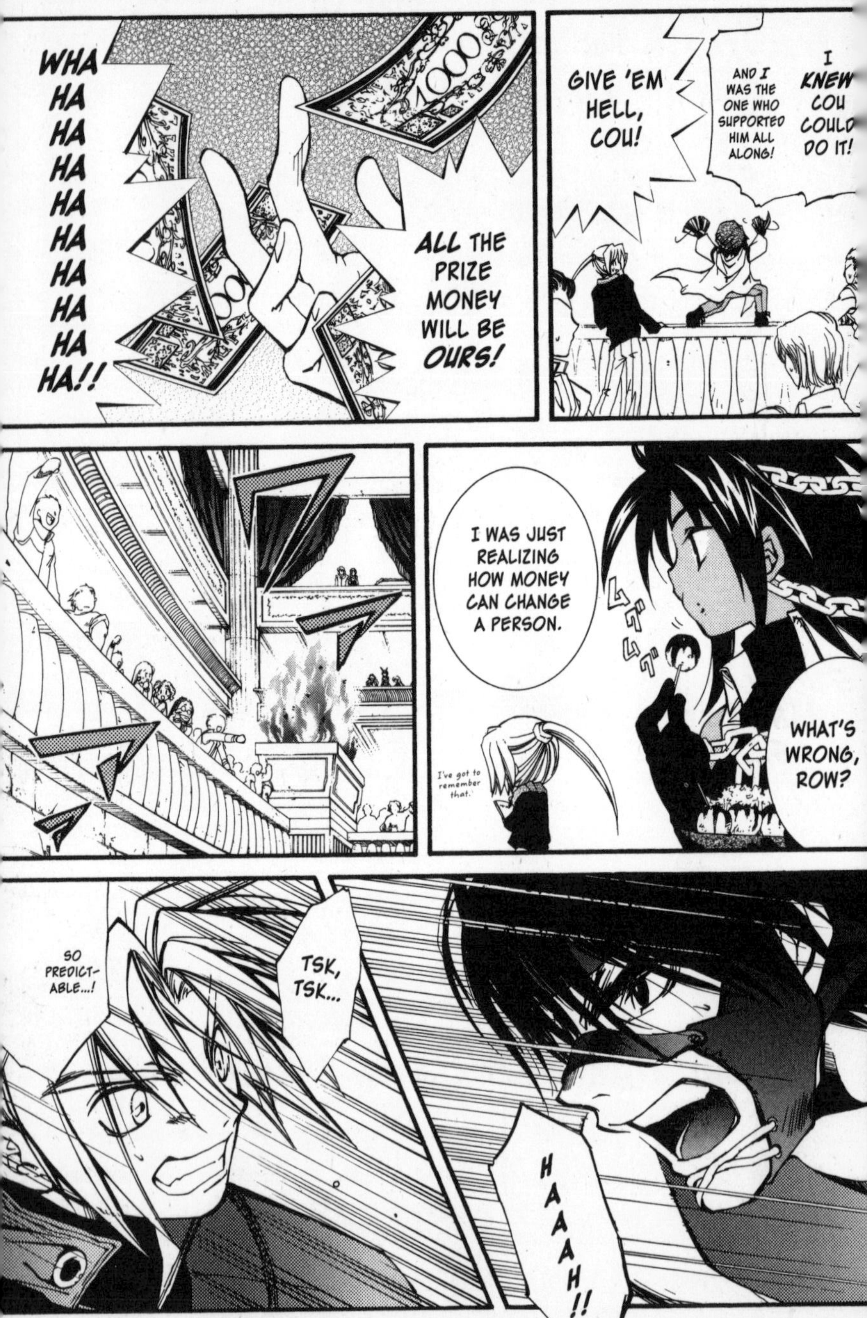
I KNEW COU COULD DO IT!
AND I WAS THE ONE WHO SUPPORTED HIM ALL ALONG!
GIVE 'EM HELL, COU!
ALL THE PRIZE MONEY WILL BE OURS!
WHA HA HA HA HA HA HA HA HA HA!!
WHAT'S WRONG, ROW?
I WAS JUST REALIZING HOW MONEY CAN CHANGE A PERSON.
I've got to remember that.
HAAAH!!
TSK, TSK...
SO PREDICT-ABLE...!

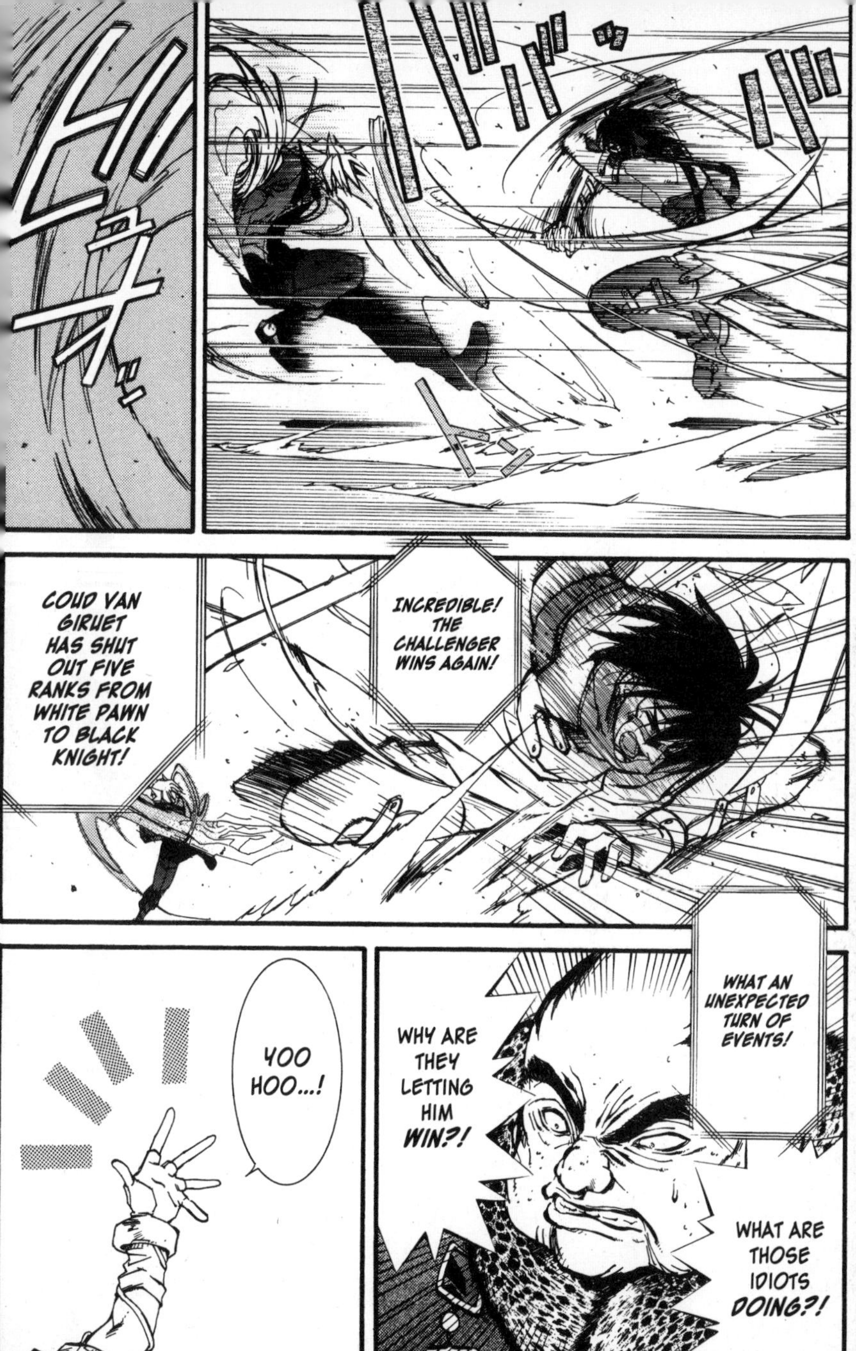
INCREDIBLE! THE CHALLENGER WINS AGAIN!
COUD VAN GIRUET HAS SHUT OUT FIVE RANKS FROM WHITE PAWN TO BLACK KNIGHT!
WHAT AN UNEXPECTED TURN OF EVENTS!
WHY ARE THEY LETTING HIM *WIN?!*
WHAT ARE THOSE IDIOTS *DOING?!*
YOO HOO...!

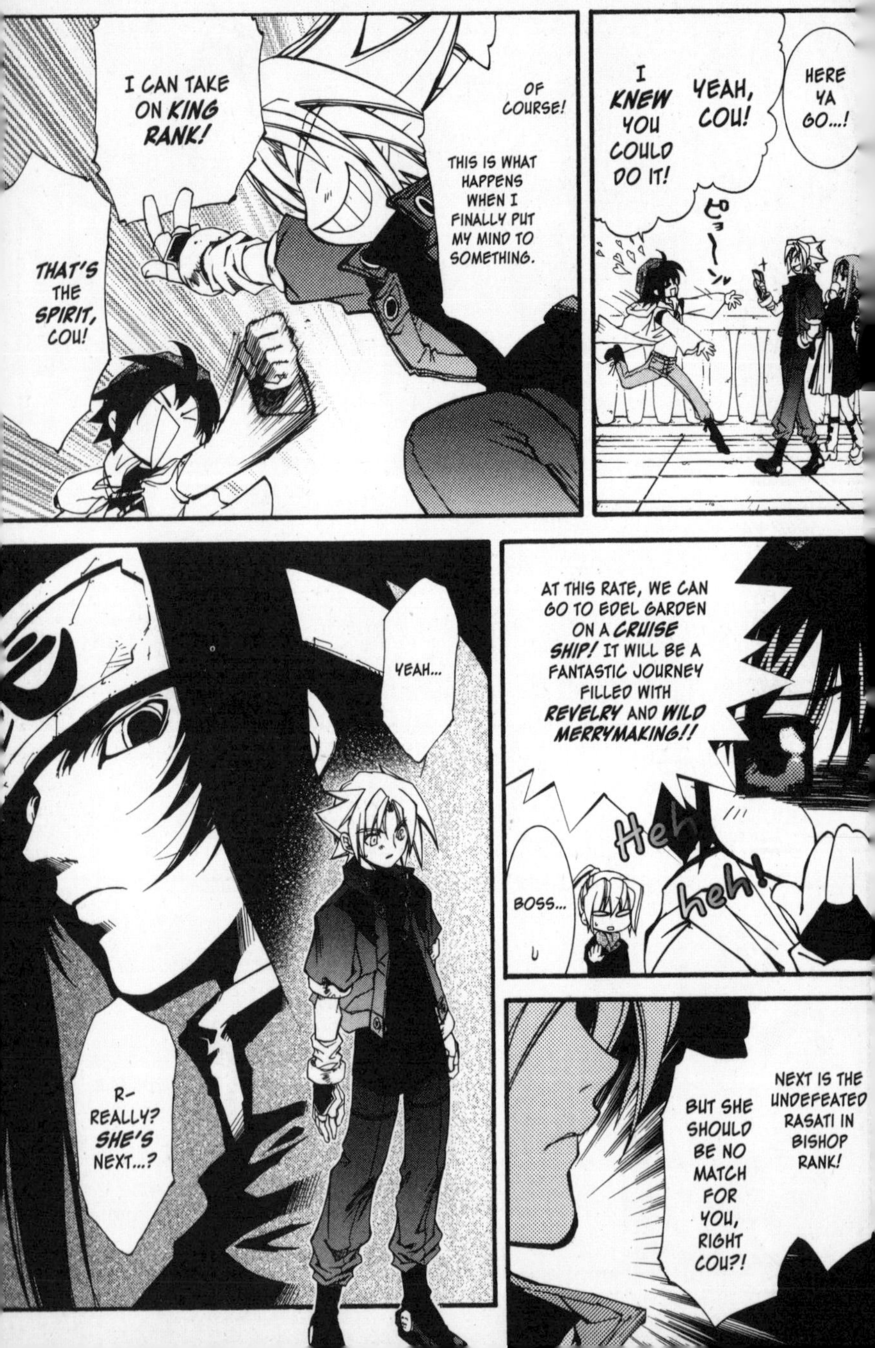
HERE YA GO...!
YEAH, COU!
I KNEW YOU COULD DO IT!
OF COURSE!
THIS IS WHAT HAPPENS WHEN I FINALLY PUT MY MIND TO SOMETHING.
I CAN TAKE ON KING RANK!
THAT'S THE SPIRIT, COU!
AT THIS RATE, WE CAN GO TO EDEL GARDEN ON A CRUISE SHIP! IT WILL BE A FANTASTIC JOURNEY FILLED WITH REVELRY AND WILD MERRYMAKING!!
Heh heh!
BOSS...
NEXT IS THE UNDEFEATED RASATI IN BISHOP RANK!
BUT SHE SHOULD BE NO MATCH FOR YOU, RIGHT COU?!
YEAH...
R- REALLY? SHE'S NEXT...?

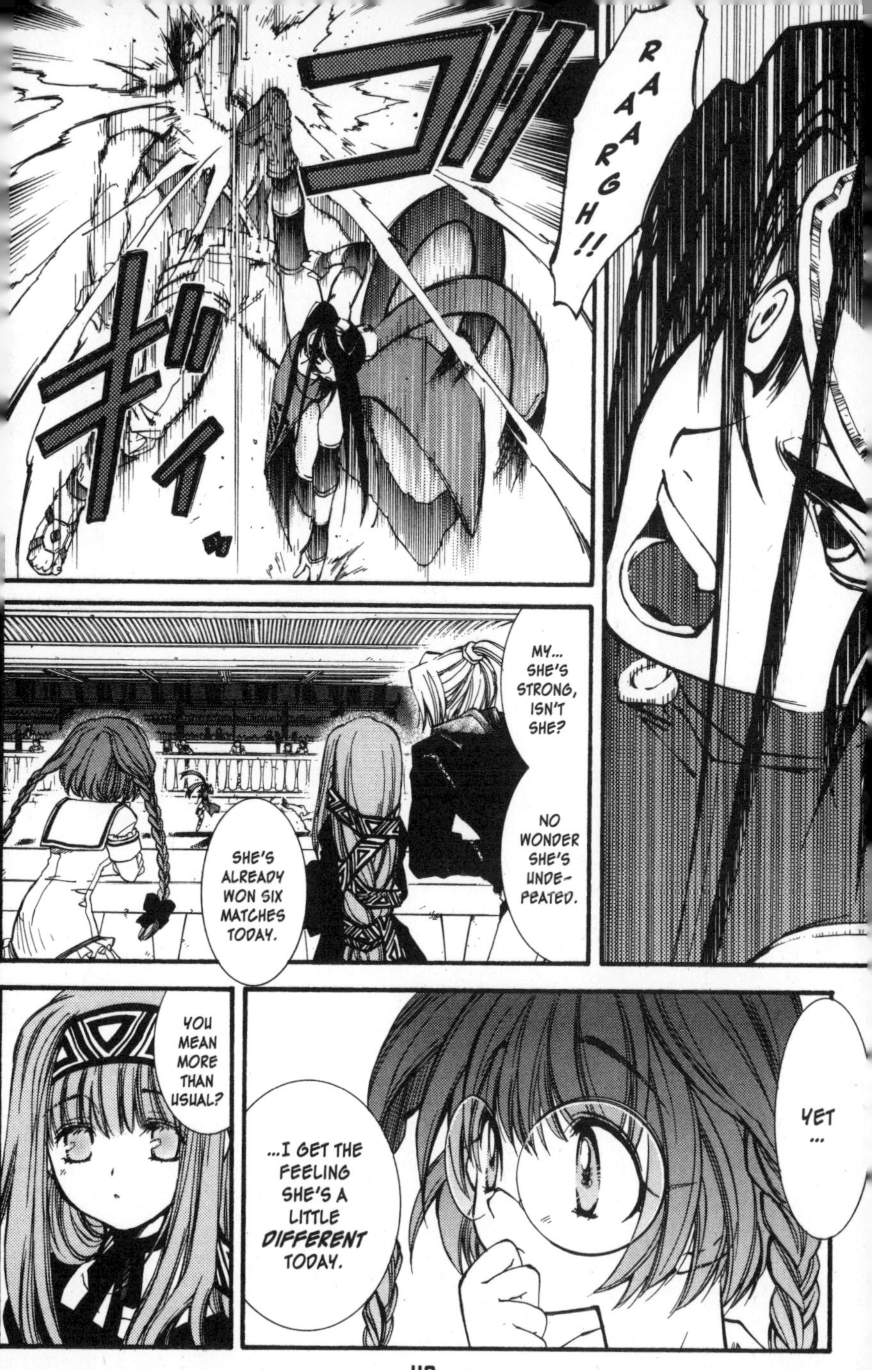
RAAARGH!!
ゴッ
ギィ
MY... SHE'S STRONG, ISN'T SHE?
NO WONDER SHE'S UNDEFEATED.
SHE'S ALREADY WON SIX MATCHES TODAY.
YET ...
...I GET THE FEELING SHE'S A LITTLE DIFFERENT TODAY.
YOU MEAN MORE THAN USUAL?

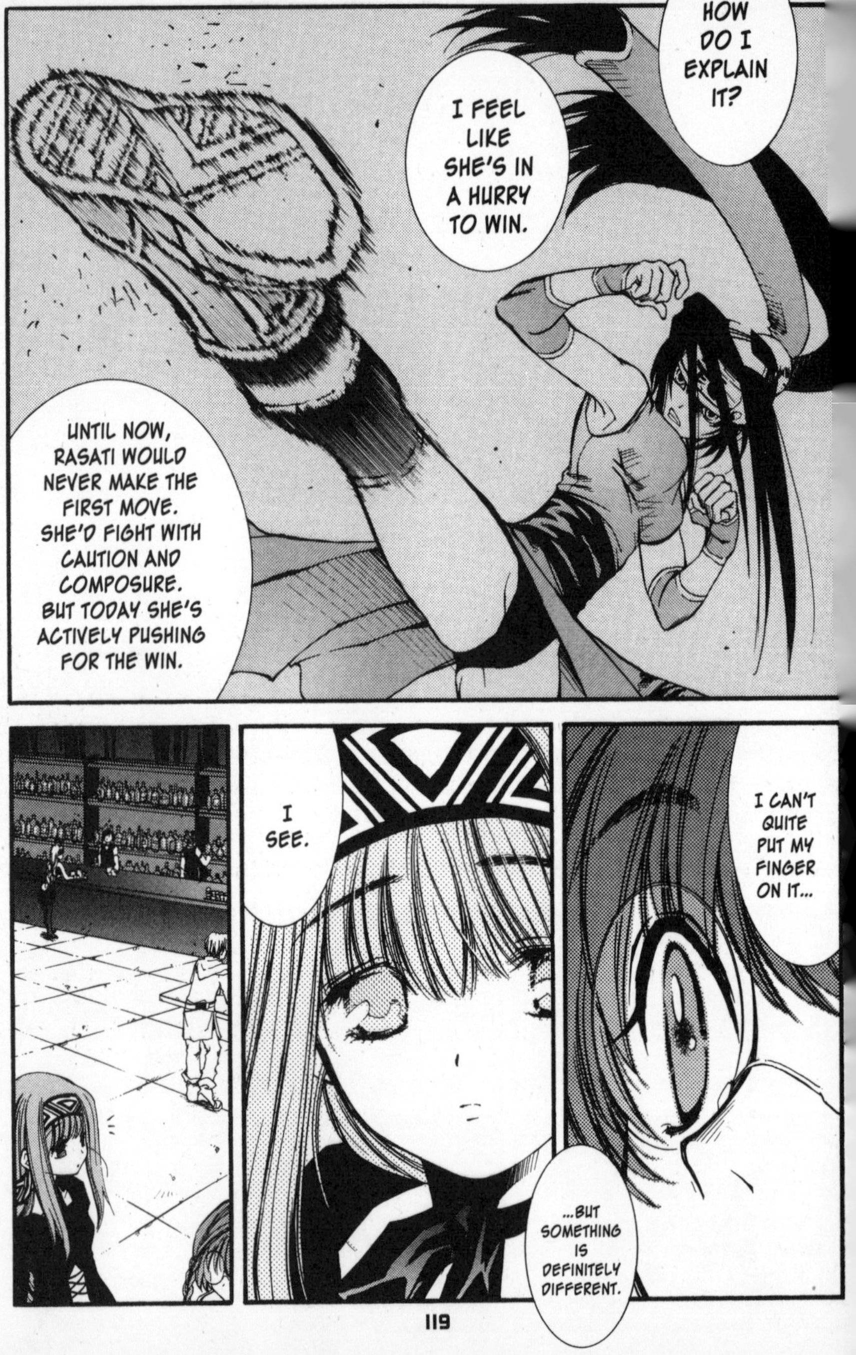
HOW DO I EXPLAIN IT?
I FEEL LIKE SHE'S IN A HURRY TO WIN.
UNTIL NOW, RASATI WOULD NEVER MAKE THE FIRST MOVE. SHE'D FIGHT WITH CAUTION AND COMPOSURE. BUT TODAY SHE'S ACTIVELY PUSHING FOR THE WIN.
I CAN'T QUITE PUT MY FINGER ON IT...
...BUT SOMETHING IS DEFINITELY DIFFERENT.
I SEE.

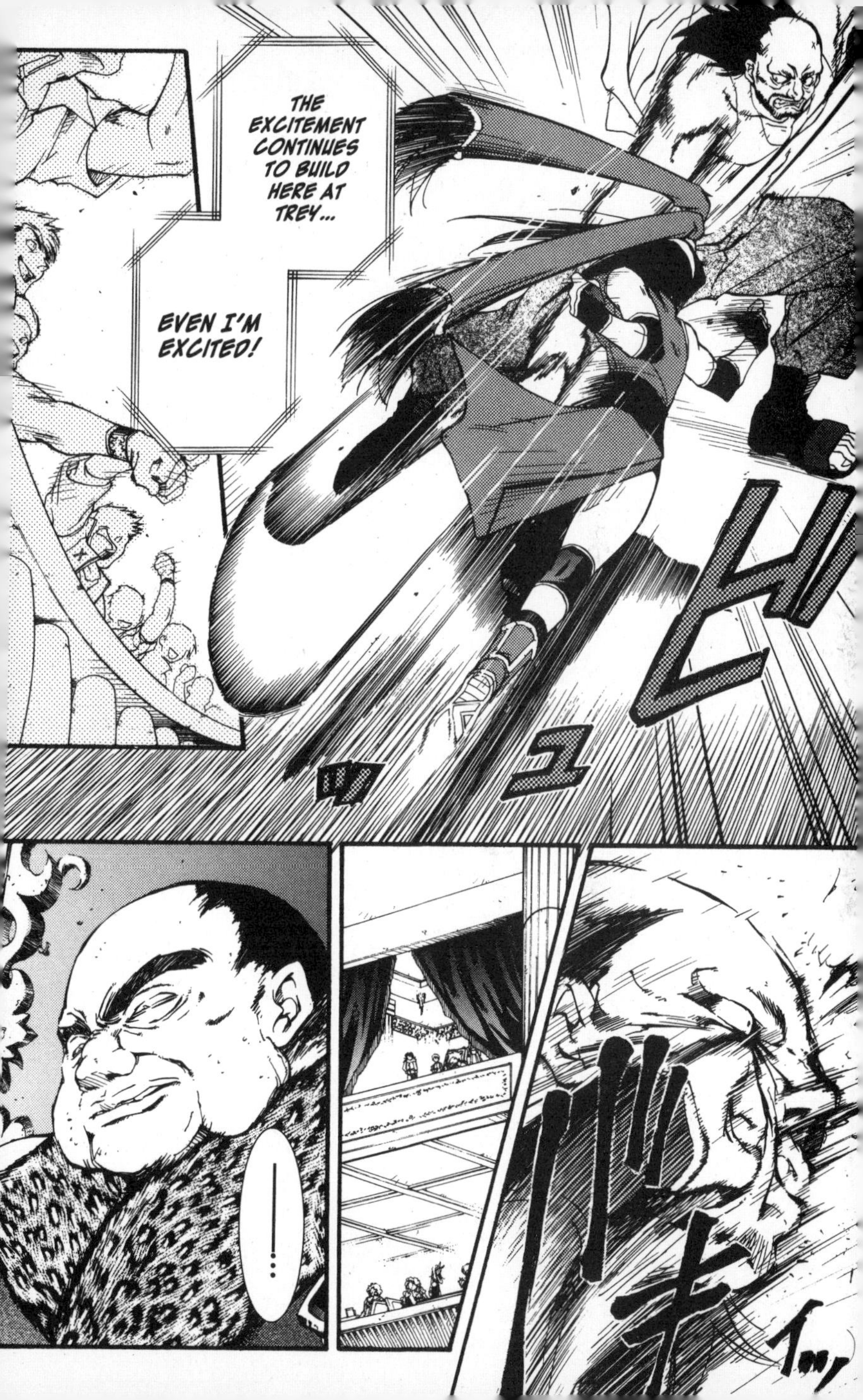
THE EXCITEMENT CONTINUES TO BUILD HERE AT TREY...
EVEN I'M EXCITED!
......

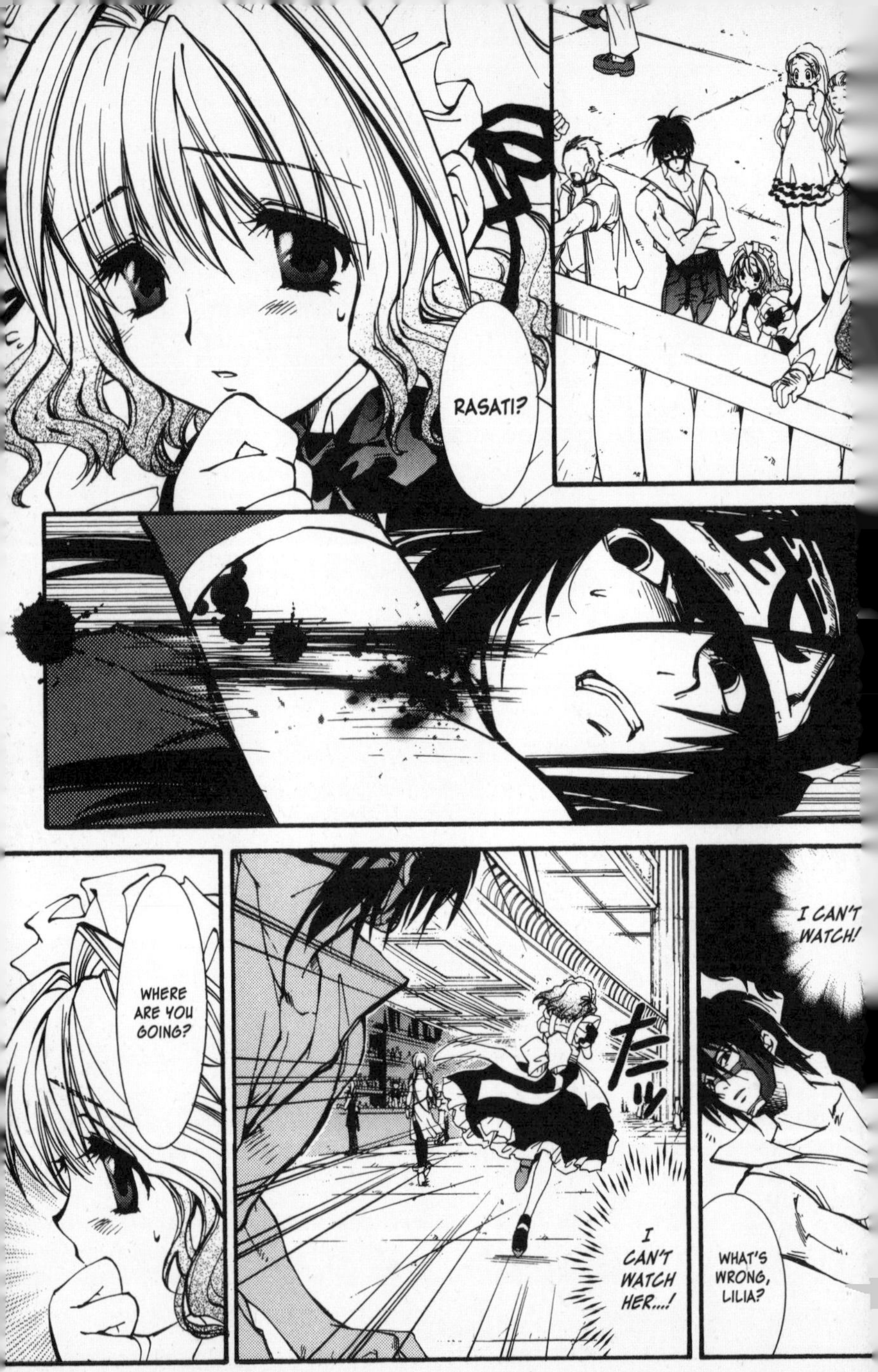
RASATI?
I CAN'T WATCH!
WHAT'S WRONG, LILIA?
たーッ
I CAN'T WATCH HER...!
WHERE ARE YOU GOING?

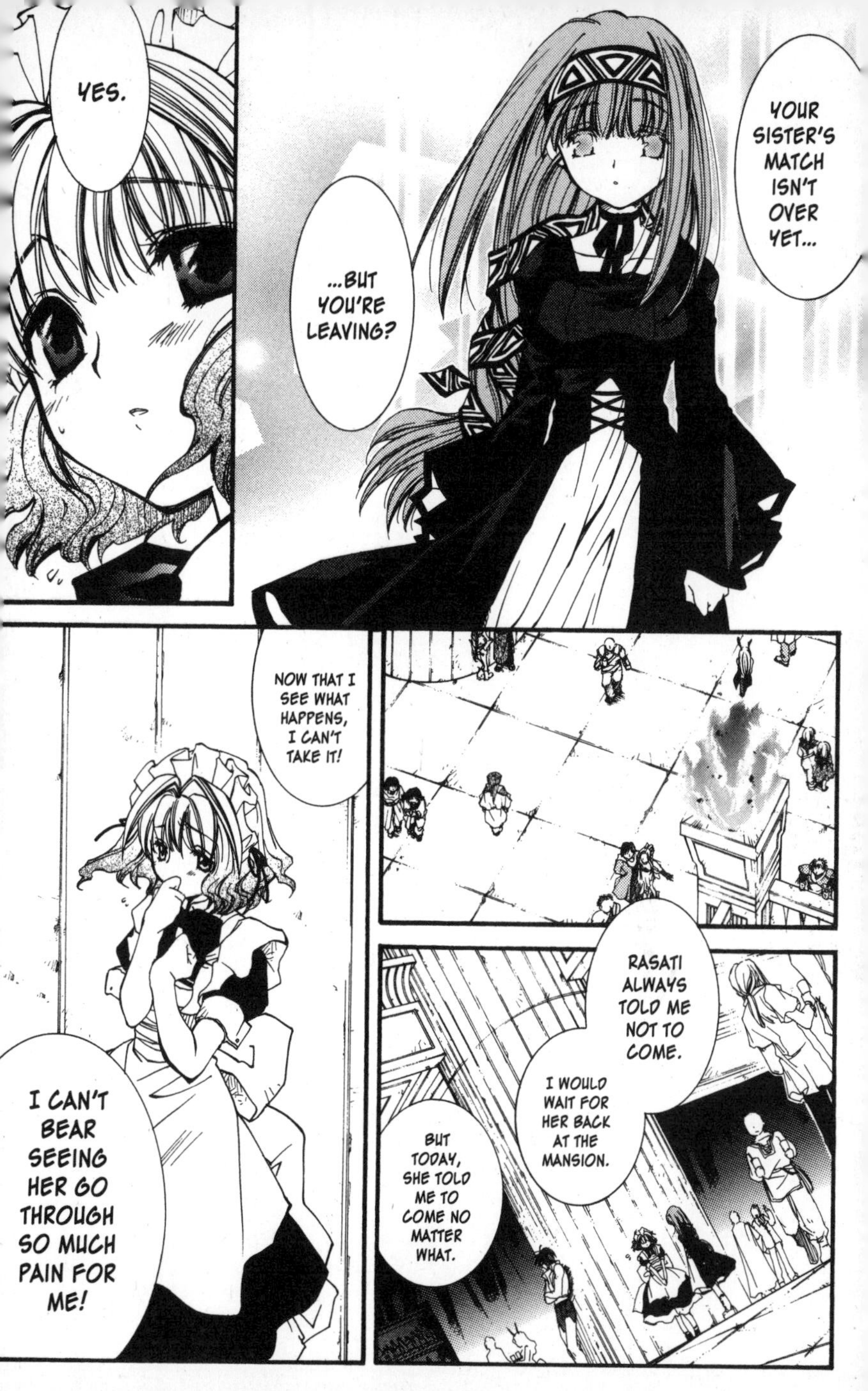
YOUR SISTER'S MATCH ISN'T OVER YET...
...BUT YOU'RE LEAVING?
YES.
RASATI ALWAYS TOLD ME NOT TO COME.
I WOULD WAIT FOR HER BACK AT THE MANSION.
BUT TODAY, SHE TOLD ME TO COME NO MATTER WHAT.
NOW THAT I SEE WHAT HAPPENS, I CAN'T TAKE IT!
I CAN'T BEAR SEEING HER GO THROUGH SO MUCH PAIN FOR ME!

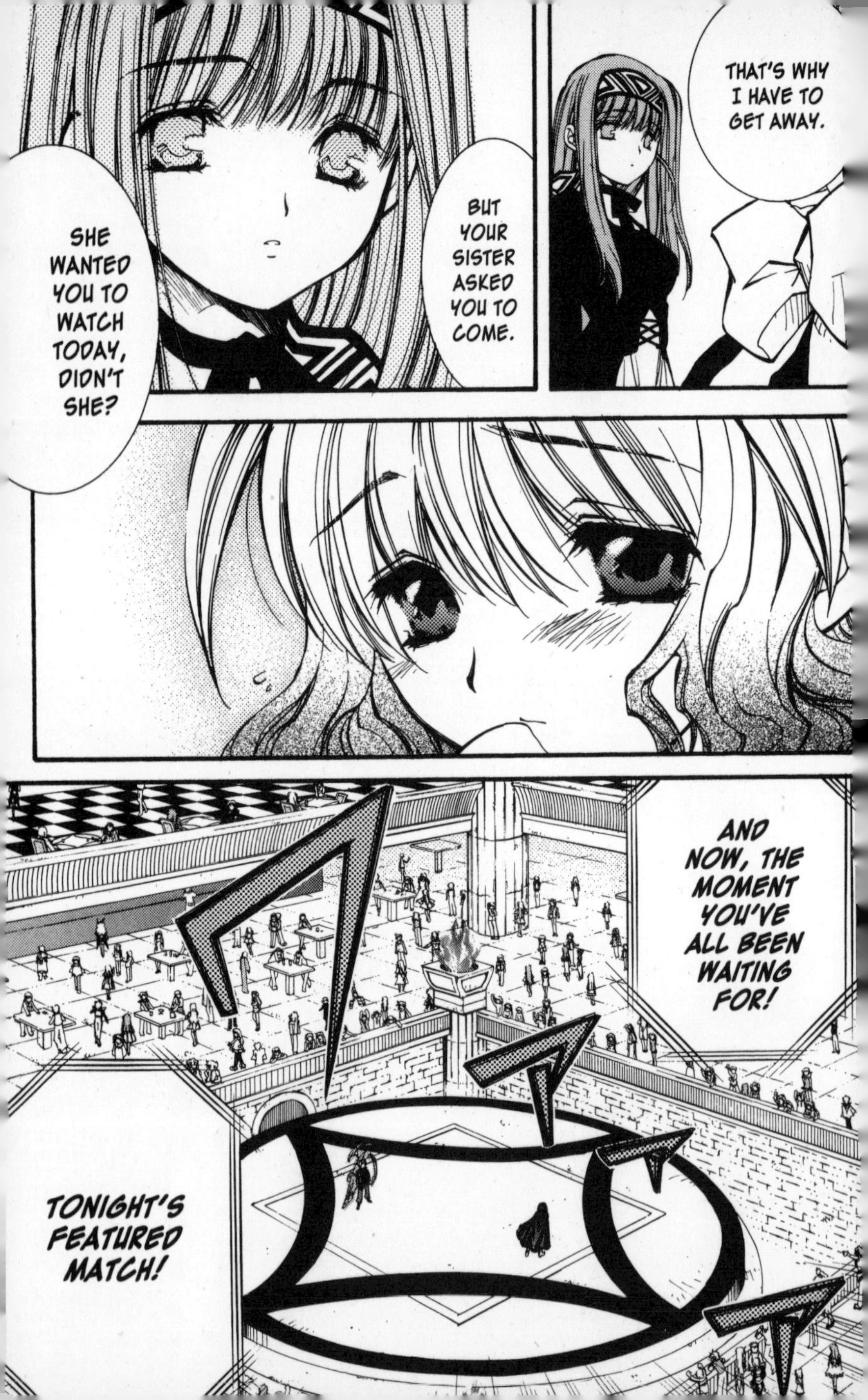
THAT'S WHY I HAVE TO GET AWAY.
BUT YOUR SISTER ASKED YOU TO COME.
SHE WANTED YOU TO WATCH TODAY, DIDN'T SHE?
AND NOW, THE MOMENT YOU'VE ALL BEEN WAITING FOR!
TONIGHT'S FEATURED MATCH!

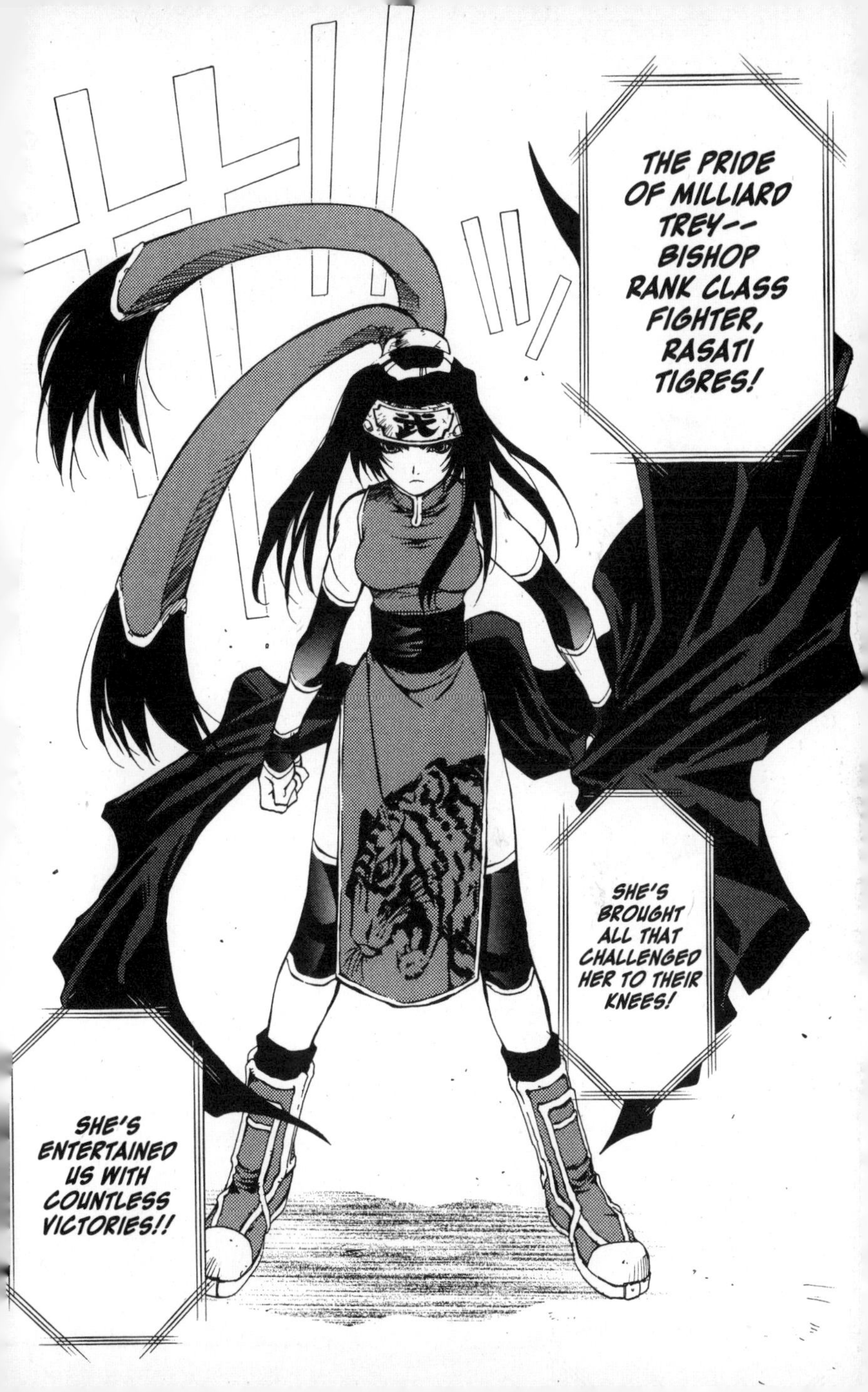
THE PRIDE OF MILLIARD TREY-- BISHOP RANK CLASS FIGHTER, RASATI TIGRES!
SHE'S BROUGHT ALL THAT CHALLENGED HER TO THEIR KNEES!
SHE'S ENTERTAINED US WITH COUNTLESS VICTORIES!!

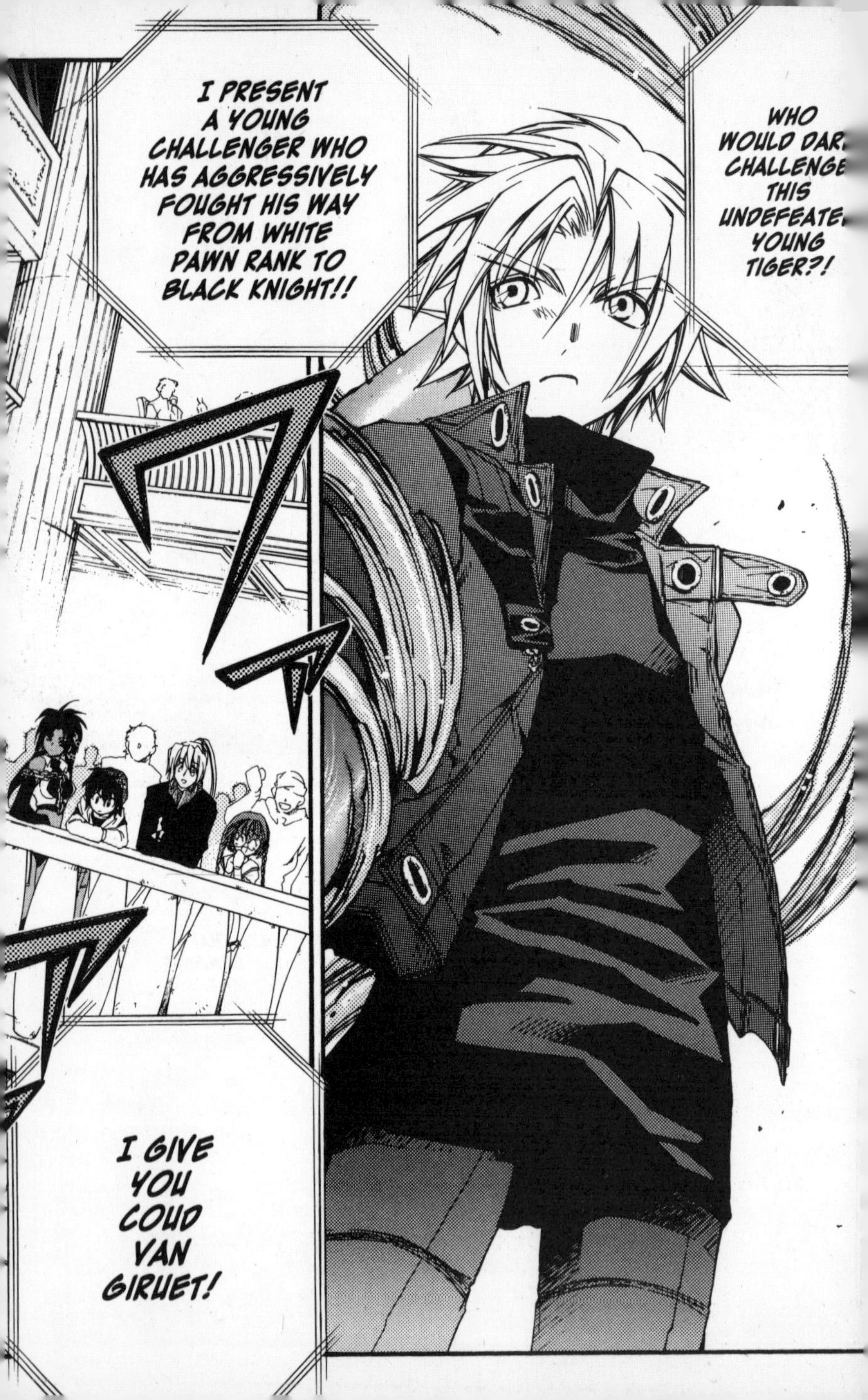
WHO WOULD DAR CHALLENGE THIS UNDEFEATE YOUNG TIGER?!
I PRESENT A YOUNG CHALLENGER WHO HAS AGGRESSIVELY FOUGHT HIS WAY FROM WHITE PAWN RANK TO BLACK KNIGHT!!
I GIVE YOU COUD VAN GIRUET!

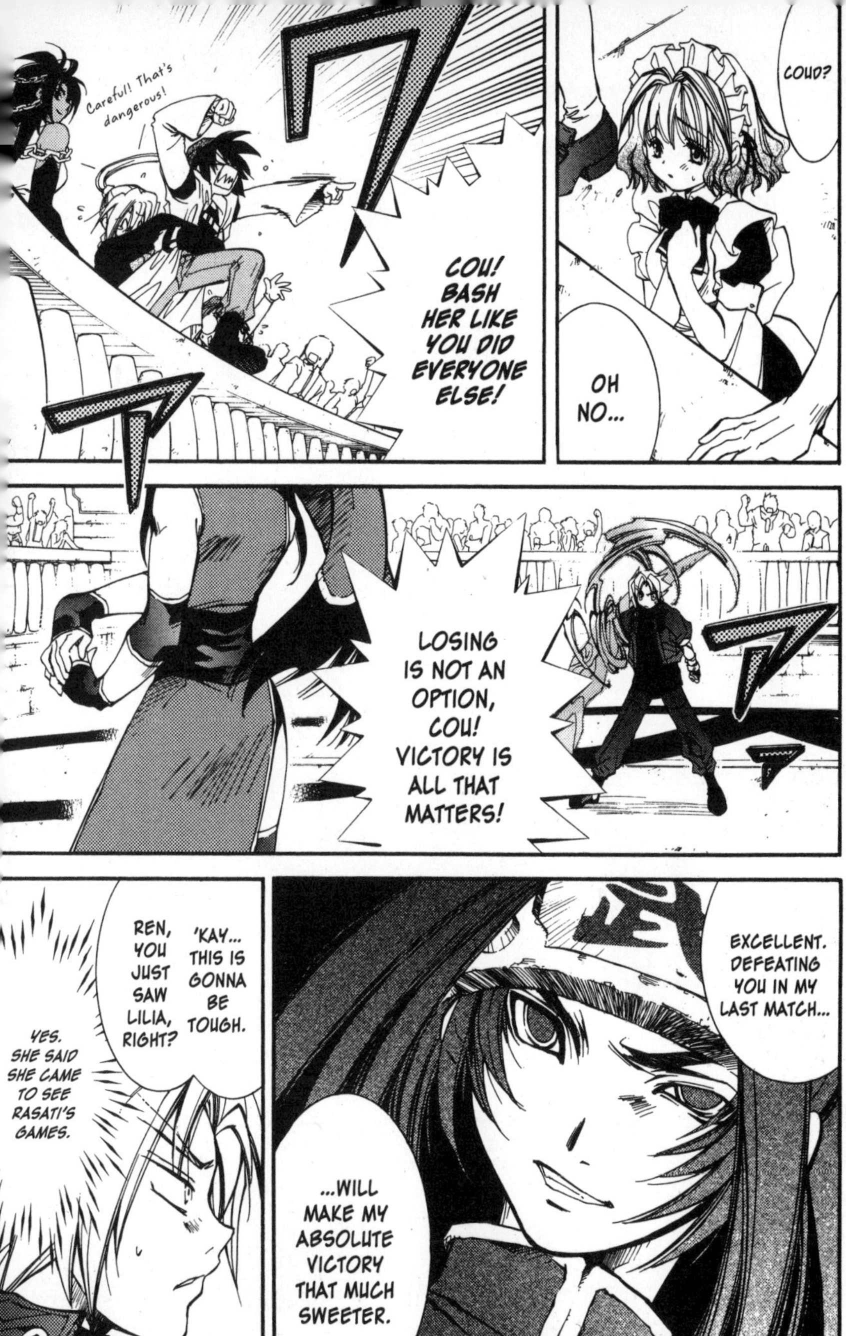
COUD?
OH NO...
COU! BASH HER LIKE YOU DID EVERYONE ELSE!
Careful! That's dangerous!
LOSING IS NOT AN OPTION, COU! VICTORY IS ALL THAT MATTERS!
EXCELLENT. DEFEATING YOU IN MY LAST MATCH...
...WILL MAKE MY ABSOLUTE VICTORY THAT MUCH SWEETER.
'KAY... THIS IS GONNA BE TOUGH.
REN, YOU JUST SAW LILIA, RIGHT?
YES. SHE SAID SHE CAME TO SEE RASATI'S GAMES.

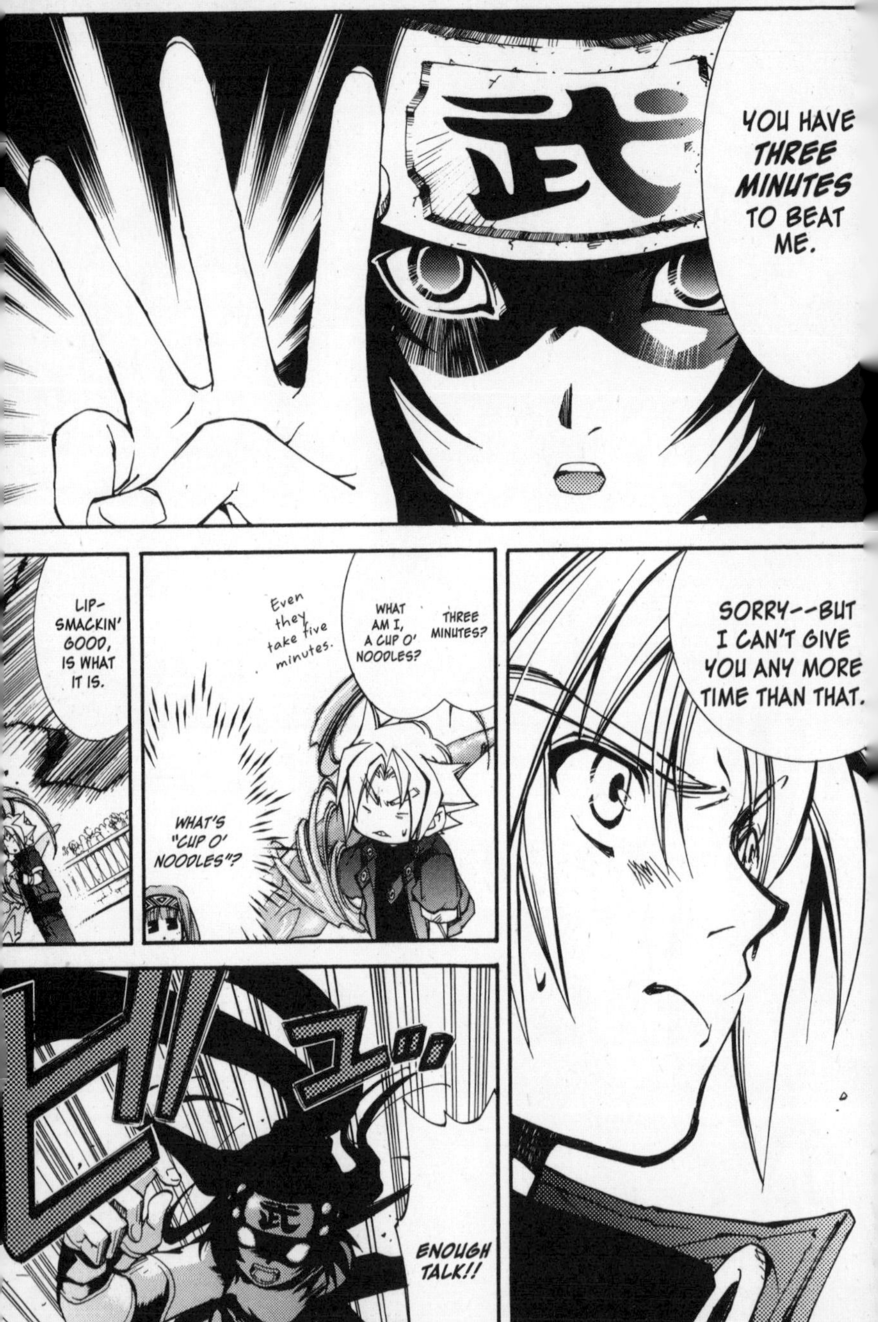
YOU HAVE THREE MINUTES TO BEAT ME.
SORRY--BUT I CAN'T GIVE YOU ANY MORE TIME THAN THAT.
THREE MINUTES?
WHAT AM I, A CUP O' NOODLES?
Even they take five minutes.
WHAT'S "CUP O' NOODLES"?
LIP-SMACKIN' GOOD, IS WHAT IT IS.
ENOUGH TALK!!

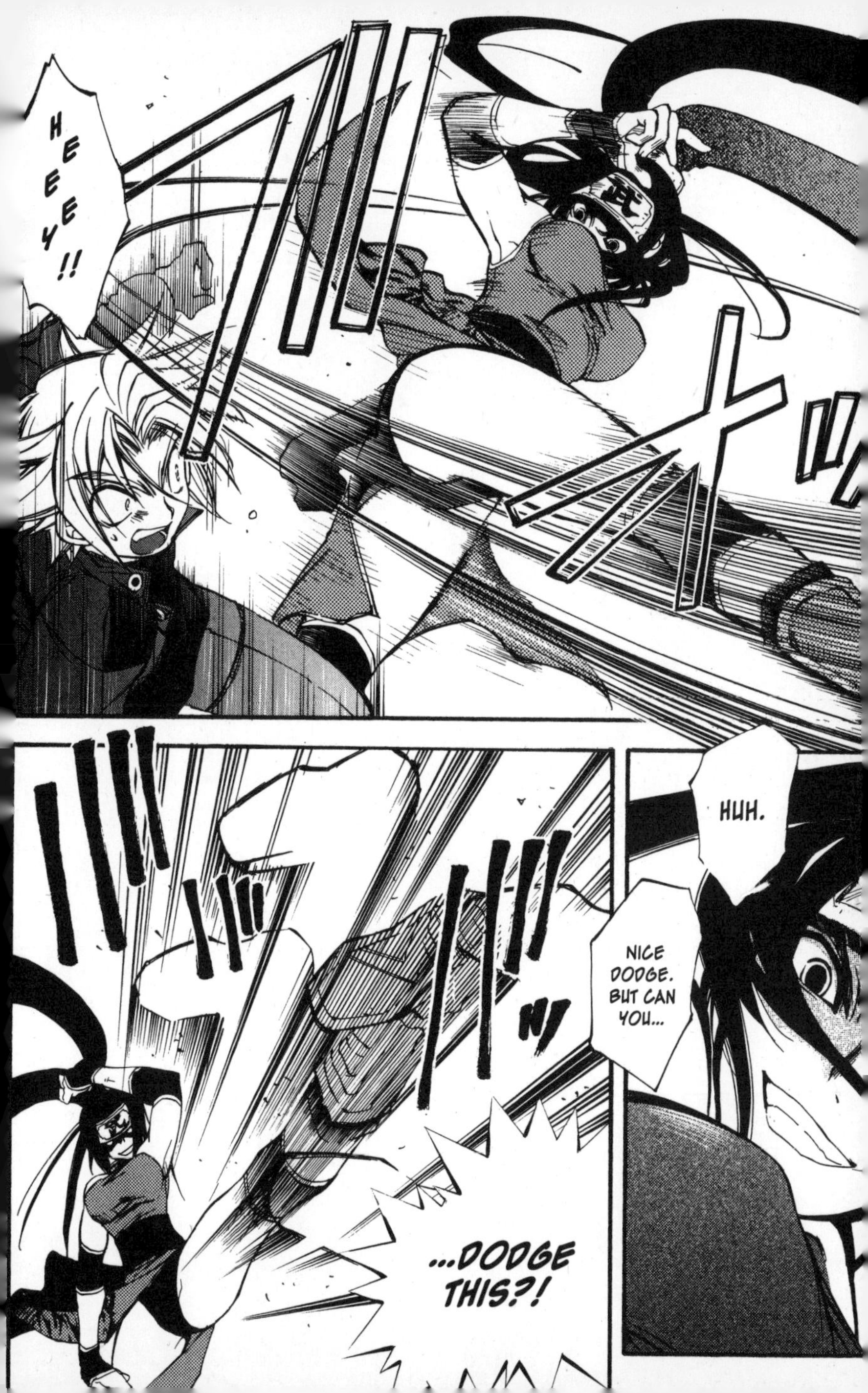
HEEEY!!
HUH.
NICE DODGE. BUT CAN YOU...
...DODGE THIS?!

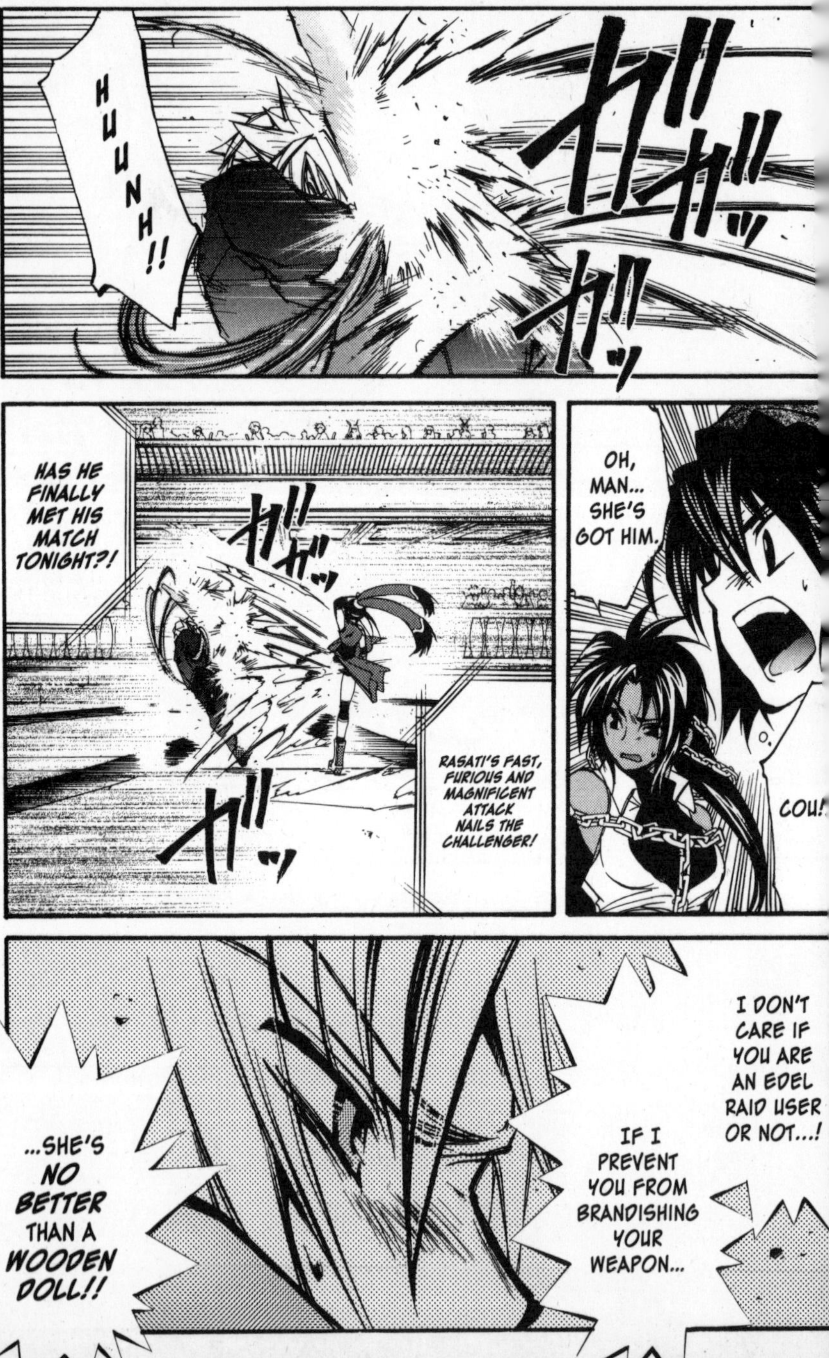
HUUNH!!
OH, MAN... SHE'S GOT HIM.
COU!
HAS HE FINALLY MET HIS MATCH TONIGHT?!
RASATI'S FAST, FURIOUS AND MAGNIFICENT ATTACK NAILS THE CHALLENGER!
I DON'T CARE IF YOU ARE AN EDEL RAID USER OR NOT...!
IF I PREVENT YOU FROM BRANDISHING YOUR WEAPON...
...SHE'S NO BETTER THAN A WOODEN DOLL!!

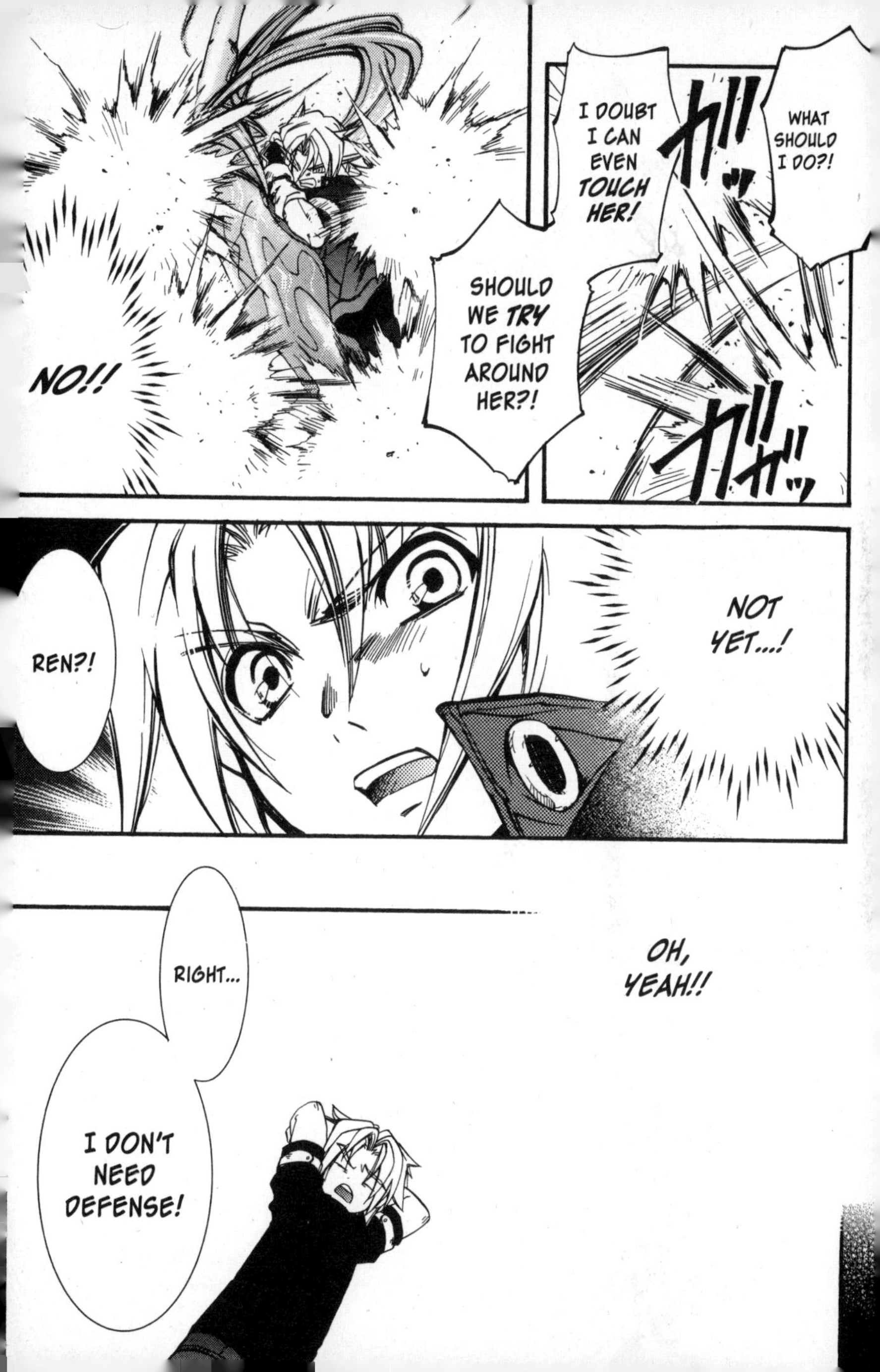
WHAT SHOULD I DO?!
I DOUBT I CAN EVEN TOUCH HER!
ガッ
ガガッ
SHOULD WE TRY TO FIGHT AROUND HER?!
NO!!
NOT YET...!
REN?!
OH, YEAH!!
RIGHT...
I DON'T NEED DEFENSE!

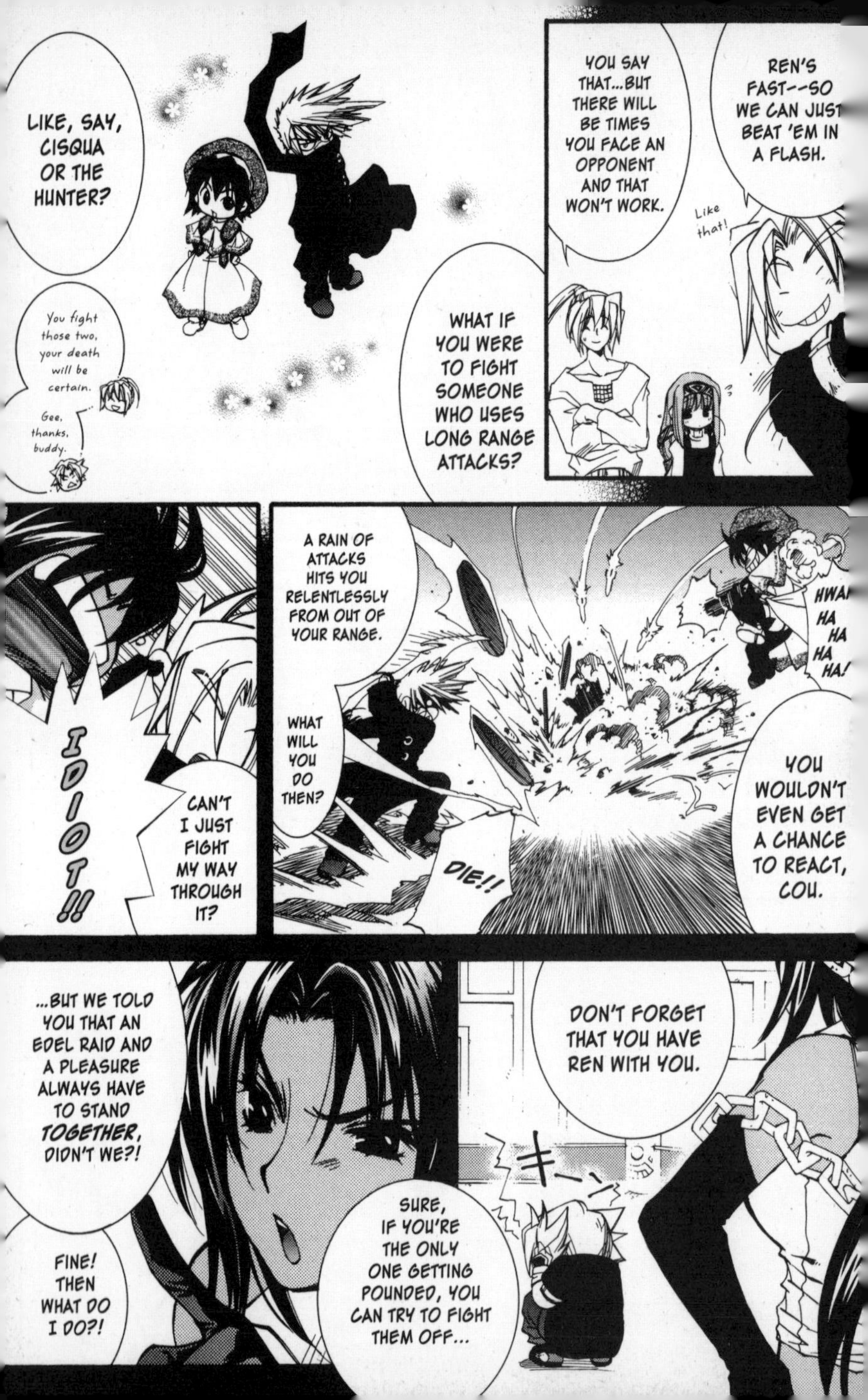
REN'S FAST--SO WE CAN JUST BEAT 'EM IN A FLASH.
Like that!
YOU SAY THAT...BUT THERE WILL BE TIMES YOU FACE AN OPPONENT AND THAT WON'T WORK.
WHAT IF YOU WERE TO FIGHT SOMEONE WHO USES LONG RANGE ATTACKS?
LIKE, SAY, CISQUA OR THE HUNTER?
You fight those two, your death will be certain.
Gee, thanks, buddy.
A RAIN OF ATTACKS HITS YOU RELENTLESSLY FROM OUT OF YOUR RANGE.
HWA HA HA HA HA!
WHAT WILL YOU DO THEN?
DIE!!
YOU WOULDN'T EVEN GET A CHANCE TO REACT, COU.
CAN'T I JUST FIGHT MY WAY THROUGH IT?
IDIOT!!
DON'T FORGET THAT YOU HAVE REN WITH YOU.
SURE, IF YOU'RE THE ONLY ONE GETTING POUNDED, YOU CAN TRY TO FIGHT THEM OFF...
...BUT WE TOLD YOU THAT AN EDEL RAID AND A PLEASURE ALWAYS HAVE TO STAND TOGETHER, DIDN'T WE?!
FINE! THEN WHAT DO I DO?!

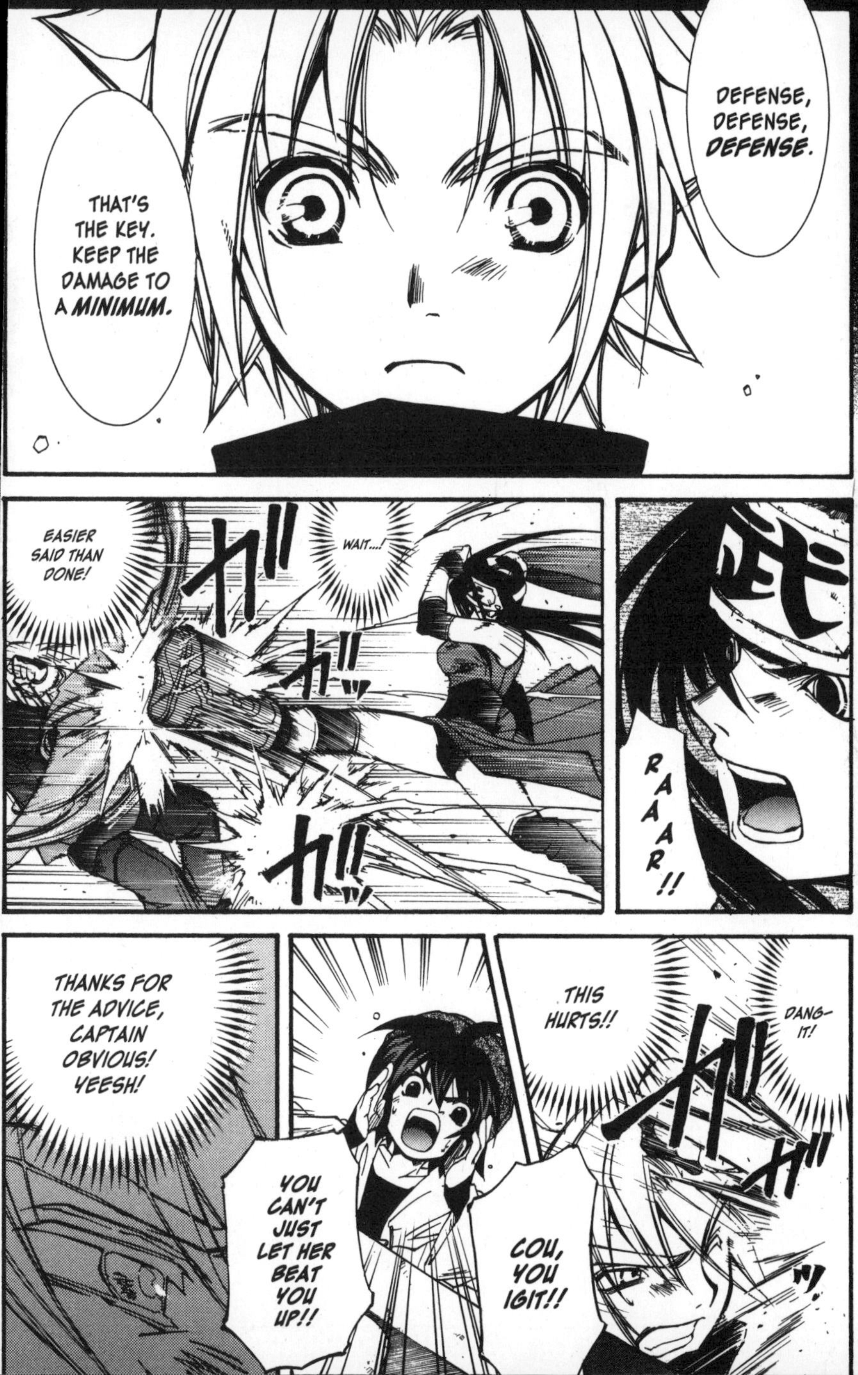

DEFENSE, DEFENSE, DEFENSE.
THAT'S THE KEY. KEEP THE DAMAGE TO A MINIMUM.
RAAAR!!
WAIT...!
EASIER SAID THAN DONE!
DANG-IT!
THIS HURTS!!
COU, YOU IGIT!!
YOU CAN'T JUST LET HER BEAT YOU UP!!
THANKS FOR THE ADVICE, CAPTAIN OBVIOUS! YEESH!

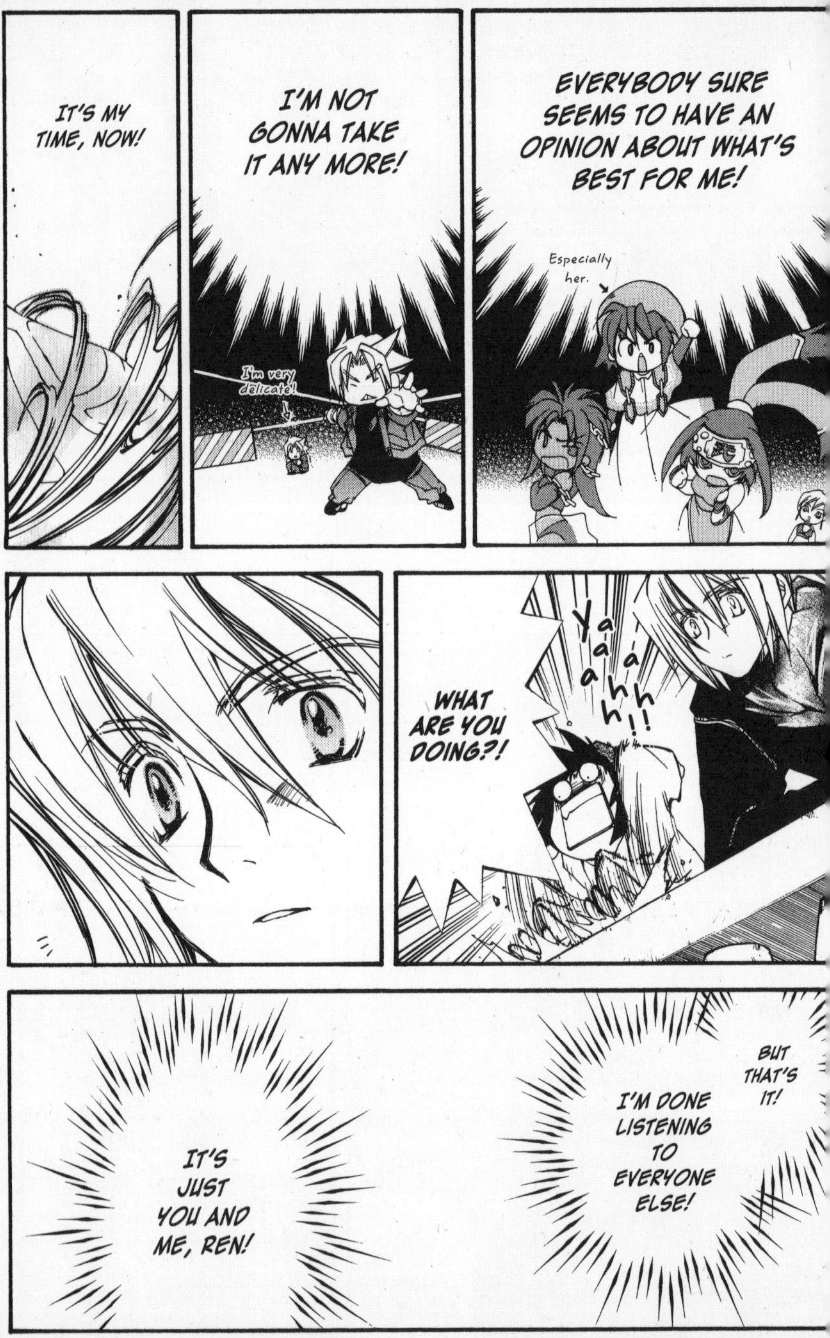
EVERYBODY SURE SEEMS TO HAVE AN OPINION ABOUT WHAT'S BEST FOR ME!
Especially her.
I'M NOT GONNA TAKE IT ANY MORE!
I'm very delicate!
IT'S MY TIME, NOW!
Yaaaahh!!
WHAT ARE YOU DOING?!
BUT THAT'S IT!
I'M DONE LISTENING TO EVERYONE ELSE!
IT'S JUST YOU AND ME, REN!

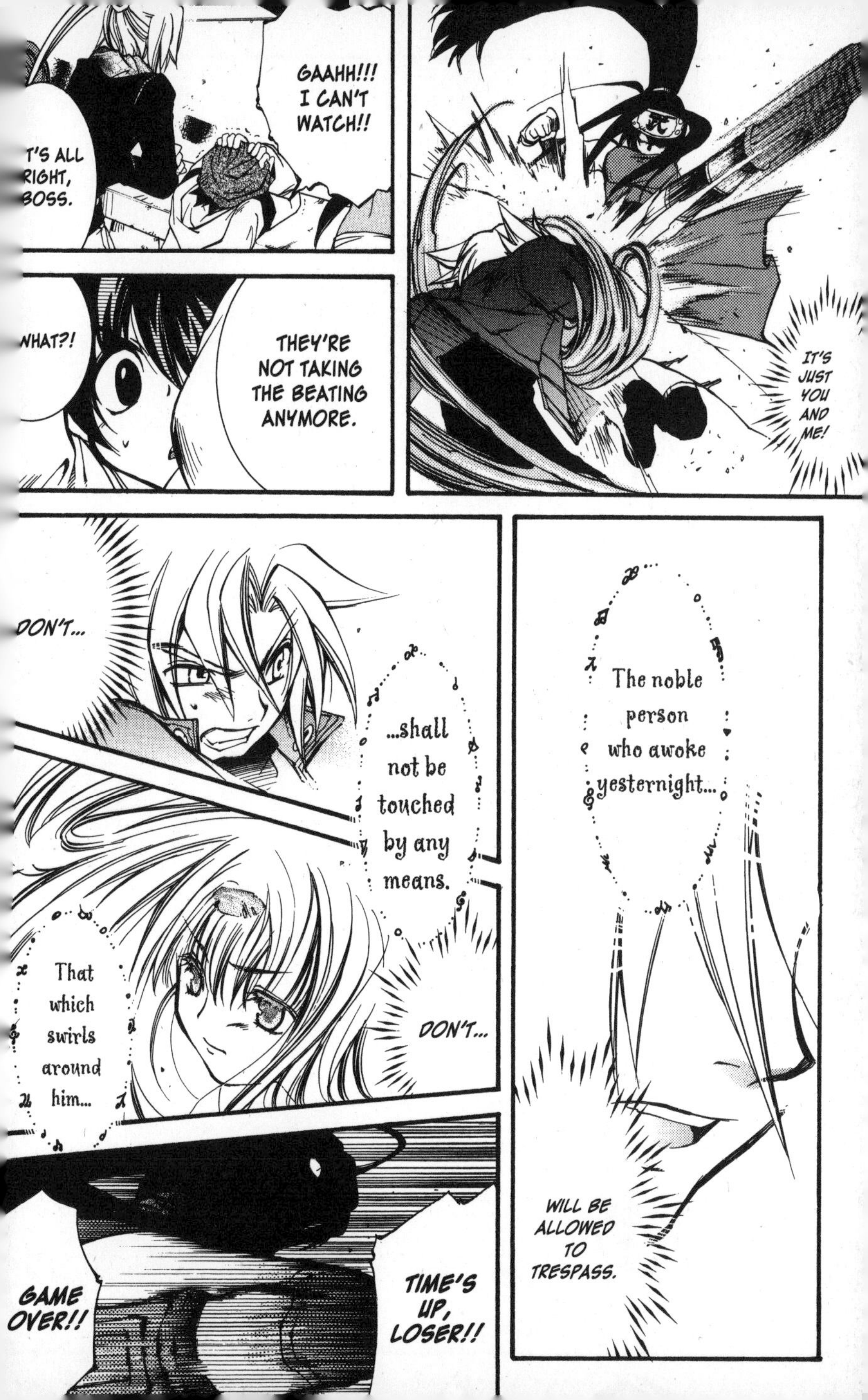
IT'S JUST YOU AND ME!
GAAHH!!! I CAN'T WATCH!!
T'S ALL RIGHT, BOSS.
THEY'RE NOT TAKING THE BEATING ANYMORE.
WHAT?!
The noble person who awoke yesternight...
WILL BE ALLOWED TO TRESPASS.
...shall not be touched by any means.
DON'T...
DON'T...
That which swirls around him...
TIME'S UP, LOSER!!
GAME OVER!!

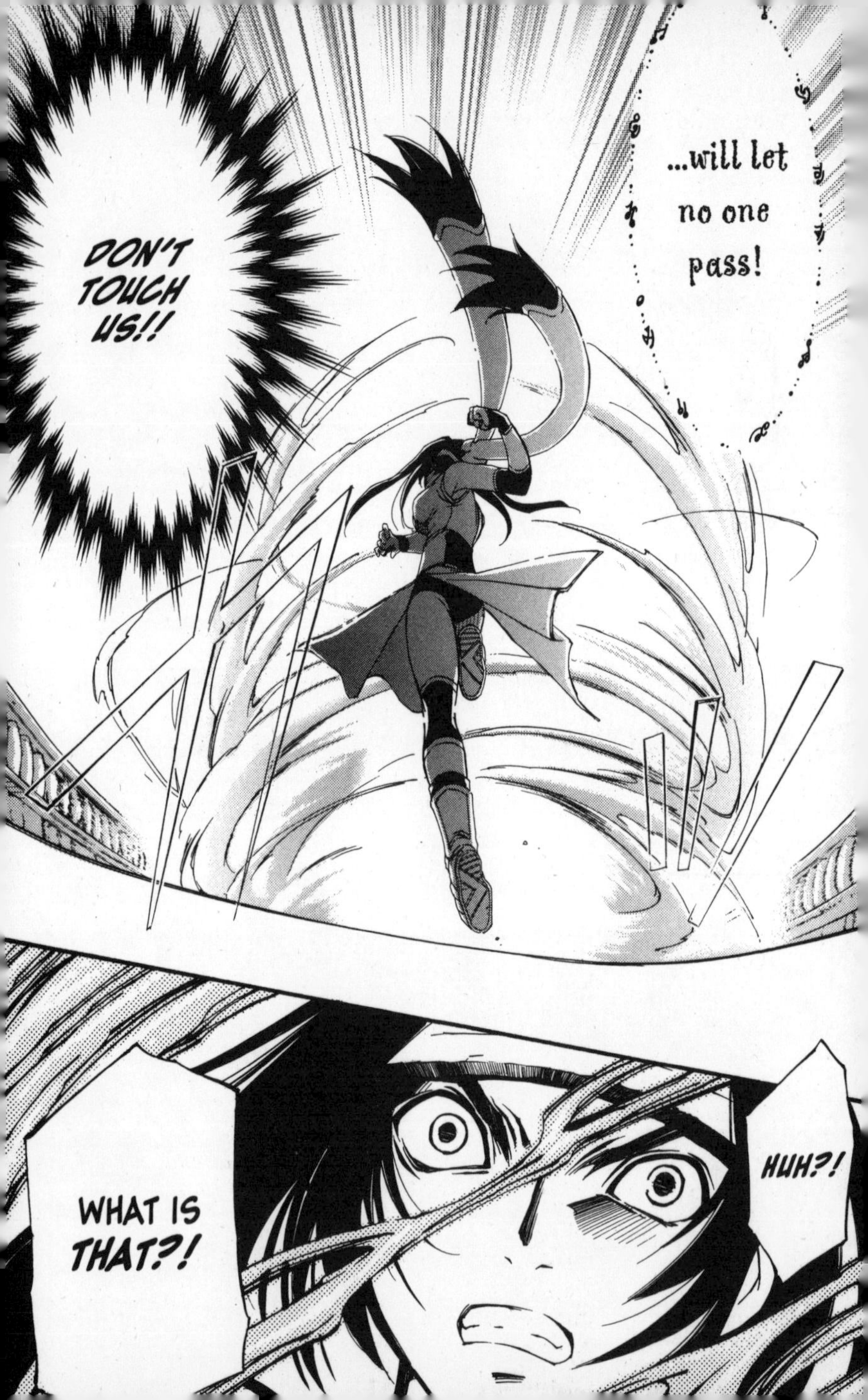
...will let no one pass!
DON'T TOUCH US!!
HUH?!
WHAT IS THAT?!

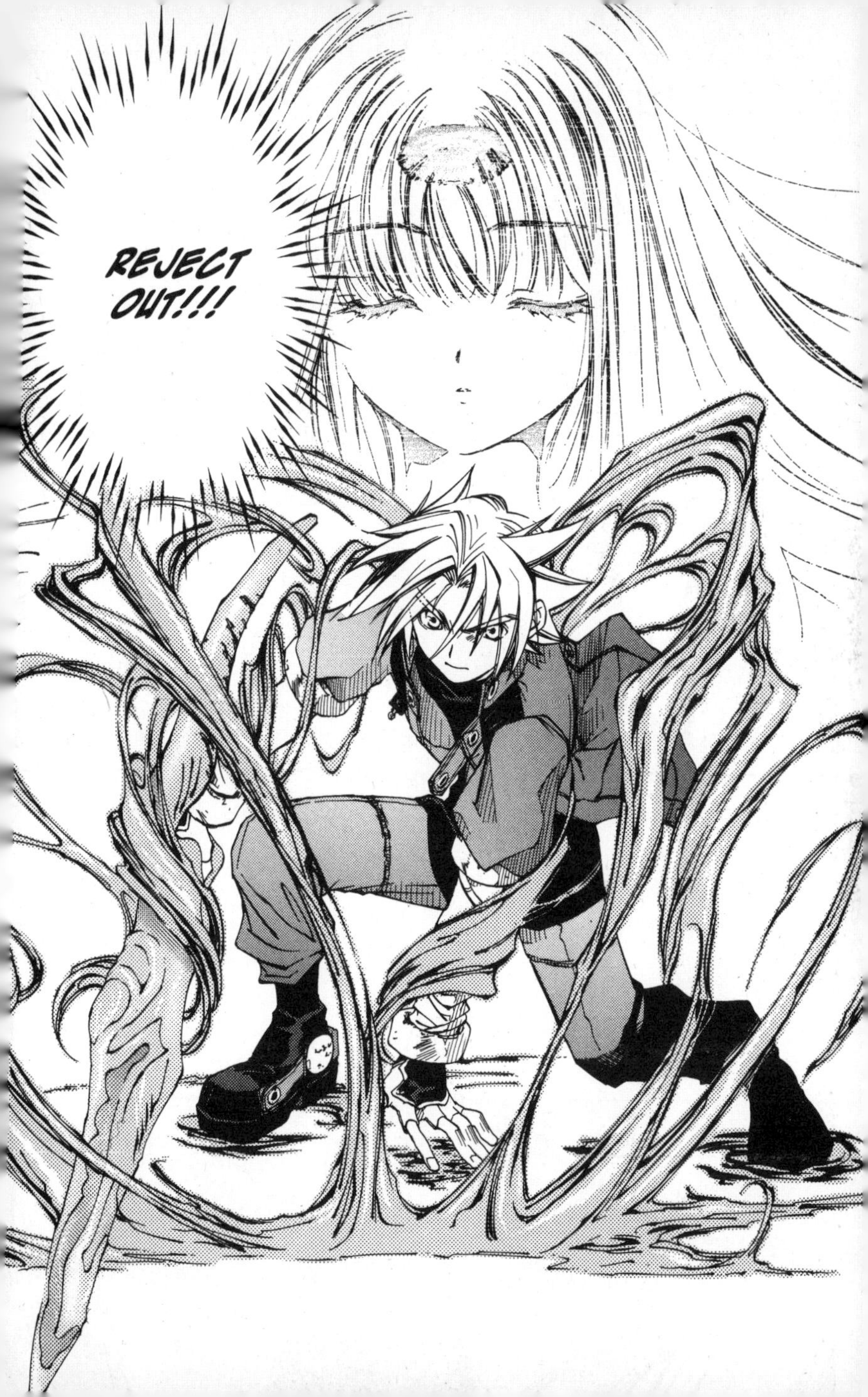
REJECT OUT!!!

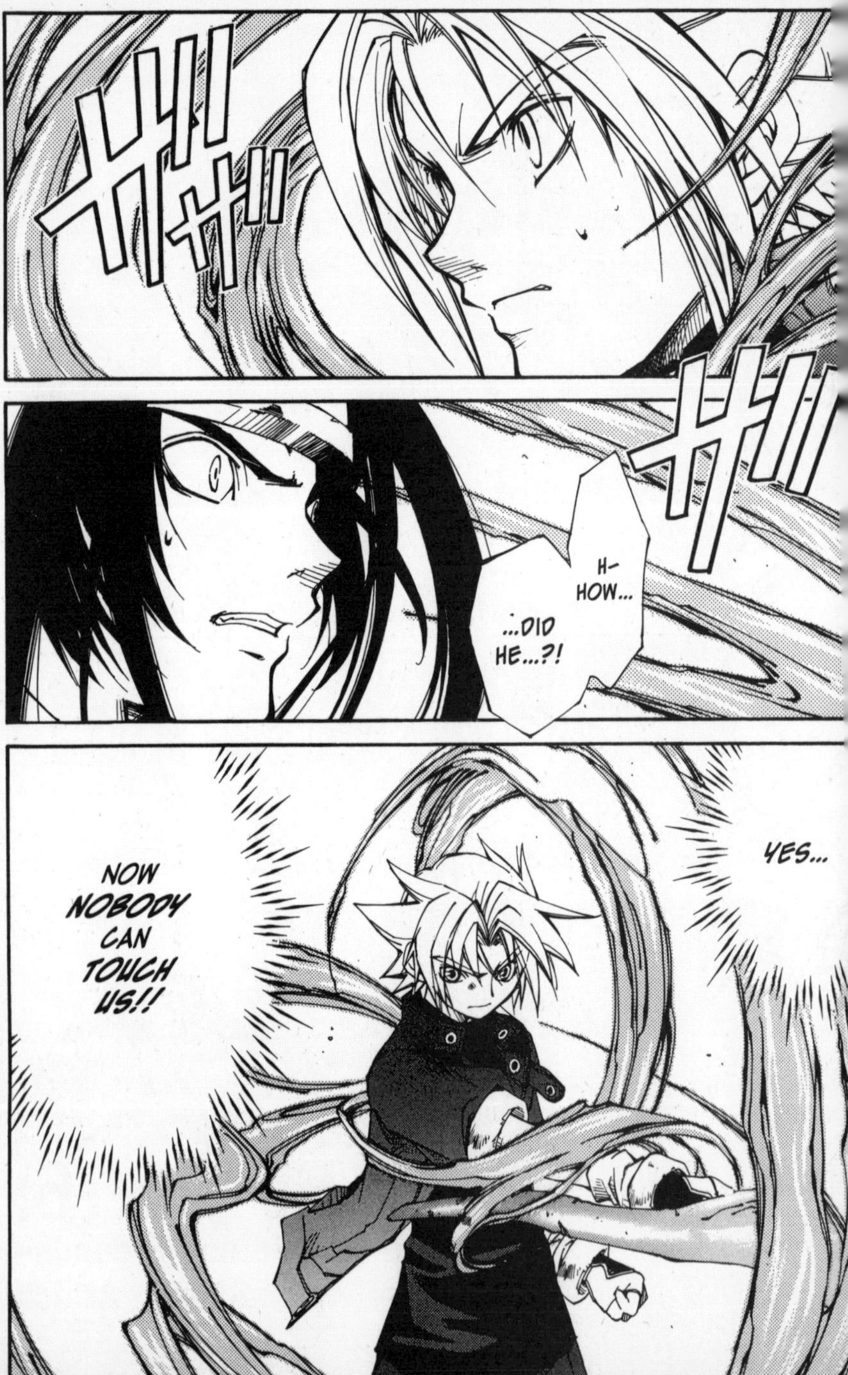
H-
HOW...
...DID
HE...?!
YES...
NOW
NOBODY
CAN
TOUCH
US!!

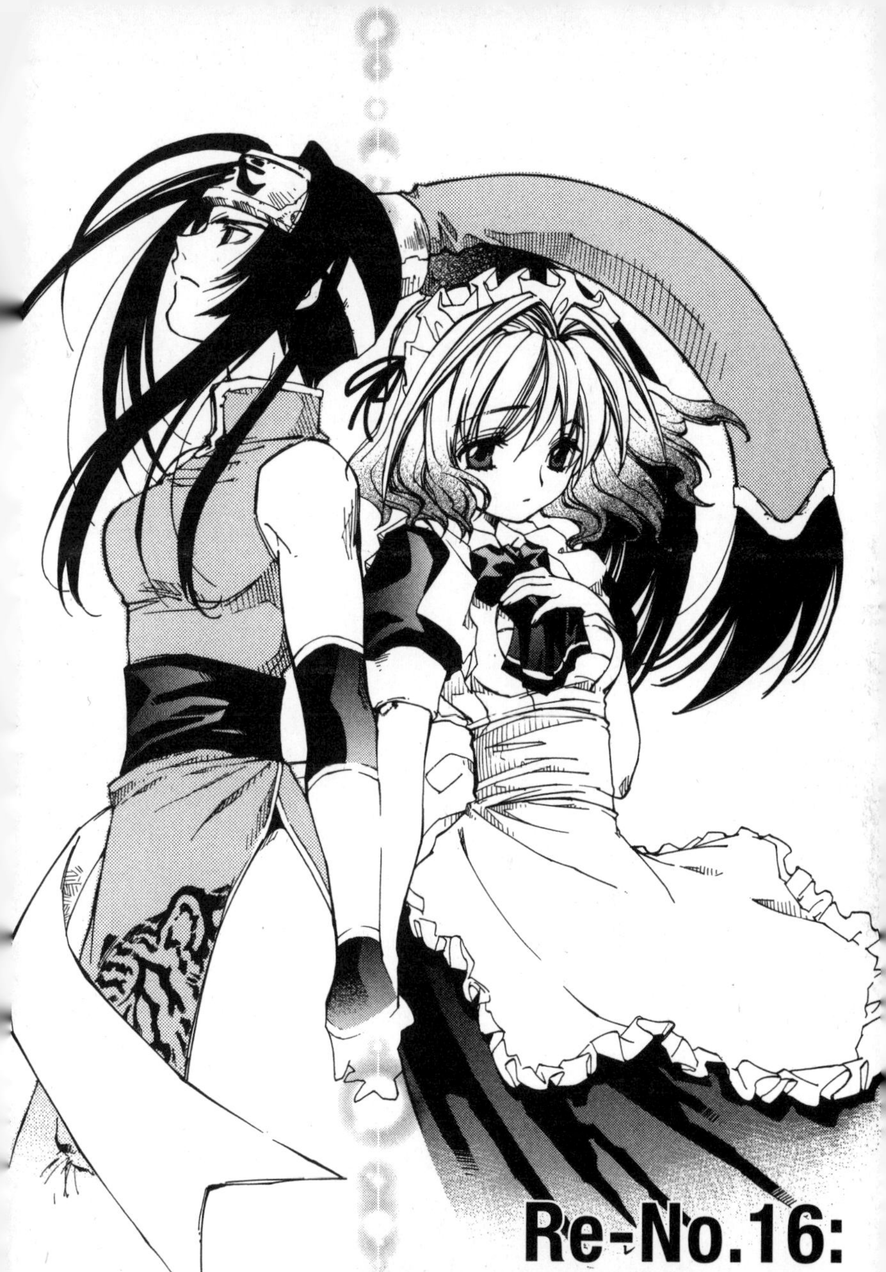

# Re-No.16:
## Milliard Trey Betting Grounds—Skewer Attack

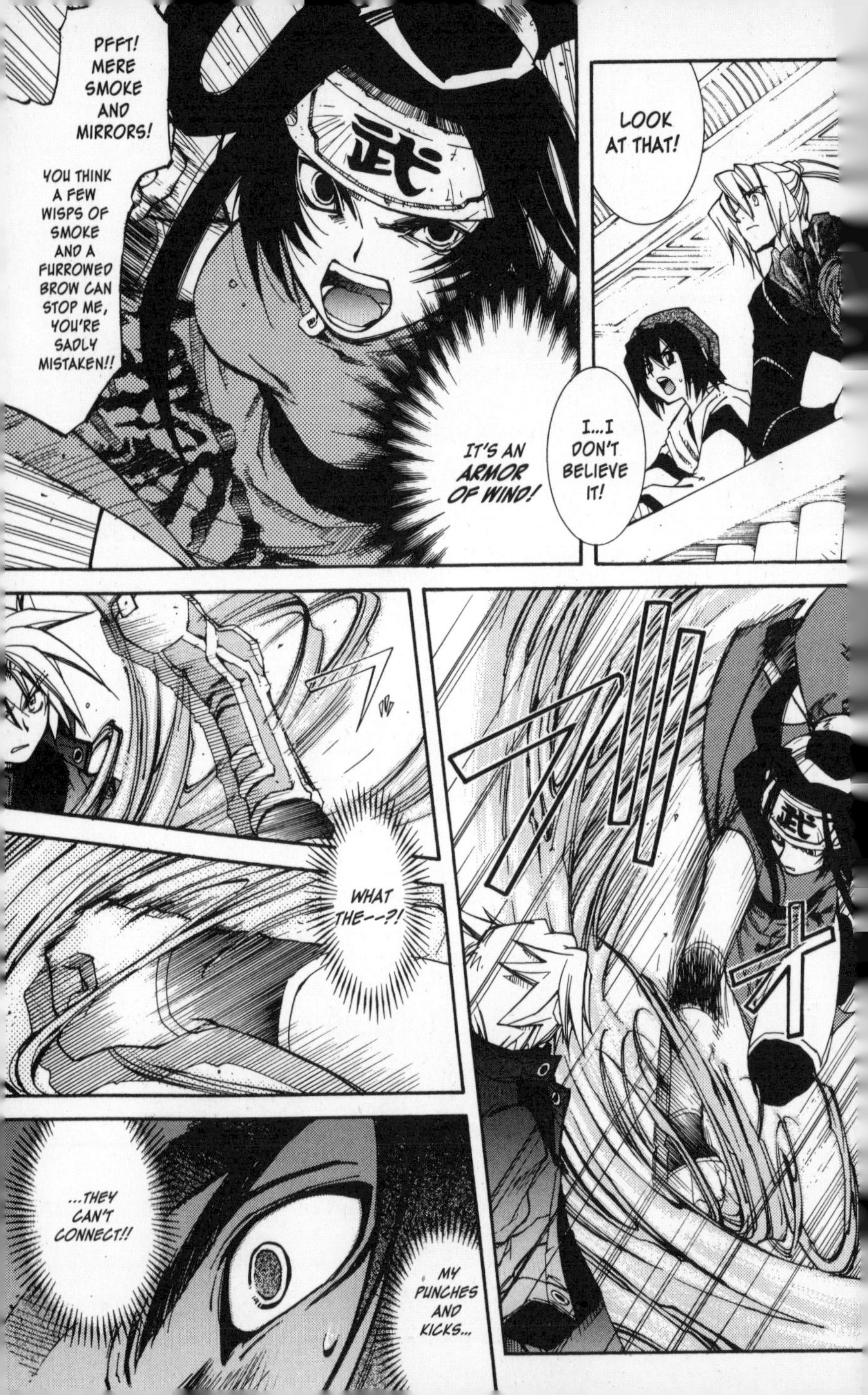
LOOK AT THAT!
I...I DON'T BELIEVE IT!
IT'S AN ARMOR OF WIND!
PFFT! MERE SMOKE AND MIRRORS!
YOU THINK A FEW WISPS OF SMOKE AND A FURROWED BROW CAN STOP ME, YOU'RE SADLY MISTAKEN!!
武
WHAT THE--?!
MY PUNCHES AND KICKS...
...THEY CAN'T CONNECT!!

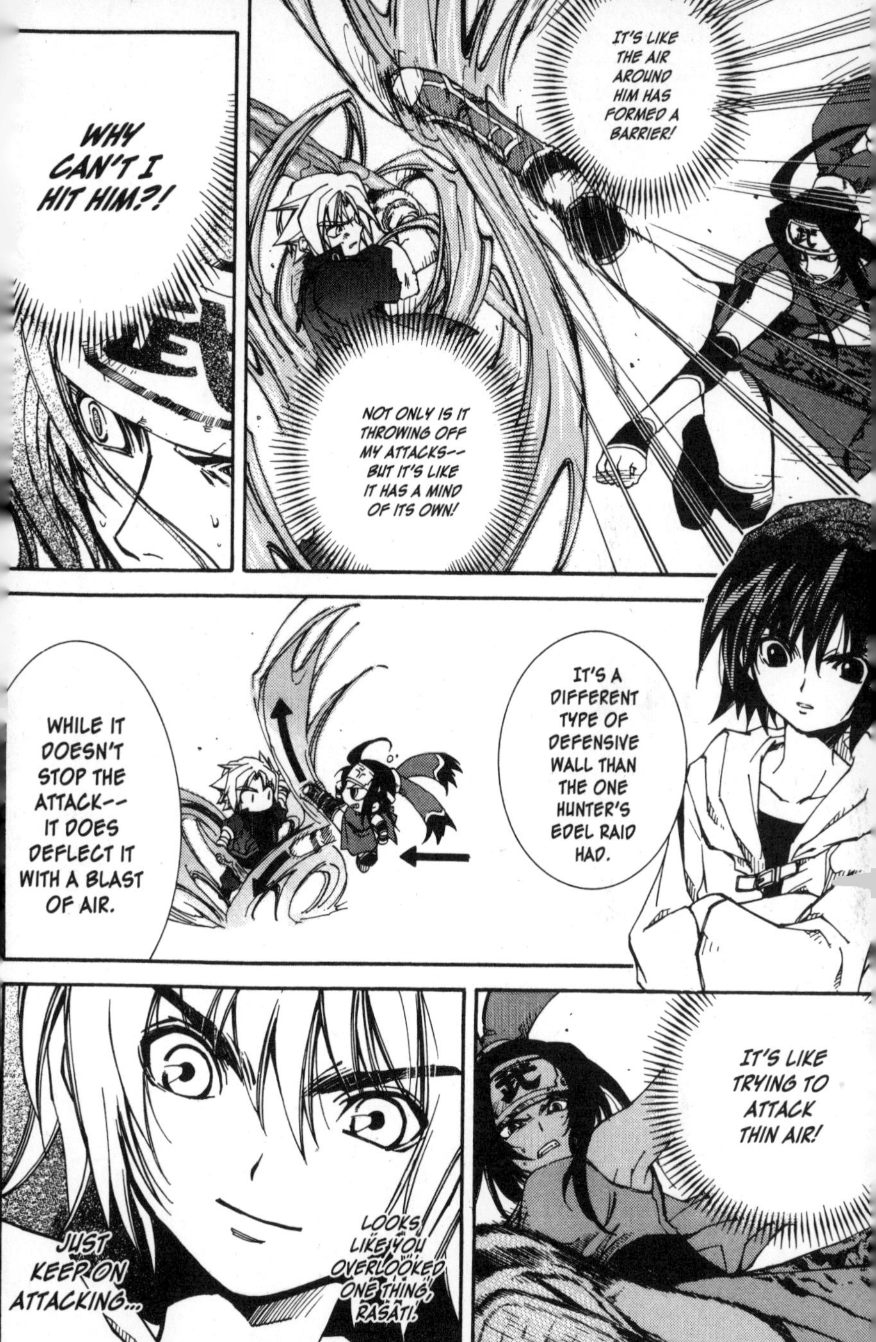
IT'S LIKE THE AIR AROUND HIM HAS FORMED A BARRIER!
NOT ONLY IS IT THROWING OFF MY ATTACKS-- BUT IT'S LIKE IT HAS A MIND OF ITS OWN!
WHY CAN'T I HIT HIM?!
IT'S A DIFFERENT TYPE OF DEFENSIVE WALL THAN THE ONE HUNTER'S EDEL RAID HAD.
WHILE IT DOESN'T STOP THE ATTACK-- IT DOES DEFLECT IT WITH A BLAST OF AIR.
IT'S LIKE TRYING TO ATTACK THIN AIR!
LOOKS LIKE YOU OVERLOOKED ONE THING, RASATI.
JUST KEEP ON ATTACKING...

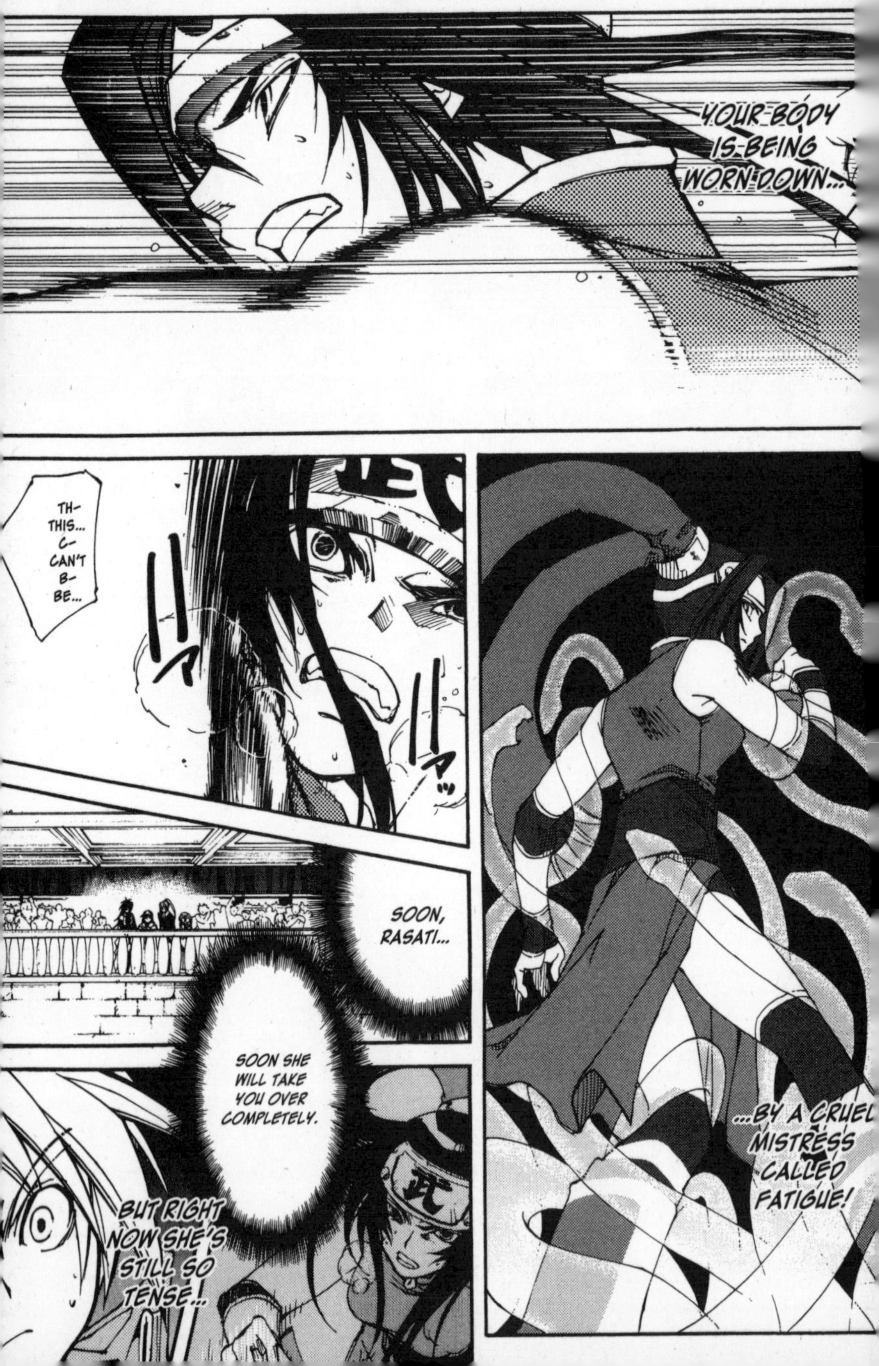

YOUR BODY IS BEING WORN DOWN...
...BY A CRUEL MISTRESS CALLED FATIGUE!
TH-THIS... C-CAN'T B-BE...
SOON, RASATI...
SOON SHE WILL TAKE YOU OVER COMPLETELY.
BUT RIGHT NOW SHE'S STILL SO TENSE...

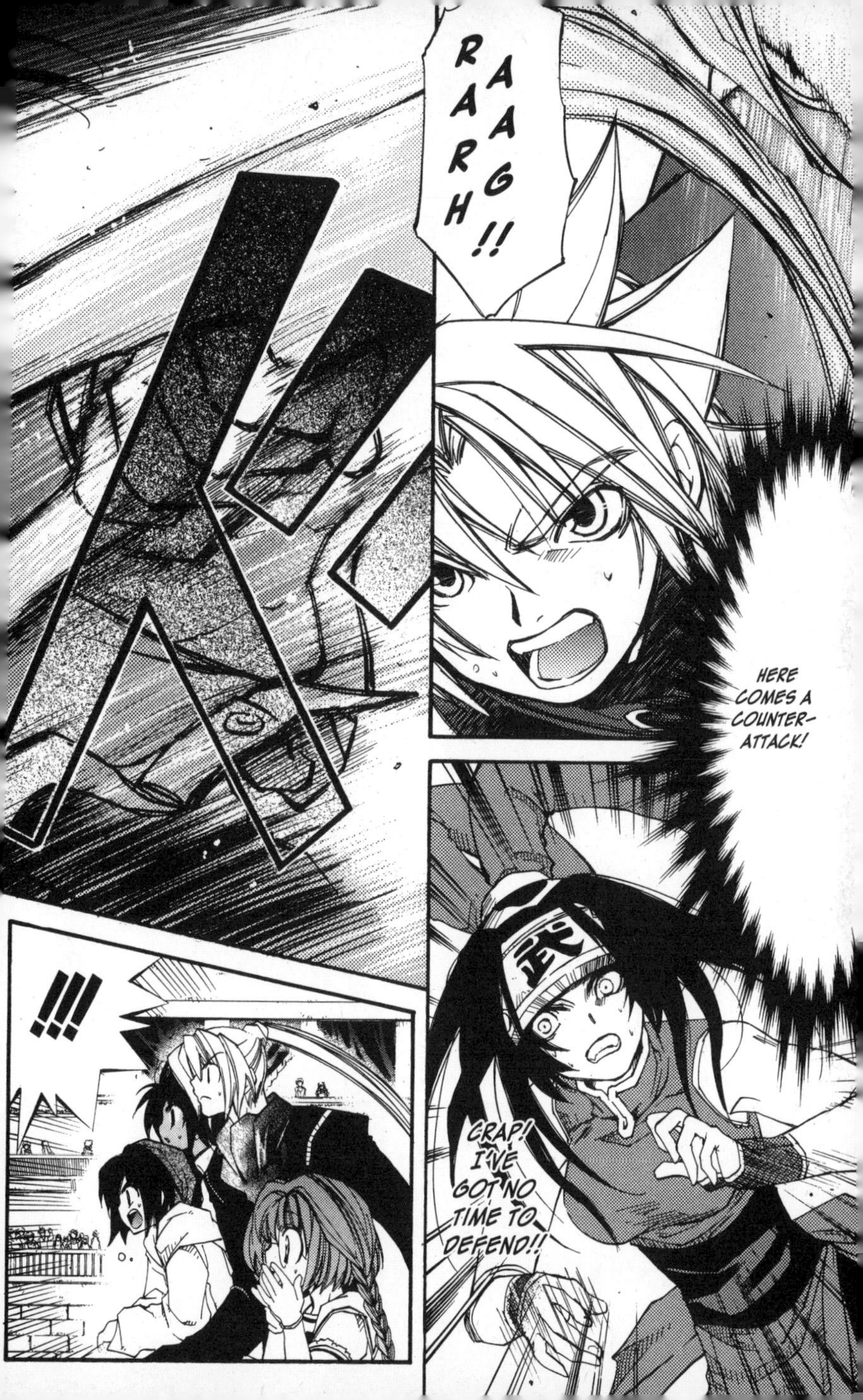
RAAARGH!!
HERE COMES A COUNTER-ATTACK!
CRAP! I'VE GOT NO TIME TO DEFEND!!
!!!

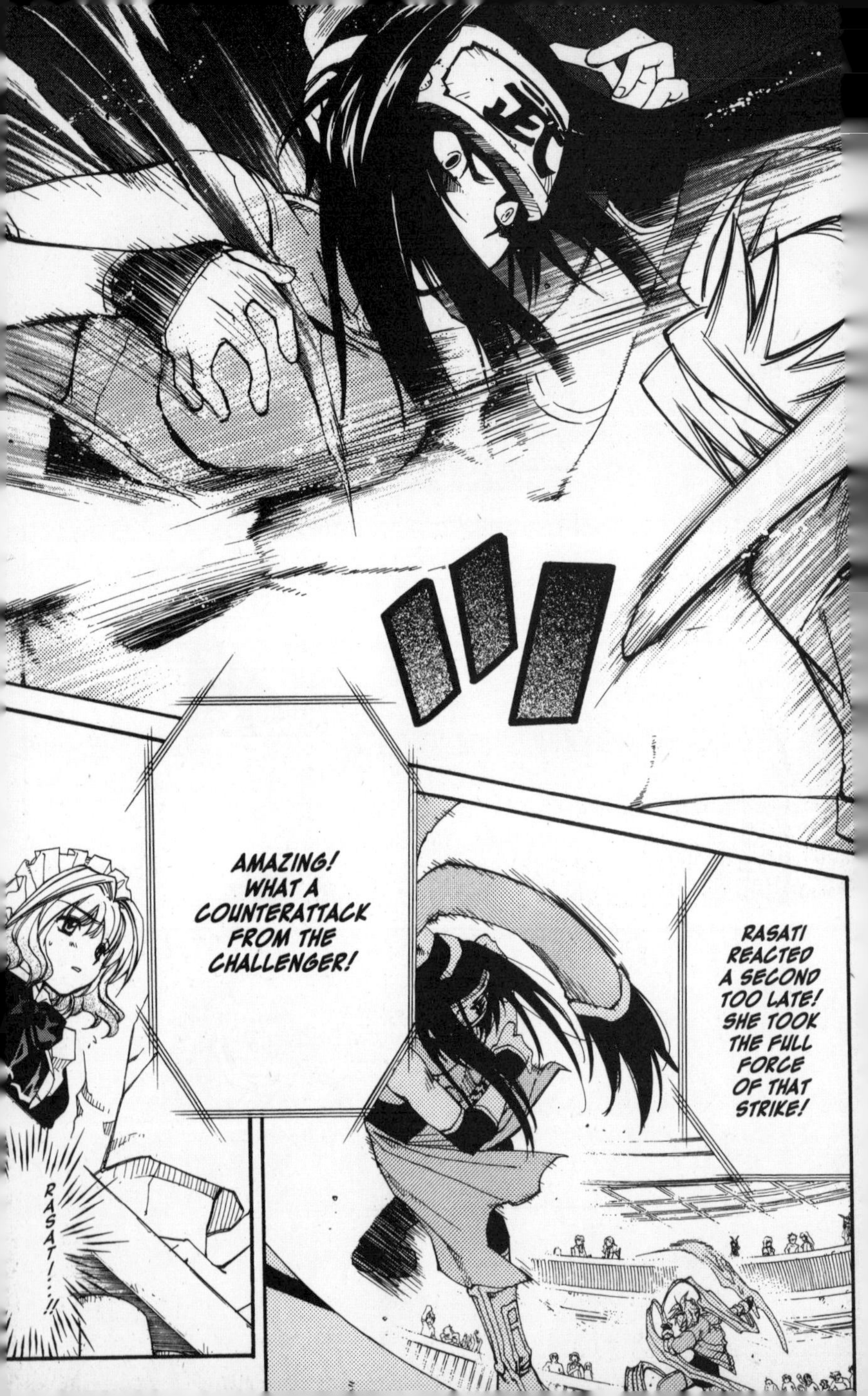
AMAZING! WHAT A COUNTERATTACK FROM THE CHALLENGER!
RASATI REACTED A SECOND TOO LATE! SHE TOOK THE FULL FORCE OF THAT STRIKE!
RASATI...!!

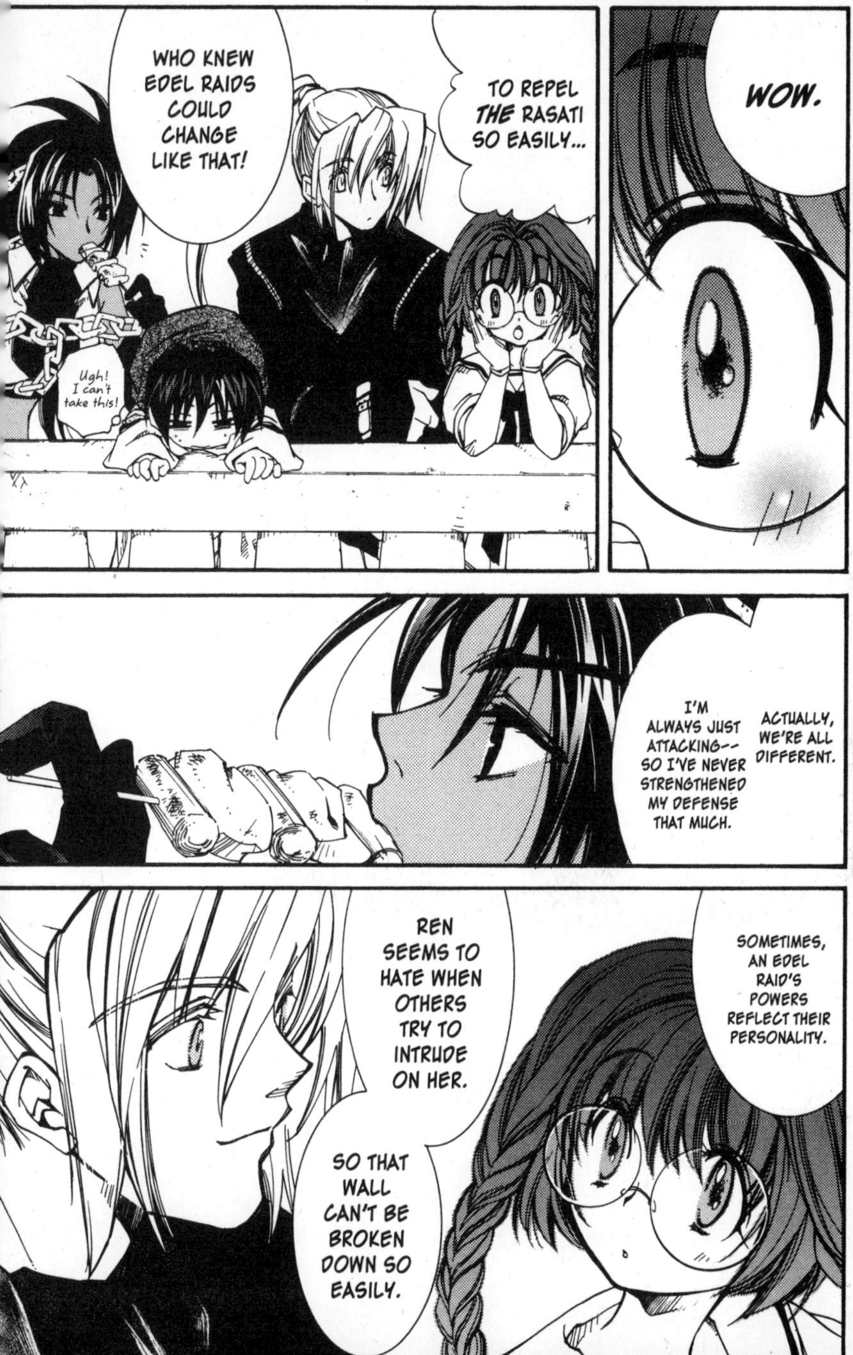
WOW.
TO REPEL *THE* RASATI SO EASILY...
WHO KNEW EDEL RAIDS COULD CHANGE LIKE THAT!
Ugh! I can't take this!
ACTUALLY, WE'RE ALL DIFFERENT.
I'M ALWAYS JUST ATTACKING-- SO I'VE NEVER STRENGTHENED MY DEFENSE THAT MUCH.
SOMETIMES, AN EDEL RAID'S POWERS REFLECT THEIR PERSONALITY.
REN SEEMS TO HATE WHEN OTHERS TRY TO INTRUDE ON HER.
SO THAT WALL CAN'T BE BROKEN DOWN SO EASILY.

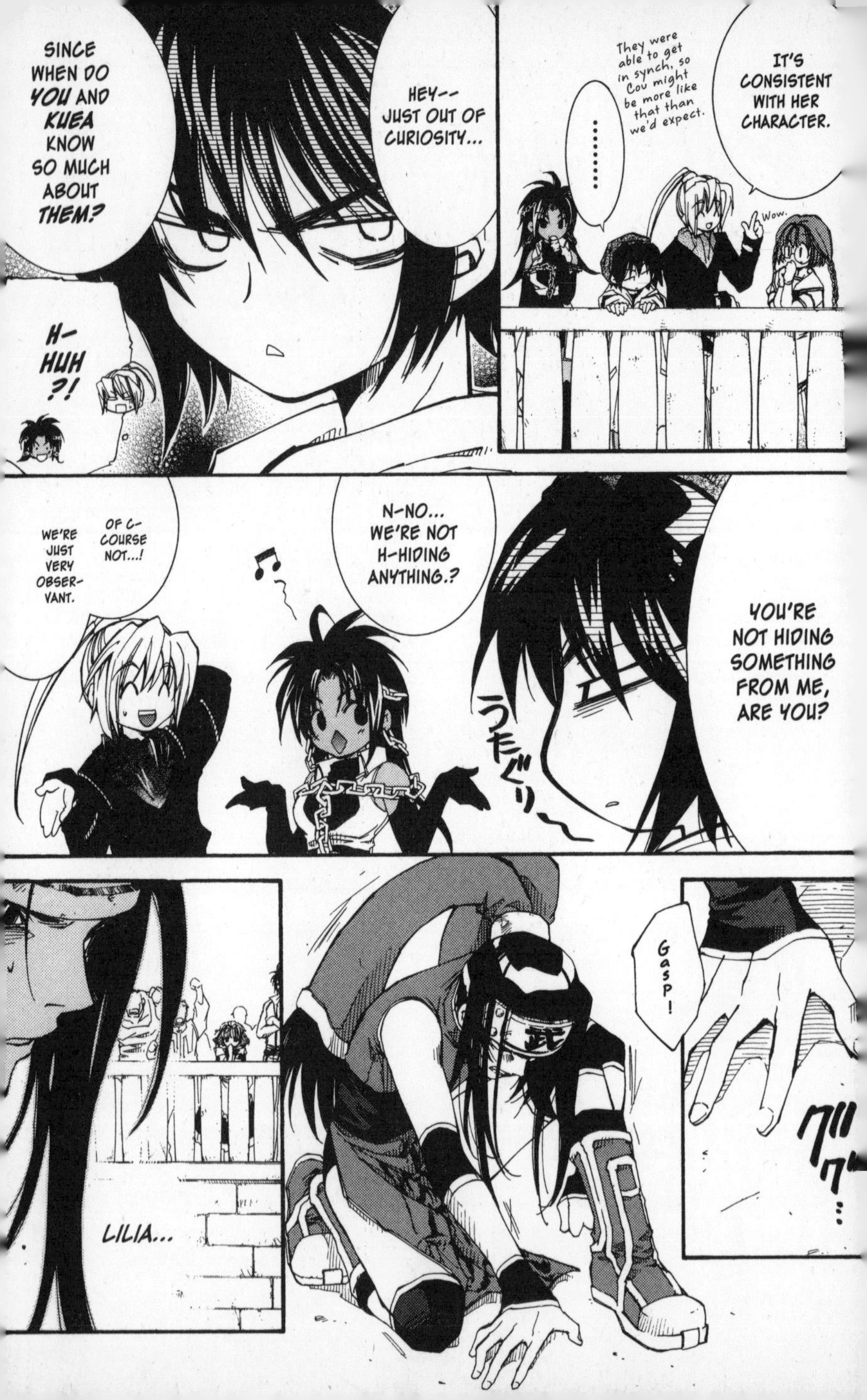
IT'S CONSISTENT WITH HER CHARACTER.
They were able to get in synch, so Cou might be more like that than we'd expect.
......
Wow.
HEY-- JUST OUT OF CURIOSITY...
SINCE WHEN DO YOU AND KUEA KNOW SO MUCH ABOUT THEM?
H-HUH?!
YOU'RE NOT HIDING SOMETHING FROM ME, ARE YOU?
うたぐりー
N-NO... WE'RE NOT H-HIDING ANYTHING.?
OF C-COURSE NOT...!
WE'RE JUST VERY OBSERVANT.
Gasp!
LILIA...

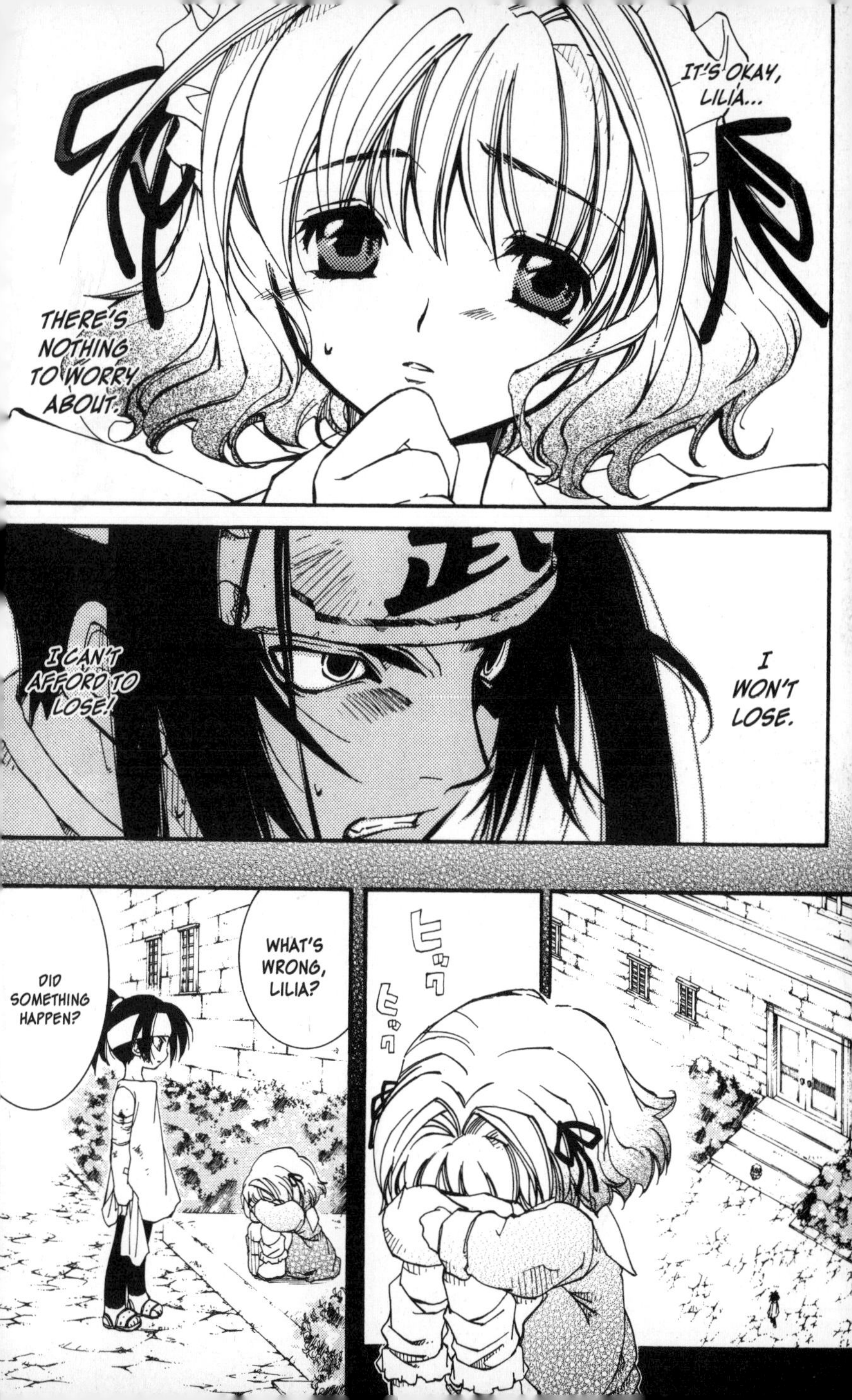
IT'S OKAY, LILIA...
THERE'S NOTHING TO WORRY ABOUT.
I WON'T LOSE.
I CAN'T AFFORD TO LOSE!
ヒック
ヒック
WHAT'S WRONG, LILIA?
DID SOMETHING HAPPEN?

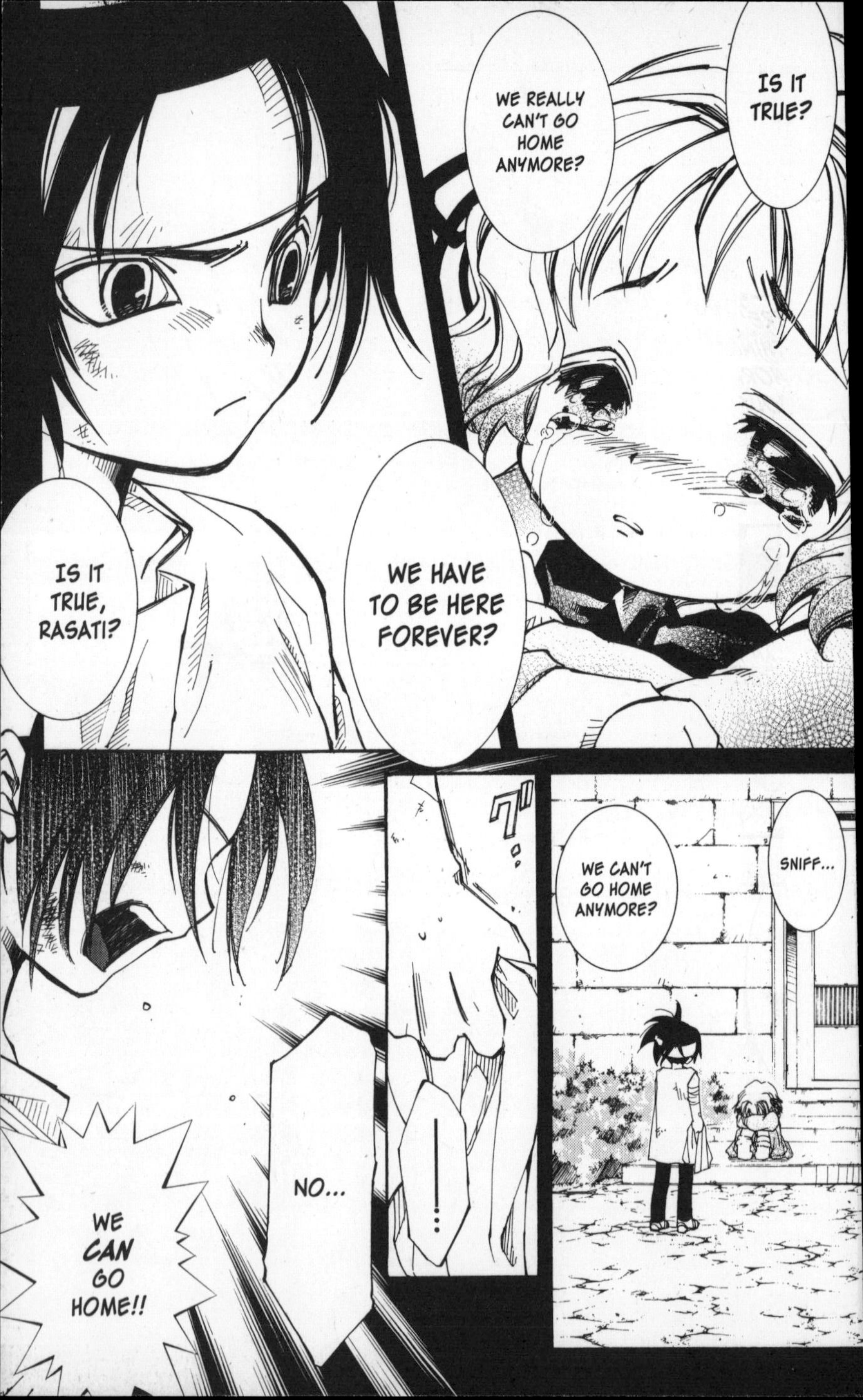
IS IT TRUE?
WE REALLY CAN'T GO HOME ANYMORE?
WE HAVE TO BE HERE FOREVER?
IS IT TRUE, RASATI?
SNIFF...
WE CAN'T GO HOME ANYMORE?
NO...
WE CAN GO HOME!!

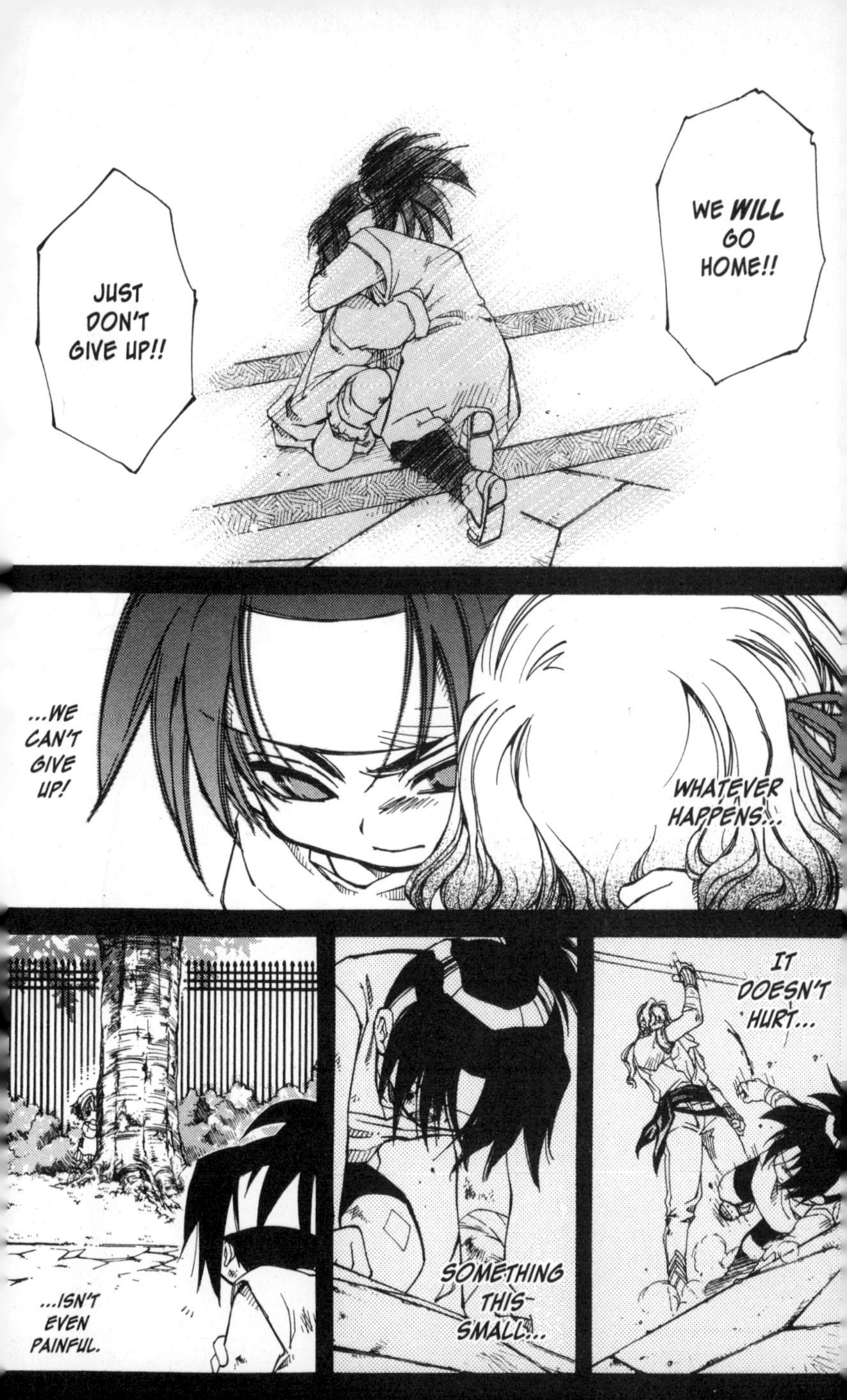
WE WILL GO HOME!!
JUST DON'T GIVE UP!!
WHATEVER HAPPENS...
...WE CAN'T GIVE UP!
IT DOESN'T HURT...
SOMETHING THIS SMALL...
...ISN'T EVEN PAINFUL.

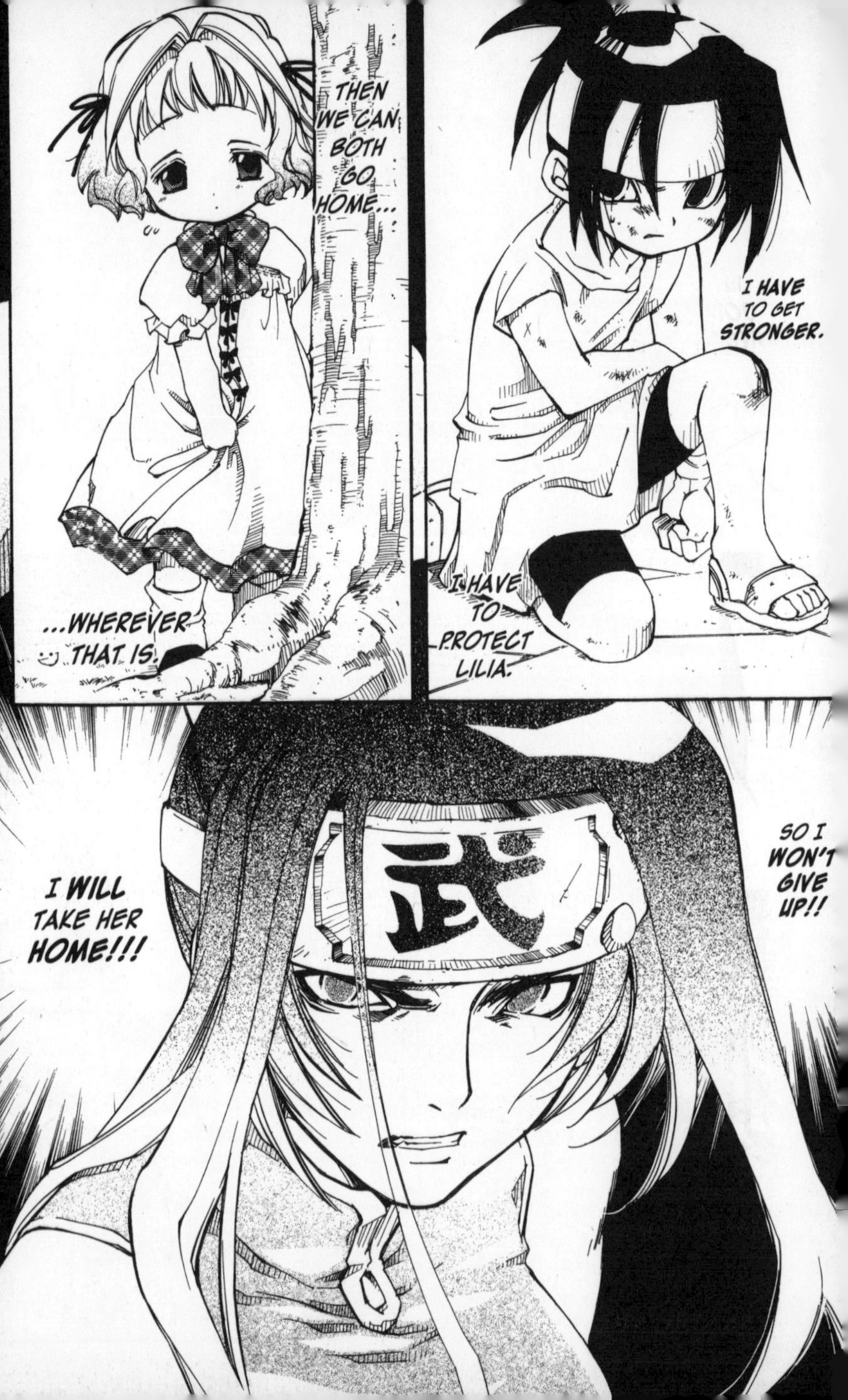
I HAVE TO GET STRONGER.
I HAVE TO PROTECT LILIA.
THEN WE CAN BOTH GO HOME...
...WHEREVER THAT IS.
SO I WON'T GIVE UP!!
I WILL TAKE HER HOME!!!

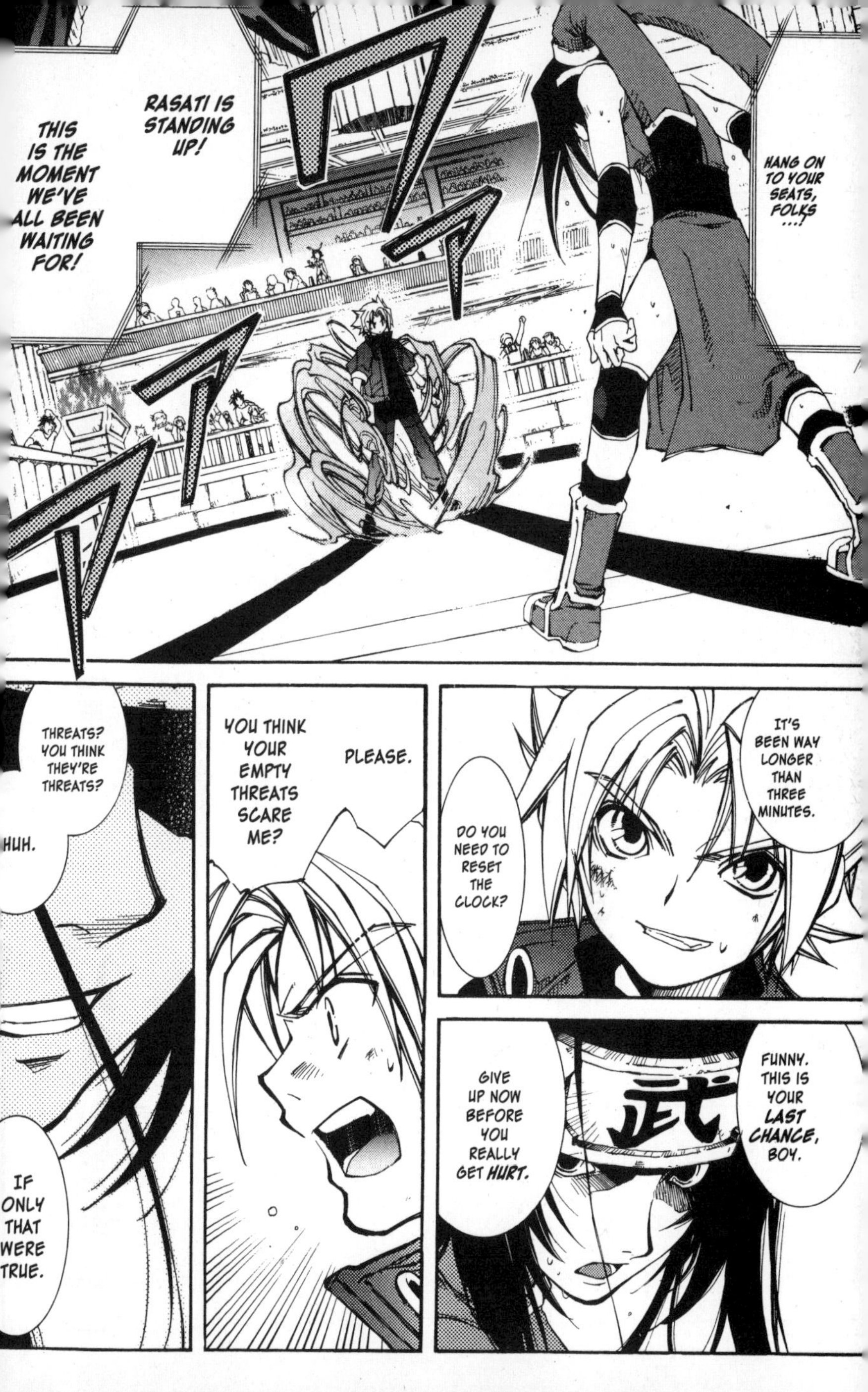
HANG ON TO YOUR SEATS, FOLKS...!
RASATI IS STANDING UP!
THIS IS THE MOMENT WE'VE ALL BEEN WAITING FOR!
IT'S BEEN WAY LONGER THAN THREE MINUTES.
DO YOU NEED TO RESET THE CLOCK?
FUNNY. THIS IS YOUR *LAST CHANCE*, BOY.
GIVE UP NOW BEFORE YOU REALLY GET *HURT*.
PLEASE.
YOU THINK YOUR EMPTY THREATS SCARE ME?
THREATS? YOU THINK THEY'RE THREATS?
HUH.
IF ONLY THAT WERE TRUE.

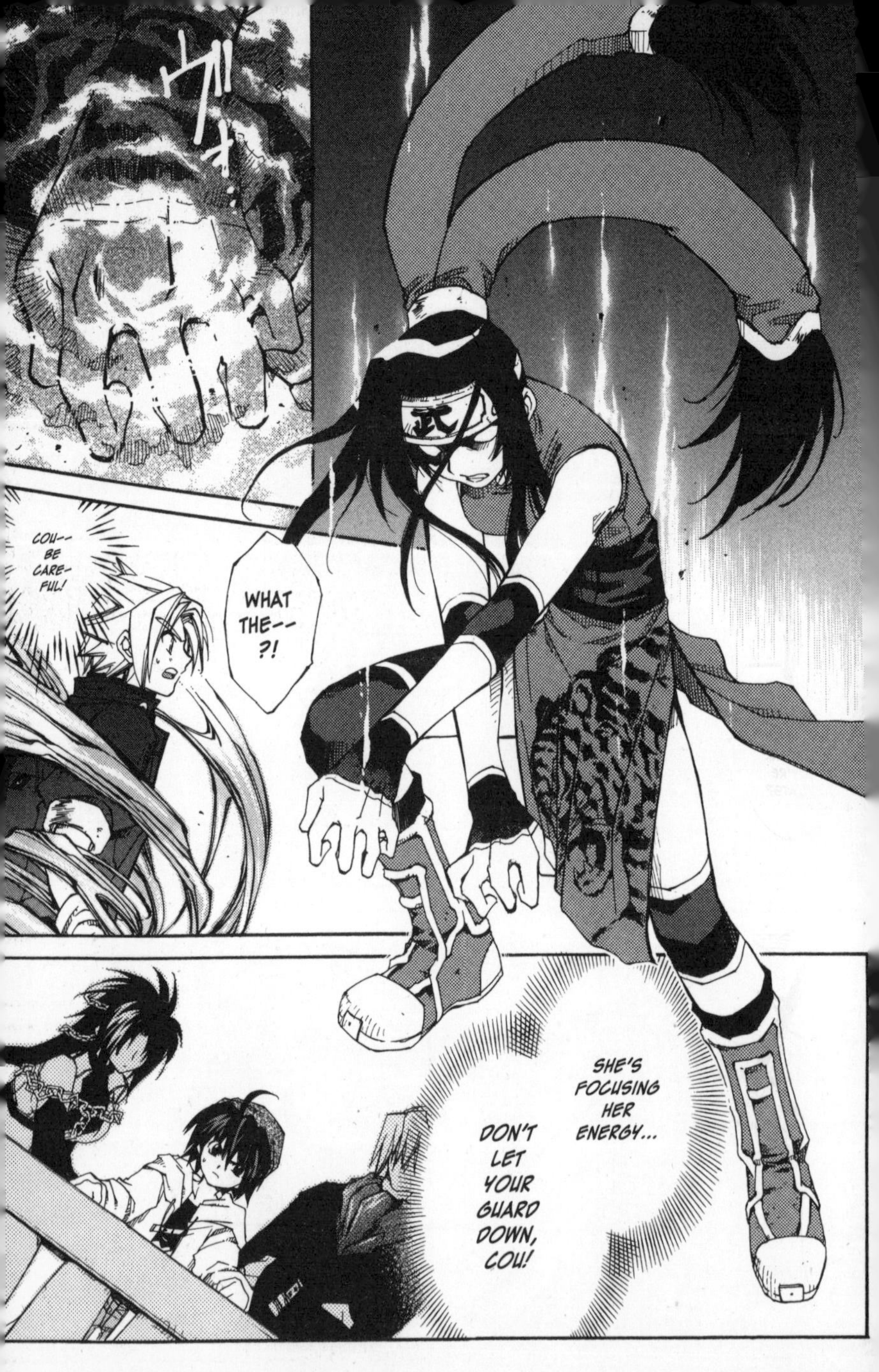
ヴォ
WHAT THE--?!
COU-- BE CAREFUL!
SHE'S FOCUSING HER ENERGY...
DON'T LET YOUR GUARD DOWN, COU!

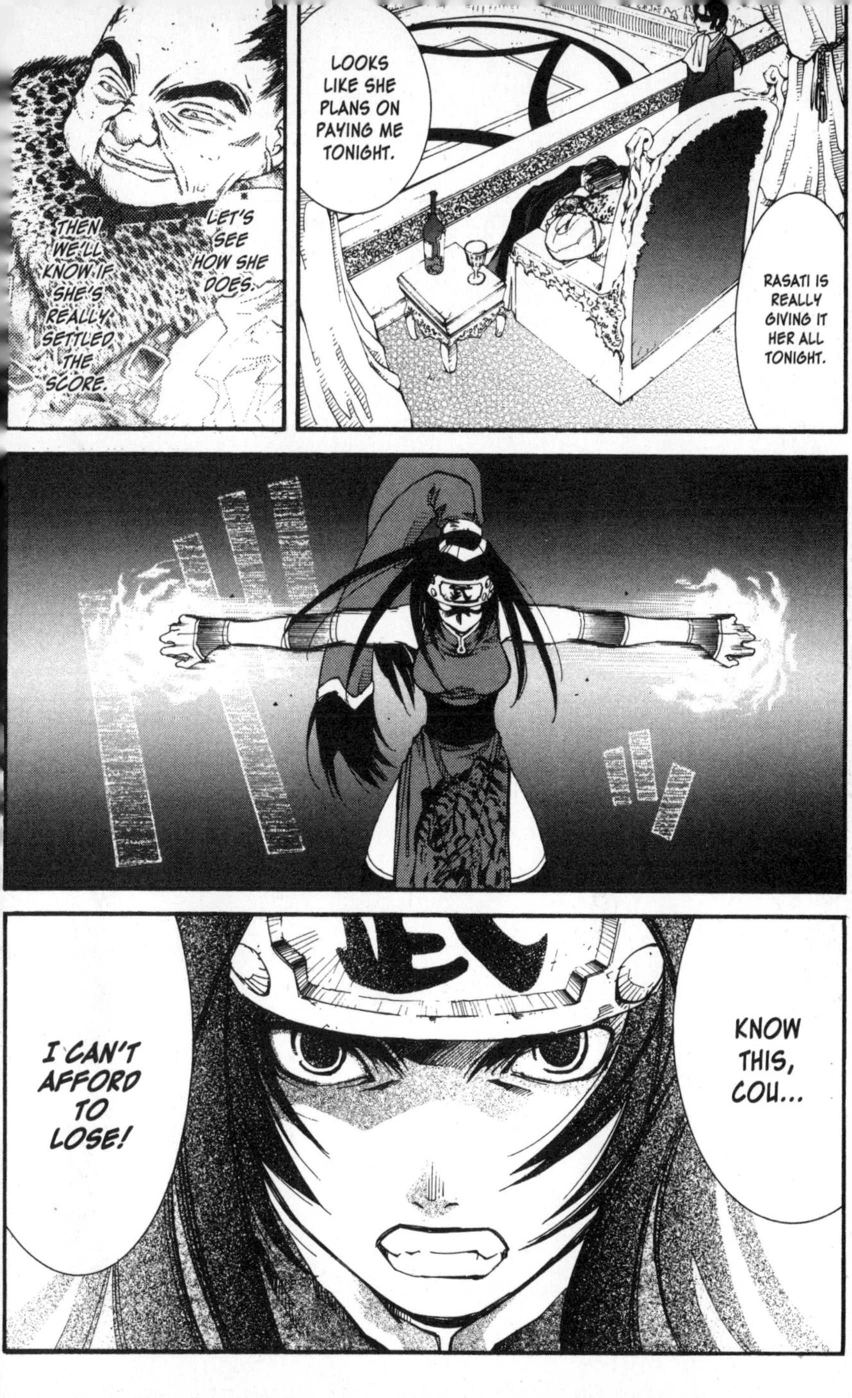
RASATI IS REALLY GIVING IT HER ALL TONIGHT.
LOOKS LIKE SHE PLANS ON PAYING ME TONIGHT.
LET'S SEE HOW SHE DOES.
THEN WE'LL KNOW IF SHE'S REALLY SETTLED THE SCORE.
KNOW THIS, COU...
I CAN'T AFFORD TO LOSE!

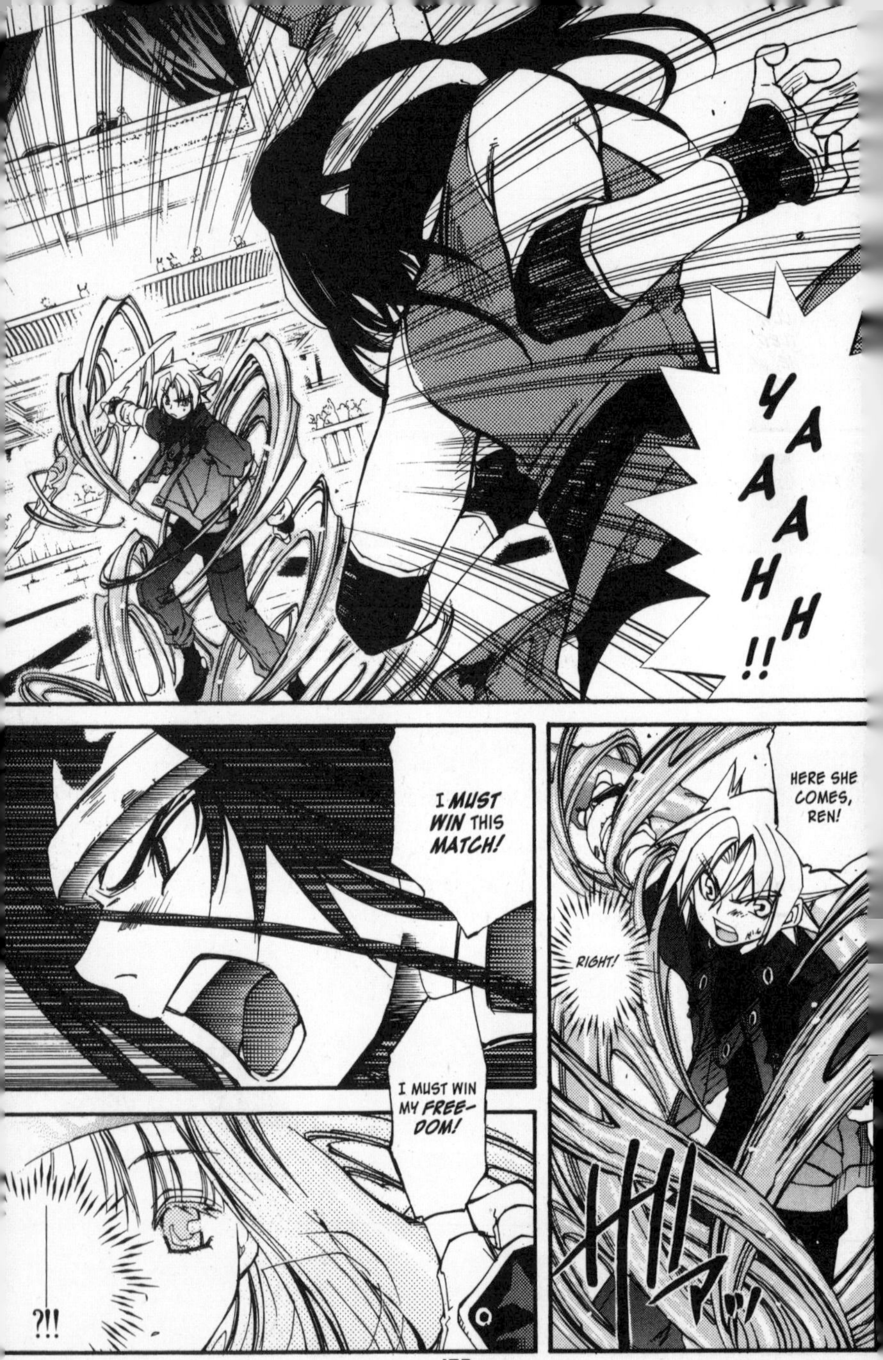
YAAAHH!!
HERE SHE COMES, REN!
RIGHT!
I MUST WIN THIS MATCH!
I MUST WIN MY FREE-DOM!
——?!!

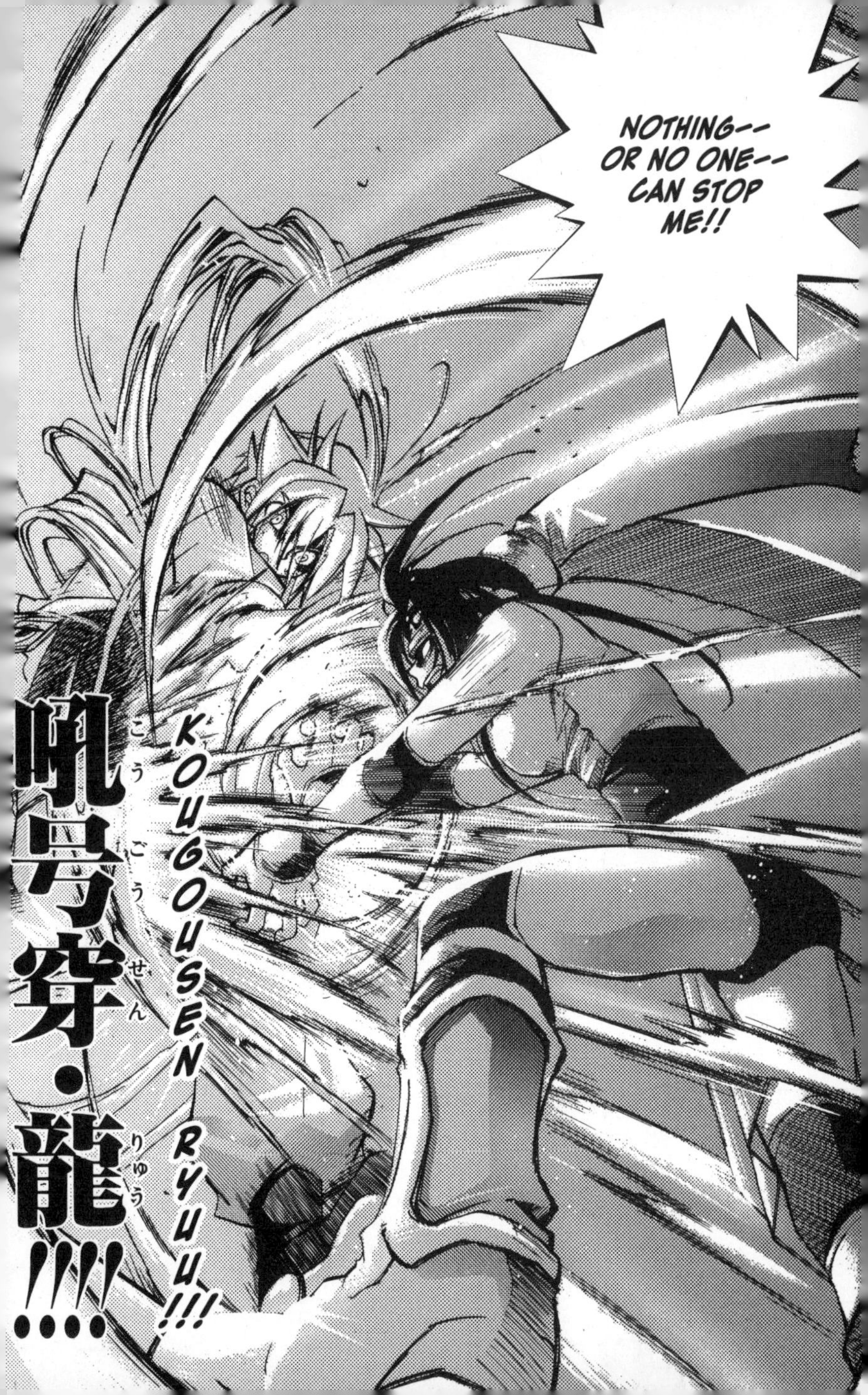

NOTHING--
OR NO ONE--
CAN STOP
ME!!
KOUGOUSEN RYUU!!!
吼号穿・龍!!!!
こうごうせんりゅう

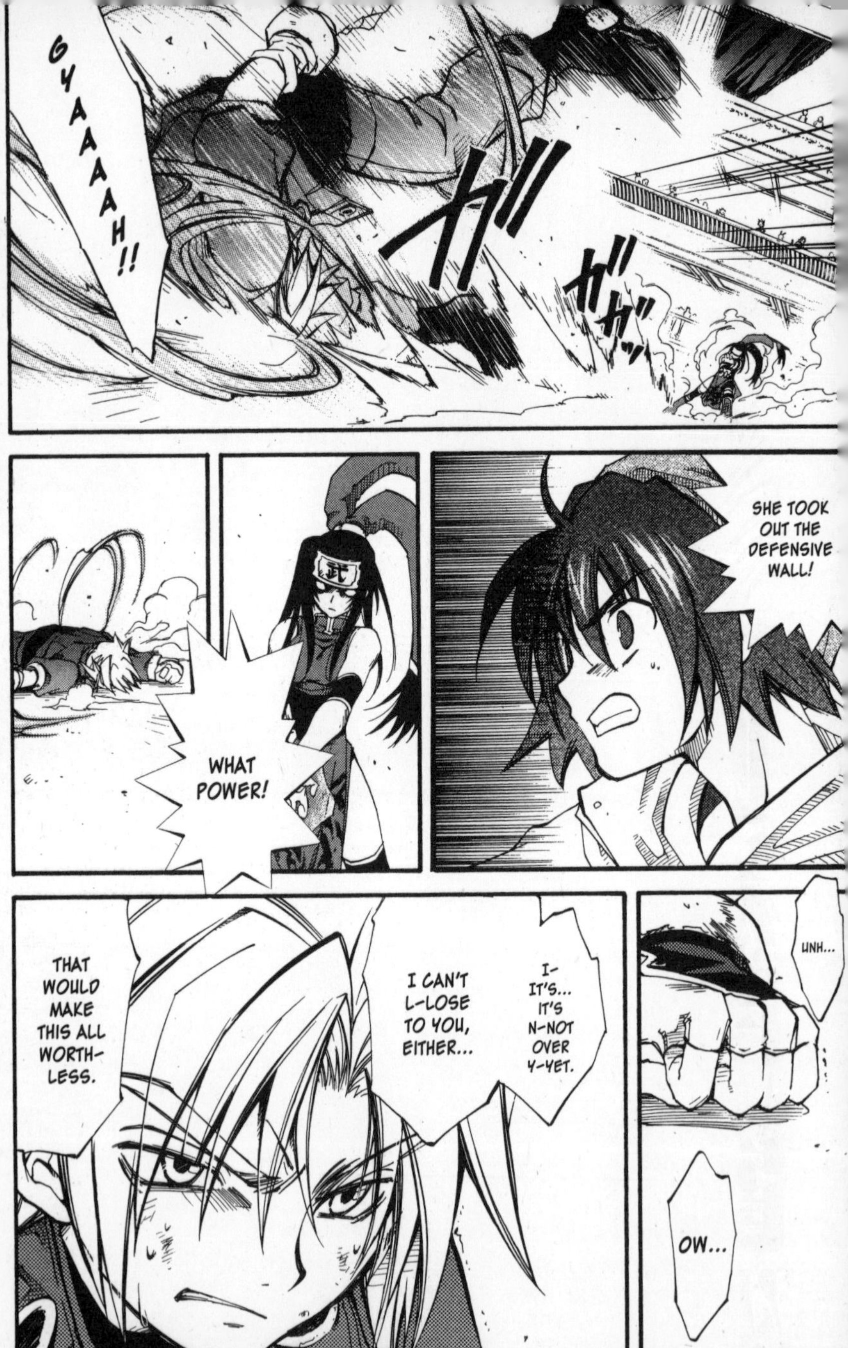
GYAAAAH!!
SHE TOOK OUT THE DEFENSIVE WALL!
WHAT POWER!
UNH...
OW...
I- IT'S... IT'S N-NOT OVER Y-YET.
I CAN'T L-LOSE TO YOU, EITHER...
THAT WOULD MAKE THIS ALL WORTH-LESS.

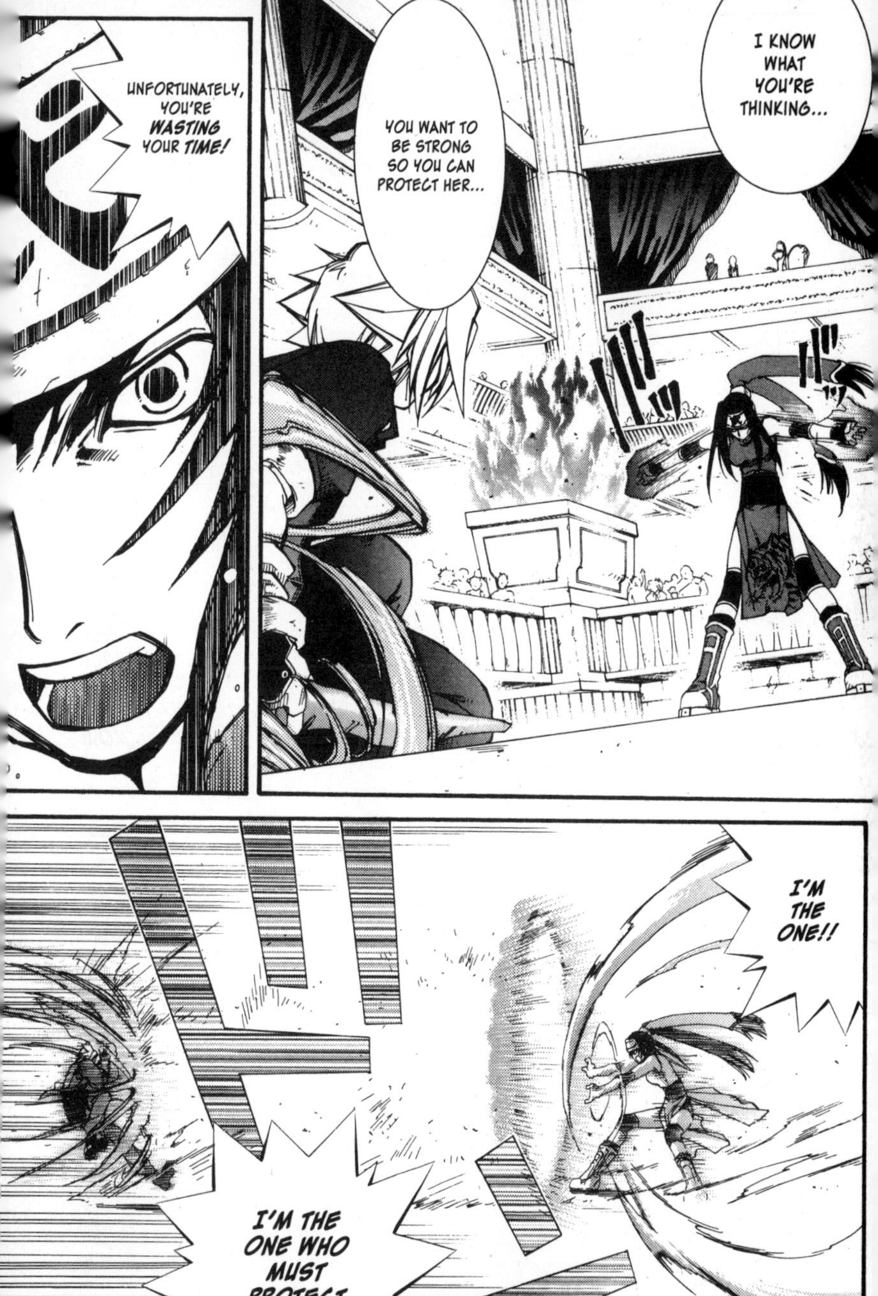
I KNOW WHAT YOU'RE THINKING...
YOU WANT TO BE STRONG SO YOU CAN PROTECT HER...
UNFORTUNATELY, YOU'RE *WASTING* YOUR *TIME!*
*I'M THE ONE!!*
*I'M THE ONE WHO MUST PROTECT HER!*

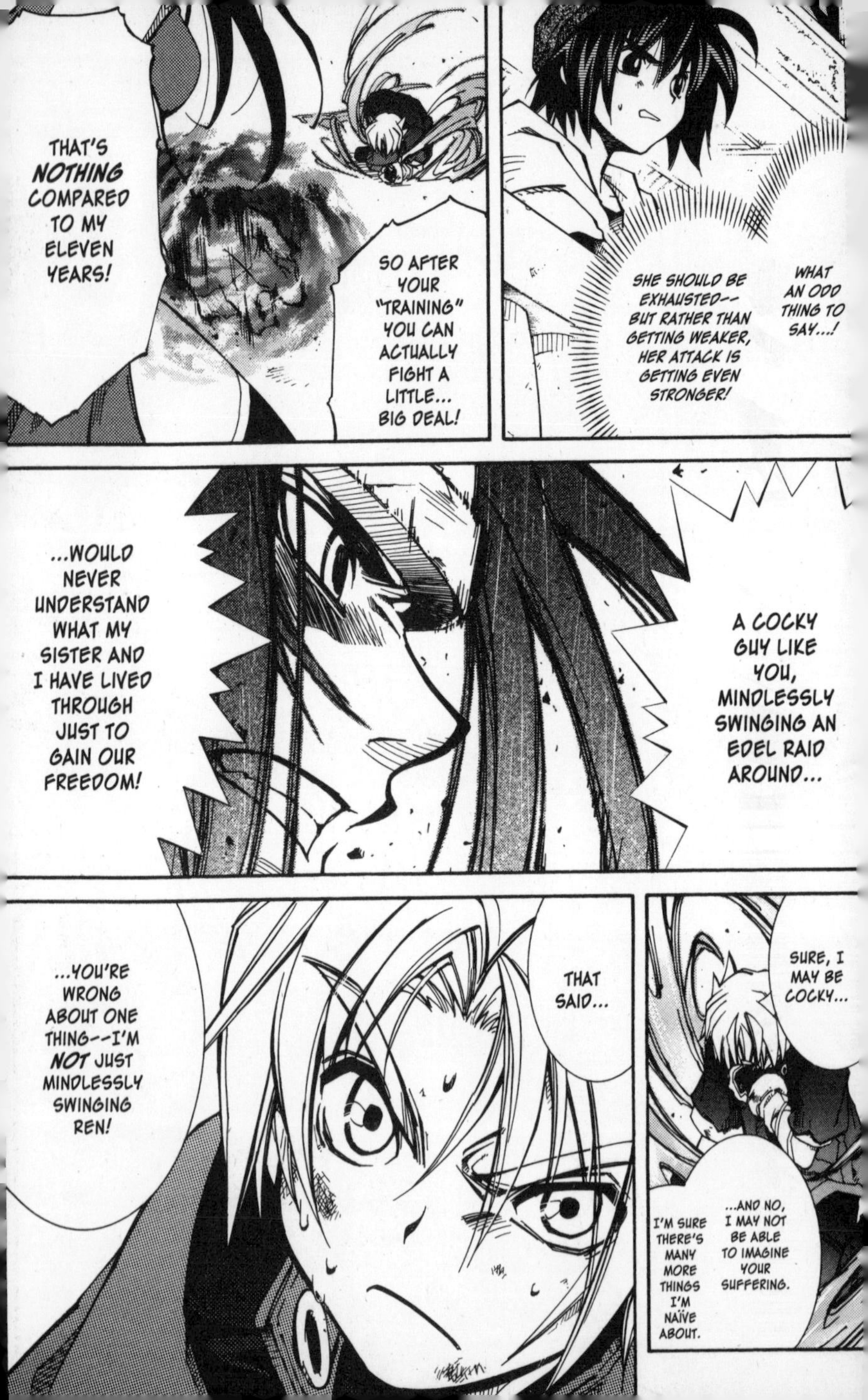
WHAT AN ODD THING TO SAY...!
SHE SHOULD BE EXHAUSTED--BUT RATHER THAN GETTING WEAKER, HER ATTACK IS GETTING EVEN STRONGER!
SO AFTER YOUR "TRAINING" YOU CAN ACTUALLY FIGHT A LITTLE... BIG DEAL!
THAT'S NOTHING COMPARED TO MY ELEVEN YEARS!
A COCKY GUY LIKE YOU, MINDLESSLY SWINGING AN EDEL RAID AROUND...
...WOULD NEVER UNDERSTAND WHAT MY SISTER AND I HAVE LIVED THROUGH JUST TO GAIN OUR FREEDOM!
SURE, I MAY BE COCKY...
...AND NO, I MAY NOT BE ABLE TO IMAGINE YOUR SUFFERING.
I'M SURE THERE'S MANY MORE THINGS I'M NAÏVE ABOUT.
THAT SAID...
...YOU'RE WRONG ABOUT ONE THING--I'M NOT JUST MINDLESSLY SWINGING REN!

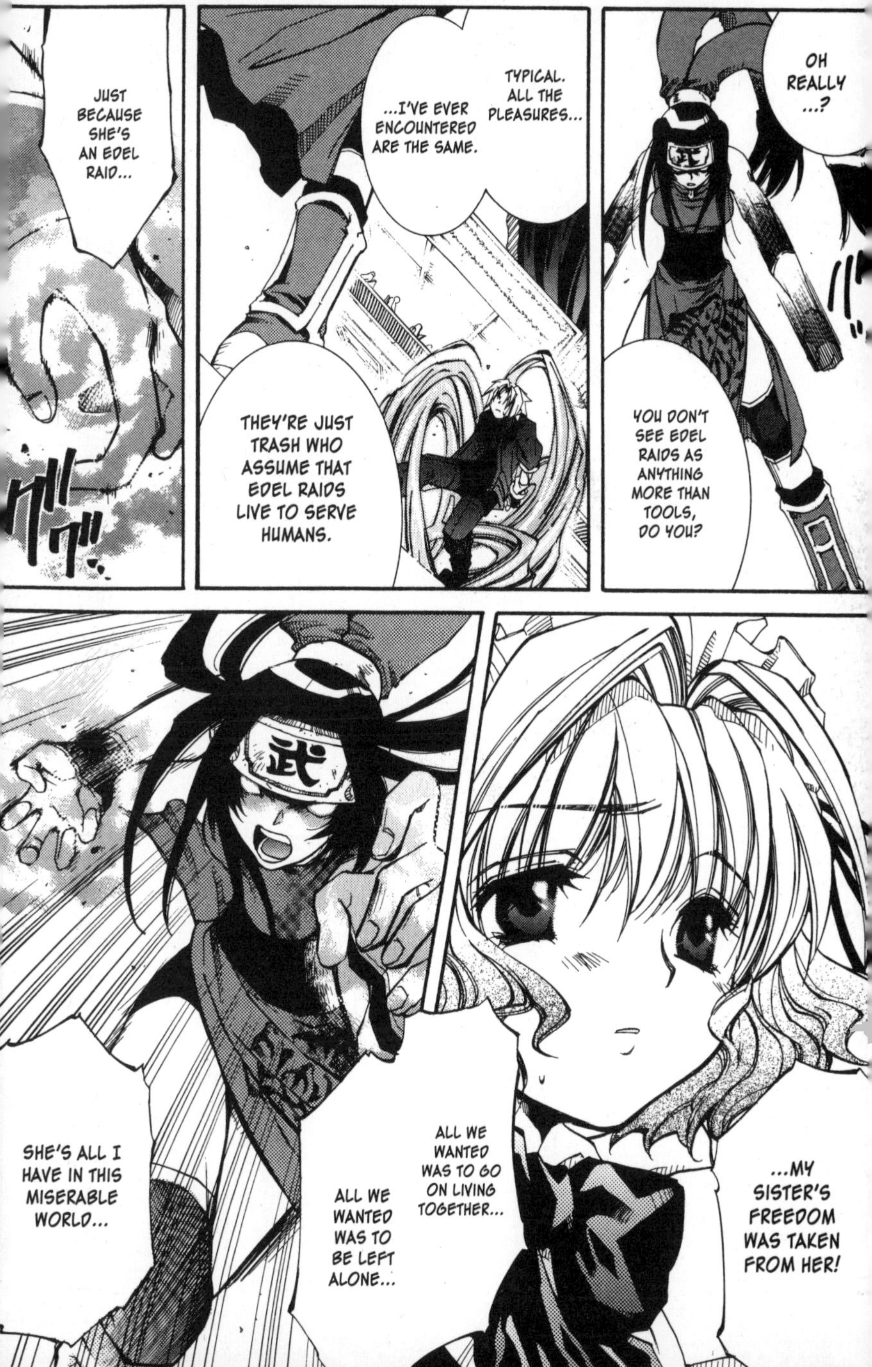
OH REALLY...?
YOU DON'T SEE EDEL RAIDS AS ANYTHING MORE THAN TOOLS, DO YOU?
TYPICAL. ALL THE PLEASURES...
...I'VE EVER ENCOUNTERED ARE THE SAME.
THEY'RE JUST TRASH WHO ASSUME THAT EDEL RAIDS LIVE TO SERVE HUMANS.
JUST BECAUSE SHE'S AN EDEL RAID...
...MY SISTER'S FREEDOM WAS TAKEN FROM HER!
ALL WE WANTED WAS TO GO ON LIVING TOGETHER...
ALL WE WANTED WAS TO BE LEFT ALONE...
SHE'S ALL I HAVE IN THIS MISERABLE WORLD...

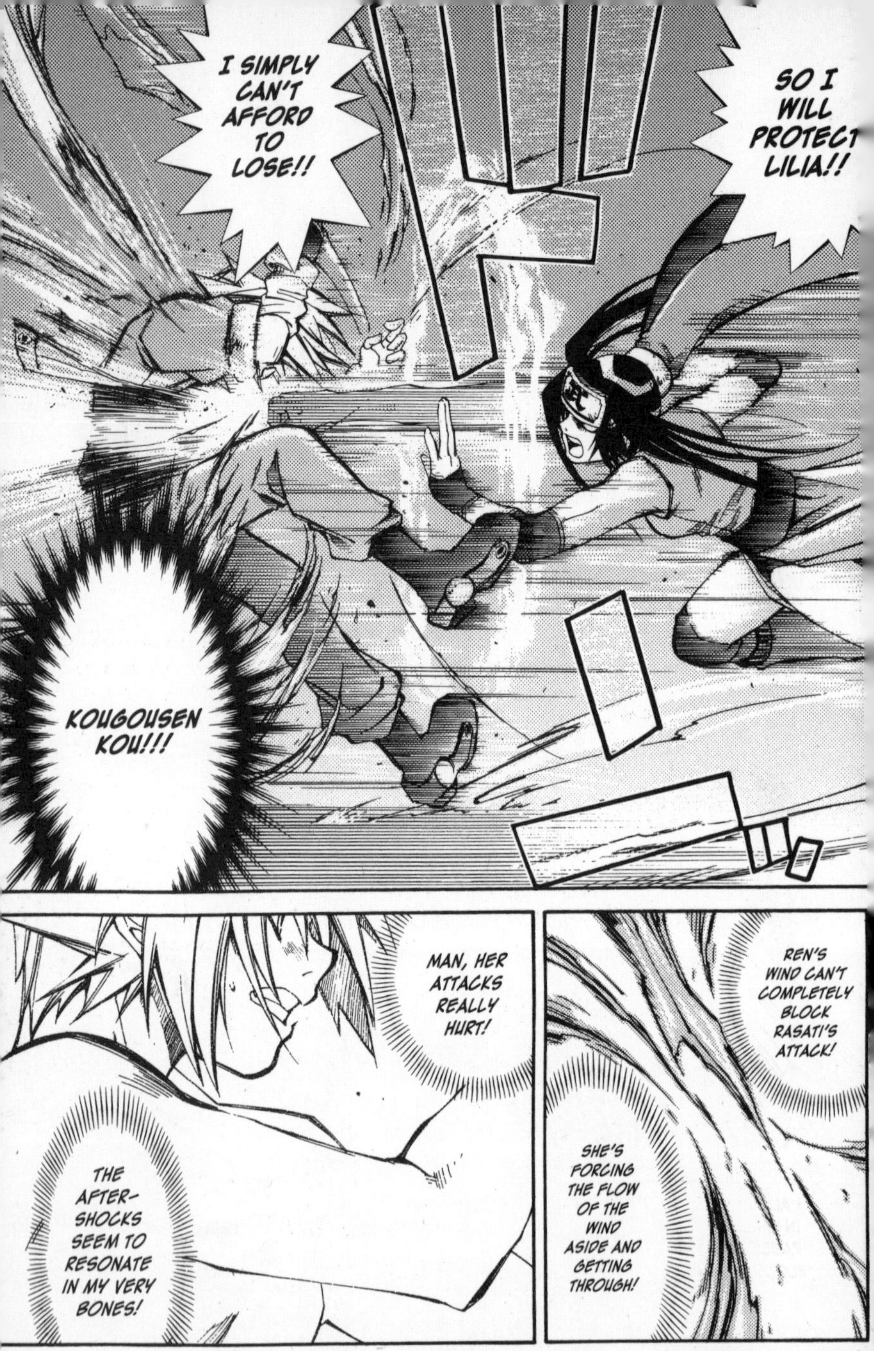
SO I WILL PROTECT LILIA!!
I SIMPLY CAN'T AFFORD TO LOSE!!
KOUGOUSEN KOU!!!
REN'S WIND CAN'T COMPLETELY BLOCK RASATI'S ATTACK!
SHE'S FORCING THE FLOW OF THE WIND ASIDE AND GETTING THROUGH!
MAN, HER ATTACKS REALLY HURT!
THE AFTER-SHOCKS SEEM TO RESONATE IN MY VERY BONES!

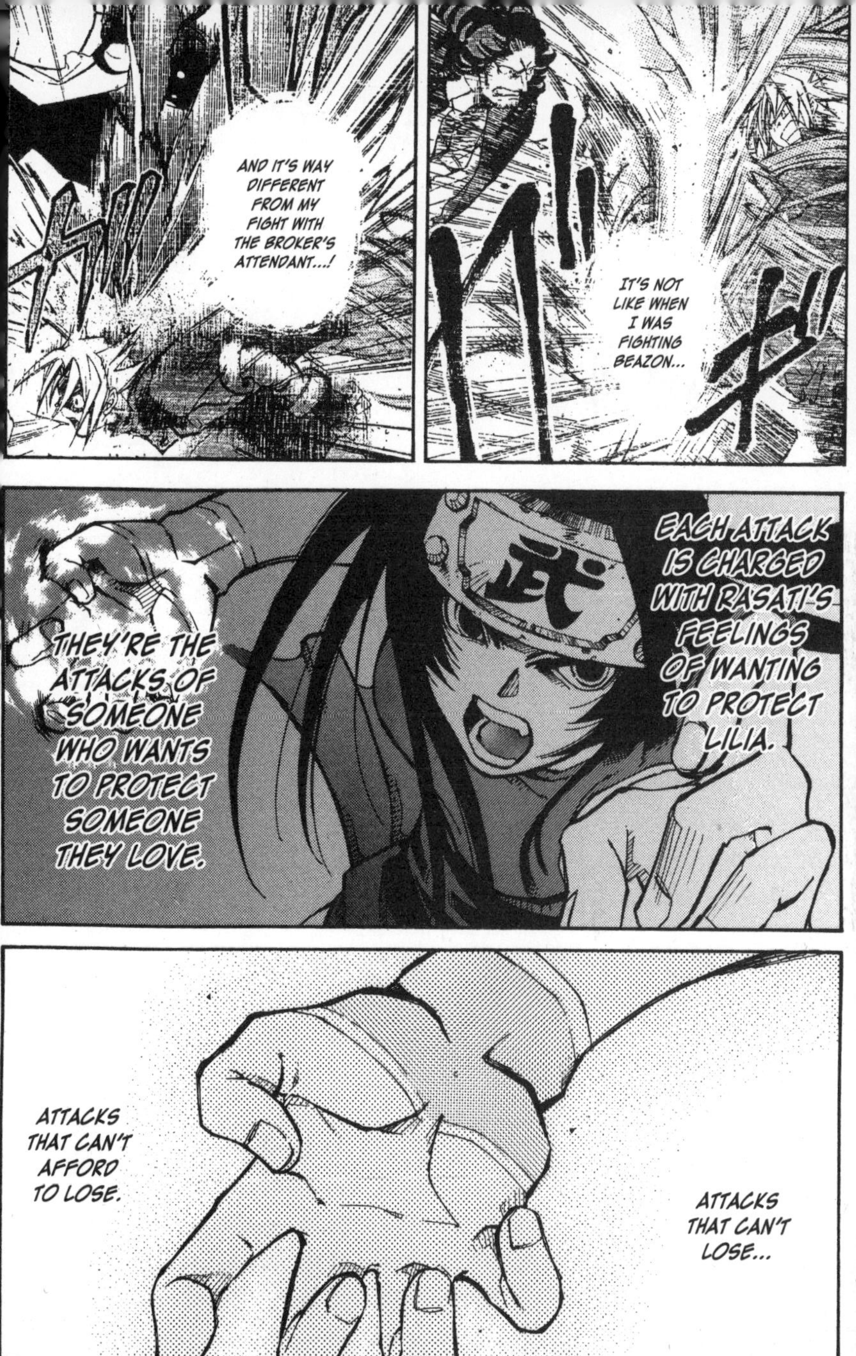
IT'S NOT LIKE WHEN I WAS FIGHTING BEAZON...
AND IT'S WAY DIFFERENT FROM MY FIGHT WITH THE BROKER'S ATTENDANT...!
EACH ATTACK IS CHARGED WITH RASATI'S FEELINGS OF WANTING TO PROTECT LILIA.
THEY'RE THE ATTACKS OF SOMEONE WHO WANTS TO PROTECT SOMEONE THEY LOVE.
ATTACKS THAT CAN'T LOSE...
ATTACKS THAT CAN'T AFFORD TO LOSE.

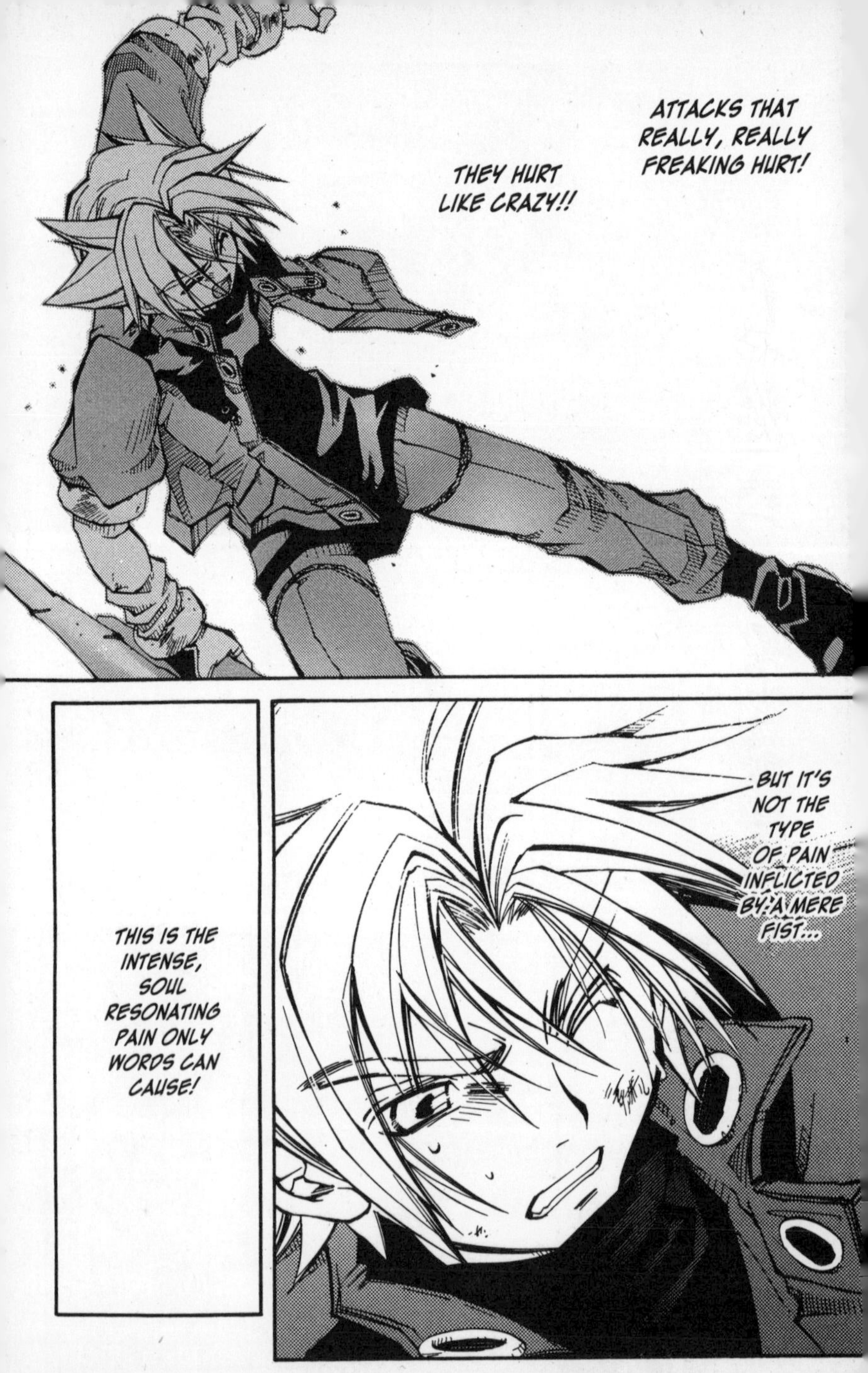
ATTACKS THAT REALLY, REALLY FREAKING HURT!
THEY HURT LIKE CRAZY!!
BUT IT'S NOT THE TYPE OF PAIN INFLICTED BY A MERE FIST...
THIS IS THE INTENSE, SOUL RESONATING PAIN ONLY WORDS CAN CAUSE!

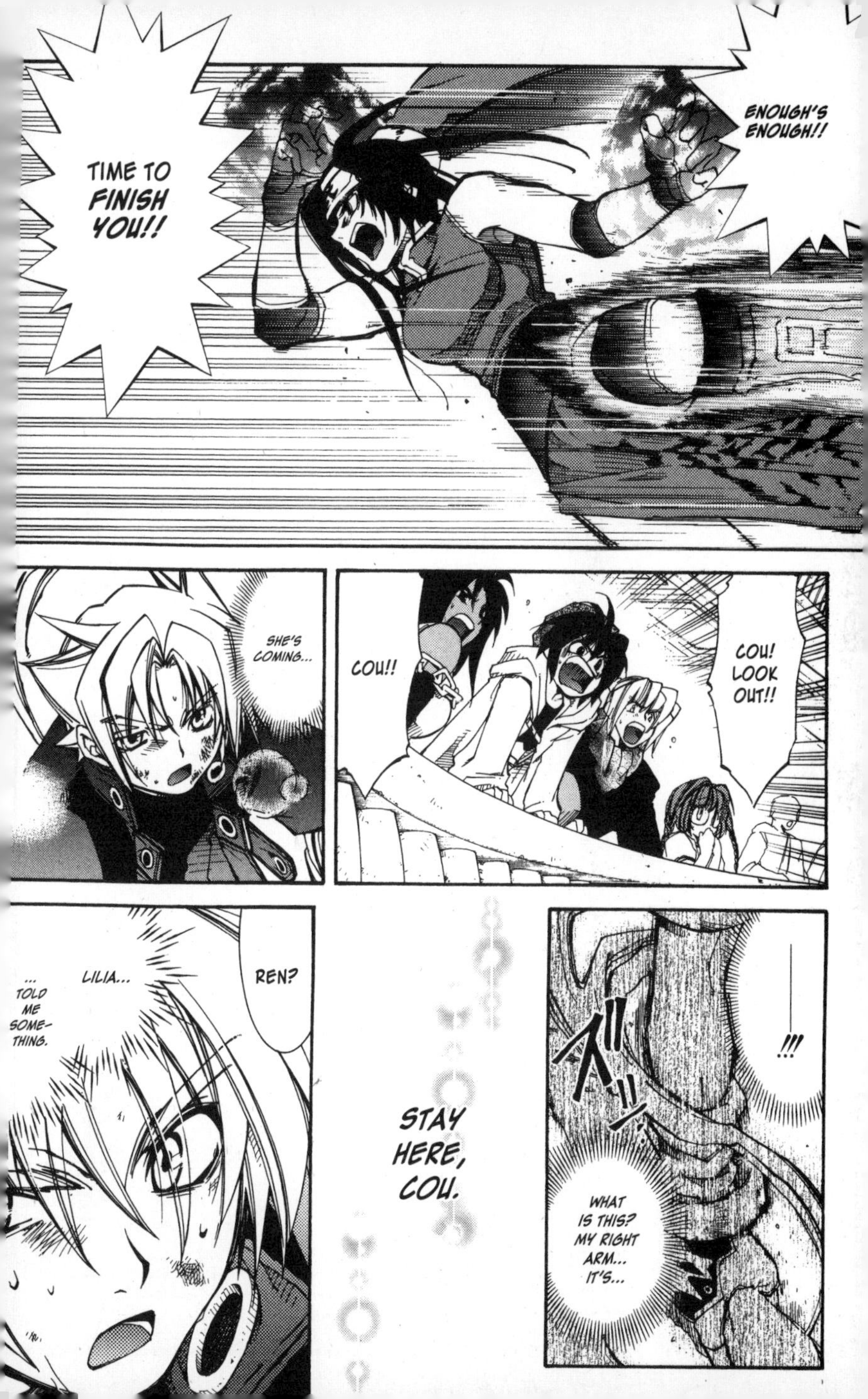
ENOUGH'S ENOUGH!!
TIME TO FINISH YOU!!
COU! LOOK OUT!!
COU!!
SHE'S COMING...
!!!
WHAT IS THIS? MY RIGHT ARM... IT'S...
STAY HERE, COU.
REN?
LILIA...
... TOLD ME SOME-THING.

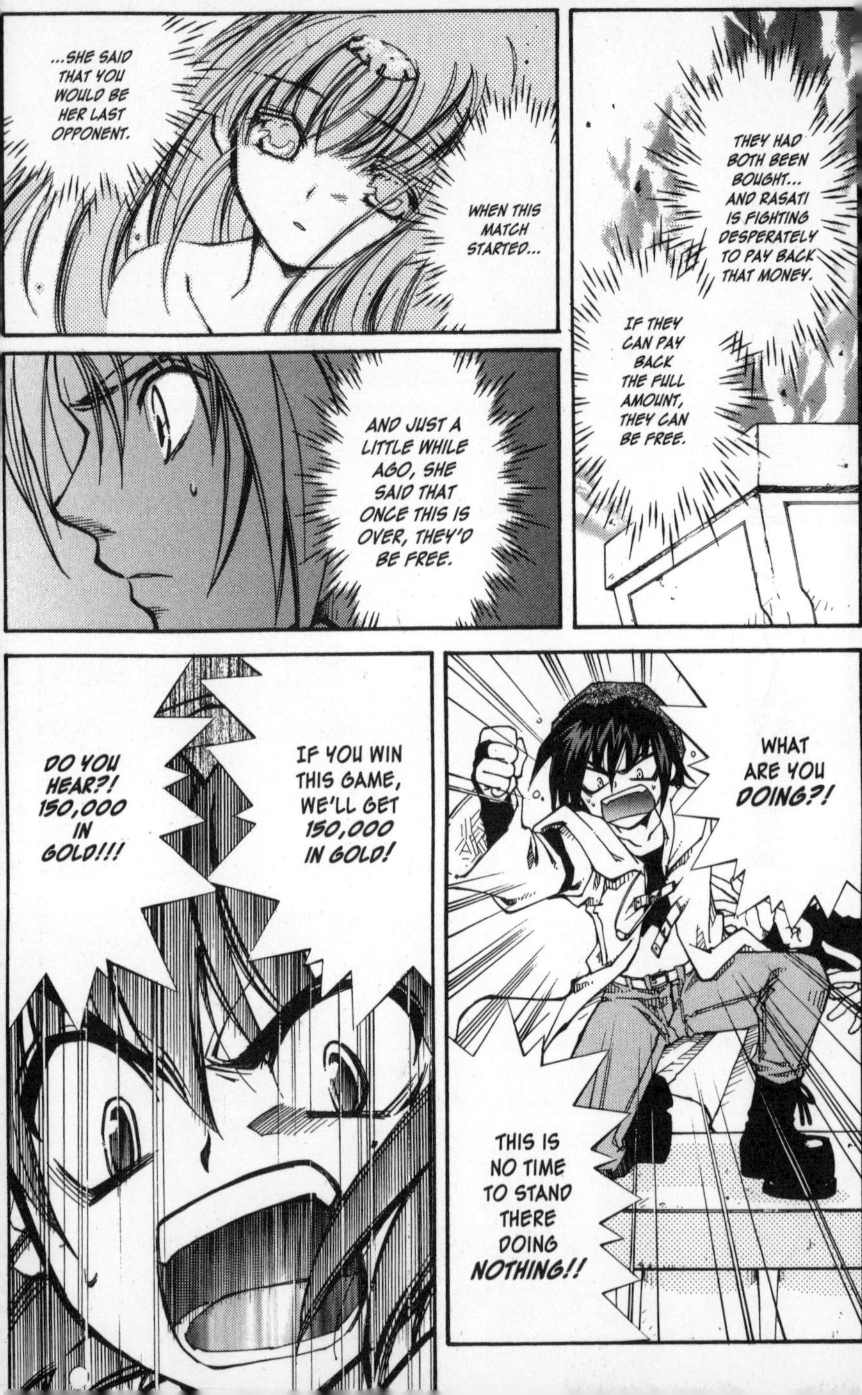
THEY HAD BOTH BEEN BOUGHT... AND RASATI IS FIGHTING DESPERATELY TO PAY BACK THAT MONEY.
IF THEY CAN PAY BACK THE FULL AMOUNT, THEY CAN BE FREE.
WHEN THIS MATCH STARTED...
...SHE SAID THAT YOU WOULD BE HER LAST OPPONENT.
AND JUST A LITTLE WHILE AGO, SHE SAID THAT ONCE THIS IS OVER, THEY'D BE FREE.
WHAT ARE YOU DOING?!
THIS IS NO TIME TO STAND THERE DOING NOTHING!!
IF YOU WIN THIS GAME, WE'LL GET 150,000 IN GOLD!
DO YOU HEAR?! 150,000 IN GOLD!!!

...WHEN I FIRST MET YOU, COU?

BACK THEN...

REMEMBER...

FREEDOM IS A WONDERFUL THING.

THAT'S WHY WE HAVE TO.

...YOU FREED ME.

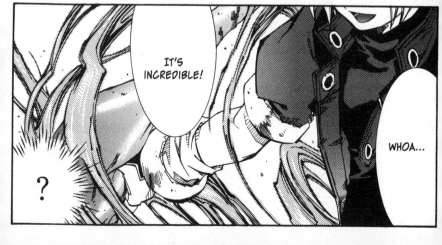

IT'S INCREDIBLE!

?

WHOA...

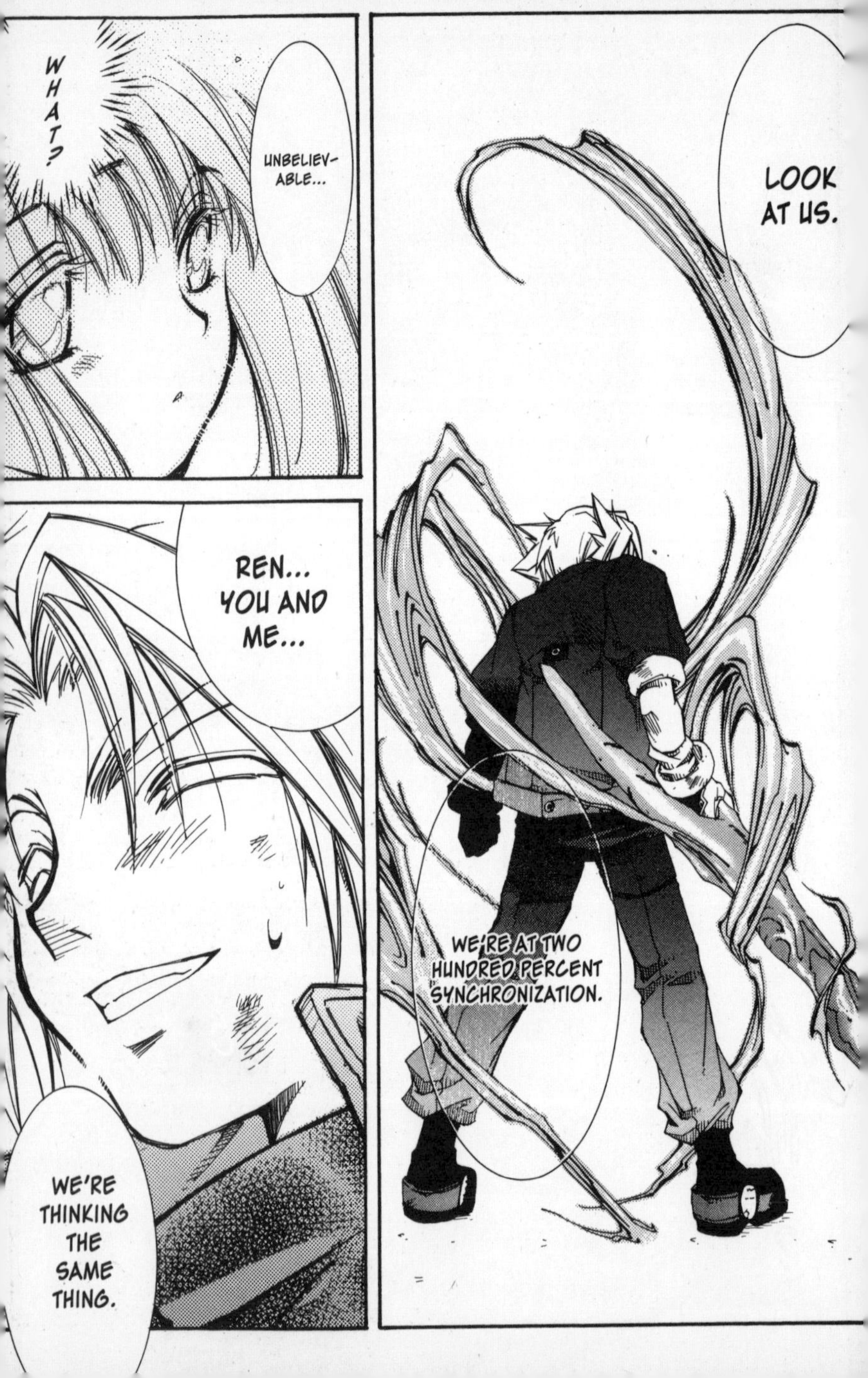
LOOK AT US.
WE'RE AT TWO HUNDRED PERCENT SYNCHRONIZATION.
UNBELIEVABLE...
WHAT?
REN... YOU AND ME...
WE'RE THINKING THE SAME THING.

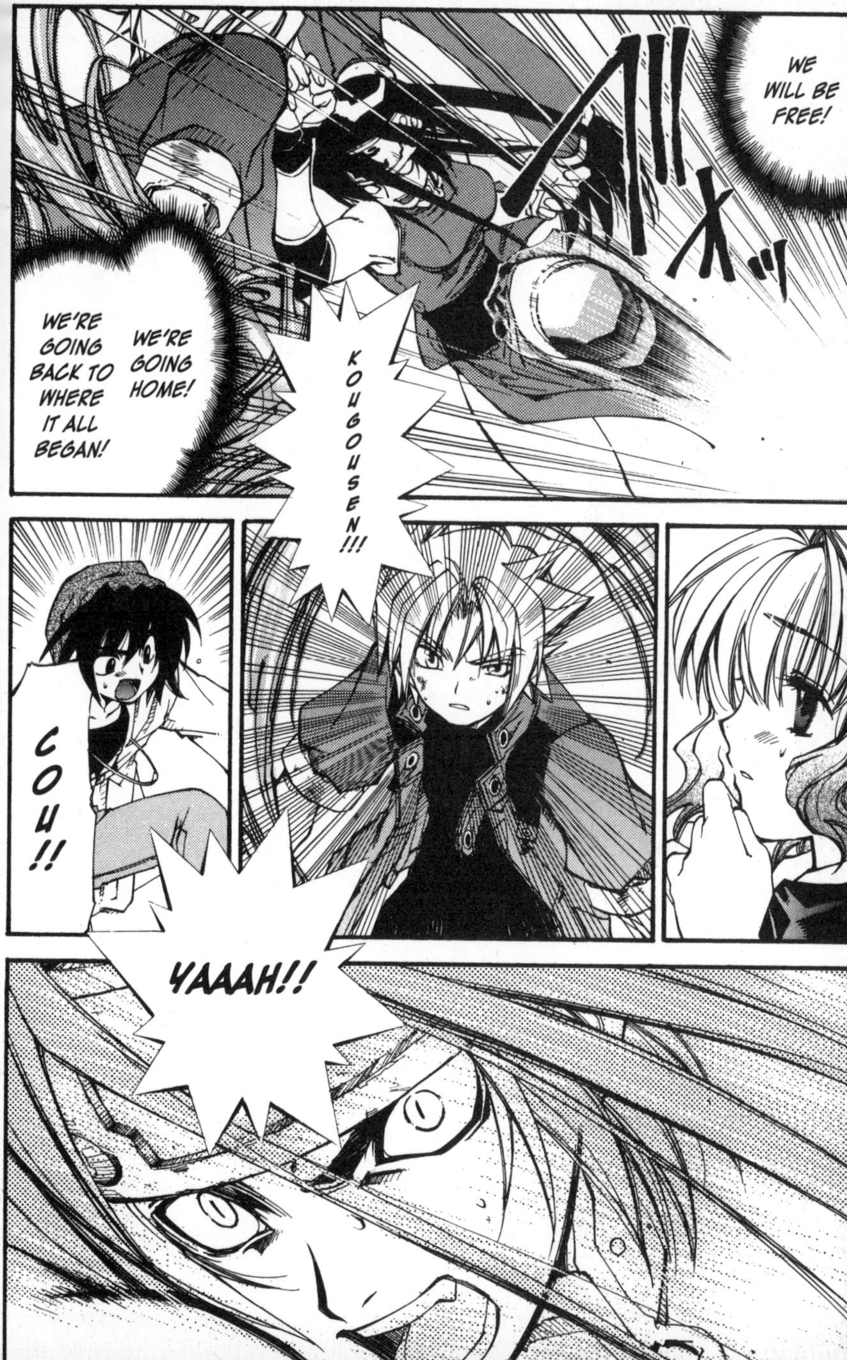
WE WILL BE FREE!
WE'RE GOING HOME!
WE'RE GOING BACK TO WHERE IT ALL BEGAN!
KOUGOUSEN!!!
COU!!
YAAAH!!

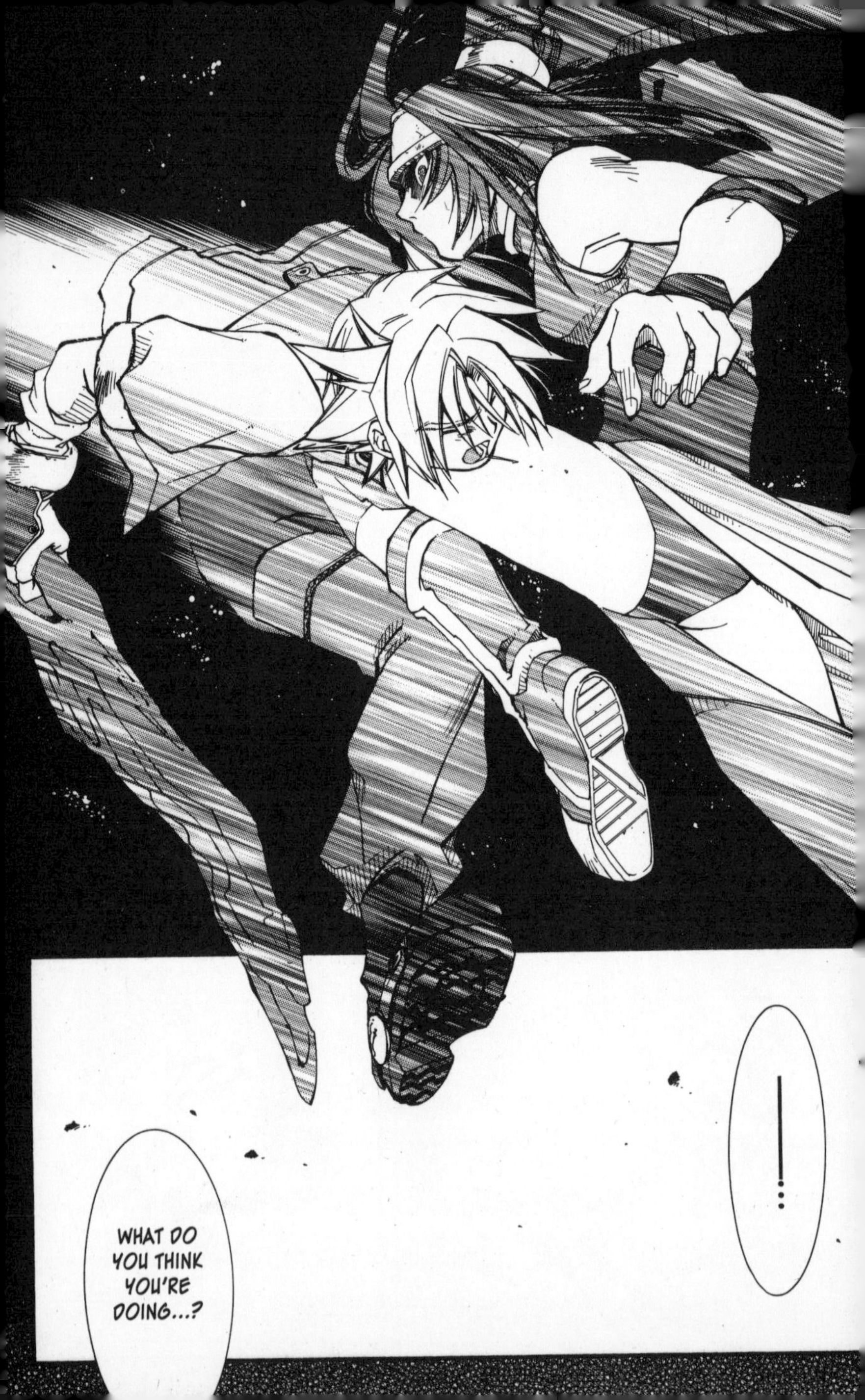

—...
WHAT DO YOU THINK YOU'RE DOING...?

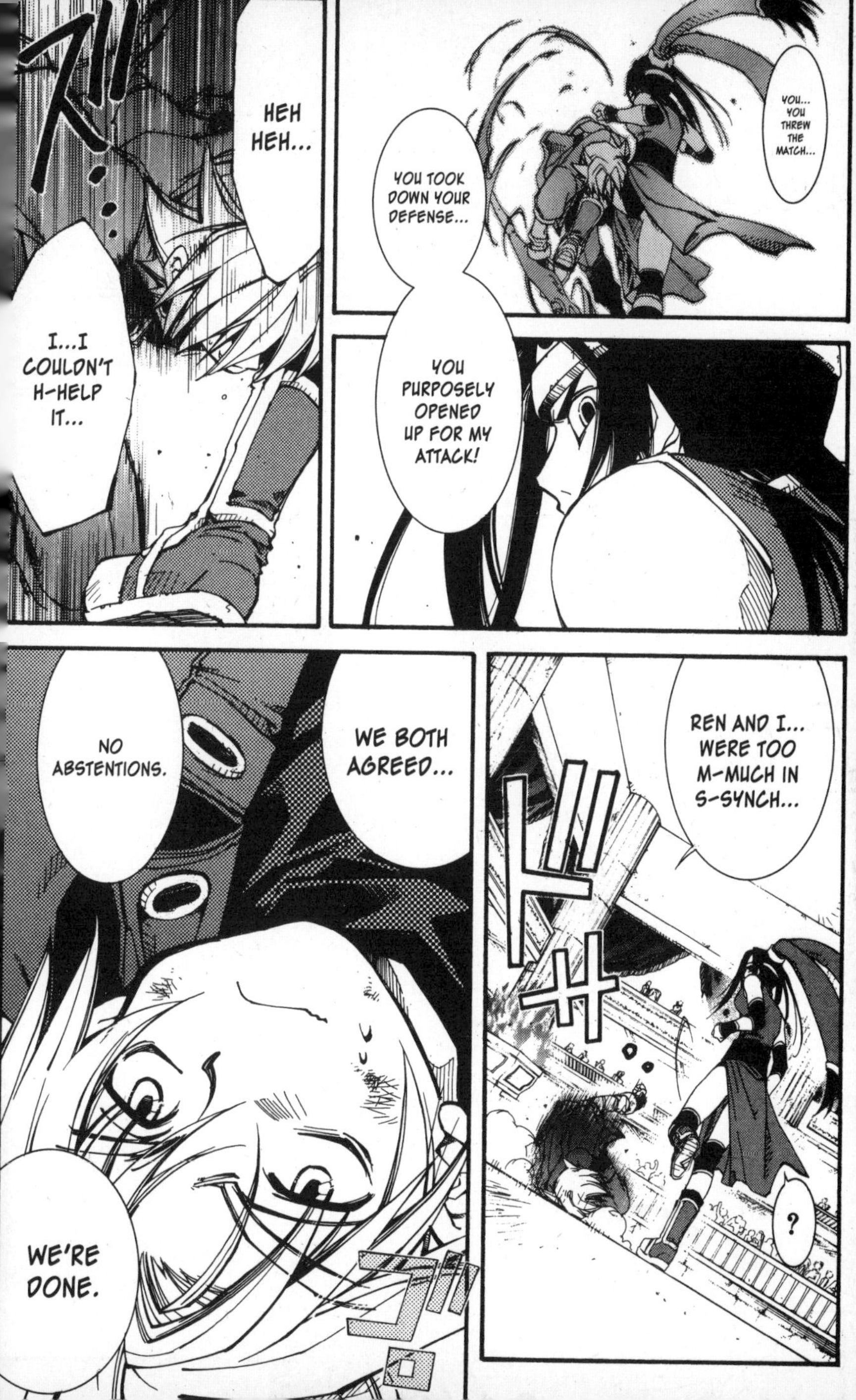
YOU... YOU THREW THE MATCH...
YOU TOOK DOWN YOUR DEFENSE...
YOU PURPOSELY OPENED UP FOR MY ATTACK!
HEH HEH...
I...I COULDN'T H-HELP IT...
REN AND I... WERE TOO M-MUCH IN S-SYNCH...
?
WE BOTH AGREED...
NO ABSTENTIONS.
WE'RE DONE.

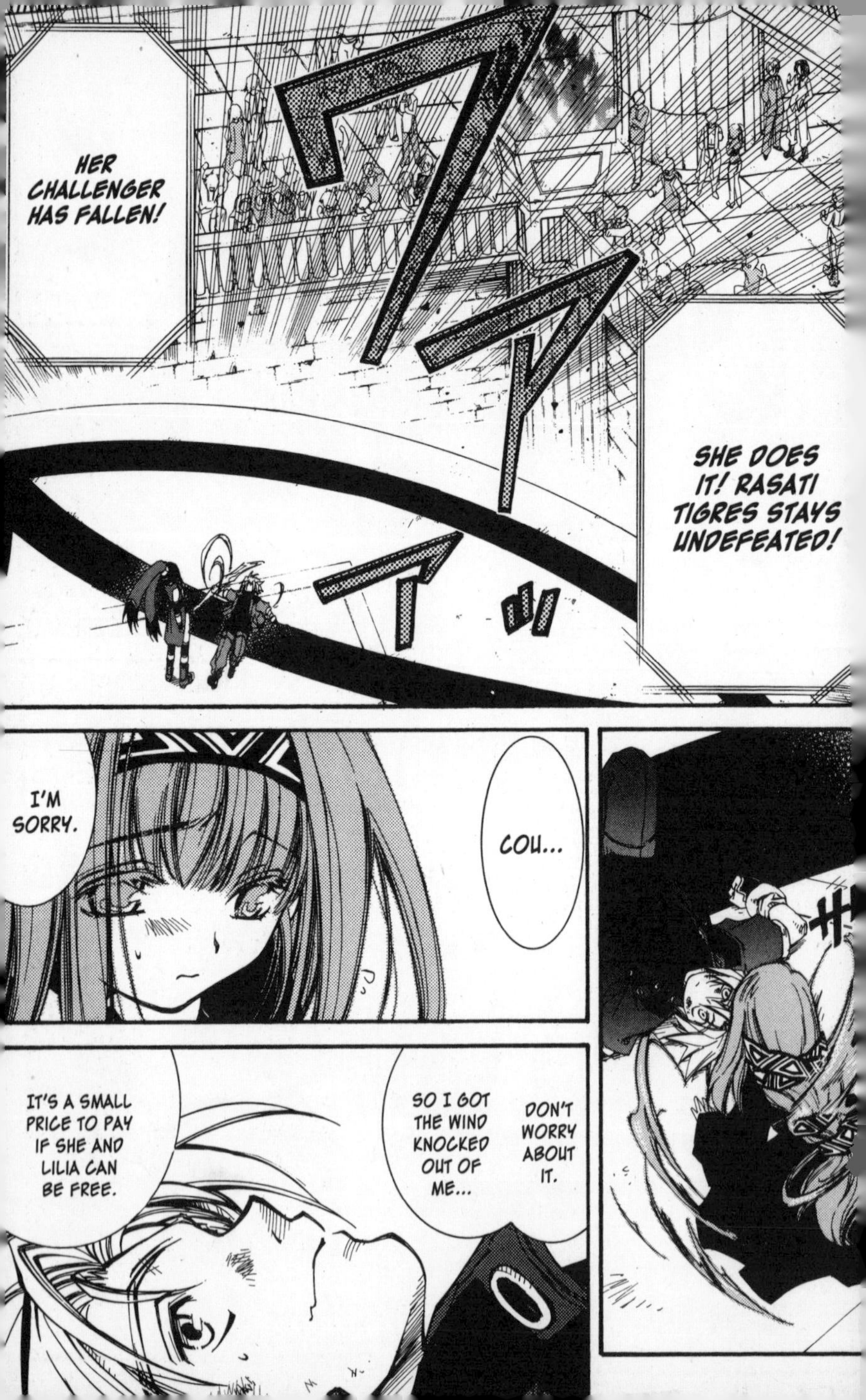
HER CHALLENGER HAS FALLEN!
SHE DOES IT! RASATI TIGRES STAYS UNDEFEATED!
COU...
I'M SORRY.
DON'T WORRY ABOUT IT.
SO I GOT THE WIND KNOCKED OUT OF ME...
IT'S A SMALL PRICE TO PAY IF SHE AND LILIA CAN BE FREE.

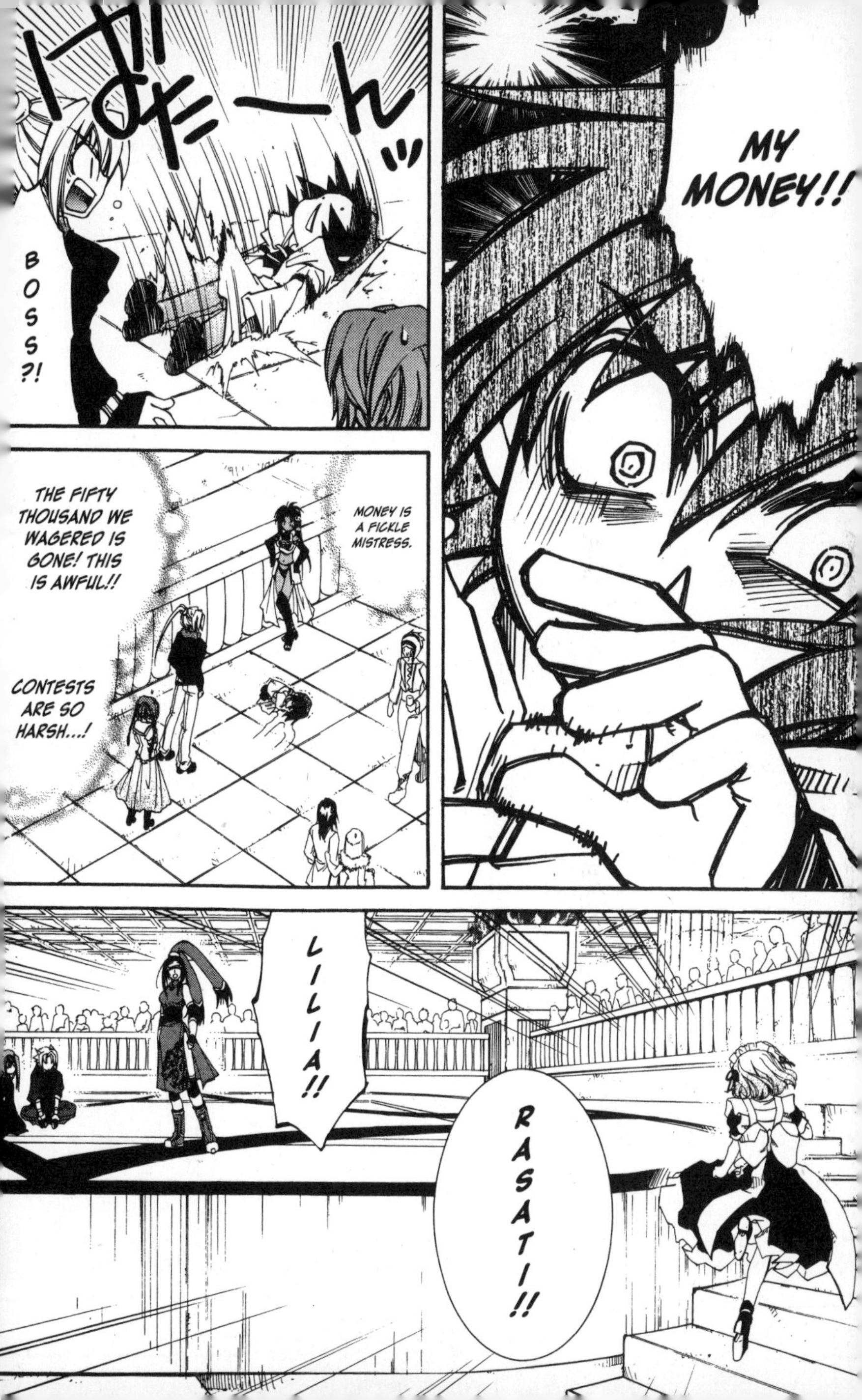
MY MONEY!!
ばたーんッ
BOSS?!
MONEY IS A FICKLE MISTRESS.
THE FIFTY THOUSAND WE WAGERED IS GONE! THIS IS AWFUL!!
CONTESTS ARE SO HARSH...!
RASATI!!
LILIA!!

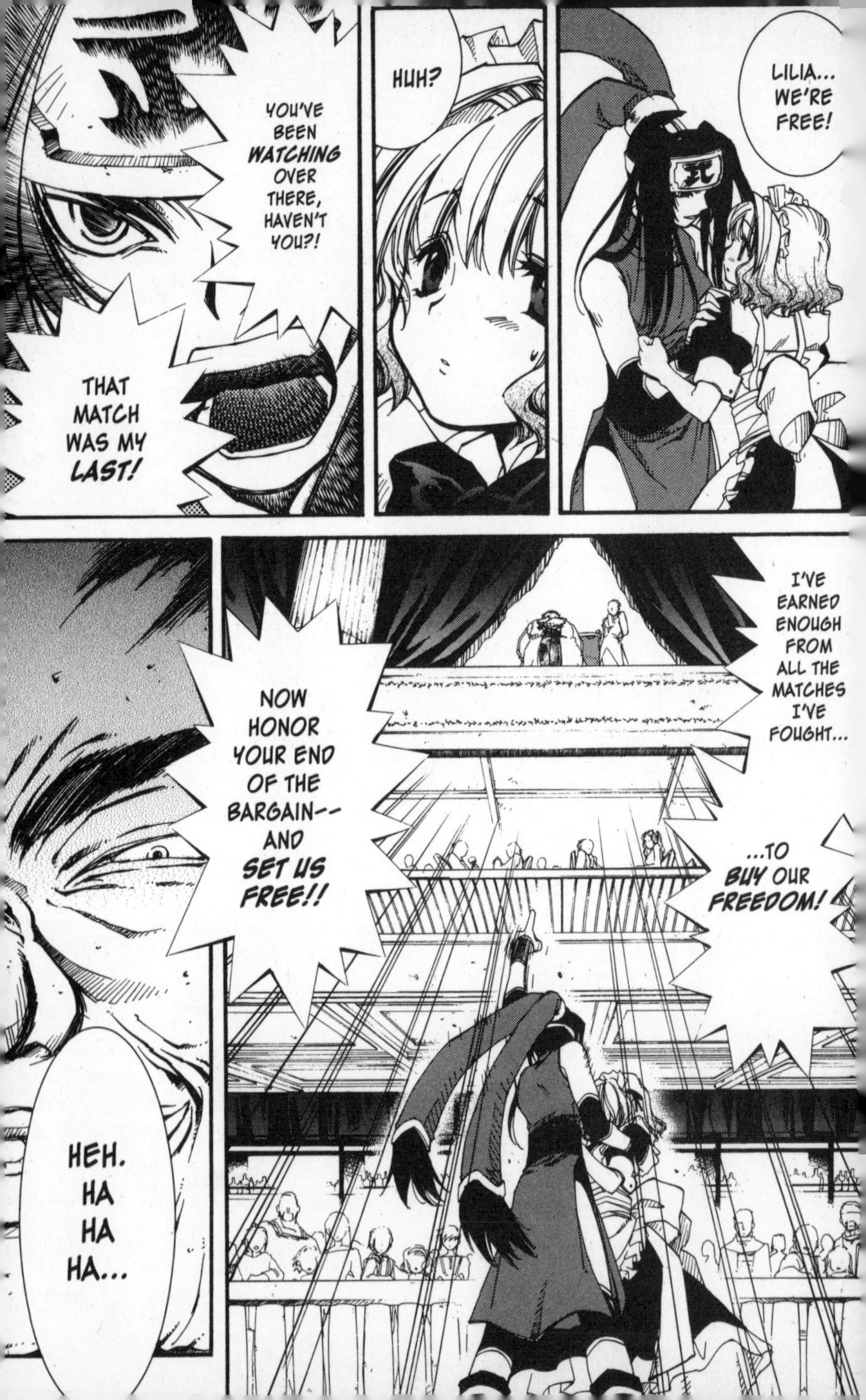
LILIA... WE'RE FREE!
HUH?
YOU'VE BEEN WATCHING OVER THERE, HAVEN'T YOU?!
THAT MATCH WAS MY LAST!
I'VE EARNED ENOUGH FROM ALL THE MATCHES I'VE FOUGHT...
...TO BUY OUR FREEDOM!
NOW HONOR YOUR END OF THE BARGAIN--AND SET US FREE!!
HEH. HA HA HA...

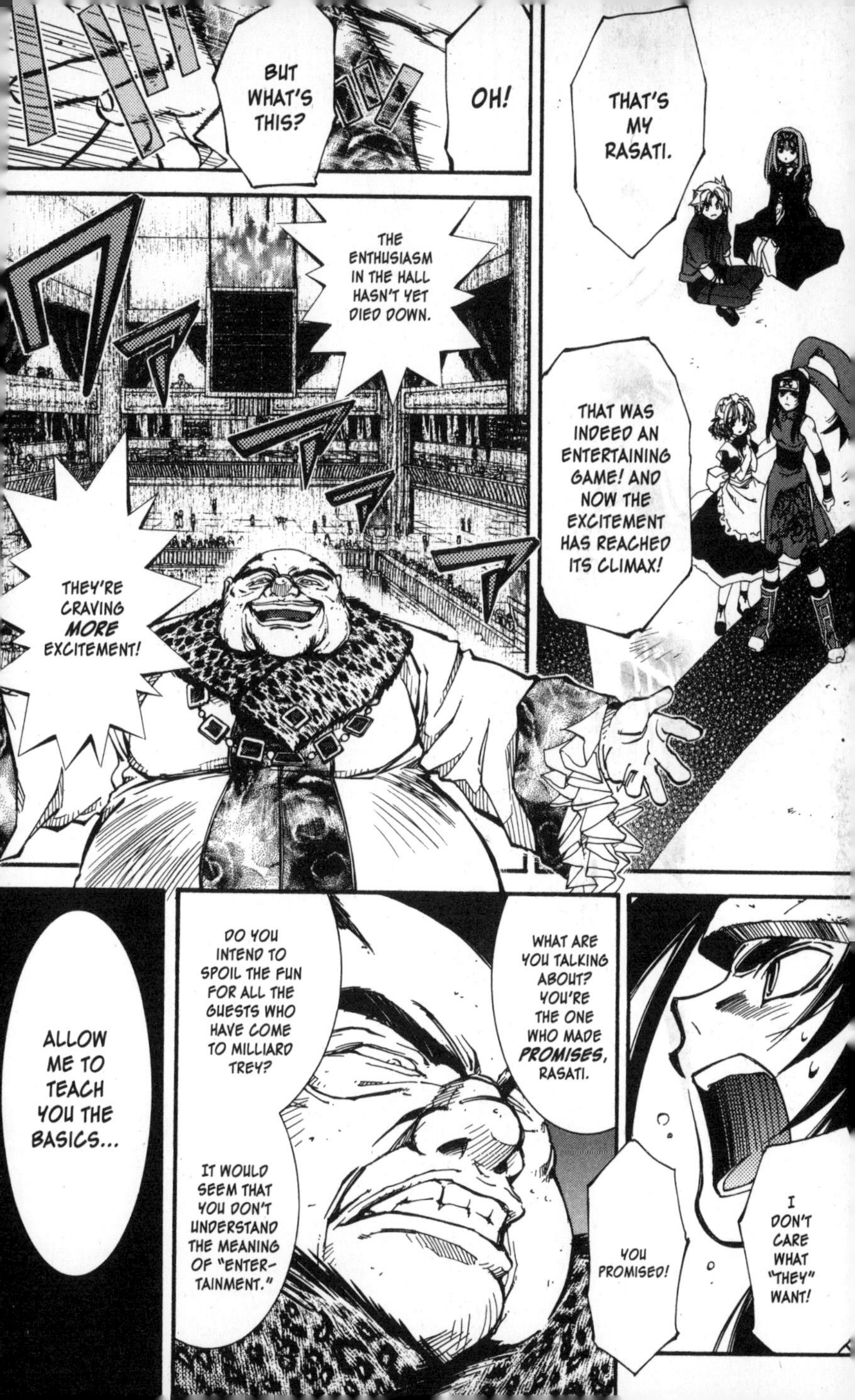
THAT'S MY RASATI.
THAT WAS INDEED AN ENTERTAINING GAME! AND NOW THE EXCITEMENT HAS REACHED ITS CLIMAX!
OH!
BUT WHAT'S THIS?
THE ENTHUSIASM IN THE HALL HASN'T YET DIED DOWN.
THEY'RE CRAVING *MORE* EXCITEMENT!
I DON'T CARE WHAT "THEY" WANT!
YOU PROMISED!
WHAT ARE YOU TALKING ABOUT? YOU'RE THE ONE WHO MADE *PROMISES*, RASATI.
DO YOU INTEND TO SPOIL THE FUN FOR ALL THE GUESTS WHO HAVE COME TO MILLIARD TREY?
IT WOULD SEEM THAT YOU DON'T UNDERSTAND THE MEANING OF "ENTER-TAINMENT."
ALLOW ME TO TEACH YOU THE BASICS...

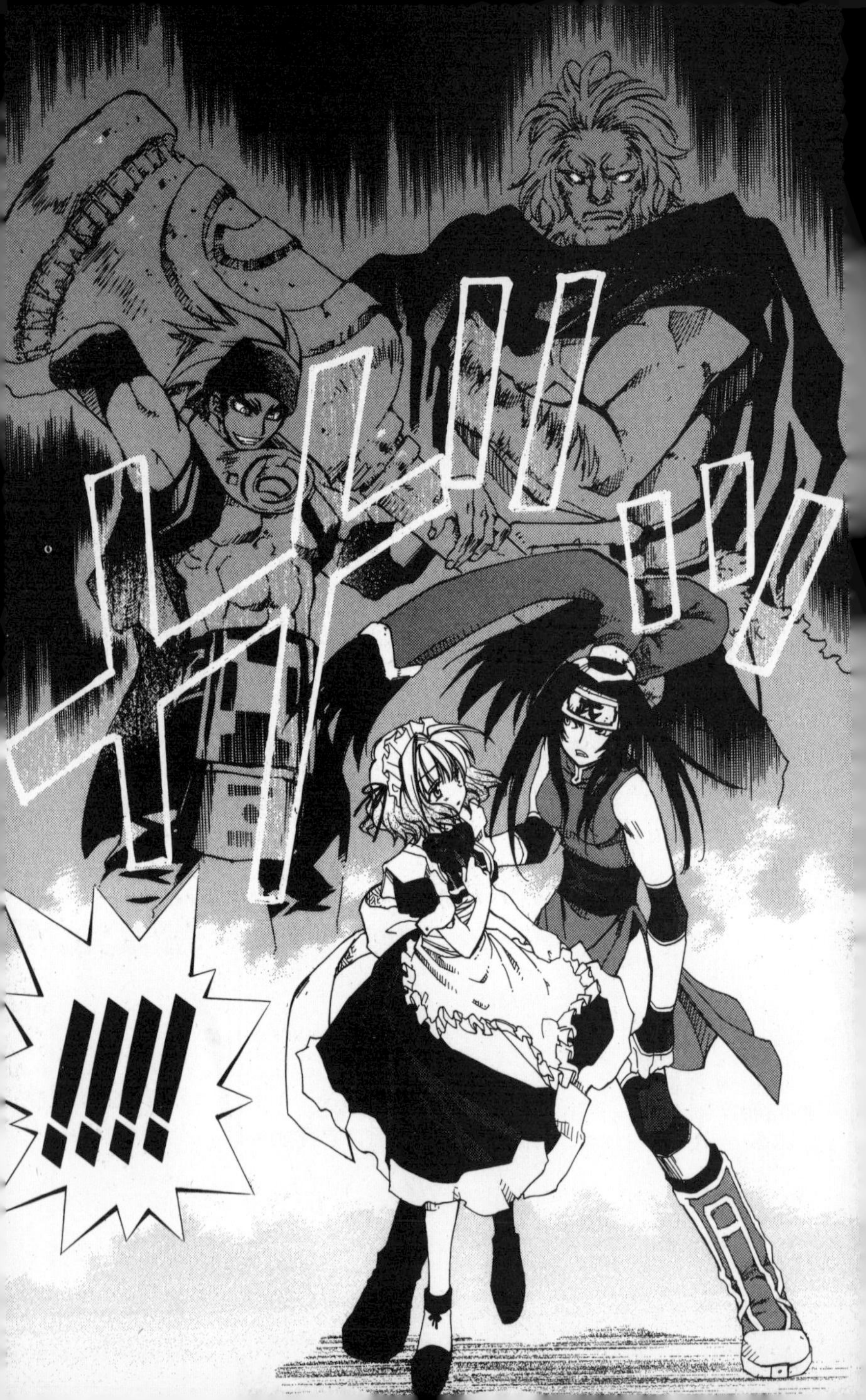
!!!!

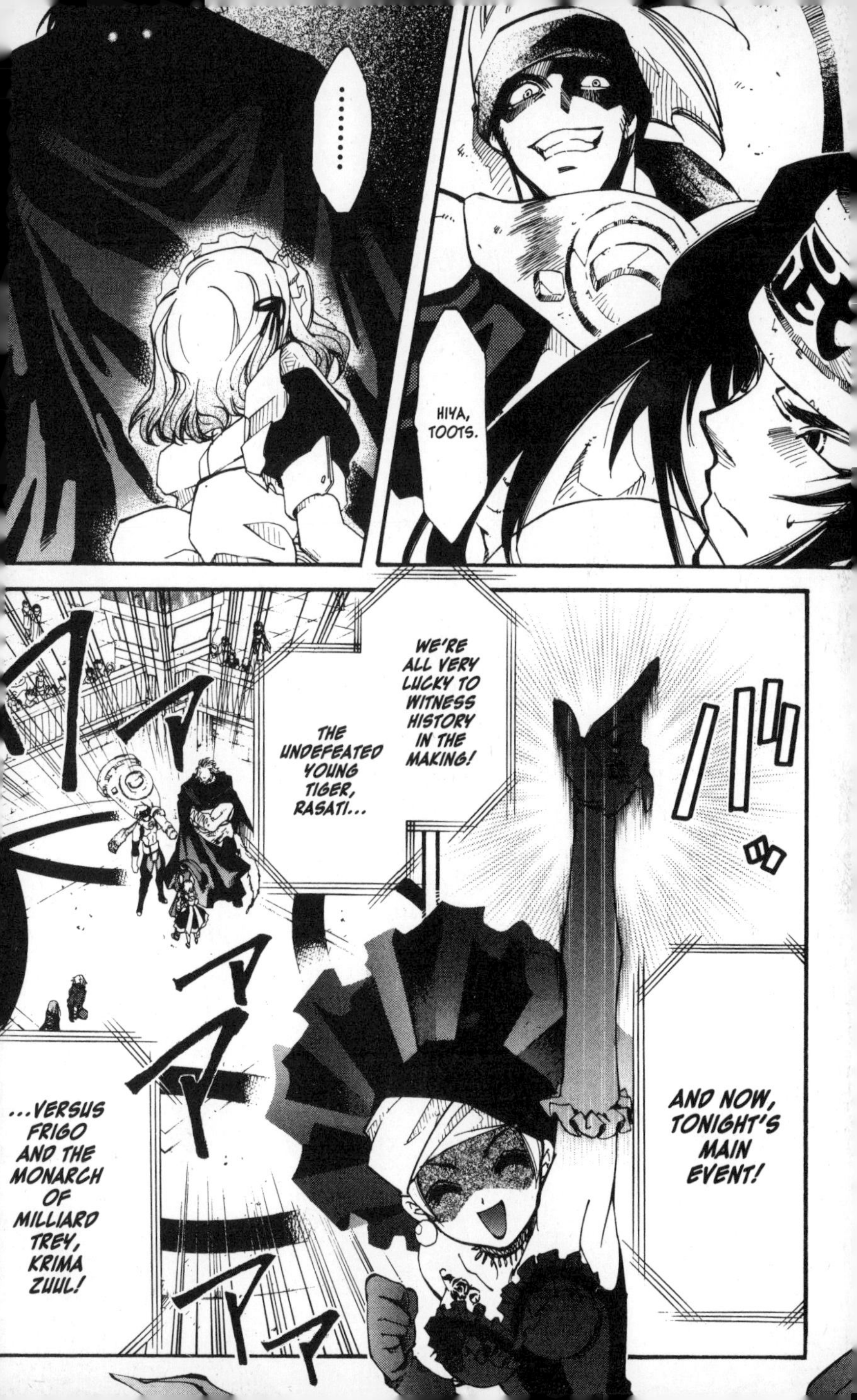
HIYA, TOOTS.
......
AND NOW, TONIGHT'S MAIN EVENT!
WE'RE ALL VERY LUCKY TO WITNESS HISTORY IN THE MAKING!
THE UNDEFEATED YOUNG TIGER, RASATI...
...VERSUS FRIGO AND THE MONARCH OF MILLIARD TREY, KRIMA ZUUL!

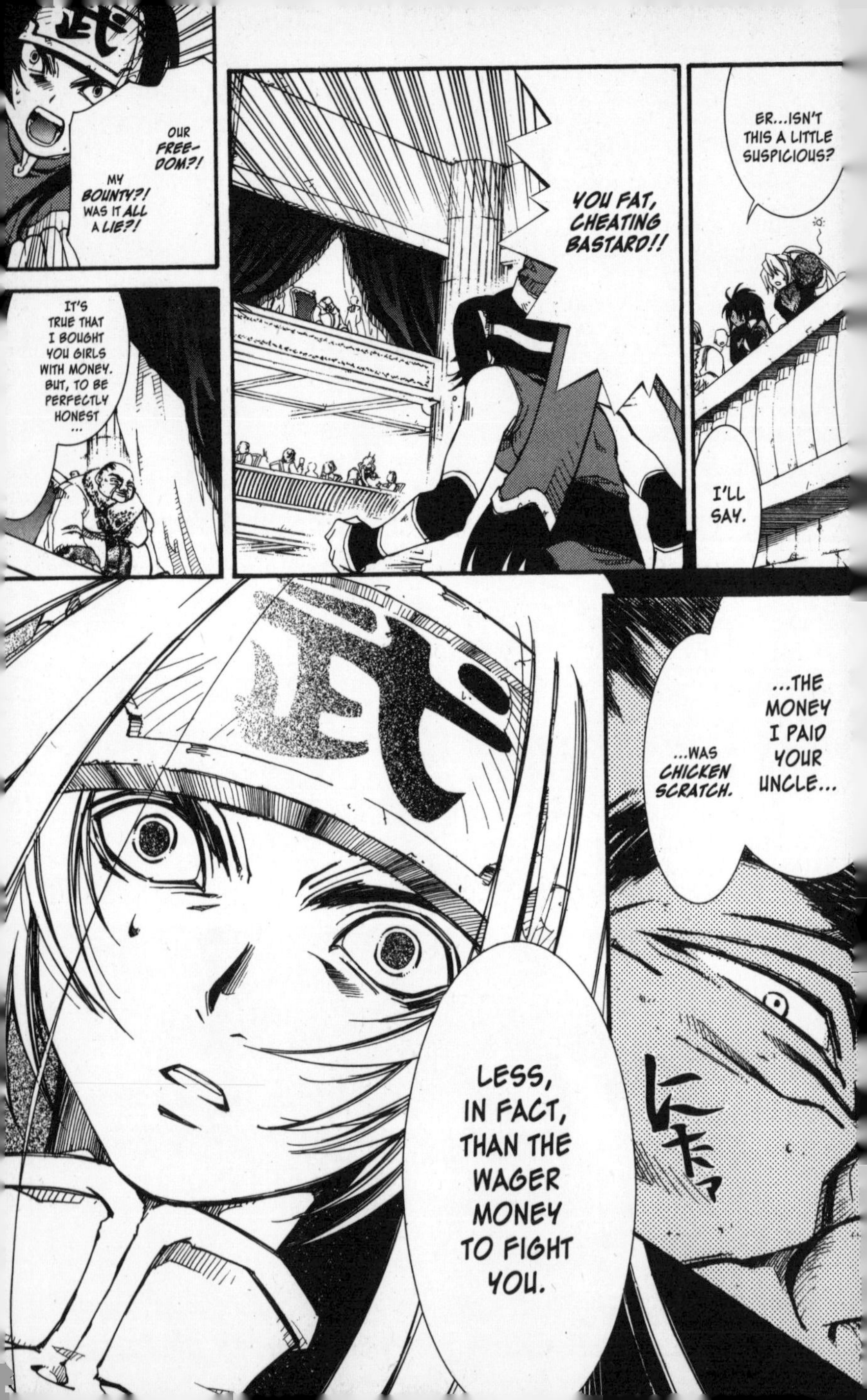
ER...ISN'T THIS A LITTLE SUSPICIOUS?
I'LL SAY.
YOU FAT, CHEATING BASTARD!!
OUR FREE-DOM?!
MY BOUNTY?! WAS IT ALL A LIE?!
IT'S TRUE THAT I BOUGHT YOU GIRLS WITH MONEY. BUT, TO BE PERFECTLY HONEST ...
...THE MONEY I PAID YOUR UNCLE...
...WAS CHICKEN SCRATCH.
LESS, IN FACT, THAN THE WAGER MONEY TO FIGHT YOU.

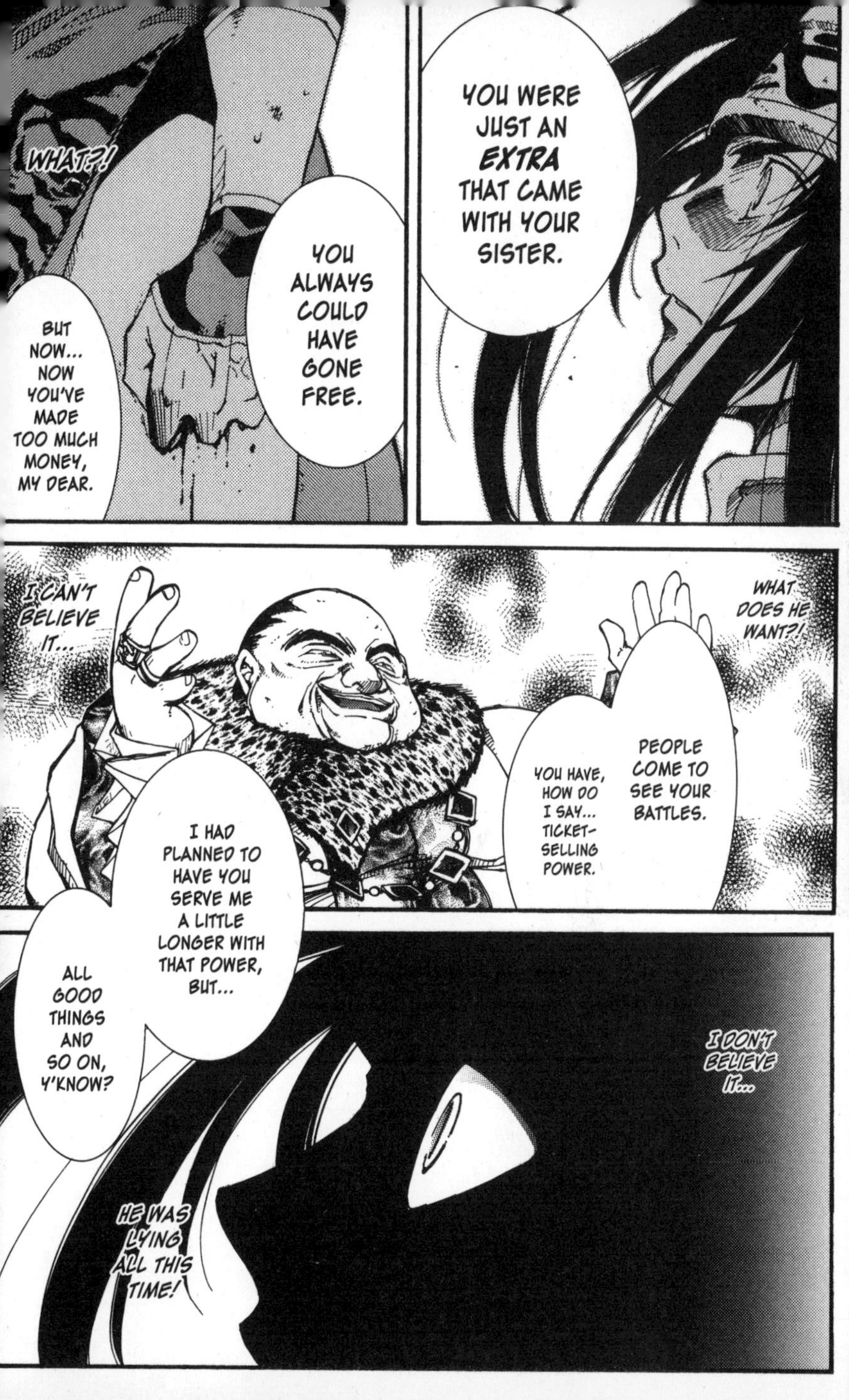
YOU WERE JUST AN **EXTRA** THAT CAME WITH YOUR SISTER.
YOU ALWAYS COULD HAVE GONE FREE.
WHAT?!
BUT NOW... NOW YOU'VE MADE TOO MUCH MONEY, MY DEAR.
WHAT DOES HE WANT?!
PEOPLE COME TO SEE YOUR BATTLES.
YOU HAVE, HOW DO I SAY... TICKET-SELLING POWER.
I CAN'T BELIEVE IT...
I HAD PLANNED TO HAVE YOU SERVE ME A LITTLE LONGER WITH THAT POWER, BUT...
ALL GOOD THINGS AND SO ON, Y'KNOW?
I DON'T BELIEVE IT...
HE WAS LYING ALL THIS TIME!

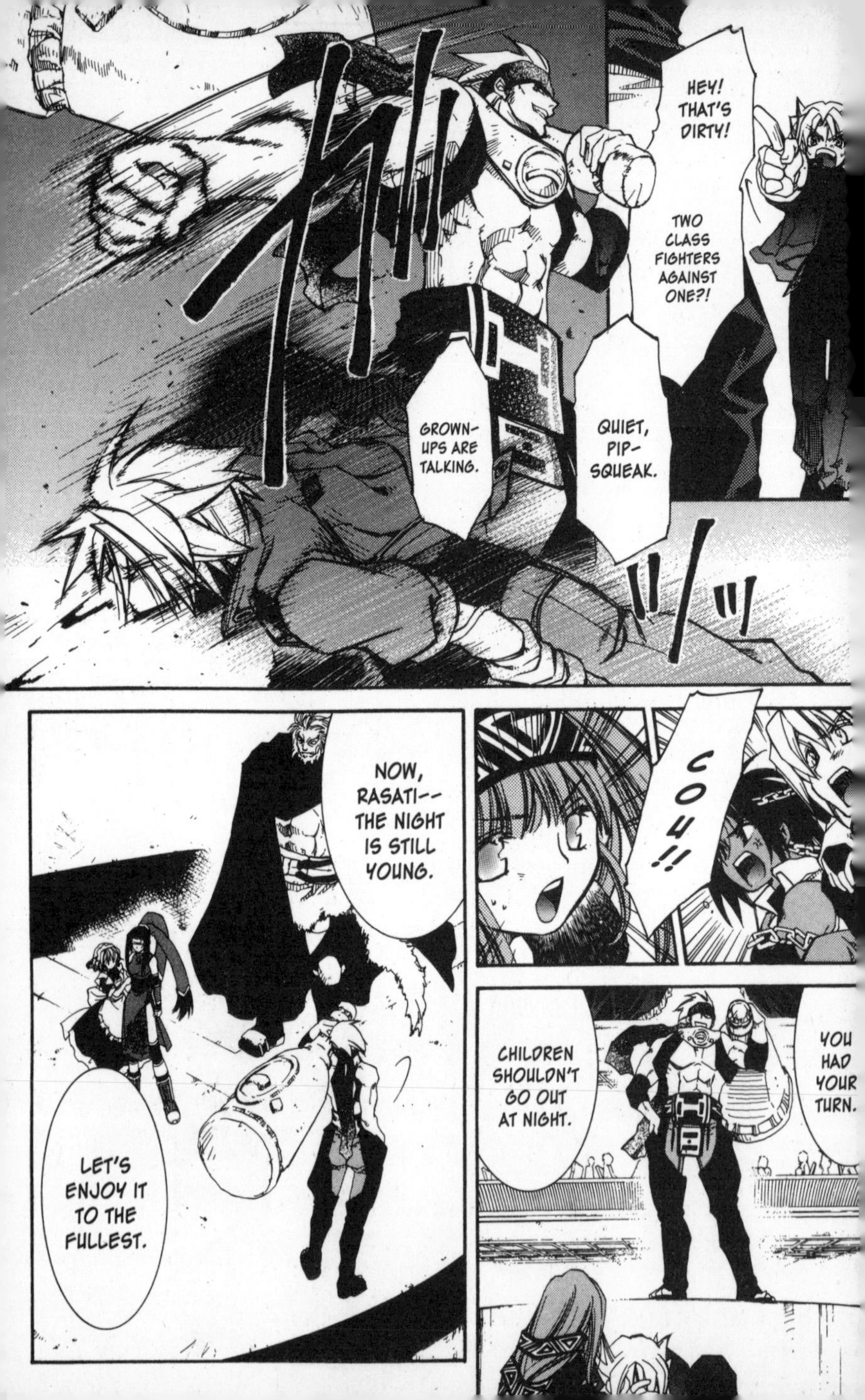
HEY! THAT'S DIRTY!
TWO CLASS FIGHTERS AGAINST ONE?!
QUIET, PIP-SQUEAK.
GROWN-UPS ARE TALKING.
COU!!
YOU HAD YOUR TURN.
CHILDREN SHOULDN'T GO OUT AT NIGHT.
NOW, RASATI-- THE NIGHT IS STILL YOUNG.
LET'S ENJOY IT TO THE FULLEST.

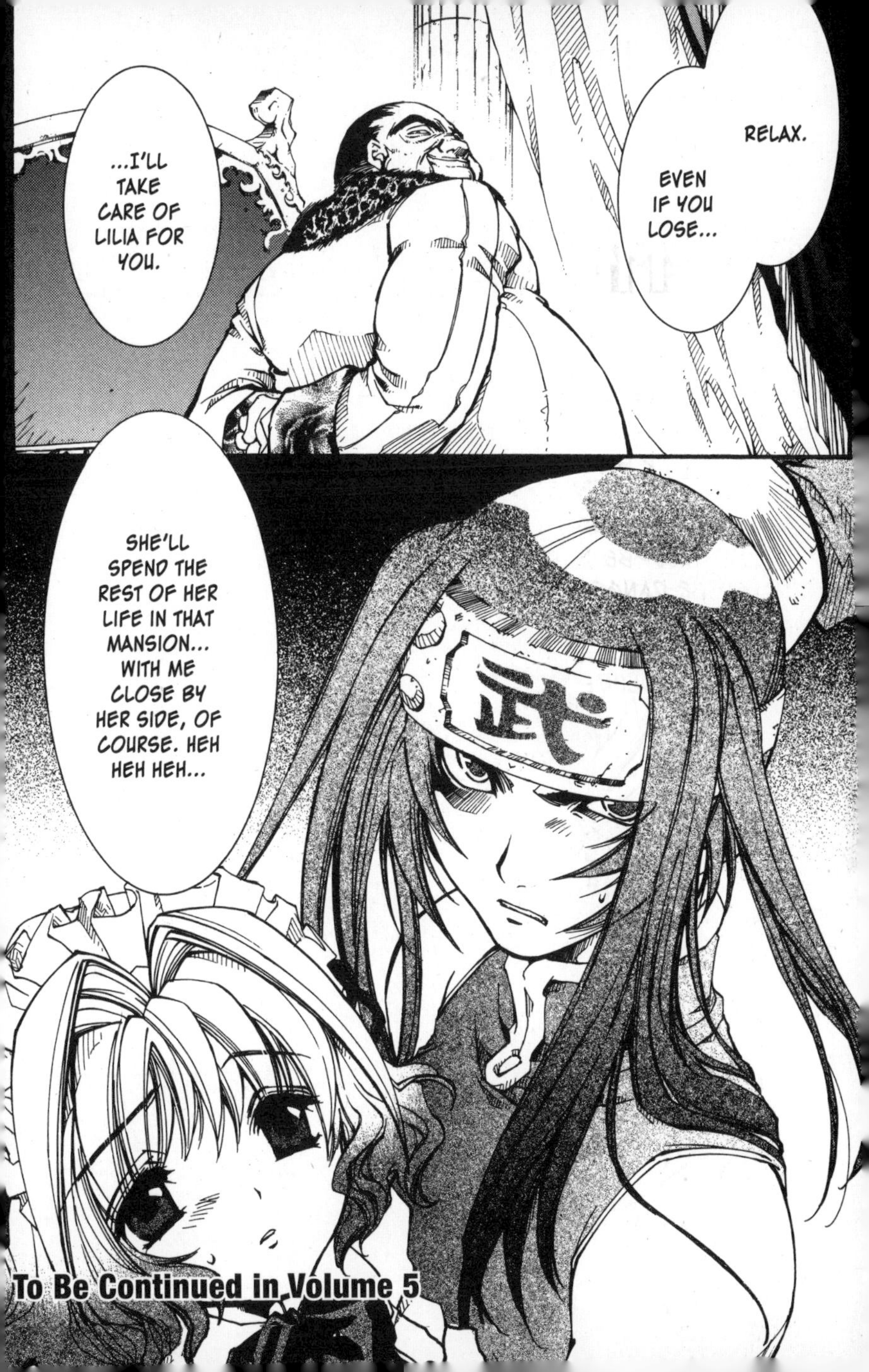
RELAX. EVEN IF YOU LOSE...
...I'LL TAKE CARE OF LILIA FOR YOU.
SHE'LL SPEND THE REST OF HER LIFE IN THAT MANSION... WITH ME CLOSE BY HER SIDE, OF COURSE. HEH HEH HEH...
To Be Continued in Volume 5

# In The Next Volume of

# ELEMENTAL GELADE

RASATI'S BATTLE FOR HER AND LILIA'S FREEDOM CONTINUES...BU
SHE CAN'T WIN THIS FIGHT ALONE. IT'S UP TO REN TO CONVINCE LILIA
TO HELP HER SISTER BEFORE IT'S TOO LATE. LATER, COUD AND REN
EXPERIENCE THEIR FIRST BOAT RIDE...BUT LITTLE DO THEY KNOW THEY
HAVE A STOWAWAY WITH AN UNSETTLING OBSESSION WITH COUD. ADD
ONE WOULD-BE ASSASSIN NAMED GRAYARTS TO THE MIX, AND YOU
HAVE ONE DANGEROUS VESSEL!

THIS SHOCKING SHIP OF SHENANIGANS SETS SAIL IN THE NEX
THRILLING VOLUME!

## Chaton Vad Walsloth

Challo, partner of Sunweld, member of the Conservation Society. She's a bright girl with a distinct will. And for someone reason, she fiercely loves Kuea. She has a faint (no, strong?!) infatuation.

tried pursuing
irlishness...but
he turned into
fairly forceful
character...
Huhhhh?

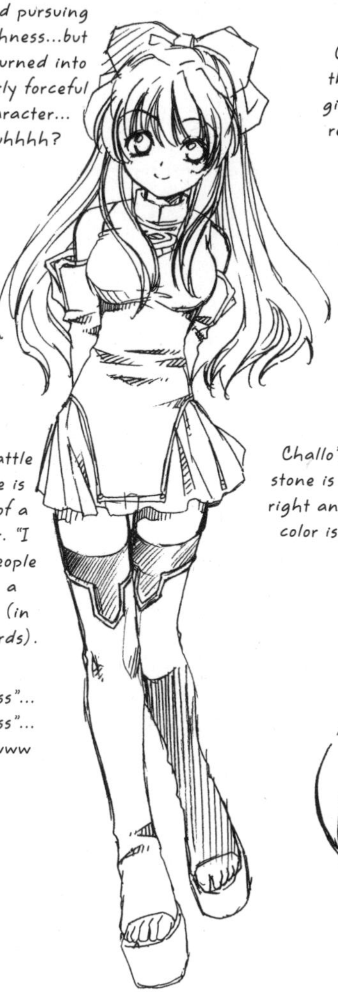

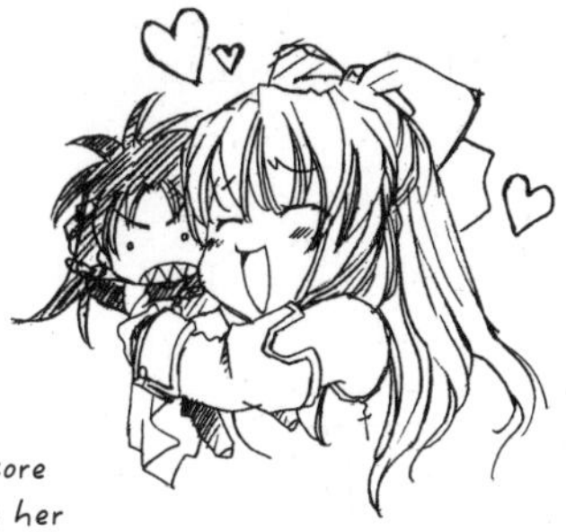

ter battle
shape is
hat of a
apier. "I
ab people
with a
ptss'" (in
er words).

Challo's core stone is on her right ankle. Its color is pink.

"ptss"...
"ptss"...
Owww

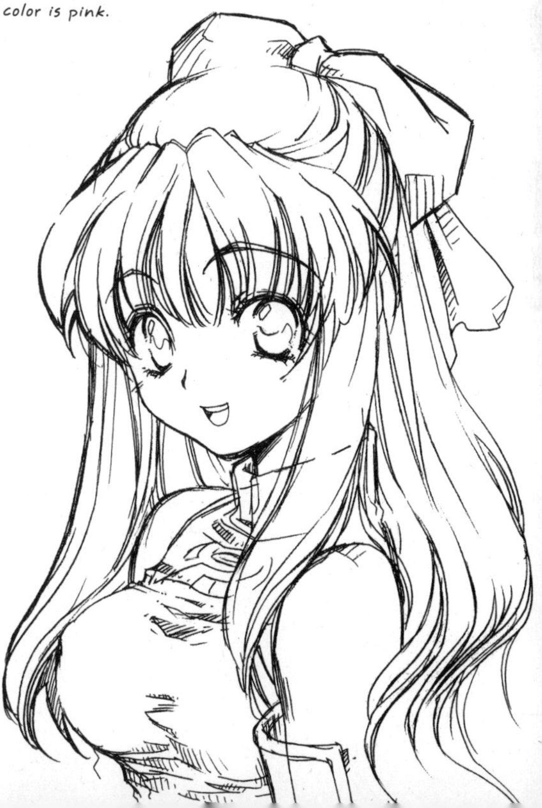

The model for Challo is an original character drawn a long time ago by Azuma's friend Mashika-san. Oh, I made sure to get permission from Mashika-san. That character has slanted eyes, and her bangs went to the side, but when you reverse those aspects, the impression is quite different, isn't it? I want to have her show up again with Sun-chan!

## Sunweld

Cisqua and Rowen's senior officer (affectionately called Sun-chan-senpai). He has an even more lukewarm personality than Rowen, and when the two are talking, then even everyone around them becomes mellow....

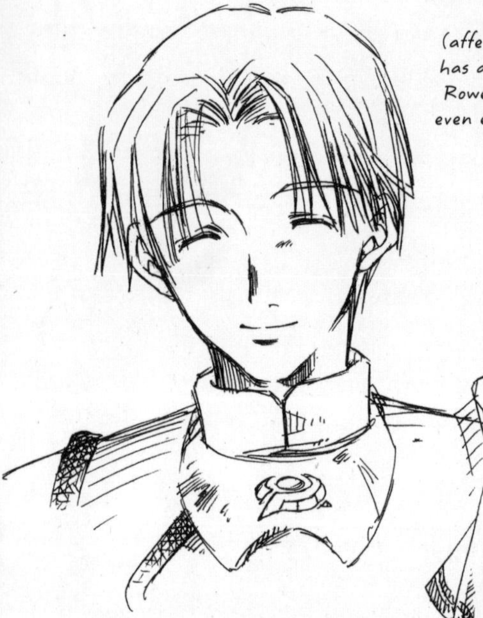

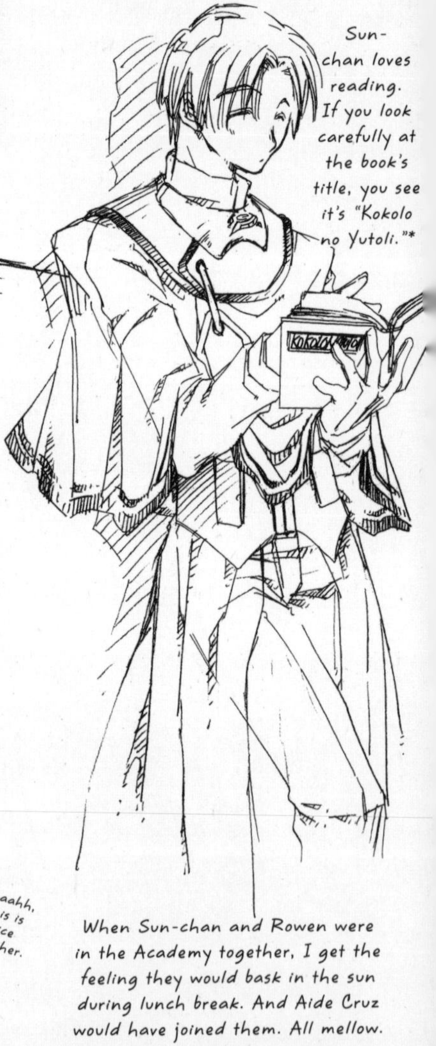

Sun-chan loves reading. If you look carefully at the book's title, you see it's "Kokolo no Yutoli."*

Sun-chan doesn't really have a model. The image came first. When I thought of "mellow" and "lukewarm," and drew what came into my head, he turned into this character. He's easy to figure out, isn't he? He seems to spoil Challo. I don't think he would ever get angry.

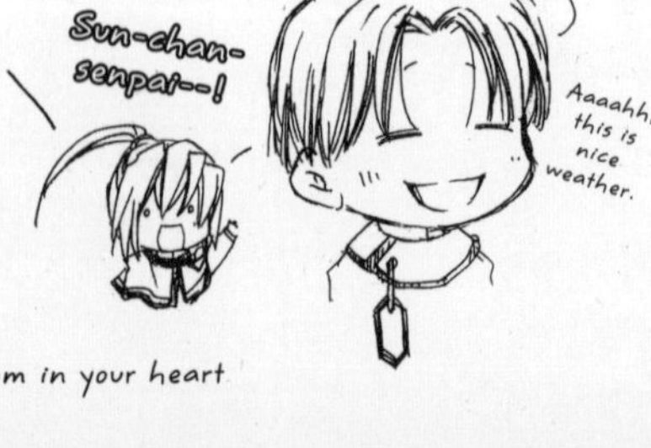
Sun-chan-senpai--!
Aaaahh, this is nice weather.

When Sun-chan and Rowen were in the Academy together, I get the feeling they would bask in the sun during lunch break. And Aide Cruz would have joined them. All mellow.

*Room in your heart

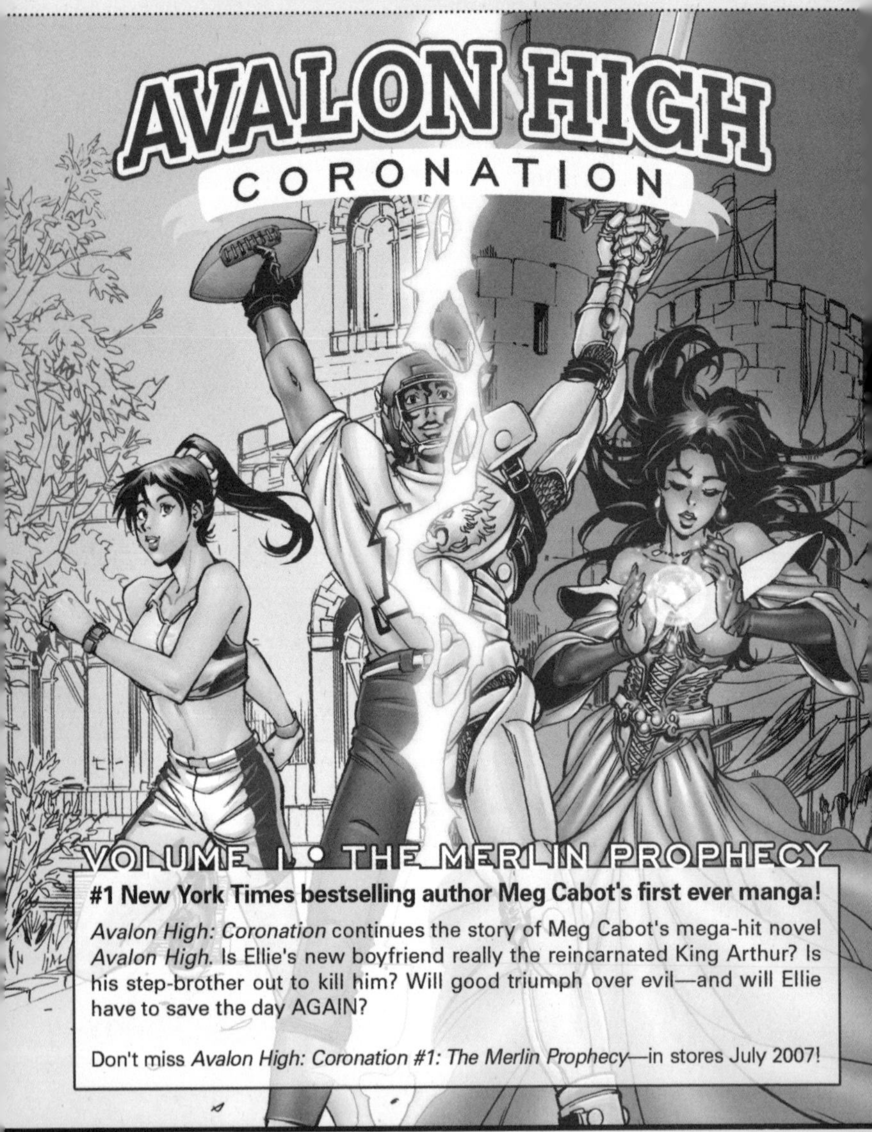
AVALON HIGH
CORONATION
VOLUME 1 • THE MERLIN PROPHECY
#1 New York Times bestselling author Meg Cabot's first ever manga!
Avalon High: Coronation continues the story of Meg Cabot's mega-hit novel Avalon High. Is Ellie's new boyfriend really the reincarnated King Arthur? Is his step-brother out to kill him? Will good triumph over evil—and will Ellie have to save the day AGAIN?
Don't miss Avalon High: Coronation #1: The Merlin Prophecy—in stores July 2007!

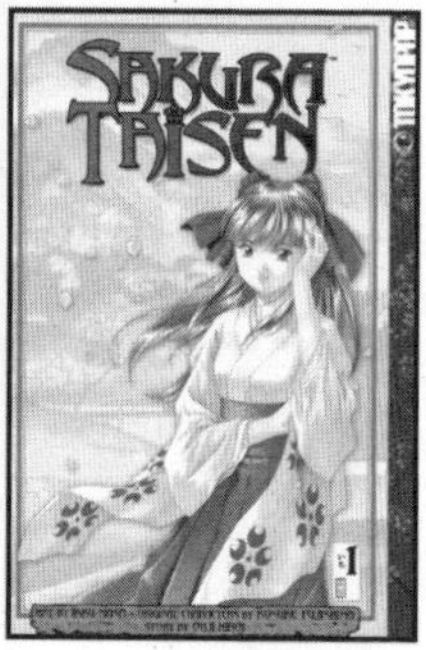
SAKURA TAISEN
TOKYOPOP

ACTION
TEEN AGE 13+

## SAKURA TAISEN

BY OHJI HIROI, IKKU MASA AND KOSUKE FUJISHIMA

I really, really like this series. I'm a sucker for steampunk-type stories, and 1920s Japanese fashion, and throw in demon invaders, robot battles and references to Japanese popular theater? Sold! There's lots of fun tidbits for the clever reader to pick up in this series (all the characters have flower names, for one, and the fact that all the Floral Assault divisions are named after branches of the Takarazuka Review, Japan's sensational all-female theater troupe!), but the consistently stylish and clean art will appeal even to the most casual fan.

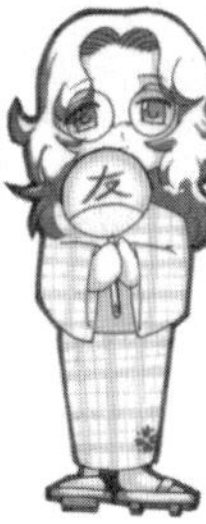

~Lillian Diaz-Przybyl, Editor

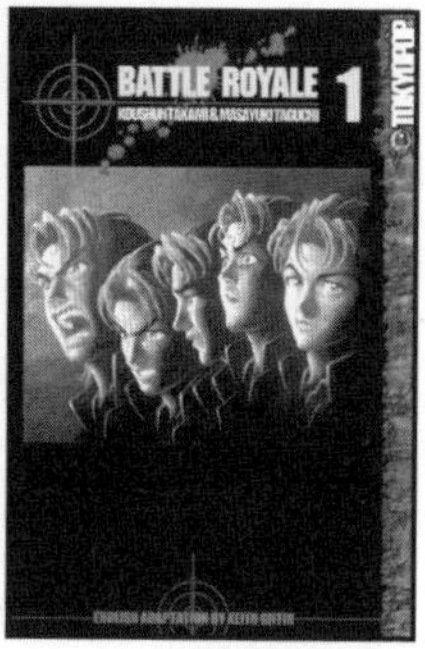
BATTLE ROYALE 1
TOKYOPOP

ACTION
MATURE AGES 18+

## BATTLE ROYALE

BY KOUSHUN TAKAMI AND MASAYUKI TAGUCHI

As far as cautionary tales go, you couldn't get any timelier than *Battle Royale*. Telling the bleak story of a class of middle school students who are forced to fight each other to the death on national television, Koushun Takami and Masayuki Taguchi have created a dark satire that's sickening, yet undeniably exciting as well. And if we have that reaction reading it, it becomes alarmingly clear how the students could so easily be swayed into doing it.

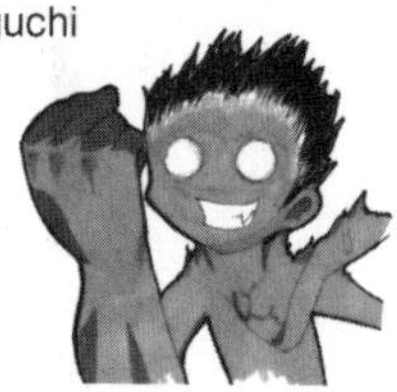

~Tim Beedle, Editor

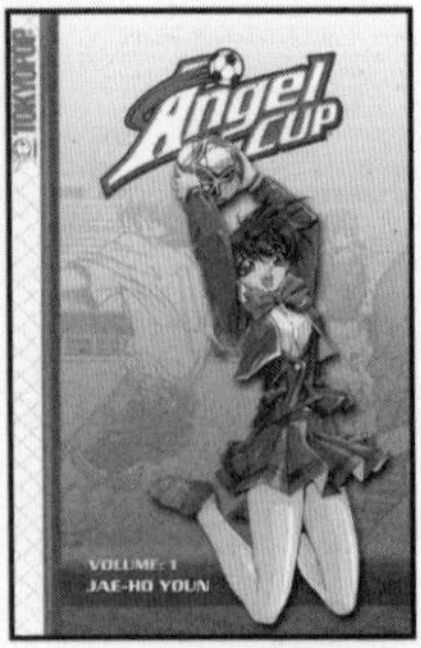
TOKYOPOP
Angel Cup
VOLUME: 1
JAE-HO YOUN

ACTION

T
TEEN AGE 13+

## ANGEL CUP

BY JAE-HO YOUN

Who's the newest bouncing broad that bends it like Beckam better than Braz—er, you get the idea? So-jin of the hit Korean manhwa, *Angel Cup!* She and her misfit team of athletic Amazons tear up the soccer field, whether it's to face up against the boys' team, or wear their ribbons with pride against a rival high school. While the feminist in me cheers for So-jin and the gang, the more perverted side of me drools buckets over the sexy bust-shots and scandalous camera angles... But from any and every angle, *Angel Cup* will be sure to tantalize the soccer fan in you... or perv. Whichever!

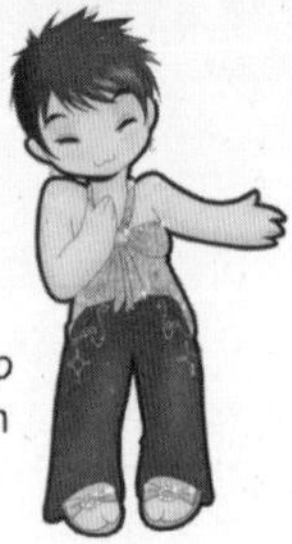

~Katherine Schilling, Jr. Editor

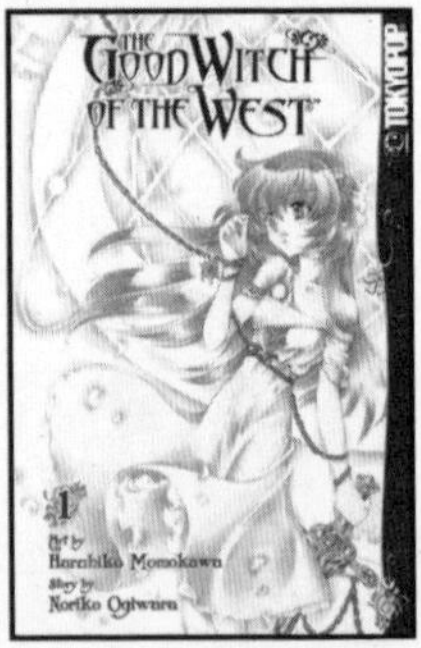
The Good Witch of the West
TOKYOPOP
1

FANTASY

T
TEEN AGE 13+

## GOOD WITCH OF THE WEST

BY NORIKO OGIWARA AND HARUHIKO MOMOKAWA

For any dreamers who ever wanted more out of a fairytale, indulge yourself with *Good Witch*. Although there's lots of familiar territory fairytale-wise—peasant girl learns she's a princess—you'll be surprised as Firiel Dee's enemies turn out to be as diverse as religious fanaticism, evil finishing school student councils and dinosaurs. This touching, sophisticated tale will pull at your heartstrings while astounding you with breathtaking art. *Good Witch* has big shoes to fill, and it takes off running.

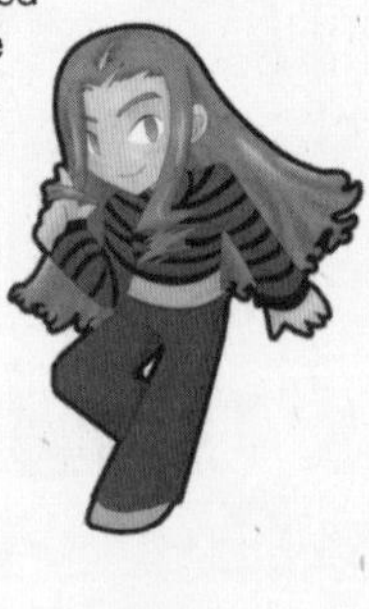

~Hope Donovan, Jr. Editor

# STOP!

## This is the back of the book.
## You wouldn't want to spoil a great ending!

This book is printed "manga-style," in the authentic Japanese right-to-left format. Since none of the artwork has been flipped or altered, readers get to experience the story just as the creator intended. You've been asking for it, so TOKYOPOP® delivered: authentic, hot-off-the-press, and far more fun!

# DIRECTIONS

If this is your first time reading manga-style, here's a quick guide to help you understand how it works.

It's easy... just start in the top right panel and follow the numbers. Have fun, and look for more 100% authentic manga from TOKYOPOP®!

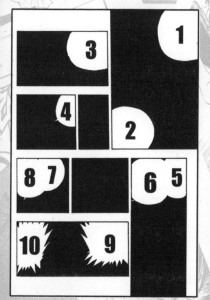